'The disruptive revenant has sparked fine Australian fiction, from Patrick White's *The Twyborn Affair* to Chris Womersley's *Bereft*. In this exhilarating debut (which won the Victorian Premier's Literary Award for an unpublished manuscript), Falk goes back to a town ravaged by feelings of resentment and distrust that are exacerbated by drought . . . A community psychologically and socially damaged, Kiewarra resembles Henry Lawson's bush. Australian novelists such as Harper, in a small and select company, are exploring disquieting imaginative territory, far from the littoral or metropolis.'

Weekend Australian

'A firecracker debut . . . Journalist Jane Harper proves literary is often mysterious, with her thriller *The Dry* capturing readers' attention both for its final twist and its depiction of a hostile small Australian town beset by drought.'

West Australian

'Every now and then an Australian crime novel comes along to stop your breath and haunt your dreams. *The Broken Shore* by Peter Temple was one, *Bitter Wash Road* by Garry Disher another. Both are books that capture something profound about the Australian landscape and the people who inhabit it. Both are not just great crime fiction, but great Australian novels. *The Dry*, by Jane Harper, is another.'

Sydney Morning Herald

'This is a story about heroism, the sins of the past, and the struggle to atone. But let's not forget the redbacks, the huntsmen, the rabbit scourge and all that makes this a quintessential Australian story beautifully told.'

D0207498

'There is about *The Dry* something mythic and valiant.'

Canberra Times

'Try to set aside one sitting to indulge in journalist Jane Harper's page-turning debut novel. The pace never falters'

Daily Telegraph

'*The Dry* is Melbourne journalist Jane Harper's first book, and sees her heading into the Peter Temple class of Australian crime fiction . . . in Aaron Falk we've been given a compelling and gritty new detective.'

The Saturday Paper

'In Jane Harper's debut, *The Dry*, long-held grudges are thrown into the mix to make for an absolute tinderbox – and a cracking read. Harper has delivered a tense, evocative thriller that paints a stark picture of what desperate times can do to a community. She slowly reveals the deep-worn tensions between characters in the small town, and it's this that makes *The Dry* such a good read . . . tension crackles . . . It's not surprising that Reese Witherspoon's production company, Pacific Standard, has already snapped up film rights for *The Dry*. It has some decidedly Australian aspects but Harper's basic point – about the desperate things people will do in desperate times – is universal.'

Adelaide Advertiser

'*The Dry* is a tightly plotted page-turner that kept me reading well into the night. Her characters are achingly real . . . shines a light on the highs and lows of rural life . . . In this cracker of a book Harper maintains the suspense, with the momentum picking up as it draws to its nerve-wracking conclusion.'

Australian Financial Review

'The book's prologue is powerful and shockingly addictive . . . wonderful debut . . . a worthy recipient of its pre-release hype.'

Queensland Times

'Debut author and journalist Jane Harper has produced a razor-sharp crime yarn dripping in the sights, sounds and smells of the Australian bush . . . action twists and turns, the pace building to a fantastic finale that will leave you breathless.'

Australian Women's Weekly Book of the Month

'A gripping crime thriller with an enigmatic protagonist and intriguing cast of characters.'

Vogue

'The taut crime thriller . . . ignited a bidding war among every major publisher in Australia, with the rights sold to more than 20 territories. *The Dry* dissects issues of masculinity, alcoholism and domestic violence . . . setting Hollywood ablaze.'

Who Weekly

'[A] devastating debut . . . From the ominous opening paragraphs, all the more chilling for their matter-of-factness, Harper . . . spins a suspenseful tale of sound and fury as riveting as it is horrific.'

Publishers Weekly starred review (US)

'A mystery that starts with a sad homecoming quickly turns into a nail-biting thriller about family, friends, and forensic accounting. Debut author Harper plots this novel with laser precision, keeping suspects in play while dropping in flashbacks that offer readers a full understanding of what really happened.

A chilling story set under a blistering sun, this fine debut will keep readers on edge and awake long past bedtime.'

Kirkus starred review (US)

'A stunner . . . It's a small-town, big-secrets page-turner with a shocker of an ending.'

Booklist starred review (US)

'One of the most stunning debuts I've ever read. I could feel the searing heat of the Australian setting. Every word is near perfect. The story builds like a wave seeking the purchase of earth before it crashes down and wipes out everything you might have thought about this enthralling tale. Read it!'

David Baldacci

'You will feel the heat, taste the dust and blink into the glare. *The Dry* is a wonderful crime novel that shines a light into the darkest corner of a sunburnt country.'

Michael Robotham

'It's extremely rare and exciting to read a debut that enthralls from the very first page and then absolutely sticks the landing. Told with heart and guts and an authentic sense of place that simply cannot be faked, *The Dry* is the debut of the year.'

C.J. Box

'Harper throws out so many teasing possibilities that it's hard to believe this is her first novel. *The Dry* is a breathless page-turner'

Janet Maslin, *The New York Times*

THE
DRY

JANE HARPER

PAN

Pan Macmillan Australia

First published 2016 in Macmillan by Pan Macmillan Australia Pty Ltd
This Pan edition published 2017 by Pan Macmillan Australia Pty Ltd
1 Market Street, Sydney, New South Wales, Australia, 2000

Reprinted 2017 (six times)

Cataloguing-in-Publication entry is available
from the National Library of Australia
http://catalogue.nla.gov.au

Typeset in Bembo by Post Pre-press Group
Printed by McPherson's Printing Group

To my parents, Mike and Helen, who always read to me.

Prologue

It wasn't as though the farm hadn't seen death before, and the blowflies didn't discriminate. To them there was little difference between a carcass and a corpse.

The drought had left the flies spoiled for choice that summer. They sought out unblinking eyes and sticky wounds as the farmers of Kiewarra levelled their rifles at skinny livestock. No rain meant no feed. And no feed made for difficult decisions, as the tiny town shimmered under day after day of burning blue sky.

'It'll break,' the farmers said as the months ticked over into a second year. They repeated the words out loud to each other like a mantra, and under their breath to themselves like a prayer.

But the weathermen in Melbourne disagreed. Besuited and sympathetic in air-conditioned studios, they made a passing reference most nights at six. Officially the worst conditions in a century. The weather pattern had a name, the pronunciation of which was never quite settled. *El Niño*.

At least the blowflies were happy. The finds that day were unusual, though. Smaller and with a smoothness to the flesh. Not that it mattered. They were the same where it counted. The glassy eyes. The wet wounds.

The body in the clearing was the freshest. It took the flies slightly longer to discover the two in the farmhouse, despite the front door swinging open like an invitation. Those that ventured beyond the initial offering in the hallway were rewarded with another, this time in the bedroom. This one was smaller, but less engulfed by competition.

First on the scene, the flies swarmed contentedly in the heat as the blood pooled black over tiles and carpet. Outside, washing hung still on the rotary line, bone dry and stiff from the sun. A child's scooter lay abandoned on the stepping stone path. Just one human heart beat within a kilometre radius of the farm.

So nothing reacted when deep inside the house, the baby started crying.

Chapter One

Even those who didn't darken the door of the church from one Christmas to the next could tell there would be more mourners than seats. A bottleneck of black and grey was already forming at the entrance as Aaron Falk drove up, trailing a cloud of dust and cracked leaves.

Neighbours, determined but trying not to appear so, jostled each other for the advantage as the scrum trickled through the doors. Across the road the media circled.

Falk parked his sedan next to a ute that had also seen better days and killed the engine. The air conditioner rattled into silence and the interior began to warm immediately. He allowed himself a moment to scan the crowd, although he didn't really have time. He'd dragged his heels the whole way from Melbourne, blowing out the five-hour drive to more than six. Satisfied no-one looked familiar, he stepped out of the car.

The late afternoon heat draped itself around him like a blanket. He snatched opened the back-seat door to get his jacket, searing his hand in the process. After the briefest hesitation, he grabbed his hat from the seat. Wide-brimmed in stiff brown canvas, it didn't go with his funeral suit. But with skin the blue hue of skimmed milk for half the year and a cancerous-looking cluster of freckles the rest, Falk was prepared to risk the fashion faux pas.

Pale from birth with close-cropped white-blond hair and invisible eyelashes, he'd often felt during his thirty-six years that the Australian sun was trying to tell him something. It was a message easier to ignore in the tall shadows of Melbourne than in Kiewarra, where shade was a fleeting commodity.

Falk glanced once at the road leading back out of town, then at his watch. The funeral, the wake, one night and he was gone. *Eighteen hours*, he calculated. No more. Keeping that firmly in mind, he loped towards the crowd, one hand on his hat as a sudden hot gust sent hems flying.

Inside, the church was even smaller than he remembered. Shoulder to shoulder with strangers, Falk allowed himself to be ferried deeper into the congregation. He noticed a free spot along the wall and darted in, carving out a space next to a farmer whose cotton shirt strained taut across his belly. The man gave him a nod, and went back to staring straight ahead. Falk could see creases at his elbows where the shirt sleeves had until recently been rolled up.

Falk removed his hat and discreetly fanned himself. He couldn't help glancing around. Faces that at first had seemed unfamiliar came more sharply into focus and he felt an illogical rush of surprise at some of the crows' feet, silver-streaked hair and gained kilos sprinkled throughout the crowd.

An older man two rows back caught Falk's eye with a nod and they exchanged a sad smile of recognition. What was his name? Falk tried to remember. He couldn't focus. The man had been a teacher. Falk could just about picture him at the front of a classroom, gamely attempting to bring geography or woodwork or something else alive for bored teenagers, but the memory kept flitting away.

The man nodded at the bench beside him, indicating he would make space, but Falk shook his head politely and turned back to the front. He avoided small talk at the best of times and this, unquestionably, was a million horrific miles from the best of times.

God, that middle coffin was small. Lying between the two full-size ones only made it look worse. If that were possible. Tiny kids with combed hair plastered to their skulls pointed it out: *Dad, look. That box is in football colours.* Those old enough to know what was inside stared in appalled silence, fidgeting in their school uniforms as they edged a little closer to their mothers.

Above the three coffins, a family of four stared down from a blown-up photograph. Their static smiles were overlarge and pixelated. Falk recognised the picture from the news. It had been used a lot.

Beneath, the names of the dead were spelled out in native flowers. *Luke. Karen. Billy.*

Falk stared at Luke's picture. The thick black hair had the odd grey line now, but he still looked fitter than most men on the wrong side of thirty-five. His face seemed older than Falk remembered, but then it had been nearly five years. The confident grin was unchanged, as was the slightly knowing look in his eyes. *Still the same*, were the words that sprang to mind. Three coffins said differently.

'Bloody tragic.' The farmer at Falk's side spoke out of nowhere. His arms were crossed, fists wedged tightly under his armpits.

'It is,' Falk said.

'You knew 'em well?'

'Not really. Only Luke, the –' For a dizzy moment Falk couldn't think of a word to describe the man in the largest coffin. He mentally grasped about but could only find clichéd tabloid descriptions.

'The father,' he landed on finally. 'We were friends when we were younger.'

'Yeah. I know who Luke Hadler is.'

'I think everyone does now.'

'You still live round this way, do you?' The farmer shifted his large body slightly and fixed Falk properly in his gaze for the first time.

'No. Not for a long time.'

'Right. Feels like I've seen you, though.' The farmer frowned, trying to place him. 'Hey, you're not one of them bloody TV journos, are you?'

'No. Police. In Melbourne.'

'That right? You lot should be investigating the bloody government for letting things get this bad.' The man nodded to where Luke's body lay alongside those of his wife and six-year-old son. 'We're out here trying to feed this country, worst weather in a hundred years, and they're crapping on about scrapping the subsidies. In some ways you can hardly blame the poor bastard. It's a fu–'

He stopped. Looked around the church. 'It's an effing scandal, that's what it is.'

Falk said nothing as they both reflected on the incompetencies of Canberra. The potential sources of blame for the dead Hadler family had been thrashed out at length over newspaper pages.

'You looking into this then?' The man nodded his head towards the coffins.

'No. Just here as a friend,' Falk said. 'I'm not sure there's anything still to look into.'

He knew only what he'd heard on the news along with everyone else. But it was straightforward according to the commentary. The shotgun had belonged to Luke. It was the same one later found clamped into what had been left of his mouth.

'No. I suppose not,' the farmer said. 'I just thought, with him being your friend and all.'

'I'm not that kind of officer anyway. Federal. With the financial intelligence unit.'

'Means nothing to me, mate.'

'Just means I chase the money. Anything ending with a few zeros that's not where it should be. Laundered, embezzled, that sort of thing.'

The man said something in reply but Falk didn't hear him. His gaze had shifted from the three coffins to the mourners in the front pew. The space reserved for family. So they could sit in front of all their friends and neighbours, who could in turn stare at the backs of their heads and thank God it wasn't them.

It had been twenty years, but Falk recognised Luke's father straight away. Gerry Hadler's face was grey. His eyes appeared sunken into his head. He was sitting dutifully in his spot in the front row, but his head was turned. He was ignoring his wife sobbing by his side and the three wooden boxes holding the remains of his son, daughter-in-law and grandson. Instead, he was staring directly at Falk.

Somewhere up the back, a few notes of music piped out from speakers. The funeral was starting. Gerry inclined his head in a tiny nod and Falk unconsciously put his hand in his pocket. He felt the letter that had landed on his desk two days ago. From Gerry Hadler, eight words written with a heavy hand:

Luke lied. You lied. Be at the funeral.
It was Falk who looked away first.

It was hard to watch the photographs. They flashed up on a screen at the front of the church in a relentless montage. Luke celebrating as an under-tens footballer; a young Karen jumping a pony over a fence. There was something grotesque now about the frozen grins, and Falk saw he wasn't the only one averting his gaze.

The photo changed again and Falk was surprised to recognise himself. A fuzzy image of his eleven-year-old face looked out at him. He and Luke were side by side, bare-chested and open-mouthed as they displayed a small fish on a line. They seemed happy. Falk tried to remember the picture being taken. He couldn't.

The slideshow continued. Pictures of Luke, then Karen, each smiling like they'd never stop, and then there was Falk again. This time, he felt his lungs squeeze. From the low murmur that rippled through the crowd, he knew he wasn't the only one shaken by the image.

A younger version of himself stood with Luke, now both long-limbed and freckled with acne. Still smiling, but this time part of a foursome. Luke's arm was slung around the slim teenage waist of a girl with baby-blonde hair. Falk's hand hovered more cautiously over the shoulder of a second girl with long black hair and darker eyes.

Falk could not believe that photo was being shown. He shot a look at Gerry Hadler, who was staring straight ahead, his jaw set. Falk felt the farmer next to him shift his weight and move a calculated half-step away. The penny had dropped for him, Falk thought.

He forced himself to look back at the image. At the foursome. At the girl by his side. He watched those eyes until they faded from the screen. Falk remembered that picture being taken. One afternoon near the end of a long summer. It had been a good day. And it had been one of the last photos of the four of them together. Two months later the dark-eyed girl was dead.

Luke lied. You lied.

Falk stared down at the floor for a full minute. When he looked back, time had moved on and Luke and Karen were smiling with stiff formality on their wedding day. Falk had been invited. He tried to remember what excuse he'd offered for not attending. Work, almost certainly.

The first pictures of Billy began to appear. Red-faced as a baby, then with a full head of hair as a toddler. Already looking a bit like his dad. Standing in shorts by a Christmas tree. The family dressed up as a trio of monsters, their face paint cracking around their smiles. Fast-forward a few years, and an older Karen was cradling another newborn to her breast.

Charlotte. The lucky one. No name spelled out in flowers for her. As if on cue Charlotte, now thirteen months old, began to wail from her front-row spot on her grandmother's lap. Barb Hadler clutched the girl tighter to her chest with one arm, jiggling with a nervous rhythm. With her other hand she pressed a tissue to her face.

Falk, no expert on babies, wasn't sure if Charlotte recognised her mother on the screen. Or perhaps she was just pissed off at being included in the memorial when she was still very much alive. She'd get used to it, he realised. She didn't have much choice. Not many places to hide for a kid destined to grow up with the label 'lone survivor'.

The last strains of music faded away and the final photos flashed up to an awkward silence. There was a feeling of collective relief when someone turned on the lights. As an overweight chaplain struggled up the two steps to the lectern, Falk stared again at those dreadful coffins. He thought about the dark-eyed girl, and a lie forged and agreed on twenty years ago as fear and teenage hormones pounded through his veins.

Luke lied. You lied.

How short was the road from that decision to this moment? The question ached like a bruise.

As an older woman in the crowd turned her gaze away from the front, her eyes landed on Falk. He didn't know her, but she gave an automatic nod of polite recognition. Falk looked away. When he glanced back, she was still staring. Her eyebrows suddenly puckered into a frown, and she turned to the elderly woman next to her. Falk didn't need to be able to lip-read to know what she whispered.

The Falk boy's back.

The second woman's eyes darted to his face then immediately away. With a tiny nod she confirmed her friend's suspicion. She leaned over and whispered something to the woman on her other side. An uneasy weight settled in Falk's chest. He checked his watch. *Seventeen hours.* Then he was gone. Again. Thank God.

Chapter Two

'**A**aron Falk, don't you bloody dare leave.'

Falk was standing by his car, fighting the urge to get in and drive away. Most of the mourners had already set off on the short trudge to the wake. Falk turned at the voice and despite himself, broke into a smile.

'Gretchen,' he said as the woman pulled him into a hug, her forehead pressed against his shoulder. He rested his chin on her blonde head and they stood there for a long minute, rocking back and forth.

'Oh my God, I'm so glad to see you here.' Her voice was muffled by his shirt.

'How are you?' he asked when she pulled away. Gretchen Schoner shrugged as she slipped off a pair of cheap sunglasses to reveal reddened eyes.

'Not good. Bad, really. You?'

'Same.'

'You certainly look the same.' She managed a shaky smile. 'Still working the albino look, I see.'

'You haven't changed much either.'

She gave a small snort, but her smile firmed. 'In twenty years? Come on.'

Falk wasn't just being flattering. Gretchen was still entirely recognisable from the photo of the teenage foursome that had flashed up during the service.

The waist Luke had thrown his arm around was a little thicker now and the baby-blonde hair might have been helped by a bottle, but the blue eyes and high cheekbones were pure Gretchen. Her formal trousers and top were a shade tighter than traditional funeral attire and she moved a little uneasily in the outfit. Falk wondered if it was borrowed or just seldom worn.

Gretchen was looking him over with the same scrutiny and as their eyes met, she laughed. She immediately looked lighter, younger.

'Come on.' She reached out and squeezed his forearm. Her palm felt cool against his skin. 'The wake's at the community centre. We'll get it over with together.'

As they started down the road, she called out to a small boy who was poking something with a stick. He looked up and reluctantly abandoned what he was doing. Gretchen held out a hand, but the child shook his head and trotted in front, swinging his stick like a sword.

'My son, Lachie,' Gretchen said, glancing sideways at Falk.

'Right. Yes.' It took Falk a moment to remember that the girl he knew was now a mother. 'I heard you'd had a baby.'

'Heard from who? Luke?'

'Must have been,' Falk said. 'A while ago now though. Obviously. How old is he?'

'Only five, but already the ringleader half the time.'

They watched as Lachie thrust his makeshift sword into invisible attackers. He had wide-set eyes and curly hair the colour of dirt, but Falk couldn't see much of Gretchen in the boy's sharp features. He scrambled to recall if Luke had mentioned her being in a relationship, or who the boy's father was. He thought not. He liked to think he'd have remembered that. Falk glanced down at Gretchen's left hand. It was ringless, but that didn't mean much these days.

'How's family life treating you?' he said finally, fishing.

'It's OK. Lachie can be a bit of a handful,' Gretchen said in an undertone. 'And it's just him and me. But he's a good kid. And we get by. For now, anyway.'

'Your parents still have their property?'

She shook her head. 'God, no. They retired and sold up about eight years ago now. Moved to Sydney and bought a tiny unit three streets away from my sister and her kids.' She shrugged. 'They say they like it. City life. Dad does Pilates apparently.'

Falk couldn't help smiling at the image of the plain-speaking Mr Schoner focusing on his inner core and breathing exercises.

'You weren't tempted to follow?' he said.

She gave a humourless laugh and gestured at the parched trees lining the road. 'And leave all this? No. I've been here too long, it's in the blood. You know what it's like.' She bit the sentence short and glanced sideways. 'Or maybe you don't. Sorry.'

Falk dismissed the remark with a wave of his hand. 'What are you doing these days?'

'Farming, of course. Trying to, anyway. I bought the Kellerman place a couple of years back. Sheep.'

'Really?' He was impressed. That was a sought-after property. Or at least, it had been when he was younger.

'And you?' she said. 'I heard you went into the police?'

'Yeah. I did. Federal. Still there.' They walked on in silence for a way. The frenetic birdsong coming from the trees sounded the same as he remembered. Up ahead, groups of mourners stood out like smudges against the dusty road.

'How are things round here?' he asked.

'Awful.' The word was a full stop. Gretchen tapped a fingertip to her lips with the nervous energy of an ex-smoker. 'God knows, it was bad enough before. Everyone's scared about money and the drought. Then this happened with Luke and his family and it's so bad, Aaron. So bad. You can feel it. We're all walking around like zombies. Not sure what to do, what to say. Watching each other. Trying to work out who'll be next to snap.'

'Jesus.'

'Yeah. You can't imagine.'

'Were you and Luke still close?' Falk asked, curious.

Gretchen hesitated. Her mouth set into an invisible line. 'No. We hadn't been for years. Not like it was when it was the four of us.'

Falk thought about that photo. Luke, Gretchen, himself. And Ellie Deacon, with her long black hair. They'd all been so tight. Teenage tight, where you believe your friends are soul mates and the bonds will last forever.

Luke lied. You lied.

'You obviously stayed in touch with him?' Gretchen said.

'On and off.' At least that was the truth. 'We caught up occasionally for a beer when he was in Melbourne, that sort of thing.' Falk paused. 'I hadn't seen him for a few years, though. It gets busy, you know? He had his family, I've been working a lot.'

'It's all right, you don't have to make excuses. We all feel guilty.'

The community centre was heaving. Falk hung back on the steps and Gretchen tugged on his arm.

'Come on, it'll be OK. Most people probably won't even remember you.'

'There'll be plenty who do. Especially after that photo at the funeral.'

Gretchen made a face. 'Yeah, I know. I got a shock too. But look, people have got plenty of things to worry about today other than you. Keep your head down. We'll go out the back.'

Without waiting for an answer she grasped Falk's sleeve with one hand and her son with the other and led them in, easing her way through the crowd. The air was stifling. The centre's air conditioner was trying its best, but fighting a losing battle as mourners huddled in the indoor shade. They were mingling solemnly, balancing plastic cups and plates of chocolate ripple cake.

Gretchen made her way to the French doors where collective claustrophobia had forced stragglers out into the patchy playground. They found a spot of shade by the fence line and Lachie ran off to try his luck on the scalding metal slide.

'You don't have to stand with me if it's going to sully your good name,' Falk said, tipping his hat a little further forward to shield his face.

'Oh shut up. Besides, I do a good enough job of that myself.'

Falk scanned the playground and spotted an elderly couple he thought might once have been friends of his father's. They were chatting to a young police officer who, suited and booted in full dress uniform, was sweating under the afternoon sun. His forehead glistened as he nodded politely.

'Hey,' Falk said. 'Is that Barberis's replacement?'

Gretchen followed his gaze. 'Yeah. You heard about Barberis?'

'Of course. Sad loss. Remember how he used to scare us all to death with horror stories about kids who mucked about with farm equipment?'

'Yeah. He'd had that heart attack coming for twenty years.'

'Still. It's a real shame,' Falk said, meaning it. 'So who's the new guy?'

'Sergeant Raco, and if it looks like he's stepped straight into the deep end, it's because he has.'

'No good? Seems like he's handling the crowd OK.'

'I don't know really. He'd only been here about five minutes when all this happened.'

'Hell of a situation to land in in your first five minutes.'

Gretchen's reply was cut short by a flurry of movement by the French doors. The crowd parted respectfully as Barb and Gerry Hadler emerged, blinking in the sunlight. Holding hands tightly they made their way around the groups of mourners. A few words, a hug, a brave nod, move on.

'How long since you last spoke to them?' Gretchen whispered.

'Twenty years, until last week,' Falk said. He waited. Gerry was still on the other side of the playground when he spotted them. He pulled away from a rotund woman mid-hug, leaving her arms embracing fresh air.

Be at the funeral.

Falk was there, as instructed. Now he watched as Luke's father approached.

Gretchen got in first, intercepting Gerry with a hug. His eyes met Falk's over her shoulder, his pupils huge and shining. Falk wondered if some form of medication was helping him through the day. When Gerry was released, he held out his hand, enclosing Falk's palm in a hot, tight grip.

'You made it then,' he said neutrally as Gretchen hovered by their side.

'I did,' said Falk. 'I got your letter.'

Gerry held his gaze.

'Right. Well, I thought it was important you be here. For

Luke. And I wasn't sure you were going to make it, mate.' The final sentence hung heavily in the air.

'Absolutely, Gerry.' Falk nodded. 'Important to be here.'

Gerry's doubts hadn't been unfounded. Falk had been at his desk in Melbourne a week earlier, staring blankly at a newspaper photo of Luke when the phone rang. In a halting voice Falk hadn't heard for two decades, Gerry had told him the funeral details. 'We'll see you there,' he'd said, without a question mark at the end. Falk had avoided Luke's pixelated gaze as he mumbled something about work commitments. In truth, he'd still been undecided. Two days later, the letter arrived. Gerry must have posted it as soon as he'd hung up the phone.

You lied. Be at the funeral.

Falk hadn't slept well that night.

They both now glanced awkwardly at Gretchen. She was frowning off into the middle distance where her son was clambering shakily over the monkey bars.

'You're staying in town tonight,' Gerry said. No question mark that time either, Falk noted.

'Above the pub.'

A wail went up from the playground and Gretchen made a noise of frustration.

'Shit. I could see that coming. Excuse me.' She jogged off. Gerry grabbed Falk's elbow and angled him away from the mourners. His hand was shaking.

'We need to talk. Before she comes back.'

Falk wrenched his arm away in a tiny controlled movement, aware of the crowd behind them. Unsure who was there, who was watching.

'For God's sake, Gerry, what is it you want?' He forced himself to stand in a way he hoped appeared relaxed. 'If this is supposed to be some sort of blackmail, I can tell you right now that's a non-starter.'

'What? Jesus, Aaron. No. Nothing like that.' Gerry looked genuinely shocked. 'If I wanted to stir up trouble I'd have done it years ago, wouldn't I? I was happy to let it lie. Christ, I would love to let it lie. But I can't now, can I? With this? Karen and Billy both dead, him not even seven years old yet.' Gerry's voice broke. 'Look, I'm sorry about the letter, but I needed you to be here. I have to know.'

'Know what?'

Gerry's eyes looked almost black against the bright sunlight. 'If Luke had killed before.'

Falk was silent. He didn't ask what Gerry meant.

'You know —' Gerry bit back his words as an officious woman wobbled up to inform him the chaplain needed to speak to him. Right away, if possible.

'Jesus, it's bloody chaos,' Gerry snapped, and the woman cleared her throat and arranged her expression into one of martyred patience. He turned back to Falk. 'I'd better go. I'll be in touch.' He shook Falk's hand, holding it a beat longer than necessary.

Falk nodded. He understood. Gerry looked hunched and small as he followed the woman away. Gretchen, having soothed her son, wandered back to Falk. They stood shoulder to shoulder as together they watched Gerry go.

'He seems dreadful,' she said in an undertone. 'I heard he was screaming at Craig Hornby in the supermarket yesterday, accusing him of making light of the situation or something. Seems a bit unlikely, Craig's been his friend for fifty years.'

Falk couldn't imagine anyone, least of all stoic Craig Hornby, making light of those three awful coffins.

'Was there really no warning at all from Luke?' He couldn't help himself.

'Like what?' A fly landed on Gretchen's lip and she brushed it away impatiently. 'Him waving a gun around in the main street threatening to do in his family?'

'God, Gretch, I'm only asking. I meant depression or something.'

'Sorry. It's this heat. It makes everything worse.' She paused. 'Look, there's barely anyone in Kiewarra who's not at the end of their tether. But honestly, Luke didn't seem to be struggling any more than anyone else. At least not in a way anyone's admitting seeing.'

Gretchen's thousand-yard stare was grim.

'It's hard to know, though,' she said after a pause. 'Everyone's so angry. But they're not just angry at Luke exactly. The people paying him out the most don't seem to hate him for what he's done. It's weird. It's almost like they're jealous.'

'Of what?'

'Of the fact that he did what they can't bring themselves to do, I think. Because now he's out of it, isn't he? While the rest of us are stuck here to rot, he's got no more worrying about crops or missed payments or the next rainfall.'

'Desperate solution,' Falk said. 'To take your family with you. How's Karen's family coping?'

'She didn't really have any, from what I heard. You ever meet her?'

Falk shook his head.

'Only child,' Gretchen said. 'Parents passed away when she was a teenager. She moved here to live with an aunt who died a few years ago. I think Karen was pretty much a Hadler for all intents and purposes.'

'Were you friends with her?'

'Not really. I —'

The clink of a fork against a wineglass rang out from the French doors. The crowd slowly fell silent and turned to where Gerry and Barb Hadler stood hand in hand. They looked very alone, surrounded by all those people.

It was only the two of them now, Falk realised. They'd also had a daughter once, briefly. She was stillborn when Luke was three. If they'd tried for more children after that they hadn't succeeded. Instead they'd channelled all their energy into their sturdy surviving son.

Barb cleared her throat, her eyes darting back and forth over the crowd.

'We wanted to thank you all for coming. Luke was a good man.'

The words were too fast and too loud, and she pressed her lips together as if to stop more escaping. The pause stretched out until it was awkward, then a little longer. Gerry stared mutely at a patch of ground in front of him. Barb prised open her lips and took a gulp of air.

'And Karen and Billy were beautiful. What's happened has been —' she swallowed, '— so terrible. But I hope eventually you can remember Luke properly. From before. He was a friend to many of you. A good neighbour, a hard worker. And he loved that family of his.'

'Yeah, 'til he butchered them.'

The words that floated from the back of the crowd were soft, but Falk wasn't the only one to whip his head around. The glares pinpointed the speaker as a large man wearing his mid-forties badly. Fleshy biceps that were more fat than muscle strained against his t-shirt as he folded his arms. His face was ruddy, with a scruffy beard and the defiant look of a bully. He stared down each person who turned to chastise him, until one by one they looked away. Barb and Gerry appeared not to have heard. Small mercies, Falk thought.

'Who's the loudmouth?' he whispered, and Gretchen looked at him in surprise.

'You don't recognise him? It's Grant Dow.'

'You're kidding.' Falk felt the hairs on his neck prickle and turned his face away. He remembered a twenty-five year old with lean muscles like barbed wire. This bloke looked like he'd had a tough two decades since. 'He looks so different.'

'Still a prize dickhead. Don't worry. I don't think he's seen you. You'd know about it if he had.'

Falk nodded, but kept his face turned. Barb started crying, which the crowd took as a sign the speech had ended, and people gravitated instinctively towards her or away, depending on their sentiment. Falk and Gretchen stayed put. Gretchen's son ran up and buried his face in his mother's trousers. She hoisted him with some difficulty onto her hip and he rested his head on her shoulder, yawning.

'Time to get this one home, I think,' she said. 'When are you off back to Melbourne?'

Falk checked his watch. *Fifteen hours.*

'Tomorrow,' he said out loud.

Gretchen nodded, looking up at him. Then she leaned forward and wrapped her spare arm around his back and pulled him close. Falk could feel the heat of the sun on his back and the warmth of her body in front.

'It's good to see you again, Aaron.' Her blue eyes wandered over his face as though trying to memorise it and she smiled a little sadly. 'Maybe see you in another twenty years.'

He watched her walk away until he couldn't see her anymore.

Chapter Three

Falk sat on the edge of the bed, listlessly watching a medium-sized huntsman perched on the wall. The early evening temperature had dropped only fractionally as the sun disappeared. He'd changed into shorts after a shower and his damp legs prickled uncomfortably against the cheap cotton bedsheet. A stern sign hanging from an egg timer next to the showerhead had ordered him to keep ablutions to three minutes. He'd started to feel guilty after two.

The dull sounds of the pub thudded up through the floor, the occasional muted voice ringing a distant bell. A small part of him was curious to see who was down there, but he felt no desire to join in. The noise was punctuated by the muffled smash of a dropped glass. There was a short pocket of silence followed by a chorus of derisive laughter. The huntsman moved a single leg.

Falk jumped as the room phone on the bedside table rang out, its tone shrill and plastic. He was startled but not surprised. He felt like he'd been waiting for it for hours.

'Hello?'

'Aaron Falk? I've a call for you.' The barman's voice was deep with a trace of a Scottish accent. Falk pictured the imposing figure who had taken his credit card details in exchange for a room key without comment two hours earlier.

Falk had never seen him before, and he was certain he would have remembered a face like that. Late forties, with broad shoulders and a full orange beard, the barman was a backpacker who had stayed and stayed, Falk guessed. He'd shown no spark of recognition at Falk's name, just an air of disbelief that anyone would use the pub for a purpose not directly linked to alcohol.

'Who's calling?' Falk asked, although he could guess.

'You'll have to ask him yourself,' the barman said. 'You want a message service, you'll have to stay in a nicer establishment, my friend. Putting him through now.' The line went silent for a long moment, then Falk heard breathing.

'Aaron? You there? It's Gerry.' Luke's father sounded exhausted.

'Gerry. We need to talk.'

'Yes. Come out to the house. Barb wants to speak to you anyway.' Gerry gave him the address. There was a long pause, then a heavy sigh. 'And listen, Aaron. She doesn't know about the letter. Or any of this. Let's keep it that way, yeah?'

Falk followed Gerry's directions along gloomy country roads and twenty minutes later turned his car onto a short paved driveway. A porch light cast an orange glow over a neat weatherboard home. He pulled to a stop and the screen door screeched open, revealing Barb Hadler's squat silhouette. Her husband appeared behind her a moment later, his taller frame throwing a long shadow onto the drive. As Falk climbed the porch steps, he could see they were both still wearing their funeral clothes. Wrinkled now.

'Aaron. My God, it's been so long. Thank you for coming. Come in,' Barb whispered, reaching out her free hand to him. She was clutching baby Charlotte close to her chest and rocking her with a vigorous rhythm. 'Sorry about the baby. She's very restless. Won't go down.'

From what Falk could see, Charlotte was fast asleep.

'Barb.' Falk leaned in over the child to give the woman a hug. 'It's so good to see you.' She held him for a long moment, her plump arm around his back, and he felt something in him relax a fraction. He could smell the sweet floral notes of her hairspray. It was the same brand she'd used when she was still Mrs Hadler to him. They moved apart, and he was able to look down at Charlotte properly for the first time. She looked red-faced and uncomfortable, pressed against her grandmother's blouse. Her forehead was creased into a tiny frown that, Falk noticed with a jolt, reminded him uncannily of her father.

He stepped into the light of the hallway and Barb looked him up and down, the whites of her eyes turning pink as he watched. She reached out and touched his cheek with the warm tips of her fingers.

'Just look at you. You've barely changed,' she said. Falk felt illogically guilty. He knew she was picturing a teenage version of her son next to him. Barb sniffed and wiped her face with a tissue, shredding little flecks of white onto her top. She ignored them, and with a sad smile gestured for him to follow. She led him down a hallway lined with framed family snaps that they both studiously ignored. Gerry trailed in their wake.

'You've got a nice place here, Barb,' Falk said politely. She had always been scrupulously houseproud, but looking around now he could see the odd sign of clutter. Dirty mugs crowded a side table, the recycling bin was overflowing, and stacks of letters stood unopened. It all told a tale of grief and distraction.

'Thank you. We wanted something small and manageable after –' She hesitated for a beat. Swallowed. 'After we sold the farm to Luke.'

They emerged onto a deck overlooking a tidy patch of garden. The wooden boards creaked beneath their feet as the night soaked some of the ferocity out of the day's heat. All around were rosebushes that were neatly pruned, but very dead.

'I tried to keep them alive with recycled water,' Barb said, following Falk's gaze. 'Heat got them in the end.' She pointed Falk to a wicker chair. 'We saw you on the news; did Gerry tell you? A couple of months ago. Those firms ripping off their investors. Stealing their nest eggs.'

'The Pemberley case,' Falk said. 'That was a shocker.'

'They said you did well, Aaron. On TV and in the papers. Got those people's money back.'

'Some of it. Some of it was long gone.'

'Well, they said you did a good job.' Barb patted his leg. 'Your dad would've been proud.'

Falk paused. 'Thanks.'

'We were sorry to hear he'd passed. Cancer is a real bastard.'

'Yes.' Bowel, six years ago. It hadn't been an easy death.

Gerry, leaning against the doorframe, opened his mouth for the first time since Falk arrived.

'I tried to keep in touch after you left, you know.' His casual tone failed to hide the note of defensiveness. 'Wrote to your dad, tried calling a couple of times. Never heard anything back, though. Had to give up in the end.'

'It's OK,' Falk said. 'He didn't really encourage contact from Kiewarra.'

An understatement. They all pretended not to notice.

'Drink?' Gerry disappeared into the house without waiting for an answer and came out a moment later with three tumblers of whiskey. Falk took his in astonishment. He had never known Gerry to drink anything much harder than a light beer. The ice was already melting by the time the glass was in his hand.

'Cheers.' Gerry tilted his head back and took a deep swallow. Falk waited for him to wince. He didn't. Falk took a polite sip and set the glass down. Barb looked at hers in distaste.

'You shouldn't really be drinking this stuff around the baby, Gerry,' she said.

'Crying out loud, love, the kid doesn't care. She's dead to the bloody world,' Gerry said, and there was a horrible pause. Somewhere in the inky garden the nocturnal insects rattled like white noise. Falk cleared his throat.

'How are you coping, Barb?'

She looked down and stroked Charlotte's cheek. Shook her head and a tear dropped onto the little girl's face. 'Obviously,' Barb began, then stopped. She blinked hard. 'I mean, *obviously* Luke didn't do it. He would never have done this. You know that. Not to himself. And certainly not to his beautiful family.'

Falk glanced at Gerry. He was still standing in the doorway, glaring down into his half-empty drink.

Barb went on. 'I spoke to Luke a few days before it happened. And he was completely fine. Honestly, he was normal.'

Falk couldn't think of anything to say so he nodded. Barb took it as a sign of encouragement.

'See, you understand, because you really knew him. But other people round here. They're not like that. They just accept what they're told.'

Falk stopped himself from pointing out that he hadn't seen

Luke in five years. They both looked up at Gerry, who continued to examine his drink. No help to be found there.

'That's why we were hoping –' Barb looked back, hesitating. '– I was hoping you'd help us.'

Falk stared at her.

'Help you how exactly, Barb?'

'Well, find out what really happened. To clear Luke's name. And for Karen and Billy. And Charlotte.'

At that she started rocking Charlotte in her arms, stroking her back and making soothing noises. The baby still hadn't moved.

'Barb.' Falk leaned forward in his chair and placed his palm on her free hand. It felt clammy and feverish. 'I am so sorry for what's happened. To you all. Luke was like a brother back then, you know that. But I am not the right person for this. If you've got concerns you've got to go to the police.'

'We've come to you.' She removed her hand. 'You're the police.'

'The police who are equipped to deal with this sort of thing. I don't do that anymore. You know that. I'm with the financial side now. Accounts, money.'

'Exactly.' Barb nodded.

Gerry made a small noise in his throat. 'Barb thinks money troubles may have played a part.' He'd aimed for a neutral tone, fallen well shy.

'Yes. Of course I do,' she snapped. 'Why is that so unbelievable to you, Gerry? Talk about burning a hole. If Luke had a dollar, he'd spend two to make sure it was gone.'

Was that true? Falk wondered. He'd never known Luke to be too keen to put his hand in his pocket.

Barb turned back to face him. 'Look, for ten years I thought we'd done the right thing selling the property to Luke. But these past two weeks I've done nothing but worry we saddled him with a burden that was too much. With the drought, who knows? Everyone is so desperate. He might well have borrowed money from someone. Or had bad debts he couldn't pay. Maybe someone he owed came looking for him.'

A silence stretched out. Falk found his glass of whiskey and took a decent swallow. It was warm.

'Barb,' he said finally. 'It might not feel like it, but the officers in charge really will have considered all these possibilities.'

'Not very bloody well,' Barb snapped. 'They didn't want to know. They drove over from Clyde and took one look and said, "Yep, another farmer gone off the rails" and that was that. Open and shut. I could see what they were thinking. Nothing but sheep and paddocks. You'd have to be half off your nut to live here in the first place. I could see it in their faces.'

'They sent a team down from Clyde?' Falk asked, slightly surprised. Clyde was the nearest big town with a fully stocked cop shop. 'It wasn't the local guy? What's his name?'

'Sergeant Raco. No. He'd only been here a week or so. They sent someone over.'

'You've told this Raco bloke you've got concerns?'

Her defiant look answered his question.

'We're telling you,' she said.

Gerry put his glass down on the deck with a thud and they both jumped.

'All right, I think we've said our piece,' he said. 'It's been a long day. Let's give Aaron a chance to think things through. See what makes sense to him. Come on, mate, I'll see you out.'

Barb opened her mouth like she wanted to protest but closed it after a look from Gerry. She laid Charlotte down on a spare chair and pulled Falk into a damp embrace.

'Just think about it. Please.' Her breath was hot against his ear. He could smell alcohol on her breath. Barb sat back down and picked up Charlotte. She rocked briskly until the child finally opened her eyes with an irritated wail. Barb smiled for the first time as she smoothed her hair and patted her back. Falk could hear her singing tunelessly as he followed Gerry down the hallway.

Gerry walked Falk right to his car.

'Barb's clutching at straws,' Gerry said. 'She's got it into her head that this is all the work of some mythical debt enforcer. It's rubbish. Luke wasn't a fool with money. Having a tough time, like everyone else, yes. And he took the odd risk, but he was sensible enough. He'd never have got mixed up in that sort of thing. Anyway, Karen did all the accounts for the farm. She would've said. Would've told us if things were that bad.'

'So what do you think?'

'I think – I think he was under a lot of pressure. And as much as it hurts me, and I tell you, it kills me, I think what happened was exactly what it looks like. What I want to know is whether I share the blame.'

Falk leaned against his car. His head was pounding.

'How long have you known?' Falk said.

'That Luke was lying when he gave you an alibi? The whole time. So what's that, twenty-odd years? I saw Luke riding his bike alone on the day it happened. Nowhere near where you boys said you were. I know you weren't together.' He paused. 'I've never told anyone that.'

'I didn't kill Ellie Deacon.'

Hidden somewhere in the dark, the cicadas screeched.

Gerry nodded, looking down at his feet. 'Aaron, if I'd thought for a second that you had, I wouldn't have kept quiet. Why do you think I didn't say anything? It would have ruined your life. The suspicion would have followed you for *years*. Would they have let you join the police? Luke would have had the book thrown at him for lying. All that for what? The girl was still dead. Killed herself, realistically, and I know a fair few others thought so too. You boys had nothing to do with it.' Gerry struck the toe of his boot against the ground. 'At least that's what I thought.'

'And now?'

'Now? Jesus. I don't know what to believe. I always thought Luke was lying to protect you. But now I've got a murdered daughter-in-law and grandchild, and my own dead son with his fingerprints all over his shotgun.'

Gerry ran a hand over his face.

'I loved Luke. I would defend him to the end. But I loved Karen and Billy as well. And Charlotte. I would have gone to my grave saying my son was incapable of something like this. But this voice keeps whispering, *Is that true? Are you sure?* So I'm asking you. Here. Now. Did Luke give that alibi to protect you, Aaron? Or was he lying to protect himself?'

'There was never any suggestion Luke was responsible for what happened to Ellie,' Falk said carefully.

'No,' Gerry said. 'Not least because you alibied each other, though, eh? You and I both knew he was lying about that, and neither of us said anything. So my question is whether that puts the blood of my daughter-in-law and grandson on my hands.'

Gerry tilted his face and his expression was lost in shadow.

'It's something to ask yourself before you go scurrying back to Melbourne. You and I both hid the truth. If I'm guilty, so are you.'

The country roads seemed even longer on the drive back to the pub. Falk flicked on his high beams and they carved a cone of white light in the gloom. He felt like the only person for miles. Nothing ahead, nothing behind.

He felt the sickening thud under the wheels almost before he registered the small blur streaking across the road. A rabbit. There, then instantly gone. His heart was pounding. He tapped the brake automatically, but was a thousand kilos and eighty kilometres an hour too late. No contest. The impact had come like a blow to the chest and it nudged something loose in Falk's mind. A memory he hadn't thought of in years slid to the surface.

The rabbit was only a baby, shivering in Luke's hands. His fingernails were thick with grime. They often were. For Kiewarra's eight-year-olds, weekend entertainment was limited. They'd been running fast through the overgrown grass, racing to nowhere, when Luke had stopped dead. He bent down among the long stalks and a moment later stood, holding the tiny creature aloft. Aaron ran over to see. They'd stroked it, each telling the other not to press so hard.

'He likes me. He's mine,' Luke said. They argued about names all the way back to Luke's house.

They found a cardboard box to put it in, and loomed over to examine their new pet. The rabbit quivered a little under their scrutiny, but mainly lay still. Fear masquerading as acceptance.

Aaron ran inside to fetch a towel to line the cardboard. It took him longer than expected and when he re-emerged into the bright sun, Luke was still. He had one hand in the box. Luke's head snapped up as Aaron approached and he snatched his hand out. Aaron walked over, uncertain of what he was seeing, but feeling the urge to delay the moment when he would look inside.

'It died,' Luke said. His mouth was a tight line. He didn't meet Aaron's gaze.

'How?'

'I don't know. It just did.'

Aaron asked a few more times but never got a different answer. The rabbit lay on its side, perfect but unmoving, its eyes black and vacant.

'Just think about it,' Barb had said as Falk had left their home. Instead, as he drove down those long country roads, the dead animal still fresh under his wheels, Falk couldn't stop thinking about Ellie Deacon and their teenage gang of four. And whether Ellie's dark eyes had looked as vacant after the water had finished filling her lungs.

Chapter Four

The yellow police tape was still hanging in strips around the door of Luke Hadler's farmhouse. It caught the morning light as Falk parked next to the police car on a patch of dead grass out the front. The sun was still some way from its peak position, but Falk's skin was already tingling from the heat as he got out of the car. He put his hat on and surveyed the house. He hadn't needed directions. He'd spent almost as much time at that house growing up as he had at his own.

Luke hadn't changed much about the place since he'd taken it over from his parents, Falk thought as he rang the bell. The chime echoed deep inside, and he was struck by the feeling of having travelled back in time. He felt such an uneasy certainty that a cocky sixteen-year-old would swing open the door that he almost took a step back.

Nothing moved. Windows shrouded by closed curtains gazed out like a pair of blinded eyes.

Falk had lain awake for most of the night thinking about what Gerry had said. In the morning he'd rung and told Gerry he could stay in town a day or two. Only until the weekend. It was Thursday. He was expected back at work on Monday. But in the meantime, he would go to Luke's property. He would look at the financials for Barb. It was the least he could do. Gerry's tone made it clear he agreed. It was almost literally the least Falk could do.

Falk waited for a moment, then made his way around the side of the building. The sky loomed huge and blue over yellow paddocks. In the distance, a wire fence kept a shadowy tangle of bushland at bay. The property was very isolated, Falk noticed properly for the first time. It had always felt full of life when he was young. His own childhood home may only have been a short bike ride away, but it was completely invisible somewhere over the horizon. Looking around now, only one other house was in sight: a sprawling grey building hunched on the side of a distant hill.

Ellie's house.

Falk wondered if her father and cousin still lived up there, and instinctively turned his head away. He wandered through the yard until he found Sergeant Greg Raco in the biggest of three barns.

The officer was on his hands and knees in the corner, rummaging through a pile of old boxes. A redback, nestled still and shiny in her web, was ignoring the activity two metres away from her. Falk rapped on the metal door and Raco twisted around, his face streaked with dust and sweat.

'Jesus, you gave me a start. Didn't hear anyone coming.'

'Sorry. Aaron Falk. I'm a friend of the Hadlers'. Your receptionist said you were here.' He pointed to the redback. 'You seen that, by the way?'

'Yeah. Thanks. There are a couple around.'

Raco stood and pulled off his work gloves. He attempted to brush the grime off his navy uniform trousers but gave up as it made things worse. His neatly pressed shirt had sweat rings under the arms. He was shorter than Falk and built like a boxer, with curls cut close to his scalp. His skin was Mediterranean olive, but his accent was pure country Australia. He had a lift to his eyes that made him look like he was smiling even when he wasn't. Falk knew, because he wasn't smiling now.

'Gerry Hadler called and said something about you stopping by,' Raco said. 'Sorry to do this, mate, but you got some ID? Had a few nut jobs prowling around. Sightseeing or something, I don't know.'

Up close he was older than Falk had first thought. Maybe thirty. Falk noticed the sergeant discreetly check him over. Open yet cautious. Fair enough. Falk handed over his driver's licence. Raco took it like he'd been expecting something else.

'I thought Gerry said you were a cop?'

'Just here in a personal capacity,' Falk said.

'So not officially.'

'Not at all.' Something flashed across Raco's face that Falk couldn't read. He truly hoped this wasn't going to descend into a pissing contest. 'I'm an old mate of Luke's. Back when we were teenagers.'

Raco looked at the licence carefully before handing it back.

'Gerry said you needed access to the bank statements. Account books, stuff like that?'

'Sounds about right.'

'Something going on there I should know about?'

'Barb asked me to have a look,' Falk said. 'As a favour.'

'Right.' Despite being several centimetres shorter, Raco almost managed to look Falk straight in the eye. 'Look, if Gerry and Barb say you're good, I'm not going to stuff you around for the sake of it. But they're pretty vulnerable right now, so you come across anything I need to hear, you make sure I hear it. Yeah?'

'No worries. Just here to help them out.'

Falk couldn't help glancing over Raco's shoulder. The cavernous barn was swelteringly hot, and plastic skylights gave everything a sickly yellow tinge. A tractor stood idle in the middle of the concrete floor and various bits of machinery Falk couldn't identify lined the walls. A hose attachment snaked out of the nearest one near his feet. He thought it might be for milking, but wasn't sure. He would have known once. Now it all looked vaguely like instruments of torture to his city eye. Falk nodded towards the boxes in the corner.

'What are you looking for in there?'

'Nice try, mate, but you said it yourself, you're here in a personal capacity,' Raco said. 'Bank statements'll be in the house. Come on. I'll show you the study.'

'It's all right.' Falk took a step back. 'I know where it is. Thanks.'

As he turned to leave, he saw Raco's eyebrows lift. If the guy had been expecting a fight over territory, Falk thought, he wasn't going to find one here. Still, he had to admire the man's dedication. It was early but it looked like Raco had been up to his elbows for hours.

Falk started towards the house. Stopped. Thought for a moment. Barb Hadler may have her doubts, but Raco seemed like a cop who took things seriously. Falk turned back.

'Listen,' he said. 'I don't know how much Gerry told you, but I know when I'm in charge, it's a hell of a lot easier when I know what's going on. Less margin for a stuff-up.'

Raco listened in silence as Falk told him Barb's theory of money troubles and debts being called in.

'You think there's anything in it?'

'I don't know. I'm sure there'll be money problems. You can tell that by looking around. Whether that means someone other than Luke pulled the trigger is another question.'

Raco nodded slowly.

'Thanks. I appreciate it.'

'No worries. I'll be in the study.'

Falk was barely halfway across the scorched yard when Raco called out.

'Hey. Wait a sec.' The sergeant wiped his face with his forearm and squinted against the sun. 'You were good friends with Luke, yeah?'

'Long time ago.'

'Say Luke wanted to hide something. Smallish. Any idea where he'd stash it?'

Falk thought for a moment; realised he didn't really need to think about it.

'Maybe. What sort of thing?'

'We find it, I'll show you.'

The last time Falk had laid on that particular patch of ground, the grass had been fresh and green. Now he could feel the yellow scrub scratching his stomach through his shirt.

He'd led Raco around to the far side of the house, testing the weatherboards with his foot. When he found the one he was looking for, he lay down and slid a stick under the bottom of the panel. It creaked a little under the strain, then gave way easily, coming loose in his hand.

Falk looked up at Raco standing over him.

'In there?' Raco asked, pulling on his heavy-duty gloves. 'What did he used to hide?'

'Anything really. Toys and junk food when we were kids. Booze a bit later. Nothing too exciting. The usual stuff kids don't want parents to see.'

Raco knelt down. He thrust his arm into the gap up to the elbow and scrabbled around, feeling blindly. He withdrew it, clutching a handful of dried leaves and an old packet of cigarettes. He dumped them on the ground by his knees and went back in. This time he pulled out the remains of a soft porn magazine. It was curled and yellowed at the edges and something had eaten holes through the important bits. He tossed it aside in irritation and tried again, pushing his arm in as far as it would go. Reluctantly he came out empty handed. Nothing.

'Here.' Falk gestured for the gloves. 'I'll have a go.'

He and Luke had never used to use gloves, Falk thought, as he thrust his hand into the dead space. Anything lurking under a house was no match for the immortality of kids and teenagers. He fumbled around, feeling nothing but flat earth.

'Give me a clue what I'm looking for,' he grunted.

'A box probably. Or some sort of packaging.'

Falk groped about, pushing his arm in as far as it would go. The hiding spot was empty. He pulled his hand out.

'Sorry,' he said. 'It's been a while.'

Raco's knees clicked as he stood from his crouched position. He opened the battered cigarette packet. Took one out, looked at it longingly, then slowly slid it back in. Neither of them spoke for a long moment.

'It's the cartridges,' Raco said finally. 'From the shotgun that killed the Hadlers. They don't match.'

'Don't match what?'

'The brand Luke Hadler used. Used for years as far as I can tell. The three shots fired that killed him and his family were

Remington. The only ammunition I can find on this entire property is Winchester.'

'Winchester.'

'Yep. I noticed when the inventory came through from Clyde and it's been picking at me ever since,' Raco said. 'So that's it. A box of Remingtons, and I'd be a happier man.'

Falk pulled off the gloves. His hands were clammy.

'Clyde couldn't send over a couple of bodies to help you do a property search?'

Raco looked away, fiddled with the cigarette packet in his hands. 'Yeah. I don't know. Probably could.'

'Right.' Falk suppressed a smile. Raco may be sporting the uniform and talking the talk, but Falk had been around long enough to know off-the-books probing when he saw it.

'Maybe Luke picked up a few odd spares somewhere,' Falk suggested.

'Yeah, definitely could have,' Raco said.

'Or the shells were the last in the box and he threw away the package.'

'Yep. Although there was no sign of that in the household rubbish or his ute. And believe me,' Raco gave a short laugh, 'I've checked.'

'Where haven't you searched yet?'

Raco nodded at the missing weatherboard.

'On this property? I think this officially makes everywhere.'

Falk frowned. 'It's a bit weird.'

'Yeah. That's what I thought too.'

Falk said nothing, just stared at him. Raco was sweating hard. His face, arms and clothes were covered in grime and dust from scrabbling around in the baking heat of the sheds.

'What else?' Falk said.

There was a silence.

'What do you mean?'

'All this effort. Down on your hands and knees all morning in a dead man's barn, in this heat,' Falk said. 'There's something more. Or at least you think there's more.'

There was a long pause. Then Raco breathed out.

'Yeah,' he said. 'There's more.'

Chapter Five

They'd sat for a while by the side of the house, backs up against the wall beside the loose panel and grass prickling the backs of their legs. Making the most of the thin slice of shade while Raco ran through the facts. He started with the slightly detached air of someone who'd said it all before.

'It was two weeks ago today,' he said, fanning himself loosely with the crinkled porn mag. 'A courier with a delivery found Karen and made the emergency call. That came in at about 5.40 pm.'

'To you?'

'And Clyde and the local GP. The dispatcher notifies us all. GP was closest so he was first on the scene. Dr Patrick Leigh. You know him?'

Falk shook his head.

'Anyway, he was first, then I turn up a couple of minutes later. I pull up and the door's open and the doc's crouched over

Karen in the hall, checking her vitals or whatever.' Raco paused for a long moment, staring out at the tree line with an unfocused gaze. 'I'd never met her, didn't even know who she was then, but he knew her. Had her blood all over his hands. And he's yelling, kind of screaming at me, you know: "She's got kids, there might be kids." So –'

Raco sighed, and flipped open Luke's aged pack of cigarettes. He put one between his lips and offered the pack to Falk, who surprised himself by taking one. He couldn't remember the last time he'd smoked. It might easily have been in this very same spot with his late best friend next to him. For whatever reason, taking one now felt right. He leaned in as Raco lit the ends. Falk took a drag and immediately remembered why he'd kicked the habit easily. But as he breathed deep and the smell of the tobacco mingled with the tang of the eucalyptus trees, the heady sensation of being sixteen again hit him like the rush of nicotine.

'So anyway,' Raco picked up. His voice was quieter now. 'The doc's yelling and I bolt off through the house. No idea who's in there, what I'm going to find. If there's someone about to step round a door with a shotgun. I want to call out to the kids but I realise I don't even know their names. So I'm yelling, "Police. It's OK, come out, you're safe," or something, but I don't even know if it's true.' He took a long drag, remembering.

'And then I hear this crying – this sort of *wailing* – so I follow it, not knowing what's waiting for me. And I go into the nursery and I see that little girl in her cot, screaming blue murder, and honestly, I've never been so glad to see a kid bawling her eyes out in all my life.'

Raco blew a plume of smoke into the air.

'Cause she was *fine*,' he said. 'I couldn't believe it. She was scared, obviously, but not hurt that I could see. And I remember thinking at that moment that it might all still be OK. Yes, it was

'sad about the mum, tragic. But *thank God*, at least the kids were
OK. But then I look across the hall and a door's ajar.'

He carefully ground his cigarette butt into the dirt, not
looking at Falk. Falk felt a cold dread seep through him, knowing
what was to come.

'And I can see it's another kid's room. All blue paint and car
posters, you know? Boy's room. And there's no sound coming
from that one. So I go across the hall and push open the door
and then it definitely wasn't OK at all.' He paused. 'That room
was like a scene from hell. That room was the worst thing I have
ever seen.'

They sat in silence until Raco cleared his throat.

'Come on,' he said, pulling himself to his feet, shaking his
arms as if shedding the memory. Falk stood and followed him
towards the front of the house.

'The response teams arrived from Clyde shortly after that,'
Raco went on as they walked. 'Police, paramedics. It was nearly
half past six by the time they got there. We'd searched the rest
of the house and there's no-one else there, thank Christ, so
everyone was desperately trying to phone Luke Hadler. At first
people are worried, you know, how are we supposed to break
this to him? But then there's still no answer and his car's not
there and he hasn't come home, and all of a sudden you could
feel the mood start to shift.'

'What was Luke supposed to have been doing then?'

'A couple of the search and rescue volunteers, mates of his,
knew he'd been helping a friend cull rabbits on his property
that arvo. A guy called Jamie Sullivan. Someone phoned and
Sullivan confirmed it, but said Luke had left his farm a couple of
hours earlier by that point.'

They'd reached the front door and Raco pulled out a set
of keys.

'When there was still no sign of Luke, and no answer on his phone, we called some more of the search and rescue team in. Paired them up with officers, sent them out looking. It was a terrible couple of hours. We had unarmed searchers tramping through paddocks and bushland, not sure what they would find. Luke dead? Alive? No idea what kind of state he'd be in. We were all panicking we'd find him holed up somewhere with a gun and a death wish. In the end one of the search guys stumbled across his ute more by luck than anything. Parked up in some crappy clearing about three kilometres away. There was no need to worry after all. Luke was dead in the back, missing most of his face. His own gun, licensed, registered, completely legit, still in his hand.'

Raco unlocked the farmhouse door and pushed it open.

'So it seemed like that was that. Pretty much done and dusted. This –' he stepped aside so Falk could see right down the long hallway, '– is where it starts to get strange.'

The entrance hall was muggy and stank of bleach. A side table piled with household clutter of bills and pens sat askew against a far wall, shoved from its original position. The tiled floor was ominously clean. The entire hallway had been scrubbed down to the original grout.

'The industrial cleaners've been through, so there aren't any nasty surprises,' Raco said. 'They couldn't save the carpet in the kid's bedroom. Not that you'd want to.'

Family photos covered the walls. The frozen poses looked somehow familiar and Falk realised he'd seen most of them at the funeral. The whole scene felt like a grotesque parody of the warm family home he'd known.

'Karen's body was found right here in the hallway,' Raco said. 'The door was open so the courier saw her straight away.'

'Was she running for the door?' Falk tried to imagine Luke chasing his own wife through their own house.

'No, that's just it. She was answering it. Shot by whoever was standing on the doorstep. You can tell from the position of the body. But tell me this, when you come home at night, does your wife answer the door to you?'

'I'm not married,' Falk said.

'Well, I am. And call me liberated, but I've got a key to my own house.'

Falk considered. 'Catch her by surprise, maybe?' he said, playing out the scenario in his mind.

'Why bother? Dad comes home waving a loaded shotgun, I reckon they'd still be pretty bloody surprised. He's got them both inside the house. Knows the layout. Too easy.'

Falk positioned himself inside the hall and opened and closed the door a few times. Open, the doorway was a rectangle of blinding light compared with the dimness of the hall. He imagined Karen answering the knock, a little distracted maybe, perhaps annoyed by the interruption. Blinking away the brightness for the crucial second it took her killer to raise a gun.

'Just strikes me as odd,' Raco said. 'Shooting her in the doorway. All it did was give that poor kid a chance to piss his pants and bolt, not necessarily in that order.'

Raco looked past Falk. 'Which brings me to my next point,' he said. 'When you're ready.'

Falk nodded and followed him down the bowels of the hall.

As Raco snapped on the light in the small blue bedroom, Falk's first dizzy impression was that someone was renovating. A child's bed had been shoved against the far wall at an angle, stripped back to the mattress. Toys were piled in boxes and stacked haphazardly beneath posters of football players and Disney characters. The carpet had been ripped out, exposing untreated floorboards.

Falk's boots left patterns in a layer of sawdust. The boards in one corner had been heavily sanded. A stain still remained. Raco lingered by the doorway.

'Still difficult for me to be in here,' he said with a shrug.

This had once been a nice bedroom, Falk knew. Twenty years ago it had been Luke's own. Falk had slept there himself many times. Whispering after lights out. Holding his breath and stifling giggles when Barb Hadler called through to them to shut up and go to sleep. Wrapped warm in a sleeping bag, not far from those floorboards with their awful stain. This room had been a good space. Now, like the hall, it stank of bleach.

'Can we open the window?'

'Better not,' Raco said. 'Got to keep the blinds down. Caught a couple of kids trying to take photos soon after it happened.'

Raco pulled out his tablet computer and tapped it a few times. He handed it to Falk. On the screen was a photo gallery.

'The little boy's body's been removed,' Raco said. 'But you can see how the room was found.'

In the photos, the blinds were wide open, spilling light onto a horrendous scene below. The wardrobe doors were flung wide open and the clothes had been roughly pushed aside. A large wicker toy box was overturned. On the bed, a spaceship duvet was rucked up on one side as though tossed back to check what was under it. The carpet was mostly beige, except for the one corner where a rich red-black pool seeped out from behind a large upended laundry basket.

For a moment Falk tried to imagine Billy Hadler's last moments. Huddled behind the laundry basket, hot urine dribbling down his leg as he tried to silence ragged breaths.

'You got kids?' Raco asked.

Falk shook his head. 'You?'

'One on the way. A little girl.'

'Congratulations.'

'We've got an army of nieces and nephews, though. Not here, back home in South Australia. A few around Billy's age, couple a bit younger,' Raco said, taking back the tablet and scrolling through the photos. 'And the thing is, my brothers know every one of their kids' hiding places. You send them blindfolded into their kids' bedrooms, and they could find them in two seconds.'

He tapped the screen.

'Every possible way I look at these photos, it looks like a search,' Raco said. 'Someone who didn't know Billy's hiding spots methodically working his way through. Is he in the cupboard? No. Under the bed? No. It's like the kid was hunted down.'

Falk stared hard at the dark smudge that had once been Billy Hadler.

'Show me where you found Charlotte.'

The nursery across the hall was decorated in yellow. A musical mobile dangled from the ceiling above an empty space.

'Gerry and Barb took the cot,' Raco explained.

Falk looked around the room. It felt so different from the others. Furniture and carpet still intact. No acrid bleach stink in there. It had the feel of a sanctuary, untouched by the horror that had unfolded outside the door.

'Why didn't Luke kill Charlotte?' Falk said.

'The popular money's on conscience and guilt kicking in.'

Falk walked out, back across the hall to Billy's bedroom. He stood at the bloodstain in the corner, turned 180 degrees and strode back across the hall into Charlotte's room.

'Eight steps,' Falk said. 'But I'm pretty tall. So we'll call it nine for most people. Nine steps from Billy's body to where Charlotte was lying like a sitting duck. And Luke would've had the adrenaline going, blood pumping, red mist, the works. So, nine steps. The question is, is that enough time for a total change of heart?'

'Doesn't sound like enough to me.'

Falk thought about the man he'd known. What had once been a clear picture was now distorted and fuzzy.

'Did you ever meet Luke?' he said.

'No.'

'He could change his mood like flipping a coin. Nine steps could be eight more than he needed.'

But for the first time since he'd returned to Kiewarra, Falk felt a pinprick of genuine doubt.

'It's supposed to be a statement, though, isn't it? Something like this. It's personal. *He murdered his entire family.* That's what you want people to say. Luke's wife of seven years is bleeding out on the hall floor and he's spent – what, two minutes? Three? – turning the bedroom upside down to murder his own son. He's planning to kill himself when he's finished. So if it was Luke –' he hesitated slightly on the word *if*, '– why does his daughter get to live?'

They stood for a moment, both looking at the mobile hanging still and silent above the empty cot space. Why slaughter a whole family bar the baby? Falk turned it back and forth in his mind until he could think of a few reasons, but only one good one.

'Maybe whoever was here that day didn't kill the baby because they just didn't need to kill the baby,' Falk said finally. 'Nothing personal about it. Doesn't matter who you are, thirteen-month-olds don't make good witnesses.'

Chapter Six

'They're not crash hot about me coming in here generally,' Raco said with a note of regret as he put two beers on the table at the Fleece. It lurched lopsidedly under the weight, slopping a centimetre of liquid over the scratched surface. He had been home to change out of his uniform, and had returned with a thick file labelled *Hadler* under his arm. 'I'm not great for business. Everyone always has to make a big show of putting their car keys away.'

They glanced over at the barman. It was the same large bearded bloke from the night before. He was watching them over the top of a newspaper.

'Policeman's lot. Cheers.' Falk raised his glass and took a long swallow. He'd always been able to take or leave the booze, but at that moment he was glad of it. It was early evening quiet in the pub and they were holed up alone in a corner. On the far side of the room three men stared with bovine blankness at greyhound racing on the TV. Falk didn't recognise them, and they ignored him in turn. In the back room, the poker machines blinked and whistled. The air conditioning was blowing Arctic cold.

Raco took a sip. 'So what now?'

'Now you tell Clyde you've got concerns,' Falk said.

'I go to the Clyde cops now, it'll send them straight into arse-covering mode.' Raco frowned. 'You know what'll be going through their heads if they think they've stuffed this up. They'll make a gymnastics team, bending over backwards to prove their investigation was sound. I know I would.'

'I'm not sure you've got a choice. Something like this. It's not a one-man job.'

'We've got Barnes.'

'Who?'

'My constable at the station. So that's three of us.'

'That's only two of you, mate,' Falk said. 'I can't stay.'

'I thought you told the Hadlers you would.'

Falk rubbed the bridge of his nose. The pokies behind him clanged more loudly. He felt like the noise was inside his head.

'For a couple of days. That means one or two. Not for the duration of an investigation. An unofficial one at that. I've got a job to get back to.'

'Fine.' Raco spoke like it was obvious. 'Stay for the couple of days then. It doesn't have to be anything on the books. Do what you said you'd do on the money side. As soon as we get something solid, I'll go to Clyde.'

Falk said nothing. He thought about the two boxes of bank statements and documents he'd taken from the Hadlers' place that were now sitting upstairs on his bed.

Luke lied. You lied.

He picked up their empty glasses and took them back to the bar.

'Same again?' The barman hauled his bulk off a stool and put his newspaper down. He was the only person Falk had seen working in the place since yesterday.

'Listen,' Falk said as he watched a clean glass put under the tap. 'That room I'm in. Likely to be available a bit longer?'

'Depends.' The barman set one beer on the counter. 'I've been hearing one or two whispers about you, my friend.'

'Have you.'

'I have. And while I welcome the business, I don't welcome trouble, see? Tricky enough running this place as is.'

'The trouble won't come from me.'

'Just comes with you?'

'Not much I can do about that. You know I'm police, though?'

'I did hear that, indeed. But out here in the sticks at midnight with a few boozed-up fellas looking for aggro, those badges mean less than they should, you get me?'

'Fine. Well. Up to you.' He wasn't going to beg.

The barman put the second glass on the counter with a half-smile.

'It's all right, mate. You can untwist your knickers. Your money's as good as the next man's and that's good enough for me.'

He gave Falk his change and picked up the newspaper. He appeared to be doing the cryptic crossword. 'Take it as a friendly warning, though, they can be a funny lot around here. You find yourself in hot water, there's not always a lot of help at hand.' He eyeballed Falk. 'Although from what I hear, you don't need telling about that.'

Falk took both glasses back to the table. Raco was staring moodily at a soggy beer mat.

'You can lose the look,' Falk said. 'You'd better fill me in on the rest.'

Raco slid the folder across the table.

'I've pulled this together from all the stuff I've got access to,' he said.

Falk glanced around the pub. It was still half-empty. No-one nearby. He flipped it open. The first page had a photo of Luke's ute taken from a distance. A pool of blood had collected by the back wheels. He closed the file.

'Just give me the highlights for now. What do we know about the courier who found them?'

'He's looking as clean as you'd want to be. Works for an established delivery firm. Has done for two years. He was delivering recipe books Karen had ordered online – that checks out. He was running late, last delivery of the day. First time he'd made a delivery to Kiewarra. Says he rocked up, saw Karen lying in the doorway, chucked up his lunch into the flowerbed and jumped back in his van. Made the emergency call from the main road.'

'He left Charlotte in the house?'

'Reckons he didn't hear her.' Raco shrugged. 'Maybe he didn't. She'd been alone for a while. Might have cried herself out by then.'

Falk turned to the first page of the file. Kept it open this time. He'd always assumed Luke had been found in the ute's driver's seat, but the images showed his body flat on its back in the cargo tray. The lip of the tray was open and Luke's legs dangled over as though he'd been sitting on the edge. A shotgun by his side pointed towards the mess where his head would have been. His face was completely missing.

'You right?' Raco was watching him closely.

'Yeah.' Falk took a long drink from his beer. The blood had spread across the bottom of the cargo tray, settling in the metal ridges.

'Forensics find anything useful in the tray?' Falk asked.

Raco checked his notes.

'Other than lots of blood – all Luke's – nothing particular noted,' he said. 'I'm not sure how well they looked, though. They had the weapon. It was a working vehicle. He had all sorts of stuff in the back.'

Falk looked again at the photo, concentrating on the area around the body. Barely visible along the left interior side of the tray were four faint horizontal streaks. They looked fresh. Light brown against the dusty white paintwork, the longest was maybe thirty centimetres, the shortest about half that. They were in pairs of two, each pair about a metre apart. The placement wasn't particularly uniform. The right-hand streaks were horizontal; those on the left had a slight tilt.

'What are these?' Falk pointed and Raco leaned in.

'I'm not sure. Like I said, ute would've carried all sorts.'

'The ute still here?'

Raco shook his head. 'Sent to Melbourne. It'll be cleaned up by now for sale or scrap, I reckon.'

Falk looked through the photos, hoping for a better view, but was disappointed. He read over the rest of the notes. Everything appeared fairly standard. Other than the hole in the front of his head, Luke Hadler was a healthy male. A couple of kilos over his ideal weight, slightly high cholesterol. No drugs or alcohol in his system.

Falk said, 'What about the shotgun?'

'Definitely Luke's gun used on all three of them. Registered, licensed. His fingerprints were the only ones on it.'

'Where did he keep it normally?'

'Secured lock box in the barn out the back,' Raco said. 'The ammo – at least the Winchester stuff I've found – was locked away separately. He was pretty big on safety by the look of things.'

Falk nodded, only half-listening. He was looking at the fingerprint report from the shotgun. Six crisp ovals embroidered with tight whorls and lines. Two less clear, slight slippage, but still confirmed as belonging to the left thumb and right little finger of Luke Hadler.

'The fingerprints are good,' Falk said.

Raco caught his tone. Looked up from his notes.

'Yeah, really solid. People didn't take too much convincing after seeing them.'

'Very solid,' Falk said, sliding the report over the table to Raco. 'Maybe too solid? The guy's supposed to have just killed his family. He would've been sweating and shaking like an addict. I've seen worse than these taken under evidence conditions.'

'Shit.' Raco frowned at the prints. 'Yeah, maybe.'

Falk turned the page.

'What did forensics find in the house?'

'They found everything. Seems like half the community had traipsed through there at one time or another. About twenty different fingerprints, not including partials, fibres everywhere. I'm not saying Karen didn't keep the place clean, but it was a farm with kids.'

'Witnesses?'

'The last person to see Luke alive was this mate of his, Jamie Sullivan. Has a property to the east of town. Luke had been helping him shoot rabbits. Arrived in the arvo about three, left about four-thirty, Sullivan reckons. Other than that, around the Hadlers' house there's really only one neighbour who could have seen something. He was on his own property at the time.'

Raco reached for the report. Falk felt a heavy weight in his stomach.

'Neighbour's a strange bloke, though.' Raco went on. 'Aggressive old bastard. No love lost for Luke, whatever that's worth. Not at all keen to assist the police with their inquiries.'

'Mal Deacon,' Falk said. He made a point of keeping his voice even.

Raco looked up in surprise. 'That's right. You know him?'

'Yeah.'

Raco waited, but Falk said nothing more. The silence stretched on.

'Well, anyway,' Raco said. 'He lives up there with his nephew – bloke called Grant Dow – who wasn't home at the time. Deacon reckons he didn't see anything. Might have heard the shots, but didn't think anything of it. Thought it was farm stuff.'

Falk just raised his eyebrows.

'Thing is, what he did or didn't see might not matter anyway,' Raco said, taking out his tablet and tapping the screen. A low-res colour image appeared. Everything was so still that it took Falk a minute to realise it was a video rather than a photograph.

Raco handed him the tablet.

'Security footage from the Hadlers' property.'

'You're kidding.' Falk gaped at the screen.

'Nothing fancy. Barely a step up from a nanny cam really,' Raco said. 'Luke installed it after a spate of equipment burglaries around here a year ago. A few of the farmers have them. Records for twenty-four hours, uploads the footage to the family computer, gets wiped after a week if no-one actively saves it.'

The camera appeared to be positioned above the largest barn. It was directed towards the yard to capture anyone coming or going. One side of the house was in shot, and in the upper corner of the screen a slim slice of driveway was visible. Raco skipped through the recording until he found the spot he was looking for, and paused it.

'OK, this is the afternoon of the shootings. You can watch the whole day later if you want, but in a nutshell the family leaves the house in the morning separately. Luke drives off in his ute just after 5 am – headed out to his own paddocks as far as I've been able to tell. Then shortly after eight, Karen, Billy and Charlotte leave for school. She worked there part-time in an admin role and Charlotte was in the on-site crèche.'

Raco tapped the screen, starting the footage. He passed Falk a pair of earphones and plugged them into the tablet. The sound was poor and muffled as wind buffeted the microphone.

'Nothing happens during the day,' Raco said. 'Believe me, I've watched the entire thing in real time. No-one comes and no-one goes until 4.04 pm, when Karen and the kids get home.'

In the corner of the screen, a blue hatchback trundled by and disappeared. It was on an angle, visible only from the bonnet down to the tyres. Falk could just make out the front number plate.

'You can read that if you freeze it and blow it up,' Raco said. 'It's definitely Karen's car.'

Above the electronic crackling, Falk heard the thud of a car door slamming, followed a moment later by a second one. Raco tapped the screen again. The image jumped.

'Then it's all quiet for nearly an hour – again, I've checked – until . . . here. 5.01 pm.'

Raco pressed play and let Falk watch. For a few long seconds all was still. Then a shape moved in the corner. The silver ute was taller than the hatchback, and only visible from the headlights down. The number plate was visible. Again, the vehicle was there and gone in less than a second.

'Luke's,' Raco said.

The image on screen was completely static, although the footage was still rolling. There was the thud of an invisible car door again, then nothing for an agonising twenty seconds. Suddenly a dull boom crashed in Falk's ears and he flinched. Karen. He felt his heart thumping in his chest.

The scene was still again as the timer continued to tick over. Sixty seconds gone, then ninety. Falk realised he was holding his breath, willing there to be a different ending. He was both frustrated and grateful at that moment for the poor sound. Billy Hadler's screams would be the haunting kind. When the second boom came it was almost a relief. Falk blinked once.

There was no movement. Then, three minutes and forty-seven seconds after the ute had first appeared, it rattled away through the corner of the screen. The back wheels, the bottom of the tray and the number plate of Luke Hadler's vehicle were all perfectly visible.

'No-one else comes or goes until the courier thirty-five minutes later,' Raco said. Falk handed the tablet back to him. He could still hear the muffled booms ringing in his ears.

'You seriously think there's doubt after seeing that?' Falk said.

'It's Luke's ute, but you can't see who's driving it,' Raco said. 'Plus the other stuff. The ammunition. Killing Karen on the doorstep. The search in Billy's room.'

Falk stared at him.

'I don't get it. Why are you so convinced it wasn't Luke? You didn't even know him.'

Raco shrugged. 'I found the kids,' he said. 'I had to see what Billy Hadler looked like after some monster killed him, and I'll never be able to unsee that. I want to make sure the right thing's been done by him. I know it seems crazy, and look, odds are Luke probably did do it. I admit that. But if there's a tiny chance that someone else has done this and got away with it –'

Raco shook his head and took a long drink.

'You know, I look at Luke Hadler and on the surface he had it all – great wife, two kids, decent enough farm, respect in his community. Why would a man like that turn around one day and destroy his family? It makes no sense. I just can't understand how someone like him could do something like that.'

Falk rubbed a hand over his mouth and chin. It felt gritty. He needed a shave.

Luke lied. You lied.

'Raco,' he said. 'There's something about Luke you need to know.'

Chapter Seven

'**B**ack when Luke and I were kids,' Falk said. 'Well, not exactly kids. Older than that, sixteen actually –'

He broke off as he sensed a swell of movement at the other end of the bar. The place had filled up without Falk noticing, and when he looked up now more than one familiar face glanced away. Falk felt the ripple of disruption a moment before he saw it. Drinkers lowered their eyes and shuffled aside without complaint as a group moved through the crowd. At the head was a meaty bloke with sludge-brown hair topped by sunglasses. Falk felt a cold trickle seep through his guts. He may not have recognised Grant Dow at the Hadlers' funeral, but there was no mistaking him now.

Ellie's cousin. They had the same eyes, but Falk knew there was absolutely nothing of her in him. Dow stopped in front of their table, his flabby frame blocking their view. His t-shirt advertised a Balinese beer brand. His features were piggy, small and cramped together in the middle of his face, while his beard straggled across a thick chin. He was wearing the same look of defiance he'd used to stare down the mourners at the wake. Dow raised his glass towards Falk in a mock salute and flashed a smile that went nowhere near his eyes.

'You've got balls turning up here,' he said. 'I'll give you that much. Don't you reckon, Uncle Mal? Give him that much, eh?'

Dow turned. An older man hidden behind him took a shaky step forward and Falk came face to face with Ellie's father for the first time in twenty years. He felt something lodge in his chest and caught himself swallowing.

Mal Deacon had a curve to his spine now but was still a tall man, with ropey arms leading to large hands. His fingers were knotted and swollen with age and were almost white as he gripped the back of a chair for support. His forehead furrowed deep into a scowl, and his exposed scalp was angry pink between strands of grey hair.

Falk braced himself for an outburst but instead a look of confusion flashed across Deacon's face. He shook his head slightly, the loose chicken flesh on his neck rubbing against a dirty collar.

'Why are you back?' Deacon's voice was slow and raspy. Deep grooves appeared on either side of his mouth as he spoke. Every single person in the pub was determinedly looking elsewhere, Falk noted. Only the barman was following the exchange with interest. He had put down his crossword.

'Eh?' Deacon slammed a gnarled hand against the back of the chair and everyone jumped. 'Why are you back? I thought you'd got the message clear enough. You brought the kid with you as well?'

It was Falk's turn to look confused. 'What?'

'That bloody son of yours. Don't act dumb with me, dickhead. He back too? Your boy?'

Falk blinked. Deacon had mistaken him for his late father. He stared at the old man's face. Deacon scowled back but there was something sluggish about his anger.

Grant Dow stepped forward and put a hand on his uncle's shoulder. For a moment he appeared to consider explaining the mistake, then shook his head in frustration and gently forced his uncle into a chair.

'Nice one, you prick, you've gone and upset him now,' Dow said to Falk. 'I've gotta ask you, mate. You think this is the best place for you to be?'

Raco pulled his Victoria Police badge out of his jeans pocket and slapped it face up on the table.

'I could ask you the same thing, Grant. This the best place for you right now, you reckon?'

Dow held up his palms, and twisted his face into a picture of innocence.

'Yeah, all right, no need for that. Me and my uncle are just out for a social drink. He's not well, you can see that yourselves. We're not the ones looking for any trouble. This one, though –' He looked straight at Falk. 'He tracks it behind him like dog shit.'

An almost imperceptible murmur rolled through the room. Falk had known the story would resurface sooner rather than later. He shifted as he felt every eye in the place glance towards him.

The hikers were hot and bored. The mosquitoes were out in force and the track by the Kiewarra River was proving slower going than they'd expected. The three of them trudged along in single file, bickering when they could be bothered to raise their voices over the sound of rushing water.

The second in line swore as he ran chest first into the group leader's backpack, spilling his open water bottle down his front. A former investment banker, he'd moved to the country for his health and had spent each day since trying to convince himself he didn't hate every minute of it. The leader held up his hand and cut short the grumbling. He pointed to the murky river water. They turned and stared.

'What the hell is that?'

'All right, we'll have none of that, thanks,' the barman called out from behind the counter. He'd got to his feet and was resting his fingertips on the countertop. Beneath his orange beard, he was unsmiling. 'This is a public bar. Anyone can drink here – him, you – and you can take it or leave it.'

'What's the third option?' Dow flashed his yellow teeth at his mates, who dutifully laughed.

'Third option is you're barred. So, your choice.'

'Yeah. Always making those promises, though, aren't you?' Dow stared at the barman. Raco cleared his throat but Dow ignored him. The barman's words came back to Falk. *Out here, those badges mean less than they should.*

'The problem's not with him being in the bar.' The room was almost silent as Mal Deacon spoke. 'It's him being back in Kiewarra at all.'

He raised a finger thick with arthritis and pointed it between Falk's eyes. 'Understand this and tell your boy. There's nothing here for you except a lot of people who remember what your son did to my daughter.'

The investment banker vomited his ham sandwiches into the bush. He and the other two were soaking wet, but he barely noticed.

The girl's body now lay on the trail, a pool of water seeping out around her. She was slim, but it had taken all three of them to drag her to the bank. Her skin was unnaturally white and a slick of hair had fallen into her mouth. The sight of it disappearing between her pale lips made the investment banker gag again. Her earlobes were red raw around her piercings. The fish had taken the opportunity. The same markings were visible around her nostrils and painted fingernails.

She was fully clothed and looked young where the water had washed her makeup away. Her white t-shirt was almost transparent as it clung to her skin, displaying her lace bra beneath. Her flat boots were still tangled with traces of the weeds that had tethered her body to the spot. Both boots and every pocket of her jeans had been packed tight with stones.

'Bullshit. I had nothing to do with what happened to Ellie.' Falk couldn't help himself and instantly regretted it. He bit down on his tongue. *Don't engage.*

'Who says?' Grant Dow stood behind his uncle. His cold grin was long gone. 'Who says you had nothing to do with it? Luke Hadler?' As he said the name it felt like air had been sucked out of the bar. 'The thing about that is, Luke's not here to say much of anything anymore.'

The fittest of the trio had run for help. The investment banker sat on the ground near his own pool of vomit. He felt safer there, engulfed in the acid stink, than near that horrific white being. The group leader paced, his feet squelching.

They could guess who she was. Her photo had been in the paper for three days. Eleanor Deacon, aged sixteen. Missing since Friday night, when she'd failed to return home. Her father had given her a night to cool whatever teenage impulse might have been keeping her away. When she didn't come home on Saturday, he'd raised the alarm.

It had seemed like an age before emergency workers arrived at the river. The girl's body was taken to the hospital. The investment banker was sent home. Within a month he'd moved back to the city.

The doctor examining Ellie Deacon's body reported the cause of death as drowning. Her lungs were soggy with the river. She appeared to have been in the water for several days, he noted, most likely since Friday. He reported some bruising on her breastbone and shoulders, and abrasions on her hands and arms. Not inconsistent with damage caused by debris rushing past in the water. There were some old scars on her forearms, possibly evidence of self-harm. She was not, he noted as an afterthought, a virgin.

At the mention of Luke's name there was a ripple around the room, and even Dow seemed to sense he'd gone too far.

'Luke was my friend. Ellie was my friend.' Falk's voice sounded strange to his own ears. 'I cared about them both. So back off.'

Deacon stood up, his chair squealing against the floorboards.

'Don't you talk to me about caring for Ellie. To me she was blood.' He was shouting, his hands shaking as he thrust a finger at Falk in accusation. Out of the corner of his eye, Falk saw Raco and the barman exchange looks.

'You reckon you and your boy had nothing to do with it,' Deacon said. 'What about the note, you lying bastard?'

He said it with a flourish, like a conversational trump card. Falk felt the air go out of him. He felt exhausted. Deacon's mouth was twisted. Next to him, his nephew was laughing. He could smell blood.

'Not so quick with an answer to that, are you?' Dow said.

Falk forced himself not to shake his head. Jesus. That bloody note.

The cops spent two hours picking apart Ellie Deacon's bedroom. Thick fingers awkwardly probed through underwear drawers and jewellery cases. The note was almost missed. Almost. It was written on a single page torn from an ordinary exercise book. It had been folded once and slipped into the pocket of a pair of jeans. On the page, written in pen in Ellie's handwriting, was the date she had disappeared. Underneath that was a single name: Falk.

'Explain that. If you can,' Deacon said. The bar was silent.

Falk said nothing. He couldn't. And Deacon knew he couldn't.

The barman banged a glass down on the counter. 'Enough.' He looked hard at Falk, considering. Raco, holding his police badge visibly in his palm, raised his eyebrows and gave a tiny shake of his head. The barman's eyes instead settled on Dow.

'You and your uncle, leave. Don't come back for two days, thanks. Everyone else, buy a drink or get out.'

The rumours started small and by the end of the day were big. Falk – sixteen and scared – holed up in his bedroom with a thousand thoughts clamouring. He jumped as a tap sounded against the window frame. Luke's face appeared, ghostly white in the evening gloom.

'You're in the shit, mate,' he whispered. 'I heard my mum and dad say. People are talking. What were you really doing on Friday after school?'

'I told you. Fishing. Up river though. Miles away, I swear.' Falk crouched by the window. His legs felt like they wouldn't hold him up.

'Anyone else asked you yet? Cops or anyone?'

'No. They're going to, though. They think I was meeting her or something.'

'But you weren't.'

'No! Course not. But what if they don't believe me?'

'You didn't meet anyone at all? No-one saw you?'

'I was on my bloody own, wasn't I?'

'Right, listen – Aaron, mate, are you listening? Right, anyone asks, you say we were shooting rabbits together. On the back paddocks.'

'Nowhere near the river.'

'No. The paddocks off Cooran Road. Nowhere near the river.

All evening. OK? We were mucking around. Like usual. We only hit one or two. Two. Say two.'

'Yes, OK. Two.'

'Don't forget. We were together.'

'Yes. I mean no. I won't forget. Jesus, Ellie. I can't –'

'Say it.'

'What?'

'Say it now. What you were doing. Practise.'

'Luke and I were shooting rabbits together.'

'Again.'

'I was with Luke Hadler. Shooting rabbits. Out on the Cooran Road paddocks.'

'Say it until it sounds normal. And don't get it wrong.'

'No.'

'You got all that, yeah?'

'Yes. Luke, mate. Thanks. Thank you.'

Chapter Eight

When Aaron Falk was eleven he'd seen Mal Deacon turn his own flock into a staggering, bleeding mess using shearing clippers and a brutal hand. Aaron had felt an ache swell in his chest as he, Luke and Ellie had watched one sheep after another brawled to the ground of the Deacons' shed with a sharp twist and sliced too close to the skin.

Aaron was a farm kid, they all were, but this was something else. A pitiful cry from the smallest ewe made him open his mouth and draw breath, but he was cut short as Ellie pulled him away by his sleeve. She looked up at him and gave a single shake of her head.

She'd been a slight, intense child at that age, prone to long bouts of silence. Aaron, who leaned towards the quiet side himself, found that suited him fine. They usually let Luke do the talking.

Ellie had barely raised her head when the noises from the barn had floated over to where the three of them had been sitting on the sagging porch. Aaron had been curious, but it had been Luke who insisted they abandon their homework to investigate. Now, with the wails of the ewes in their ears and Ellie's face fixed into an expression he hadn't seen before, Aaron knew he wasn't the only one wishing they hadn't.

They turned to leave and Aaron jumped as he saw Ellie's mother watching silently from the barn's doorway. She was jammed up against the frame, wearing an ill-fitting brown jumper with a single greasy stain on it. She took a sip of amber liquid from a glass without taking her eyes off the shearing. Her facial features were shared by her daughter. They had the same deep-set eyes, sallow skin and wide mouth. But to Aaron, Ellie's mother looked a hundred years old. It was years before he realised on that day she would not even have been forty.

As he watched, Ellie's mother closed her eyes and tilted her head back sharply. She took a deep breath, her features creasing. When she opened her eyes again, they fixed on her husband, staring at him with a look so pure and undiluted Aaron was terrified Deacon would turn and see it for himself. Regret.

The weather that year had made the work harder for everyone, and a month later Deacon's nephew Grant had moved into their farmhouse to lend a hand. Ellie's mother left two days after that. Perhaps it had been the final straw. One man to resent was plenty enough for anyone.

Throwing two suitcases and a clinking bag of bottles into an old car, she had tried half-heartedly to stem her daughter's tears with weightless vows that she would be back soon. Falk wasn't sure how many years it had been until Ellie had stopped believing it. He wondered if part of her might have believed it until the day she died.

★

Falk now stood on the porch of the Fleece with Raco while the sergeant lit a cigarette. He offered the packet and Falk shook his head. He'd spent enough time down memory lane for one night.

'Smart choice,' Raco said. 'I'm trying to quit. For the baby.'

'Right. Good on you.'

Raco smoked slowly, blowing the vapour into the hot night sky. The pub noise had ratcheted up a notch. Deacon and Dow had taken their time leaving and the hint of aggression still hung in the air.

'You should've told me earlier.' Raco took a drag. Suppressed a cough.

'I know. I'm sorry.'

'You have anything to do with it? That girl's death?'

'No. But I wasn't with Luke when it happened. Not like we said.'

Raco paused.

'So you lied about your alibi. Where was Luke?'

'I don't know.'

'You never asked?'

'Of course I did, but he —' Falk paused, remembering. 'He always insisted on sticking to our story. Always. Even when it was only the two of us. He said it was safer to be consistent. I didn't push it. I was grateful to him, you know? I thought it was for my benefit.'

'Who else knew it was a lie?'

'A few people suspected. Mal Deacon, obviously. Some others. But no-one knew for certain. At least that's what I always thought. But now I'm not sure. It turns out Gerry Hadler knew all along. Maybe he's not the only one.'

'Do you think Luke killed Ellie?'

'I don't know.' He stared out at the empty street. 'I want to know.'

'You think all this is connected?'

'I really hope not.'

Raco sighed. He stubbed the cigarette out carefully, then doused the butt with a splash of beer.

'All right, mate,' he said. 'Your secret's safe with me. For now. Unless it needs to come out, in which case you sing like a canary and I knew nothing about any of it, right?'

'Yes. Thank you.'

'Meet me at the station at nine tomorrow morning. We'll go and have a chat to Luke's mate, Jamie Sullivan. The last person who admits seeing him alive.' He looked at Falk. 'If you're still in town.'

With a wave, he headed off into the night.

Back in his room, Falk lay on his bed and pulled out his mobile. He held it in his palm but didn't dial. The huntsman had disappeared from above the lamp. He tried not to think about where it was now.

If you're still in town, Raco had said. Falk was all too aware he had the choice. His car was parked right outside. He could pack his bag, pay the bearded bartender and be on the road to Melbourne inside fifteen minutes.

Raco might roll his eyes, and Gerry would try to call. But what could they do? They wouldn't be pleased, but he could live with that. Barb, though – Falk could picture her face with unwelcome clarity – Barb would be dismayed. And he wasn't entirely sure he could live with that. Falk shifted uncomfortably at the thought. The room felt airless in the heat.

He had never known his own mother. She had died in a haemorrhaging pool of her own blood less than an hour after he was born. His dad had tried – tried hard, even – to fill the gap. But any sense Falk had growing up of maternal tenderness, every warm cake from the oven, every over-perfumed cuddle, had come from Barb Hadler. She may have been Luke's mother, but she had always made time for him.

He, Ellie and Luke had spent more time at the Hadlers' house than at any of the others'. Falk's own home was often silent and empty, his father trapped for hours by the demands of the land. Ellie would shake her head at suggestions they go to her house. *Not today*, she'd say. When he and Luke had insisted for variety, Falk always found himself regretting it. Ellie's house was messy, with a whiff of empty bottles.

The Hadlers' place was sunlit and busy, with good things coming from the kitchen and clear instructions about homework and bedtime and orders to turn off that damn TV and get some fresh air. The Hadlers' property had always been a haven — until two weeks ago, when it had become a crime scene of the worst kind.

Falk lay unmoving on the bed. Fifteen minutes had passed. He could be on the road by now. Instead, he was still there.

He sighed and rolled over, his fingers hovering over his phone as he considered who he needed to inform. He pictured his St Kilda flat, the lights off, front door locked up tight. Big enough for two, but for the past three years home only to him. No-one was waiting there anymore. No-one fresh from the shower, with music playing and a bottle of red breathing on the kitchen counter. No-one eager to answer the phone and interested to hear why he was staying a few extra days.

Most of the time, he was fine with that. But at that moment, lying in a pub room in Kiewarra, he wished he'd built a home a little more like Barb and Gerry Hadlers' than one just like his father's.

He was due back at work on Monday, but they knew he'd been at a funeral. He'd avoided saying whose. He could stay, he knew. He could take a few days. For Barb. For Ellie. For Luke, even. He'd built up more overtime and goodwill on the Pemberley case than he could use. His latest investigation was a slow burn at best.

Falk mulled it over, and another fifteen minutes passed. Finally, he picked up his phone and left a message for the financial division's long-suffering secretary, informing her he'd be taking a week's leave for personal reasons, effective immediately.

It was hard to say which one of them was more surprised.

Chapter Nine

Jamie Sullivan had been at work for more than four hours by the time Falk and Raco tramped across his paddocks. He was on one knee, his bare hands deep in the dry dirt, checking the soil with scientific scrutiny.

'We'll go into the house,' he said when Raco told him they had questions about Luke. 'I need to check on my gran anyways.'

Falk studied Sullivan as they followed him towards the low brick building. Late twenties, he had a dusting of straw-blond hair that was prematurely thinning at the crown. His torso and legs were wiry, but his arms were built like pistons, giving him the shape of an inverted triangle.

At the house, Sullivan led them into a cluttered hallway. Falk took off his hat and fought to keep the look of surprise off his face. Behind him, he heard Raco swear under his breath as his shin connected with a footstool lurking by the door. The hallway was chaotic. Every surface was crammed with ornaments and knick-knacks gathering dust. Somewhere deep in the house, a television blared.

'It's all Gran's.' Sullivan answered the question that neither of them had asked out loud. 'She likes them. And they keep her –' he considered, '– present.'

He led them through to the kitchen where a birdlike woman was standing at the sink. Her blue-veined hands trembled under the weight of a filled kettle.

'All right there, Gran? Fancy a cuppa? Let me.' Sullivan hastily took the kettle from her.

The kitchen was clean but disorganised, and above the stove a large scorch mark stained the wall. The paint had blistered and was peeling away like an ugly grey wound. Mrs Sullivan glanced at the three men and then back at the door.

'When's your dad getting home?'

'He's not, Gran,' Sullivan said. 'He died, remember? Three years now.'

'Yes. I know.' It was impossible to tell whether she was surprised by the news or not. Sullivan looked at Falk and nodded towards a doorway.

'Could you take her through? I'll be in in a minute.'

Falk could feel the bones through the loose skin of the old woman's arm as she leaned on him. The living room felt claustrophobic after the brightness of the kitchen, and everywhere half-empty cups jostled with blank-eyed china figurines for precious space. Falk led the woman to a threadbare armchair near the window.

Mrs Sullivan sat down shakily with an irritated sigh.

'You officers are here about Luke Hadler, are you? Don't touch those,' she snapped as Raco went to move a pile of dog-eared newspapers from a chair. Her vowels carried a trace of an Irish lilt. 'No need to look at me like that. I'm not completely daft yet. That fella Luke was round here then went off and did away with his family, didn't he? Why else would you be here? Unless our Jamie's been up to something he shouldn't.'

Her laugh sounded like a rusty gate.

'Not that we know of,' Falk said, exchanging a glance with Raco. 'Did you know Luke well?'

'I didn't know him at all. Other than he was friends with our Jamie. Came round from time to time. Gave him a hand on the farm.'

Sullivan came through carrying a tea tray. Ignoring his gran's protests, he cleared a space on the sideboard and waved at Falk and Raco to sit down on the battered couch.

'Sorry about the mess,' Sullivan said, handing around cups. 'It gets a bit tricky –' He glanced towards his gran and turned his focus instead to the teapot. He had shadows under his eyes that made him look older, Falk noticed. But he had a confidence about him, the way he took stock of the situation and managed the room. Falk could imagine him away from all of this, wearing a suit in a city office somewhere. Making six figures and blowing half of it on expensive wines.

Sullivan finished passing out the drinks and pulled up a cheap wooden chair. 'So what do you want to know?'

'We're tidying up one or two loose ends,' Raco said.

'For the Hadlers,' Falk added.

'Right. No worries. If it's for Barb and Gerry,' Sullivan said. 'But look, the first thing I want to say, and what I told the Clyde cops, is that if I'd known – if there'd been any suggestion that Luke was about to go off and do what he did – I'd never have let him leave. I want to say that straight off.'

He looked down and fiddled with his mug.

'Of course, mate, no-one's saying you could have stopped what happened,' Raco said. 'But if you could run through it one

more time that would be helpful. So we can hear for ourselves.
Just in case.'

Rabbits, Sullivan told them. That was the problem. One
of them, at least. Hard enough to get through the drought
without them attacking everything worth eating. He'd been
complaining in the Fleece the night before and Luke had
offered to give him a hand.

'Anyone hear you making the arrangements?' Falk said.

'Probably. I don't remember specifically. But it was pretty
busy. Anyone could've heard if they'd bothered listening.'

*Luke Hadler pulled up at the entrance to the paddock and climbed out of
his ute. He was five minutes early, but Jamie Sullivan was already there.
The pair each raised a hand in greeting. Luke reached into the cargo tray
for his shotgun and took the ammunition Sullivan handed him.*

*'Come on, let's get these bastard bunnies of yours,' Luke said,
flashing his teeth.*

'You supplied the ammo?' Raco asked. 'What kind?'

'Winchester. Why?'

Raco caught Falk's eye. Not the missing Remingtons then.

'Did Luke bring any of his own?'

'I don't think so. My bunnies, my bullets, was my way of
thinking. Why?'

'Just checking. How did Luke seem to you?'

'I don't know really. I've gone over that in my head a lot since
then. But I suppose I'd have to say that he seemed fine. Normal.'
Sullivan thought for a minute. 'By the time he left, at least.'

*Luke's first few shots were poor, and Sullivan glanced over. Luke was
chewing on the skin around his thumb. Sullivan said nothing. Luke shot
again. Missed.*

'*All right, mate?*' *Sullivan said reluctantly. He and Luke tended to confide in each other as much as Sullivan did with any of his friends, which was to say hardly at all. On the other hand, he didn't have all day to get these rabbits dealt with. The sun bored down on their backs.*

'*Fine.*' *Luke shook his head, distracted. 'You?*'

'*Yeah, same.*' *Sullivan hesitated. He could easily leave it there. Luke shot and missed again. Sullivan decided to try to meet the man halfway.*

'*My gran's getting a bit on the frail side these days,*' *Sullivan said. 'Can be a handful.*'

'*She OK?*' *Luke said without taking his eyes off the rabbit warren.*

'*Yeah. It's just a bit tricky looking after her sometimes.*'

Luke nodded vaguely and Sullivan realised he was only half-listening.

'*That's bloody women for you,*' *Luke said. 'At least yours can't run around carrying on about God knows what anymore.*'

Sullivan, who had never once in his life considered his gran to be in the same category as 'women', struggled to think of a response.

'*No. I suppose not,*' *he said. He felt they had somehow strayed into uncharted waters. 'Everything OK with Karen?*'

'*Oh. Yeah. No worries.*' *Luke levelled his gun, pulled the trigger. Better this time. 'You know. Karen's Karen. Always something happening.*' *He took a breath as if to say something else, then stopped. Changed his mind.*

Sullivan fidgeted. Definitely uncharted waters. 'Right.'

He tried to think of something else to add, but his mind was blank. He glanced over at Luke, who had lowered his gun and was watching him. Their eyes met for a moment. The atmosphere had become decidedly uncomfortable. Both men turned back to the warren.

'"Always something happening"?' Raco said. 'What did he mean by that?'

Sullivan looked at the table miserably. 'I don't know. I didn't ask. I should've asked, shouldn't I?'

Yes, Falk thought. 'No,' he said. 'It probably wouldn't have made a difference.' He didn't know whether that was true. 'Did Luke say anything else about it?'

Sullivan shook his head. 'No. We got back onto the weather. Like always.'

An hour later Luke stretched.

'I think that's made a dent in them.' He checked his watch. 'Better make a move.' He handed the spare ammunition back to Sullivan. They walked together back to the ute, any earlier tension now dissolved.

'Quick beer?' Sullivan took off his hat and wiped his face with his forearm.

'No, I should get home. Things to do, you know.'

'Right. Thanks for your help.'

'No worries.' Luke shrugged. 'Finally got my eye in, at least.'

He put his unloaded gun in the footwell of the ute's passenger seat and climbed in. Now that he'd made up his mind to go he seemed in a hurry to leave. He rolled down the window and gave a short wave as he pulled away.

Sullivan stood alone in the empty paddock and watched the silver ute disappear.

They mulled the scenario over in silence. By the window, Mrs Sullivan's teacup rattled against the saucer as she placed it down on a pile of novels. She glared at it.

'What happened then?' Raco said.

'A while later the Clyde police rang, looking for Luke,' Sullivan said. 'I told them he'd left a couple of hours earlier. The news was everywhere about five minutes after that though.'

'What time was that?'

'Probably about six-thirty, I reckon.'

'You were here?'

'Yeah.'

'And before that, when Luke left, you did what?'

'Nothing. Work. Here on the farm,' Sullivan said. 'I finished up outside. Had dinner with Gran.'

Falk blinked as his eye caught a tiny movement.

'It was just the two of you here?' Falk kept his voice light. 'You didn't leave at all? No-one else came by?'

'No. Just us.'

It would have been easy to miss, but when Falk thought about it afterwards, he felt sure. In the corner of his vision, Mrs Sullivan had jerked her pale gaze up in surprise. She'd stared at her grandson for barely half a moment before casting her eyes back down. Falk had watched closely, but she didn't look up again once. For the short remainder of their visit, she appeared to be sound asleep.

Chapter Ten

'I tell you, I would be climbing the bloody walls.' Raco shuddered behind the steering wheel. Outside, a thin wire fence protecting yellow scrub flashed past. Beyond, the paddocks were beige and brown. 'Cooped up in the middle of nowhere with no-one but the old lady. That house was like a weird museum.'

'Not a fan of china cherubs?' Falk said.

'Mate, my gran is more Catholic than the Pope. When it comes to quasi-religious ornaments, I can see you and raise you,' Raco said. 'It just doesn't seem like much of a life for a guy his age.'

They passed a fire warning sign by the side of the road. The alert level had been lodged at severe since Falk arrived. The arrow pointed insistently at the bright orange segment of the semicircle. Prepare. Act. Survive.

'Was he being straight with us, you reckon?' Falk explained how Sullivan's grandmother had reacted to his claim he'd been at home that evening.

'That's interesting. She's quite batty, though, isn't she? Bit of a mean streak as well. There was nothing in the reports suggesting Sullivan was out and about, but that doesn't really mean anything. He probably wasn't checked too thoroughly, if at all.'

'The thing is,' Falk leaned forward to fiddle with the air conditioner. 'If Sullivan wanted to kill Luke, it would have been easy. They were out in the middle of nowhere with shotguns for over an hour. It's an open invitation to stage an accident. His gran could have pulled it off out there.'

Falk gave up on the air conditioner and wound down his window a crack, letting in a stream of boiling air. He hastily rolled it back up.

Raco laughed. 'And I thought the heat was bad in Adelaide.'

'That's where you were? What brought you all the way out here?'

'First chance for a sergeant's posting. Seemed like a good opportunity to run my own station, and I was a country kid anyway. You always worked in Melbourne?'

'Mostly. Always been based there.'

'You like doing the financial stuff?'

Falk smiled to himself at Raco's tone. Polite yet complete disbelief that anyone had chosen that route. It was a familiar reaction. People were always surprised to discover how often the banknotes he handled were sticky with blood.

'It suits me,' he said. 'Speaking of, I started going through the Hadlers' financial records last night.'

'Anything interesting?'

'Not yet.' Falk stifled a yawn. He'd stayed up late peering at the numbers under the weak wattage of his room's main light. 'Which is telling in itself. The farm was struggling, that's obvious, but I'm not sure it was doing much worse than any of the others round here. At least they'd planned for it a bit. Put some money away during the good times. Their life insurance policy was nothing special. Just the basic attached to their super.'

'Who gets that?'

'Charlotte, via Luke's parents. It's pretty minimal, though. It'll probably pay off the mortgage and not much more. She'll get the property, I guess, whether she likes it or not. So far no other real red flags – multiple accounts, large withdrawals, third party debts, that sort of stuff. I'll keep at it.'

The main thing Falk had learned from the exercise was that Karen Hadler was a competent and thorough bookkeeper. He'd felt a pang of affinity with her as he'd followed her ordered numbers and careful pencil markings.

Raco slowed as he approached a deserted junction and checked his watch.

'Seven minutes gone.'

They were following Luke's route home from Sullivan's place. Raco turned left onto the road towards the Hadlers' farmhouse. It was paved, but not well. Deep cracks showed where the bitumen had swelled and shrunk with the seasonality of a crop.

It was technically a two-way road, but was barely wide enough for two vehicles to pass side by side. A head-on meeting would force one to take a neighbourly dip into the scrub, Falk imagined. He didn't get the opportunity to find out. They didn't meet a single vehicle the whole way.

'Nearly fourteen minutes, door to door,' Falk said as Raco pulled up at the Hadlers' driveway. 'All right. Let's see where Luke's body was found.'

It was barely even a clearing.

Raco managed to shoot past it and swore quietly, screeching to a halt. He reversed a few metres and pulled over at the side of the road. They got out, not bothering to lock the doors. There was no-one else around. Raco led the way to a gap in the tree line.

'It's in here.'

There was a pocket of eerie silence as invisible birds were momentarily stilled by the sound of his voice. The gap opened into a small space, big enough for a vehicle to drive in but not turn around. Falk stood in the centre. It was fractionally cooler here, shaded on all sides by a sentry line of ghost gums. The road was completely hidden by the thick growth. Something in the bush rustled and scurried away. The yellow earth was baked solid. No tracks or wheel marks.

Directly beneath Falk's feet, in the centre of the clearing, lay a dusting of loose sand. He realised what it had been put down to cover and hastily stepped off. The area had been trampled over by dozens of boots recently, but other than that it looked ill-used.

'Pretty miserable place to spend your last moments,' Falk said. 'Was this spot supposed to mean anything to Luke?'

Raco shrugged. 'Hoping you might have some idea about that.'

Falk searched his memory for old camping trips, boyhood adventures. Nothing came to mind.

'He definitely died here? In the back of the ute?' Falk said. 'No chance he was shot somewhere else and moved?'

'None at all. Blood pattern was definitive.'

Falk tried to organise the timeline in his head. Luke had left Jamie Sullivan's around 4.30 pm. Luke's ute was on camera at the Hadlers' farm about thirty minutes later. Longer than it had taken Falk and Raco to drive the same distance. Two gunshots, four minutes, and the ute had driven away.

'It's fairly straightforward if Luke shot his family,' Falk said. 'He drove himself to the house, taking the scenic route for whatever reason, killed them, then drove himself here.'

'Yeah. Gets a lot more complicated if it was someone else, though,' Raco said. 'The killer had to be inside Luke's ute at some point soon after he left Sullivan's, because Luke had the murder weapon with him. So who drove it to the farmhouse?'

'And if it wasn't Luke behind the wheel, where the hell was he while his family was being murdered? Sitting in the passenger seat watching it happen?' Falk said.

Raco shrugged. 'Maybe he was? I mean, it's a possible scenario. Depending on who the other person was, what kind of hold they might have had over him.' They looked at each other, and Falk knew Raco was also thinking about Sullivan.

'Or the killer could have physically overpowered him,' Raco said. 'Might have taken a bit of effort, but some people could do it. You saw Sullivan's arms. Like walnuts packed into a sock.'

Falk nodded and thought back to the report on Luke's body. He was a decent-sized bloke. A healthy male, other than the gunshot wound. No defensive marks on his hands. No sign of ligature marks or other restraints. He pictured Luke's corpse lying flat on its back in the ute's cargo tray. The blood pooled around him and the four unexplained streaks on the side of the metal tray.

'"Bloody women",' Falk said out loud. 'What do you think he meant by that?'

'I dunno,' Raco said, glancing at his watch. 'But we're set to meet someone who might later this arvo. I thought it could be worth seeing what Karen Hadler kept in her desk drawer.'

Chapter Eleven

The wattle sapling looked a little less sickly once it was in the ground, but not much. Uniformed schoolchildren looked on in bewilderment as mulch was shovelled around its base. Teachers and parents stood in loose groups, some crying openly.

A handful of the wattle's fuzzy yellow buds gave up the fight immediately and fluttered to the ground. They settled near a plaque with the fresh engraving:

> *In memory of Billy Hadler and Karen Hadler.*
> *Much loved and missed by our school family.*

The sapling didn't stand a chance, Falk thought. He could feel the heat through the soles of his shoes.

Back on the grounds of his old primary school, Falk was again struck by the feeling that he could be thirty years in the past. The asphalt playground was a miniature version of the one he remembered and the water fountains seemed absurdly low. But it was instantly familiar, sparking half-remembered flashes of faces and events he'd long forgotten.

Luke had been a good ally to have back then. He was one of those kids with an easy smile and a sharp wit who could navigate the jungle law of the playground effortlessly. *Charismatic* would have been the word, if they'd known it at that age. He was generous with his time, his jokes, his belongings. His parents. Everyone was welcome at the Hadler household. He was loyal almost to a fault. When Falk had once taken a stray football in the face, he'd had to drag Luke off the kid who'd kicked it. Falk, tall and awkward then, was always aware he was lucky to have Luke on his side.

Falk shifted uncomfortably as the ceremony came to a close.

'Scott Whitlam, principal,' Raco said, nodding as a fit-looking man in a tie politely extracted himself from a crowd of parents.

Whitlam came over, one hand extended. 'Sorry to keep you waiting,' he said after Raco introduced Falk. 'Everyone wants to talk at a time like this.'

Whitlam was in his early forties and moved with the easy energy of a retired athlete. He had a broad chest and a wide smile. Half an inch of clean brown hair was visible under the bottom of his hat.

'It was a nice service,' Falk said, and Whitlam glanced back at the sapling.

'It's what we needed.' He lowered his voice. 'Tree hasn't got a hope in hell, though. God knows what we're supposed to tell the kids when it dies. Anyway —' He nodded towards the blond-brick building. 'We've gathered together anything belonging to Karen and Billy, like you asked. There's not a lot, I'm afraid, but it's in the office.'

They followed him across the grounds. A bell rang somewhere in the distance. End of the school day. Up close, the buildings and play equipment made a depressing sight. Paint had chipped from every surface and the exposed metal was red with rust. There were cracks in the plastic slide and only one end of the basketball court had a hoop. The signs of a community in poverty were everywhere.

'Funding,' Whitlam said when he saw them looking around. 'There's never enough.'

Around the back of the school building a few sad sheep stood in brown paddocks. Beyond, the land rose sharply to a chain of hills covered with bushland.

The principal stopped to fish a handful of leaves out of the sheep's water trough.

'Do you still teach farm skills these days?' Falk remembered checking a similar water trough once upon a time.

'Some. We try to keep it light, though. Have some fun. The kids get enough of the gritty realities at home,' Whitlam said.

'You teach it?'

'God, no, I'm a humble city slicker. We moved up from Melbourne eighteen months ago and I've just about learned to tell one end of a cow from the other. My wife fancied a change of scenery from the city.' He paused. 'We got one all right.'

He pushed open a heavy door to a hallway that smelled like sandwiches. Along the walls, kids' paintings and drawings were pinned up.

'Jesus, some of these are depressing,' Raco murmured.

Falk could see what he meant. There were stick figure families in which every face had a crayon mouth turned downwards. A painting of a cow with angel wings. *Toffee My Cow in Heaven*, the shaky caption read. In every attempt at landscape, the paddocks were coloured brown.

'You should see the ones we didn't put up,' Whitlam said, stopping at the office door. 'The drought. It's going to kill this town.'

He took an enormous bunch of keys from his pocket and let them in to his office. Pointing them to a couple of chairs that had seen better days, he disappeared into a store cupboard. He emerged a moment later carrying a sealed cardboard box.

'Everything's in here. Bits and pieces from Karen's desk, some of Billy's school work. Mostly paintings and worksheets, I'm afraid.'

'Thanks.' Raco took it from him.

'They're missed.' Whitlam leaned against his desk. 'Both of them. We're all still reeling.'

'How closely did you work with Karen?' Falk asked.

'Reasonably so, we've only got a small staff. She was excellent. She looked after the finances and accounts. Good at it, too. Too smart for this job really, but I think it suited her with childcare and things.'

The window was open a crack and the sounds from the playground drifted through. 'Look, can I ask why you're here?' Whitlam said. 'I thought this was resolved.'

'It involved three members of the same family,' Raco said. 'Unfortunately something like that's never clear-cut.'

'Right. Of course.' Whitlam sounded unconvinced. 'The thing is, I've got an obligation to make sure students and staff are safe, so if –'

'We're not suggesting there's anything to worry about, Scott,' Raco said. 'If there's something you need to know, we'll make sure you know it.'

'All right, message received,' Whitlam said. 'What can I do to help you?'

'Tell us about Karen.'

The knock was quiet but firm. Whitlam looked up from his desk as the
door opened. A blonde head poked around.

'Scott, have you got a minute?'

Karen Hadler stepped into his office. She wasn't smiling.

'She stopped by to speak to me, the day before she and Billy
were killed,' Whitlam said. 'She was worried, of course.'

'Why "of course"?' Raco asked.

'Sorry, I didn't mean that to sound facetious. But you saw
those kids' pictures on the wall. I meant everyone's scared. The
adults are no different.'

He thought for a moment.

'Karen was a really valued team member. But she'd become
quite stressed in those last couple of weeks. She was snappy, which
was unusual. Definitely distracted. And she'd been making one
or two errors in the accounts. Nothing serious, we caught them.
But again, it was unlike her. It bothered her. She was normally
so precise. So she came to see me about it.'

Karen shut the door behind her. She chose the seat closest to Whitlam's
desk. She sat straight-backed and crossed her legs neatly at the ankles. Her
wraparound dress was flattering but modest, with a subtle print of white
apples against a red background. Karen was the kind of woman whose
youthful good looks had been softened by age and childbirth into something
less defined, but just as appealing in their own way. She could easily be
cast as a how-does-she-do-it mum in a supermarket ad. Anyone could have
confidence in a brand of detergent or cereal Karen Hadler recommended.

Now she was clutching a small stack of papers on her lap.

'Scott,' she began, then stopped. He waited. She took a deep breath.
'Scott, to be honest, I wasn't sure about coming to you with this. My
husband —' Karen held his gaze, but Whitlam felt she was forcing herself.
'Luke, well. Look, he wouldn't be happy.'

Raco leaned forward. 'Did she sound scared of her husband?'

'I didn't think so at the time.' Whitlam pinched the bridge of his nose. 'But knowing what happened the next day makes me realise I probably wasn't listening closely enough. I worry that I missed the signs. I've asked myself that every day. But I want to be clear that if I'd suspected for a minute they were in danger, I'd obviously never have let her and Billy go home.' Whitlam's words unconsciously echoed Jamie Sullivan's.

Karen fiddled with her wedding ring.

'You and I have worked together for a while – worked together well, I would say –' She looked up and Whitlam nodded. 'I feel I have to say something.'

She paused again, and took a deep breath.

'I know there have been some issues lately. With me, and my work. A few mistakes here and there.'

'One or two perhaps, but there's no harm done, Karen. You're a good worker, everyone can see that.'

She nodded once, dropping her eyes. When she looked up, her face was set.

'Thank you. But there is a problem. And I can't turn a blind eye to it.'

'She said the farm was going under,' Whitlam said. 'Karen thought they had six months, maybe less. She said Luke didn't believe it. Apparently he was sure things would turn around, but she said she could see it coming. She was worried. She actually apologised to me.'

Whitlam made a little noise of disbelief.

'It seems absurd now. But she said she was sorry she'd been so distracted. Karen asked me not to tell Luke that she'd told me. Not that I would have, of course. But she said he'd be upset if he thought she'd been spreading it around town.'

Whitlam chewed his thumbnail.

'I think she needed to get it off her chest. I got her a glass of water, listened for a while. Reassured her that her job wasn't at risk, that sort of thing.'

'Did you know Luke Hadler well?' Falk said.

'Not well. I met him a few times, of course. Parents' night. I'd see him down the pub occasionally, but not really to chat to. He seemed nice enough, though. Active parent as well. I couldn't believe it when I got that call. It's bad enough to lose a member of staff, but to lose a student. It's a teacher's worst nightmare.'

Falk said, 'Who told you what had happened?'

'Someone from Clyde police phoned the school. I suppose because Billy was a pupil. It was late-ish by then, close to seven. I'd been about to leave for the night but I remember sitting here instead, trying to process it. Trying to work out how to tell the children the next day.'

He shrugged sadly.

'There is no good way. Billy and my daughter were quite good friends, you know? They were in the same class. That's why it was such a shock to hear Billy was caught up in it.'

'What do you mean?' asked Raco.

'Because he was supposed to be round at our place that afternoon,' Whitlam said, as if it were obvious. He looked back and forth between Falk's and Raco's blank faces. He held out his hands, confused.

'Sorry, I thought you knew. I told the Clyde officers. Billy was supposed to come over and play that day but Karen called my wife and cancelled at the last minute. She said Billy had been under the weather.'

'He was well enough to come to school though. Did you and your wife believe her?' Falk asked, leaning forward.

Whitlam nodded. 'Yes. We still do, for the record. There'd been a mild bug going round. She might have decided he needed an early night. I think it was just one of those sad coincidences.'

He rubbed his hand over his eyes.

'But something like that,' he said. 'Knowing how close he came to not being there. God, it leaves you with a lot of what ifs.'

Chapter Twelve

'We'd have known that if we were liaising with Clyde,' Falk said when they got outside. He tucked the box of Karen's and Billy's belongings under his arm. The cardboard stuck uncomfortably to his clammy skin.

'Yeah, well, no harm done. We found out anyway.'

'Eventually. I don't know. It might be time to bring them in.'

Raco looked at him.

'You honestly feel confident that we've got enough to make that phone call? Bearing in mind how they'll react?'

Falk opened his mouth to reply when a voice rang out across the playground.

'Hey, Aaron! Wait.'

Falk turned to see Gretchen Schoner jogging over. He felt his mood lift fractionally. The funeral attire had been swapped for shorts and a fitted blue shirt, rolled up at the elbows. It suited her much better, Falk thought. Raco took the box from him.

'I'll meet you back at the car, mate,' he said tactfully, with a polite nod at Gretchen. She stopped in front of Falk and pushed her sunglasses up, catching her blonde hair in a complicated bundle on top of her head. The blue of the shirt set off her eyes, he noticed.

'Hey, what are you still doing here? I thought you'd left.' She was frowning and smiling at the same time. She reached out as she spoke and touched his elbow. He felt a pang of guilt. He should have let her know.

'We were having a word with Scott Whitlam,' he said. 'The principal.'

'Yeah, I know who Scott is. I'm on the school board. I mean, what are you doing in Kiewarra?'

Falk looked past her. A gaggle of mums had their heads turned towards them, their eyes hidden behind sunglasses. He took Gretchen's arm and turned slightly so their backs were to the group.

'It's a bit complicated. The Hadlers asked me to look into what happened with Luke.'

'You're kidding. Why? Has something come up?'

Falk had a powerful urge to blurt out the whole story. About Ellie, the alibi, the lies. The guilt. Gretchen was part of the original foursome. She was a balancing force. The light to Ellie's dark, the calm to Luke's craziness. She would understand. Over her shoulder, the mums were still watching.

'It's about the money,' Falk said with a sigh. He gave her a watered down version of Barb Hadler's concerns. Bad debts gone wrong.

'Jesus.' She blinked, still for a moment as she processed the information. 'You think there's anything in it?'

Falk just shrugged. The conversation with Whitlam had thrown some new light on the suggestion. 'We'll see. But do me a favour and keep it to yourself for now.'

Gretchen frowned. 'It might be too late for that. Word's gone round that some cops were at Jamie Sullivan's earlier.'

'Christ, how's that got out already?' Falk asked, knowing the answer. Small town, fast gossip. Gretchen ignored the question.

'Just tread lightly.' She reached out and brushed away a fly that had settled on Falk's shoulder. 'People are wound up pretty tight at the moment. It wouldn't take much to set them off.'

Falk nodded. 'Thanks. Understood.'

'Anyway –' Gretchen paused as a swarm of small boys careered by in a chaotic game of football, the weight of the memorial service already lifting from their small shoulders as the weekend came into sight. She shaded her eyes and waved at the group. Falk tried to pick her son from the pack, but couldn't. When he looked back Gretchen was watching him.

'How long do you think you'll be around for?'

'A week.' Falk hesitated. 'No more than that.'

'Good.' Her mouth turned up at the corners, and it could have been twenty years ago.

When she walked away a few minutes later, Falk was clutching a scrap of paper with her mobile number and an arrangement to meet the following night on it, both scrawled in Gretchen's distinctive handwriting.

'You gone and made yourself a new friend, mate?' Raco said lightly as Falk climbed into the car.

'Old friend, thanks,' Falk said, but he couldn't help smiling.

'So what do you want to do?' Raco said, more serious now. He nodded at the cardboard box in the back seat. 'You want to call Clyde and tie yourself up to the arse in red tape convincing them they might've stuffed up, or do you want to go to the station and check out what's in the box?'

Falk looked at him for a moment, imagining that phone call. 'Yeah, all right. Station. Box.'

'Good decision.'

'Just drive.'

The police station was a low red-brick building at the far end of Kiewarra's main street. The shops on either side had closed for good, their windows empty. Across the road was a similar story. Only the milk bar and the bottle shop seemed to be enjoying any real trade.

'Christ, it's dead around here,' Falk said.

'That's the thing about money problems. They're contagious. Farmers have no cash to spend in shops, the shop goes under and then you've got yourself more people with no money to spend in shops. Apparently they've been falling like dominoes.'

Raco pulled on the station door. It was locked. He swore and dug out his keys. On the door was a notice with station hours: Monday to Friday, 9 am to 5 pm. Out of hours, victims of crime had to try their luck with Clyde, according to the sign. Falk looked at his watch. 4.51 pm. A mobile number for emergencies had been written in pen underneath. Falk bet it was Raco's.

'Knocking off early?' Raco called when they got inside, the annoyance evident in his tone.

The receptionist, in her sixties but with the improbable coal-coloured hair of a young Elizabeth Taylor, raised her chin defiantly.

'I was in early,' she said, stiffening slightly in her position behind the counter. Handbag over her shoulder like a soldier's weapon. Raco introduced her as Deborah. She didn't shake hands.

In the office space behind her, Constable Evan Barnes looked up guiltily, clutching his car keys.

'Afternoon, boss,' Barnes said. ''Bout that time, isn't it?' His voice was overly casual and he made a big show of checking his watch. 'Oh. Yeah. Still a couple of minutes to go yet.'

A big man with a fresh-faced complexion and curly hair that stuck out in unfortunate tufts, he sat back down at his desk and started shuffling paper. Raco rolled his eyes.

'Oh, go on, bugger off,' he said, lifting the counter hatch. 'Have a good weekend. We'll just have to hope the town doesn't burn to the ground at one minute to five, won't we?'

Deborah straightened her spine like a woman fortified by the knowledge she'd been in the right all along.

'Bye then,' she said to Raco. She gave Falk a tiny curt nod, her gaze firmly on his forehead rather than his eyes.

Falk felt a cold bead of understanding drop somewhere in his chest. She knew. He wasn't really surprised. Assuming Deborah was Kiewarra born and bred, she was the right age to remember Ellie Deacon. It had been the most dramatic thing ever to happen in Kiewarra, at least until the Hadlers' deaths. She'd probably tutted over coffee as she'd read the newspaper articles under Ellie's black and white photo. Traded nuggets of gossip with neighbours. Perhaps she'd known his dad. Before it happened, of course. She wouldn't have admitted to knowing the Falk family afterwards.

Hours after Luke's face had disappeared from his bedroom window, Aaron lay awake. The events ran through his head on a loop. Ellie, the river, fishing, the note. Luke and I were shooting rabbits together.

He waited for it all night, but when the knock came at last, it wasn't for him. Falk watched in mute horror as his father was forced to wash the paddocks from his hands and accompany the officers to the station. The name on the note did not specify which Falk, they said, and at sixteen, the younger one was technically still a child.

Erik Falk, a willowy and stoic man, was kept in the station for five hours.

Did he know Ellie Deacon? Yes, of course, she was a neighbour's child. She was a friend of his son's. She was the girl who was missing.

He was asked for an alibi for the day of her death. He'd been out much of the afternoon buying supplies. In the evening he had popped into the pub. Had been seen by a dozen people in a handful of locations. Tight enough, if not quite watertight. So the questions continued. Yes, he had spoken to the girl in the past. Several times? Yes. Many times? Probably. And no. He could not explain why Ellie Deacon had a note with his name on it and the date of her death.

But Falk wasn't only his name, was it? the officers said pointedly. At that, Aaron's father fell silent. He clamped down and refused to say another word.

They let him go, and then it was his son's turn.

'Barnes is on secondment from Melbourne,' Raco said as Falk followed him under the hatch to the office. Behind them, the station door slammed shut and they were alone.

'Really?' Falk was surprised. Barnes had the wholesome milk-fed look of a homegrown country boy.

'Yeah, his parents are in farming, though. Not here, somewhere out west. I think that made him the obvious choice for the placement. I feel for the guy really; his backside barely touched the ground in the city before they sent him up here. Having said that –' Raco glanced towards the closed station door, then reconsidered. 'Never mind.'

Falk could guess. It was a rare day when a city force sent its best officer on a country secondment, especially to a place like Kiewarra. Barnes was unlikely to be the sharpest knife in the drawer. Raco may have been too tactful to say it, but the message was clear. In this station, he was pretty much on his own.

They put the box of Karen's and Billy's belongings on a spare desk and opened it. The fluorescent lights hummed overhead. At the window, a fly bashed itself repeatedly against the glass.

Aaron sat on a wooden chair, his bladder nervous and aching, and stuck to the plan. I was with Luke Hadler. Shooting rabbits. Two, we got two. Yes, Ellie is – was, I mean – my friend. Yes, I saw her at school that day. No! We didn't fight. I didn't even see her later. I didn't attack her. I was with Luke Hadler. I was with Luke Hadler. We were shooting rabbits. I was with Luke Hadler.

They had to let him go.

Some of the whispers took on a new shape then. Not murder, perhaps, but suicide. A vulnerable girl led up the path by the Falk boy was a popular version. Pursued and used by his slightly odd father was another. Who was to say? Either way, between them they as good as killed her. The rumours were fed well by Ellie's father Mal Deacon, and grew fat and solid. They sprouted legs and heads and they never died.

One night a brick was thrown through the Falks' front window. Two days later, Aaron's father was turned away from the corner shop. Forced to walk out empty handed with burning eyes and his groceries piled on the counter. The following afternoon, Aaron was followed home from school by three men in a ute. They crept behind him as he pedalled his bike faster and faster, wobbling every time he dared look over his shoulder, his breath loud in his ears.

Raco reached into the box and laid out the contents in a line on the desk.

There was a coffee mug, a stapler with 'Karen' written on it in white-out, a heavy-knit cardigan, a small bottle of perfume called Spring Fling, and a framed picture of Billy and Charlotte. It was a meagre offering.

Falk opened up the frame and looked behind the photo. Nothing. He put it back together. Across the desk, Raco took the cap off the perfume and sprayed it. A light citrusy scent floated into the air. Falk liked it.

They moved on to Billy's belongings: three paintings of cars, a small pair of gym shoes, a beginner's reading book and a pack of colouring pencils. Falk turned over the pages of the book, not at all sure what he was looking for.

It was around that time he realised his father was watching him. From across the room, through a window, over his newspaper. Aaron would get the feathery sense across the back of his neck and would look up. Sometimes Erik's gaze would flick away. Sometimes it wouldn't. Contemplative and silent. Aaron waited for the question but it didn't come.

A dead calf was left on their doorstep, its throat cut so deep that the head was almost severed. The next morning, father and son bundled what they could into their truck. Aaron said a hasty goodbye to Gretchen and a longer goodbye to Luke. None of them mentioned why he was leaving. As they drove out of Kiewarra, Mal Deacon's white ute followed them for a hundred kilometres past the town limits.

They'd never gone back.

'Karen made Billy come home that afternoon,' Falk said. He'd been thinking it over since leaving the school. 'He was supposed to be out playing with his friend and she kept him home on the day he was killed. How do you feel about chalking that up to coincidence?'

'Not good.' Raco shook his head.

'Me neither.'

'But if she'd had any idea what was going to happen, surely she'd have got both kids as far away as possible.'

'Maybe she suspected something was up, but didn't know what,' Falk said.

'Or how bad it was going to be.'

Falk picked up Karen's coffee mug and put it down again. He checked the box, felt around the edges. It was empty.

'I was hoping for something more,' Raco said.

'Me too.'

They stared at the items for a long time, then one by one, put them back.

Chapter Thirteen

The cockatoos were shrieking in the trees when Falk left the station. They called each other home to roost in a deafening chorus as the early evening shadows grew. The air felt clammy and a line of sweat ran down Falk's back.

He wandered along the main street, in no rush to reach the pub waiting at the other end. It wasn't late, but few people were about. Falk peered into the windows of the abandoned shops, pressing his forehead against the glass. He could still remember what most of them used to be. The bakery. A bookshop. Many had been completely stripped out. It was impossible to tell how long they'd stood bare.

He paused as he came to a hardware store displaying a line of cotton work shirts in the window. A grey-haired man, wearing one of the very same shirts under an apron with a name badge, had his hand on the OPEN sign hanging on the door. He paused mid-flip as he noticed Falk assessing the merchandise.

Falk plucked at his own shirt. It was the same one he'd worn to the funeral and was stiff from being rinsed out in the bathroom sink. It stuck under his arms. He went inside.

Under the harsh shop lights, the man's warm smile froze mid-grin as recognition kicked in a moment later. His eyes darted around the deserted shop, which Falk suspected had been as empty for most of the day. A moment's hesitation, then the smile continued. Easier to have principles when you've got dollars in the till, Falk thought. The shopkeeper guided him through the store's limited apparel selection with the thoroughness of a gentleman's tailor. Falk bought three shirts, because the man seemed so grateful that he was prepared to buy one.

Back on the street, Falk tucked the purchases under his arm and continued on. It wasn't much of a walk. He passed a takeaway that seemed to offer cuisine from any corner of the world as long as it was fried or could be displayed in a pie warmer. A doctors' surgery, a pharmacy, a tiny library. A one-stop store that appeared to sell everything from animal feed to gift cards, several boarded-up shopfronts and he was back at the Fleece. That was it. Kiewarra's main hub. He looked back, toying with the idea of giving it another pass, but couldn't work up the enthusiasm.

Through the window of the pub he could see a handful of men staring indifferently at the TV. His bare room was all that was waiting for him upstairs. He put his hand in his pocket and felt his car keys. He was halfway to Luke Hadler's place before he knew it.

The sun was lower in the sky when Falk parked his car out the front of the Hadlers' farmhouse in the same spot as before. The yellow police tape still hung from the door.

This time, he ignored the house and walked straight over to the biggest of the barns. He peered up at the tiny security camera installed above the door. It looked cheap and functional. Fashioned from dull grey plastic with a single red light glowing, it would be easy to miss if you didn't know it was there.

Falk imagined Luke up on a ladder, fixing it to the wall, angling it just right. It had been positioned to capture as much as possible of the entrances to the barns and the shed, where the valuable farm equipment was stored. The house was merely an afterthought, the small slice of driveway captured by accident. The property wouldn't go under if thieves stole the five-year-old TV. Losing the water filter from the barn would be another story.

If someone else had come along that day, had they been aware of the camera? Falk wondered. Could they have been there before and known what would be captured? Or had they just been lucky?

Luke would have known his ute's number plate would be recorded, if he had been the one behind the wheel, Falk thought. But by that point, maybe he simply didn't care. Falk walked across the yard and did a complete circuit of the outside of the house. Raco had been as good as his word at keeping out prying eyes. Every blind was drawn and every door locked tight. There was nothing to see.

Needing to clear his head, Falk left the house behind him and tramped out across the paddocks. The property shouldered the Kiewarra River and up ahead he could see a copse of gums marking the boundary. The summer sun hung low and orange in the sky.

He often did his best thinking on his feet. Usually that involved pounding the streets around his city office block, dodging tourists and trams. Or clocking up kilometres around the botanic gardens or the bay when he was really stumped.

Falk knew he used to be at home in the paddocks, but now it all seemed very different. His head still felt crowded. He listened to the rhythm of his steps against the hard ground and the bird calls echoing from the trees. The shrieks seemed louder out here.

He was nearly at the boundary when he slowed his pace, then stopped altogether. He wasn't sure what made him hesitate. The line of trees in front of him stood shadowy still. Nothing moved. An uneasy feeling crept up Falk's shoulders and neck. Even the birds suddenly seemed hushed. Feeling a little foolish, he glanced over his shoulder. The paddocks stared back blankly. The Hadler farm lay lifeless in the distance. He'd walked the whole way around it, Falk told himself. There was no-one there. There was no-one left in that place.

He turned back in the direction of the river, a feeling of foreboding still fluttering in his chest. When the answer came, it crept up slowly, then thundered home all at once. Where Falk stood now, he should be hearing the rush of water. The distinct sound of the river carving its way through the country. He closed his eyes and listened, seeking it out, willing it to materialise. There was only an eerie nothingness. He opened his eyes and took off at a run.

He plunged into the tree line, pounding along the well-worn trail, ignoring the whip and sting of the occasional overgrown branch. He reached the river bank breathing fast, and pulled up short at the edge. There was no need.

The huge river was nothing more than a dusty scar in the land. The empty bed stretched long and barren in either direction, its serpentine curves tracing the path where the water had flowed. The hollow that had been carved over centuries was now a cracked patchwork of rocks and crabgrass. Along the banks, gnarled grey tree roots were exposed like cobwebs.

It was appalling.

Struggling to accept what his eyes were telling him, Falk clambered into the cavity, hands and knees scraping against the baked bank. He stopped in the dead centre of the river, in the open void where the heavy ribbon of water had once been deep enough to close over his head.

The same water he and Luke had dived into every summer, wallowing and splashing as they soaked up its coolness. The water he had stared into for hours on bright afternoons, fishing lines dangling hypnotically, with his father's sturdy weight at his shoulder. The water that had forced its way down Ellie Deacon's throat, greedily invading her body until there was no room left for the girl herself.

Falk tried to take a deep breath but the air tasted warm and cloying in his mouth. His own naivety taunted him like a flicker of madness. How could he have imagined fresh water still ran by these farms as animals lay dead in the paddocks? How could he nod dumbly as the word *drought* was thrown around, and never realise this river ran dry?

He stood on shaky legs, his vision blurred as all around the cockatoos whirled and screamed into the scorching red sky. Alone, in that monstrous wound, Falk put his face in his hands and, just once, screamed himself.

Chapter Fourteen

Falk sat for a long while on the river bank, letting a numbness seep over him as the heavy sun dipped lower. Eventually he forced himself to his feet. He was losing the light. He knew where he was headed next, but couldn't be sure of finding it in the dusk.

He turned his back on the path leading to the Hadlers' property and instead headed in the other direction. Twenty years ago there'd been a small river trail. Now Falk had to rely on his memory, picking his way over exposed roots and dry undergrowth.

He kept his head down, focused on not losing his way. Without the great river flowing alongside as a beacon, he caught himself nearly wandering off track several times. The surroundings looked different now, and markers that had once been familiar failed to appear. As he was beginning to worry he'd gone too far, he found it. He felt a sharp rush of relief. It was a short distance from the bank, almost overrun by scrub. As he trampled his way through the thicket, a spark of happiness raced through him, and for the first time since he had arrived in Kiewarra he felt the stirrings of homecoming. He put his hand out. It was still there, it was still the same.

The rock tree.

'Shit, where did they go?'

Ellie Deacon frowned and delicately kicked aside a small pile of leaves with the toe of one beautiful boot.

'They're down there somewhere. I heard them hit the ground.' Aaron scrambled around the rock tree. He crouched, scouring the ground and sifting through dried leaves for Ellie's house keys. She watched through hooded eyes and half-heartedly turned over a small stone with her foot.

Falk ran his hand over the rock tree and smiled properly for what felt like the first time in days. As a child, it had seemed like a miracle of nature. A huge eucalyptus had grown tightly against a solid boulder, its trunk curving around to trap the two in a gnarled embrace.

When he was younger, Falk had been at a complete loss to explain others' lack of fascination with the tree. Hikers walked past every week with barely a glance, and even to other kids it was little more than a quirky landmark. But every time Falk saw it he wondered how many years it had taken for the rock tree to form. Millimetre by millimetre. It gave him the free-falling sensation that he himself was a tiny dot in time. He liked it. More than twenty years later, he looked at the rock tree and could feel it anew.

Aaron was alone with Ellie that day, which at sixteen was a scenario he both craved and feared. He chattered incessantly, annoying even himself.

But the bottom kept dropping out of the conversation, like an unexpected pothole in the road. It had never used to happen, but recently it seemed to creep into all their interactions like a fault line.

Aaron frequently found himself casting around for something to say that would elicit more than a raised eyebrow or a nod. Occasionally, he'd strike gold, and the corner of her mouth would lift.

He loved those moments. He would make a mental note of what he'd said, storing it to analyse later. Hoping to find a pattern on which he could build a whole repertoire of banter so witty that she couldn't help but smile. So far, the pattern was disappointingly random.

They'd spent much of the afternoon leaning against the rock tree in the shade. Ellie had seemed more distant than normal. Twice that afternoon he'd asked her something and she hadn't appeared to even hear him. Eventually, terrified of boring her, he'd suggesting tracking down Luke or Gretchen. To his relief she shook her head.

'I don't think I could face the chaos right now,' she'd said. 'It's all right with just us, isn't it?'

'Yeah, of course.' Of course it was. He tried to keep his voice light. 'What have you got planned for tonight?'

She made a face. 'I'm working.' For the past year she'd had a part-time job which mainly involved standing disinterestedly behind the counter of the milk bar.

'Didn't you work last night?'

'Milk bar opens every day, Aaron.'

'I know, but —' It was more work than usual. Out of nowhere he wondered if she was lying to him, then felt ridiculous. She wouldn't bother.

He watched as she repeatedly tossed her key ring idly in the air and caught it, her shiny purple nails reflecting the afternoon sunlight. He was trying to work up the courage to reach up and snatch the key ring from her in midair. He could tease her gently, the way Luke would do. And then — well, then Aaron wasn't sure what. So it had almost been a relief when Ellie threw it too high and it sailed backwards over their heads.

The keys clanged once off the boulder and they heard the metallic thump as they hit the ground.

Falk crouched by the rock tree and shifted position a few times until he found the right angle. He let out a little grunt of surprise and satisfaction when he finally saw it.

The gap.

'Hey, look at this.' Aaron leaned back and forth from where he was kneeling. A deep crevasse in the heart of the rock tree appeared, then disappeared as he moved to a slightly different angle. He'd never noticed it before. A single sweet spot where the base of the tree was curved out rather than flush with the rock. An optical illusion, it was almost invisible from all but one angle.

Aaron peered into the dead space. It was big enough to squeeze his arm, shoulder and head through, if he'd wanted to. Instead, he saw what he was looking for tucked right inside the entrance. He triumphantly closed his hand around Ellie's keys.

Falk peered into the mouth of the gap. He could see nothing beyond the entrance. He found a small stone and tossed it in, listening to it rattle off the sides. Nothing scurried or slithered out.

Falk hesitated, then rolled his sleeve down as far as it would go, and dipped his hand into the inky entrance. The tips of his fingers landed on an object – small and square and unnatural – and he scooped it up. As he did, something invisible scuttled across his wrist and he snatched his hand out. He straightened, laughing at his pounding heart.

Falk opened his palm and felt a jolt of recognition. It was a small metal cigarette lighter. Battered, weather-beaten, but still with a working hinge. Falk grinned and turned it upside down, knowing what he would find. There, in an earlier version of his own writing were scratched the initials: *A.F.*

Never a keen smoker, he'd had it mainly for show, and one day towards the end had hidden it rather than risk getting caught with it by his dad. Falk opened the lid, but didn't dare light it. Not in these conditions. He rubbed his palm over the metal, and debated slipping the lighter into his pocket. But it felt like it belonged here, in a different time. After a moment, he reached into the gap and put it back.

Ellie crouched, her hand hot on his shoulder as she wobbled and steadied herself. She was close enough that he could see the mascara coating the individual lashes as she narrowed her eyes and peered in. Her shoulder pressed painfully into his own as she tentatively reached into the gap with her hand, checking out its size.

'That's pretty cool,' she said, deadpan. It was difficult to tell if she meant it.

'I found your keys,' Aaron said, holding them up. She turned to face him. He could see the little specks in the corners of her eyes where her makeup had bled. She'd cut back on the booze lately and up close her skin looked smooth and clear.

'So you did. Thank you, Aaron.'

'You're welcome, Ellie.' He smiled. He could feel her breath on his cheeks. He wasn't sure if he actually moved his head, or just wanted to, but suddenly her face was closer and she was kissing him, pressing those pink lips hard against his. Lusciously sticky with a hint of artificial cherry. It was better than he'd imagined and he pushed back, wanting to taste more, feeling the fizz and pop of pure joy.

He lifted a hand to her shiny hair but as he slipped it gently around the back of her head she gasped a little, her mouth still on his, and jerked away. She sat back on the ground with a thump, and lifted her fingers first to her mouth and then to her hair. Aaron was frozen, crouched down

*with his open mouth still tasting of her, as horror flooded through him.
She was looking up at him.*

'I'm sorry, Ellie. I'm –'

'No, I'm sorry, I didn't mean –'

'– so sorry. It's my fault, I thought you wanted –'

'Aaron, no, honestly, it's fine. It just –'

'What?'

A breath.

'Took me by surprise.'

'Oh.' Then: 'Are you all right?'

*'Yes.' She opened her mouth as though about to say something more,
but the silence stretched out. He thought for a heart-stopping moment
there were tears in her eyes, but she blinked and they were gone.*

*Aaron stood and offered a hand to help her up from the ground. For a
terrible second he thought she might not take it, but she slipped her palm into
his and hauled herself up. He took a step back, giving her some distance.*

'I'm sorry,' he repeated.

'Please don't say that.'

'OK. Are we OK?'

*To his surprise, she took one small step in, closing the distance between
them. Before he knew what was happening, her mouth pressed softly,
briefly, to his, and the taste of cherries was back.*

*'We're OK.' She stepped away as quickly as she'd stepped in. 'I told
you. It took me by surprise.'*

*By the time Aaron's mind had caught up it was all over. She was
leaning down, brushing the dirt off her jeans.*

*'I'd better get going. But thanks.' She didn't look up. 'For finding
my keys, I mean.'*

He nodded.

*'Hey.' Ellie said as she turned to leave. 'Let's not tell anyone about
this. Keep it just for us.'*

'Which . . .? The gap or –'

She gave a laugh. 'The gap.' Ellie looked at him over her shoulder. 'But maybe the other thing as well. For now, anyway.'

Both corners of her mouth were turned up a tiny bit.

He wasn't entirely sure, but he thought on balance it had been a good day.

Falk had never told anyone else about the gap. Or their kiss. He was fairly sure Ellie hadn't either. Not that she'd had long to keep the secret. Three weeks later and twenty metres from where he stood, Ellie's pale pickled body was dragged from the river. Falk had never come down here again after she was found. He hadn't had much chance even if he'd wanted to. Within a month, he and his father were five hundred kilometres away in Melbourne.

He'd always felt glad he and Ellie had discovered the gap when they had, just the two of them. There would have been plenty of opportunity when they were younger, hanging around the rock tree in a tight trio with Luke. But then, by default, it would have automatically become Luke's find. He would have claimed full custody when, around the age of twelve, the three-some developed a crack neatly along the gender divide.

None of them noticed until it was too late. Ellie was gradu-ally inducted into the foreign world of girls and skirts and clean hands and conversations that made Aaron and Luke exchange looks of bewilderment. It was a slow migration, but one day Aaron looked up and realised it was just him and Luke, and had been for months. They barely missed a beat. She was only a girl. It was probably for the best that she didn't tag along.

Ellie melted out of their consciousness with an ease Falk now found staggering, but for three years he barely recalled thinking about her once. He must have seen her out and about – there was no way they could have avoided it. But when she re-emerged in his life at fifteen, it was like she'd been reborn, fully formed and trailing fascination and mystery behind her like perfume.

It had been yet another Saturday night for him and Luke, sitting on the back of a bench in Centenary Park. Feet on the seat like true rebels, one eye out for the local cop like true small-town boys.

A crunch of gravel and a shifting shadow, and Ellie Deacon had appeared as if from nowhere. Her hair was now an artificial jet black, and the split ends almost touched her elbows. It shone dully under the orange park lamps. She was alone.

She sauntered over, jeans tight, boots artfully scuffed, lace bra strap peeking out from the wide neckline of her top. She ran her eye-lined gaze over the two boys as they stared back, mouths ever so slightly agape. Ellie raised an eyebrow at the can of warm beer they were sharing, reached into her fake leather bag and pulled out a mostly full bottle of vodka.

'Room for one more?' she said. They'd nearly fallen off the bench in their haste to shuffle over. The years disappeared with the vodka and by the time they'd made a dent in the bottle, the trio was reformed.

But tiny variances in their friendship hinted at new paths to be explored. Conversations had a fresh edge. The boys still occasionally spent time as a pair, but Aaron found himself going to significant lengths to limit opportunities for Luke and Ellie to be together without him. He never discussed it with Luke, but the rate at which his own attempts at time alone with her were thwarted made him suspect his friend was running a similar covert operation. The group dynamics had taken a subtle but definite shift, with none of them quite yet sure where they had landed.

Ellie never really explained why she'd returned to the boys. When Aaron once asked, she rolled her eyes skywards.

'Bunch of bitches,' she said. 'If it doesn't involve their reflection in a mirror, they're not interested. At least you two don't care if I cramp your style.' She lit a cigarette and looked at him frankly as though that explained everything, and maybe it did.

The friendship was still being cemented as it faced its first real test. When the pressure was applied, it came unexpectedly from the heel of Gretchen Schoner's hot-pink shoes.

Even in Kiewarra, social hierarchies had to be observed, and Gretchen was a creature most commonly sighted tossing back her golden hair and laughing amid a crowd of followers. So Aaron and Ellie had sat open-mouthed as Luke rocked up at Centenary Park one night with his arm flung around the girl's shoulders.

A sharp growth spurt had put Luke half a head above most of their classmates, and filled out his shoulders and chest in the right ways. In the shadowy park that night, with Gretchen's hair falling in a tousled curtain over his jacket sleeve, and a definite swagger in his step, Aaron realised for the first time how much his friend looked like a man.

Gretchen was flushed and giggling as Luke introduced them. He caught Aaron's eye over the top of her head and gave a not-so-subtle wink. Aaron nodded, duly impressed. There were a thousand places Gretchen Schoner could be on a Saturday night and yet she was there, by Luke's side.

Having rarely been invited to exchange words with Gretchen in the past, Aaron had been pleasantly surprised. She was charming and unexpectedly quick-witted. She chatted easily and within moments had made him laugh. He could see why people flocked to be near her. She radiated an energy that begged to be basked in.

Behind Aaron, Ellie cleared her throat with a tiny noise and he realised with a start that he'd almost forgotten she was there. Her look as he turned was one of mild disdain but not surprise, as though he and Luke had failed a test they hadn't been expected to pass. His gaze jumped from Gretchen's smile to Ellie's cold expression, red flags popping up loud and bright but far too late. He glanced at Luke, expecting to see the same realisation dawning. Instead, Luke was watching with curious amusement. For a tense moment, no-one said anything.

Gretchen suddenly flashed the other girl a conspiratorial smile and made a spectacularly bitchy comment about one of Ellie's former friends. There was a pregnant pause, then Ellie gave a small snort of laughter. Gretchen sealed the deal by passing around her own cigarettes. A space was made for her on the park bench, that night and every Saturday night for the next year.

'Jesus, she's the human equivalent of bubble bath,' Ellie whispered to Aaron one evening shortly after, but she couldn't hide the tiny smile as she spoke. They'd all been laughing at Gretchen's story of an older boy who'd asked her out by carving words into crops and ruined his father's whole field in the process. Now she and Luke were deep in conversation, heads so close they were nearly touching. Gretchen gave a playful laugh and cast her eyes down as Luke murmured something Aaron didn't catch. He turned back to Ellie.

'You and I could go somewhere else if she's annoying you,' Aaron said. 'We don't have to hang around here.'

Ellie regarded him through a veil of smoke for a moment, then shook her head. 'No. She's OK,' she said. 'Bit of an airhead. But she's harmless.'

'Fair enough.' Aaron sighed silently and took the cigarette she offered him. He turned to light it, and saw Luke slip his arm around Gretchen's shoulders and lean in for a quick kiss. As Luke sat back, he glanced over the top of Gretchen's head in their direction. Ellie, who was examining the lit tip of her cigarette with a faraway look in her eye, didn't react.

It was there and gone in a flash, but Aaron saw the frown flit across his friend's face. It occurred to him that he wasn't the only one a little put out that the girls seemed to be getting on so well.

Chapter Fifteen

Falk leaned against the rock tree, staring down at the dusty river. The Hadlers' place and his car were down the path to his left. To his right, the hint of a forgotten trail led away from the river and deeper into the bushland. It had all but disappeared over the past twenty years but to Falk it was a tattoo on the landscape. He had walked it a thousand times. He stood for a long time, arguing with himself. Finally he stepped to the right. A thousand times. Once more couldn't hurt.

It took only a few minutes to reach the end of the trail, but when Falk emerged from the trees the sky was already a deep indigo. Across a paddock, a family farmhouse shone grey in the twilight. Falk cut straight over the paddock, like he always had. His pace slowed as he got closer, until he came to a halt about twenty metres from the building. He stared at what had been his childhood home.

The porch door that used to be yellow was now an insipid shade of blue, he noted with something like indignation. It had pockmarks where the paint was peeling. He could see flashes of yellow underneath, gaping like fatty scars. The wooden steps where he'd sat fiddling with toys and footy cards now sagged with age. Underneath, a beer can nestled in the flaxen grass.

He fought the sudden urge to pick it up and find a bin. To paint the wood. Fix the steps. Instead, he stayed where he was. The windows were all unlit but one, which glowed with a television blue.

Falk felt a sharp pang of longing for what might have been. He could see his father standing at the screen door in the evenings, a tall figure framed with the glow of light from the house. Calling him to leave his games and come in. Time for dinner, Aaron. Bath, bed. In you come, son. Time to come home. His dad rarely spoke of Aaron's mother, but when Aaron was younger he'd like to pretend he could feel her in the house. He had run his fingers over things he knew she would have touched – the kitchen taps, the bathroom fittings, the curtains – and imagined her in the same spot.

They'd been happy there once, Falk knew. Him and his father, at least. Looking at the house now, it was like a line in his life. A marker at the cusp of before and after. A surge of anger fizzed, directed at least partly at himself. He didn't know why he'd come. He took a step back. It was just another building in need of repair. There was nothing of him or his dad left there.

He was turning to leave when the screen door screeched open. A woman stepped out, her squashy figure backlit by the television glow. Dull chestnut hair was scraped back in a limp ponytail and her hips spilled over the top of her waistband. Her face was the purple-red of a woman whose drinking was crossing the line from social to serious. She lit a cigarette and inhaled deeply, staring at Falk in cold-eyed silence.

'Help you, mate?' She exhaled, her eyes narrowing into slits as the smoke drifted across her face.

'No, I —' He stopped, mentally kicking himself. He should have thought of something. Some excuse for lurking outside a stranger's door as night fell. He studied her expression. There was suspicion, but not recognition. She didn't know who he was. That helped. He considered and rejected telling her the truth in a single moment. He could always flash the badge. He would if he had to. But Falk the cop was embarrassed to find himself there.

'Sorry,' he said. 'I used to know the people who lived here.'

The woman said nothing, took another drag from the cigarette. With her spare hand she reached behind and thoughtfully plucked the seat of her shorts from between her buttocks. She never took her narrowed eyes off Falk.

'Me and my hubby are the only ones here. Been here five years. And the place was his mum's for fifteen or so before that.'

'It's been about that long,' Falk said. 'The people before her.'

'They're gone,' she said, with the tone of someone forced to state the obvious. She dabbed her index finger and thumb to her tongue and removed a piece of tobacco.

'I know.'

'So?'

It was a good question. Falk wasn't sure of the answer himself. The woman twisted around at a noise from inside the house. She opened the screen door wide enough to poke her head back indoors.

'Yeah, love,' Falk heard her say. 'I'm sorting it. It's fine. No-one. Go back in. No, just — go back in, will you?' The woman waited a moment then re-emerged, red-faced and scowling. She turned back to Falk and stepped off the porch towards him. Stopped a few metres away.

'You'd better leave right now, if you know what's good for you.' Her voice was quiet but hostile. 'He's had a few and he's not going to be happy if he has to come out here, right? We've got bugger all to do with any of that stuff that happened back then. Understand? Never have. His mum neither. So you can take your bloody press pass or spray paint or bag of dog shit or whatever you're here for and piss off, all right?'

'Look, I'm sorry.' Falk took a big step back, showed her his palms. Unthreatening. 'I didn't mean to upset you. Either of you.'

'Yeah, well, you have. This is our home, right? Bought and paid for. And I'm buggered if we're going to be harassed. It's been twenty years. Aren't you dickheads bored of it by now?'

'Look, fair enough. I'll go —'

She took a single step forward, pointed to the house with one hand and held out her mobile phone with the other.

'Too right you will. Or it won't be the cops I'll be calling. It'll be him inside and some of his mates who'll be all too happy to get the message across. You hear me? Get. Lost.' She took a deep breath, her voice louder now. 'And you can share that with whoever needs to know. We've got nothing to do with them that lived here. Nothing to do with those freaks.'

The word seemed to echo across the paddocks. Falk stood frozen for a moment. Then without a reply, he turned and walked away.

He didn't look back once.

Chapter Sixteen

Gretchen's blonde hair bobbed through the pub crowd, and Falk felt a swift stab of gratitude that he hadn't given in to his urge to cancel.

Leaving his old house behind the night before, he'd walked straight to his car and stood there for a long time, fighting the temptation to drive all the way back to Melbourne. After a restless night, he'd spent the day holed up in his room, poring over the stack of documents he'd taken from the Hadlers' farm. It had been a fairly fruitless search, but he'd continued to work through methodically, making the odd note when something caught his eye. Head down, get the job done. Emerging briefly only to get food, he'd ignored the weekend bustle on the street and, after a moment's guilt, turned his phone to silent when Gerry had called. Falk would do what he'd promised. That didn't mean he wanted to talk about it.

Now, downstairs in the pub, for the first time all day he didn't feel in quite such a hurry to get away. Gretchen found him sitting at a table tucked into the back corner, his hat pulled forward. She was back in black, but a dress this time. It was short with a hem that skimmed her bare legs as she walked. It suited her far better than her funeral clothes. A few heads among the Saturday night crowd turned as she passed. Not as many as in high school, Falk noted, but some.

'You look nice,' he said.

Gretchen seemed pleased and gave him a peck on the cheek as he stood up to get the drinks. She smelled good. Something flowery.

'Thanks. So do you. I like the shirt. Very cutting-edge Kiewarra.' She nodded at his recent purchase and he grinned. She edged into the corner seat. 'Was this the only table left or are you hiding?'

'Hiding. Sort of.' Falk smiled despite himself. 'I went back to my old house last night.'

She raised her eyebrows. 'And?'

'It wasn't quite what I expected.'

'It never is.'

He went to the counter and let the bearded barman pour him a beer and slightly suspect white wine. When he returned, Gretchen lifted her glass.

'Cheers. Remember when we couldn't wait to be able to get served in here? All those nights in the park downing whatever we could get our hands on.' She widened her blue eyes in mock disbelief as she gestured at their surroundings. 'Now look at us. Living the dream.'

Falk laughed and their eyes met as they thought back. Falk knew Gretchen's glossy-lipped, long-limbed teenage years gave her a deeper well of youthful joy to draw on than most. But looking at her now in her dress, he was struck by the thought that those years, before Ellie died and before everything changed, may have been her happiest. He hoped not. He hoped she'd had more. He frowned involuntarily and the moment was lost.

Gretchen leaned in. 'Listen, you should know. The cat's definitely out of the bag. It's all round town that you're nosing around what happened to the Hadlers. You and the sergeant.'

'It's nothing official.'

'And you think that matters?'

Falk nodded. Fair point. 'What's the general feeling?'

'It depends who you ask. Some people think it couldn't come soon enough. Others are pretty sure you of all people should be minding your own business.' She lowered her voice. 'And everyone's shitting themselves about what it means if someone else killed them.'

Falk felt a pang of guilt at the string of missed calls from Gerry Hadler on his phone. He resolved to call him first thing in the morning.

'What do you think about it?' Falk asked, curious.

'I think you should be careful.' She fiddled with the stem of her wineglass. 'Don't get me wrong, I'd love to know Luke didn't do it.'

'You think he did?'

She frowned. Thought before answering. 'I don't know. I couldn't believe it when I heard the news. But it was more disbelief that something like that had happened at all. From what we were all hearing, it seemed pretty clear-cut. I didn't really stop to think whether or not Luke had actually been responsible, you know?'

'Neither did most people. Neither did I.'

She gave a twisted little smile. 'I wouldn't say this to anyone but you, but that's partly Luke's own fault for being such an arsehole.'

The paddocks below them glowed silver in the moonlight, the occasional farmhouse standing out like a smudge on the land. The foursome sat on the edge of the rocky outcrop, dangling their feet over the edge. Luke had been the first one to climb over the fence, kicking the 'Keep Out' sign with his foot as he did. He deliberately hadn't shaved for a few days, Aaron noted with annoyance, and had a dusting of stubble shading his chin. It was more visible in the moonlight as he stood near the rocky edge and stretched his arms out wide, surveying the view.

Aaron had felt his stomach flip at the sight of the unguarded drop, but hoisted himself over the fence without a glance at the others. Ellie was right behind him. Luke made a big show of putting his arm out to help Gretchen. She didn't need it, but she took it with a smile. Now they sat talking and laughing, their insides warm from the half-empty bottle they were passing around. Only Ellie shook her head when the bottle came her way. They took it in turns daring each other to lean forward and stare over the precipice. Full of bluster and bullshit. Scary but not scared.

Falk raised his eyebrows a fraction, but didn't disagree. 'There's a big gap between arsehole and murderer,' he said. Gretchen nodded.

'And listen, I'm not saying he did it. But was he capable of it?' Gretchen glanced around the room, as though Luke might materialise and overhear her. 'That's a completely different question.'

Luke had his arm around Gretchen's waist, Aaron could see out of the corner of his eye. Luke leaned in to murmur something and Gretchen glanced down coyly, her eyelashes casting blue shadows on her cheeks.

Aaron could feel Ellie next to him, but didn't move. It was the first time he'd seen her properly since their kiss a week earlier at the rock tree, and he still felt on shaky ground. She'd said she'd been working every night. He'd allowed himself to go to the shop only once. She'd waved from behind the till, but it wasn't a place they could talk.

On the walk up to the lookout he'd hung back, hoping to engineer a few minutes alone with her, but Luke had stuck maddeningly by his side. Ellie gave no sign she was thinking about what had happened at the tree. By the time they'd reached the hill, Aaron was starting to feel he'd imagined the whole thing.

They'd trudged up the trail, Aaron half-listening as Luke loudly told some story. Suddenly Ellie looked over and caught his gaze across Luke's head. She rolled her eyes with exaggerated suffering. Then smiled. A pure, knowing, secret smile meant just for him.

Buoyed now by the memory, Aaron shifted, looking to move a little closer. He turned but stopped short, the movement frozen before it had begun. The light was poor, up there on the lookout, but it was bright enough for Aaron to see some things clearly. Among them, Ellie's eyes, and the way they were focused on Luke Hadler as he whispered in Gretchen's ear.

'Luke could be so selfish sometimes,' Gretchen said. She ran a finger through a condensation ring on the table, ruining it. 'He would put himself first, second and third and not even realise it. Didn't he? It wasn't just me?' She looked gratified when Falk nodded.

'Sorry,' she said. 'I'm having trouble separating the Luke I knew from what people are saying. The Luke I thought I knew, anyway.'

'I always thought Luke was pretty straightforward when we were younger,' Falk said. 'He was very open, said what he thought. You might not have always liked it, but at least you knew where you were with him.'

'And now?'

'I don't know. His bravado drove me nuts, but underneath that I always felt he was one of the good guys.'

'Well. Let's hope so.' Gretchen rolled her eyes. 'I'd hate to think he wasn't worth it.'

'What do you mean?'

'Oh, nothing.' She looked embarrassed. 'Stupid stuff. I just meant becoming friends with him in the first place. And you and Ellie. It changed a lot for me. Kids I wouldn't give the time of day to started shunning me after Ellie died. Like I was tainted by association. But they were dumb teenage problems compared with everything else. Nothing worth worrying about.'

She couldn't completely disguise the wistful note in her voice. Falk thought about her wide social circles that had seemed to shrink when she'd become a firm member of their ill-fated foursome. It occurred to him for the first time that without him and without Ellie, golden-haired Gretchen may in fact have found herself lonely. He'd never considered the possibility before. He stretched out his hand and touched her arm.

'I'm sorry I wasn't better at keeping in touch. It wasn't that I didn't care, it was just –' He stopped. 'I didn't think. I should have made the effort.'

Gretchen gave a small smile. 'Forget it. I was no better. I blame age and hormones. We were all stupid back then.'

Luke stood and gave an exaggerated stretch. 'Going for a piss,' he announced. His teeth glowed white in the shadows. 'Don't get into trouble while I'm gone.'

He disappeared into the bushes, and the remaining three sat shoulder to shoulder. Aaron and Gretchen passed the bottle between them and he could hear her humming tunelessly to herself. On his other side, Ellie had fixed the horizon with a thousand-yard stare.

The tranquillity was broken by a heavy crash and a loud scream. It echoed in the silence. The three looked at each other, faces silvery and shocked, then Aaron was on his feet and running on rubbery vodka legs towards the sound. He pulled ahead of the girls, and could hear someone's panicked raspy breath behind him. He skidded to a halt at the edge of a sheer drop. The bushes were torn and flattened in a rough patch. Branches near the edge were snapped clean off.

'Luke!' Gretchen appeared by his side and screamed into the void. Her voice bounced back, crying his name on repeat. There was no reply. Falk dropped onto all fours and crept to the edge. He peered down, afraid of what he would see. The drop was more than a hundred metres. The bottom disappeared in the gloom.

'Luke! Mate! Can you hear me?' he yelled.

Gretchen was crying, her face a wet mess. Ellie arrived behind her, edging through the bushes. Walking, not running. Falk's breath was a deafening roar in his ears. Ellie's sober gaze wandered over the trampled bush. She turned and surveyed the bushland behind them, her eyes lingering on the shadows of the trees. Stepping towards the edge of the cliff, she peered once into the abyss. She looked straight at Aaron and gave a tiny shrug.

'The dickhead's faking it.'

She turned and picked something invisible off one of her fingernails.

'I actually wondered if you and Luke would stay together,' Falk said. 'He was self-centred but he always had a genuine soft spot for you.'

Gretchen's small laugh had a bite to it.

'And be a sidekick in the Luke Show, twenty-four seven? No thanks.' She sighed. Her voice lost its edge. 'We did try for a couple of years, after you left. It felt serious at the time, but it was kids' stuff really. I think at heart we were both trying to keep the foursome together somehow. It fell apart, though. Of course.'

'Bad ending?'

'Oh. No.' She looked up and gave a tight smile. 'Not especially. No worse than the usual, anyway. We just grew up. He got married, I had Lachie. Anyway, Luke was never right for me.

I know that now.' She blinked. 'I mean, even before all this with Karen and Billy happened.'

There was a clumsy pause.

'So Luke never spoke about me? After you left, I mean.' Gretchen's casual tone failed to mask her curiosity.

Falk hesitated. 'We didn't really discuss Kiewarra at all if we could help it. Kind of made a point of it. I'd ask after you, of course, and he said you were well, that he'd seen you out and about. That sort of thing, but –' He trailed off, keen not to hurt her feelings. In fact, Luke had barely mentioned Gretchen unless prompted. Falk was surprised to learn now that they'd continued to date for more than a few months. Luke had always made their relationship sound like something soon abandoned.

'I was quite surprised Luke ended up staying in Kiewarra,' Gretchen said. 'After you left, for a while all he talked about was getting out. He had plans to go to Melbourne and study engineering. Work on the big projects.'

'Did he?' That was news to Falk. Luke had never mentioned it. Never once asked for his help, a job reference, a place to crash in the city. 'Why didn't he go?'

Gretchen shrugged.

'I guess eventually he met Karen. It's always been hard to know what Luke really wanted, though.' She paused. Repositioned her wineglass on the table. 'You know, I reckon if she'd lived, Luke would actually have ended up with Ellie. She was more his type than me. Probably more his type than Karen even, for that matter.'

Falk sipped his drink and wondered if that were true.

Gretchen was hysterical. Her colour was high and her blonde hair was damp with sweat. Falk realised she was more drunk than she'd seemed.

His own head was spinning. He kept creeping up and looking down at the drop, yelling Luke's name.

'Will you keep back from there?' Ellie called as he nearly lost his footing for a third time. 'If you go over there really will be something to worry about.'

Aaron wished he could be as calm as she was. At first he'd felt a spark of hope she might be right, Luke could be faking it. But as the minutes ticked on, he became less and less sure. Luke knew his way around, but the cliffs were notoriously unstable. They'd been told that, warned to keep away. More than once. And the booze they'd shared was already rolling around in his stomach. Maybe Ellie was right, but what if −? Gerry's and Barb's faces sprang into his mind, and he couldn't complete the thought.

'We have to − for God's sake, Gretchen, shut up for a second − we have to go and get help,' he said. Ellie merely shrugged. She walked to the cliff and lined up the toes of her boots right on the edge. She looked over for a long moment, then took a step back. She lifted her chin slightly.

'You hear that, Luke?' she called in a clear voice that echoed and bounced off the rock face. 'We're heading down. Everyone's shitting themselves. Last chance.'

It felt to Aaron like nothing moved while he held his breath and waited. The lookout remained silent.

'All right,' Ellie called. She sounded sad rather than angry. 'You've made your choice. I hope you're happy.'

The accusatory inflection rolled through the valley below.

Aaron stared at her for a moment, right into her cold gaze, then grabbed Gretchen's hand and started running down the trail.

'Sometimes it feels like you were the only person Luke was loyal to,' Gretchen said. 'The way he stood by you around Ellie's death. He copped a load of grief for that after you left. All kinds of people were leaning on him to change his story, give you up.'

She drained her wineglass and peered at Falk over the rim. 'He never would.'

Falk took a breath. Now was the time to tell her. *Luke lied. You lied.* 'Listen, Gretch, about that –'

'You were lucky really,' she cut him off. Her voice had lowered a notch. 'Lucky you were with him, for starters. But the amount of flak he got round here, it would've been far easier for him to roll over and change his story. Without Luke, I reckon the Clyde cops would have pinned that on you, no question.'

'Yeah. I know. But listen, Gretch –'

She glanced around the bar. More than one or two watching faces hastily turned away.

'Look, Luke stuck to his guns – stuck by you, really – for twenty years,' she said, quieter now. 'That's more or less the only thing standing between you and a whole lot of problems round here. So a word to the wise, I'd be making sure I was singing pretty loud and long from the same song sheet.'

As they rounded the corner at the bottom of the hill, Aaron couldn't believe it, then immediately could believe it. Luke was lounging on a rock, in perfect health, with a grin on his face and a cigarette in one hand.

'Hey,' he laughed. 'What took you guys so long, you –'

Aaron lunged at him.

'Jesus, Gretchen, I am,' Falk said, trying to keep his tone light. But her message was clear. *Don't ask, don't tell.* 'Why wouldn't I be?'

They stared at each other for a moment. Then Gretchen sat back in her seat and smiled at him, properly. 'Good. No reason at all. I just want to make sure you're being sensible. Better safe than sorry.' She lifted her wineglass, realised it was empty, and put it down. Falk drained his own and went to the bar for two more.

'If everyone was so sure about me,' he said, when he returned, 'I'm surprised they didn't run Luke out of town as well.'

Gretchen took the glass, her smile fading.

'Some tried, you know. At first,' she said. 'Pretty hard. But you know how Luke was, he brazened it out. He didn't wobble, didn't waver. Eventually they kind of accepted it. They pretty much had to.'

She glanced around the pub again. Fewer faces were watching now.

'Look, if they're honest with themselves, most people know Ellie killed herself. She was a sixteen-year-old girl who needed support that she obviously didn't get, and yeah, we should all feel guilty about that. But people don't generally like feeling guilty, and ultimately it was your name on the note. There never really was an explanation for that —' She paused and raised her eyebrows slightly.

Falk gave a tiny shake of his head. He couldn't explain it then, he couldn't explain it now. He had racked his brain over the years. Reliving his last conversations with Ellie, trying to decipher a message or a meaning. To her, he had been Aaron, not Falk. What had been going through her mind when she wrote it? Sometimes he wasn't sure what disturbed him more: the trouble it had caused, or the fact he'd never know the reason why.

'Well,' Gretchen said. 'It doesn't really matter. She was thinking about you in some way around the time she died, and for anyone looking to point the finger, it was enough. Like it or not, Luke was a big character, he was involved in the community. He became a bit of a leader in this town, and we couldn't afford to lose many of them. I think by and large people just chose to put it out of their minds.'

She shrugged. 'It's the same reason everyone round here puts up with morons like Dow and Deacon. It's Kiewarra. It's tough. But we're all in it together. You were gone, Luke stayed. You got the blame.'

Aaron lunged at him and Luke stepped back.

'Watch it,' he said as Aaron grabbed his shoulders. They stumbled, falling backwards to the ground. They landed with a thud and Luke's cigarette rolled out of his fingers. Ellie stepped over and ground it out.

'Watch the sparks, will you? You've already managed to scare them, try not to burn us all to death as well.'

Aaron, pinning Luke under his own weight, felt him bristle at her tone. It was one he'd heard her use on farm animals.

'Jesus, Ellie, what's crawled up your arse? You can't take a joke all of a sudden?' Luke aimed for light-hearted bravado, fell short. Aaron could smell the alcohol in his sweat.

'Did no-one tell you?' Ellie snapped. 'A joke's supposed to be funny.'

'Christ, what the hell's wrong with you these days? You don't like a drink, don't like a laugh. You hardly come out, you're always working at that stupid shop. You're so boring now, Ellie, maybe you and Aaron should just get together and be done with it. Perfectly bloody suited.'

Boring. As the word landed, Aaron felt like Luke had hit him. He stared at his friend in disbelief, then grabbed the front of his shirt and pushed him away so hard Luke's head hit the ground with a smack. He rolled away from Luke, his breathing ragged, not trusting himself to look over.

Ellie stared down at Luke sprawled in the dust, her face showing something worse than anger. Pity. All around, everything seemed still.

'That's what you think?' She stood over him. 'You think your friends are boring because they're loyal to you? Because they show some sense once in a while? The only joke round here is you, Luke. The fact you think it's OK to use people for your own amusement.'

'Get stuffed. I don't.'

'You do,' Ellie went on. 'You do it to all of us. Me. Aaron. Your girlfriend over there. You think it's normal to frighten the people who care about you? To play people off against each other?' She shook her head. 'And to you it's all just a big game. That's the scariest thing about you.'

No-one said anything for a long moment. The words hung between them in the air like mist as each of the four avoided looking at the others. Ellie moved first, turning sharply, and without a second glance, she walked off. Luke and Aaron stared after her from the ground, then clambered to their feet. Aaron still couldn't bring himself to look at Luke.

'Bitch,' he heard Luke mutter at Ellie's back.

'Hey. Don't you call her that,' Aaron said, his voice sharp.

Ahead, Ellie gave no sign whether she'd heard either of them and continued walking at a steady pace. Luke turned and flung his arm around Gretchen, whose sobs had been stunned into silence.

'I'm sorry if I gave you a bit of a scare, babe. You knew it was meant to be a bit of fun, didn't you?' He bent his head and pushed his lips against her cheek. His face shone with sweat and was an angry red. 'But fair enough. Maybe things went a bit far. Said a couple of things I shouldn't have. Maybe I owe you guys an apology.' He sounded like he'd never meant anything less.

'You certainly owe them something.' Ellie's voice drifted back in the night air.

None of them had mentioned the argument again, but it had clung to them like the heat. Ellie spoke to Luke only when she had to, and always with the same polite but distant tone. Aaron, embarrassed around Ellie and pissed off with Luke, kept to himself a little more. Gretchen found herself cast in the role of middleman, and Luke simply pretended not to notice anything had changed.

It would probably all blow over, Aaron told himself, but in reality he wasn't sure. The cracks had been exposed, and they were deeper than he'd realised. He never found out whether he was right or not. Ellie had only another two weeks to live.

Gretchen reached out across the scarred table and touched the edge of Falk's fingers. The noise of the pub faded a little into the background. She had hard-working hands. Her nails were bare and clean, and the pads of her fingertips were rough against his own office-blanched skin.

Ellie had been wrong about her, Falk knew. Gretchen was never an airhead. She was made of much sterner stuff than that. She had stayed and faced the music. She'd built a life in a community that had got the better of others, not least himself and possibly now Luke Hadler. Gretchen was tough. She was a fighter. And she was smiling at him.

'I know it wasn't easy for you to come back here, but it really is good to see you,' she said. 'You were always the only one of us who had any sense. I wish —'

She paused. Shrugged. One tanned shoulder lifted against the strap of her dress. 'I wish you'd been able to stay. Maybe then everything would have been different.'

They looked at each other until Falk felt heat creep up his chest and neck. He cleared his throat and was still thinking of a response when a figure stepped in front of him.

Chapter Seventeen

Grant Dow placed a half-empty beer glass firmly on the table between them with a bang. He was wearing the same shorts and Balinese beer t-shirt as the day before. Falk groaned.

'I thought you were barred,' he said, keeping his voice as neutral as he could.

'I generally find that's more of a suggestion round here.'

Falk looked past Dow to where the barman was watching with a resigned look. Falk raised his eyebrows, but the barman just shrugged. *What can you do?* Across the table, Gretchen caught Falk's eye. She gave a tiny shake of her head. When she spoke, her voice was light.

'What do you want, Grant?'

'I'll tell you what *you* want, Gretch. You want to be more careful who you choose for your boyfriends.' Dow had some of Mal Deacon's arrogance, Falk noticed, but while his uncle's mean streak was reptile cold, Dow was definitely hot-blooded.

Up close, his face was a flushed mess of broken veins and high blood pressure. 'Girls who hang around this bloke tend to end up dead.'

Behind him, his mates sniggered, their reaction a fraction late. Falk wasn't sure if they were the same gang Dow had been with the previous night. They looked wholly interchangeable. The barman had stopped serving as he watched the exchange.

'Thanks, Grant. But I'm a big girl. I can make my own decisions,' Gretchen said. 'So if you've said your piece, why don't you get on with your night and leave us to get on with ours.'

Dow's laugh exposed a mouthful of neglected teeth. His beery breath wafted towards Falk.

'I'll bet you will, Gretch,' he said, giving her a wink. 'You're looking particularly fancy tonight, if I may say so. We don't normally see you all frocked up round here.' He looked at Falk. 'That dress must be all for you, you dickhead. Hope you appreciate it.'

Gretchen's cheeks coloured and she avoided Falk's eye. Falk stood up and took a single step closer to Dow. He was gambling that Dow's desire to avoid the hassle of arrest would outweigh the temptation to throw a punch. He hoped he was right. Falk knew he was a man of some skills, but pub fighting was not among them.

'What is it you want, Grant?' Falk said calmly.

'As it happens,' Dow said, 'I think we got off on the wrong foot yesterday. So I've come to give you a chance to make amends.'

'For what?'

'You know what.'

They looked at each other. Grant Dow had always been older, bigger, stronger. Constantly hovering on the cusp of anger, he sent people scurrying to the other side of the street as he approached. Now older, fatter and with the faint whiff of chronic ill-health on the horizon, the bitterness seemed to seep from his pores.

'Is that all?' Falk said.

'No, that's not bloody all. Take my advice. Take my uncle's advice. For what it's worth these days. Leave.' Dow's voice was low. 'That sack of shit Hadler's not worth the trouble you're going to find yourself in, mark my words.'

Dow glanced over his shoulder at his cronies. Out of the pub window was nothing but night. Falk knew beyond the main street, the town was all but deserted. *Out here, those badges don't mean as much as they should.* Maybe so, but they still meant something.

'I'll be leaving when we've got some clarity about the Hadlers' deaths,' Falk said. 'Not before.'

'This has bugger all to do with you.'

'A family shot dead in a small town like this? I'd say that has something to do with everyone. And you seem to have some strong thoughts on the matter, so maybe we start with you. Make this thing official. What do you reckon?'

Falk reached into his pocket and pulled out a small notebook and pencil. He wrote *Hadler Inquiry* across the top of the page. Directly underneath he wrote Dow's name in large capitals so the man could see it.

'All right, calm down, dickhead.' He was rattled, as Falk knew he would be. There was something about seeing a name on paper that said 'on the record'.

'Confirm your address?'

'I'm not giving you my address.'

'No problem.' Falk didn't miss a beat. 'Luckily, I know it.' He wrote down the details of Deacon's farmhouse. He looked past Dow to his group of followers. They had taken a step away from the exchange. 'I'll take your mates' names as well. If they're so keen to weigh in?'

Grant looked around. His gang had lost their vacuous expressions and were glaring at him.

'You trying to stitch me up?' Dow said. 'Trying to find yourself a scapegoat?'

'Grant,' Falk said, fighting the urge to roll his eyes. 'You're the one who came over to our table.'

Dow looked him up and down, his expression thunderous. He'd closed his right fist. Seemed to be deciding whether it was worth it. He glanced over his shoulder. The barman was still watching them, his hands braced on the countertop. He gave Dow a stern look and nodded towards the door. There'd be no more drinks for them tonight.

Dow loosened his fist and took a casual step away. Like it was hardly worth his effort.

'You're as full of lies and bullshit as ever,' he said to Falk. 'Well. You'll need to be. Might give you a fighting chance here.'

With a jerk of his head his mates followed him out of the pub. The general noise level, which had dimmed during the exchange, gradually swelled to normal.

Falk sat back down. Gretchen was watching him, mouth open a fraction. He grinned, but as he put his notebook away he kept his hand in his pocket until he was sure it had stopped shaking.

Gretchen shook her head in disbelief. 'Jesus. Some welcome back. Well done.' She gave him a wink. 'I told you you were the only one with any sense.' She went up and got the next round.

Later, when the pub was closing, Falk walked her to her car. The street was quiet. Under the streetlights Gretchen's hair glowed like a halo. They stood there, a foot apart, looking at each other, every move awkward and overthought until eventually she laughed and put both hands on his shoulders. She leaned in and kissed him on the cheek, catching the very corner of his mouth. He slipped his arms around her and they held each other close for a moment, heat on heat in the warm night air.

Finally with a small sigh, she pulled herself away, got into her car and with a smile and a wave was gone. Falk stood alone under the swathe of stars thinking, of all things, about Grant Dow. The man talked a lot of shit, that was certain. But he'd said one thing that Falk had caught and kept, and now took out and examined in his mind, turning it over like a find.

That dress must be all for you, you dickhead.

He grinned the whole way back to the pub.

Falk had one foot on the staircase leading to his room when the barman's voice called out.

'In here a minute, mate. If you don't mind.'

Falk sighed, hand on the bannister. He looked longingly up the stairs. A badly framed portrait of the Queen gazed down unsympathetically from the landing. He turned and trudged back through to the bar. The place was empty now. There was the acid lemon scent of cleaning fluid as the barman ran a cloth over the countertop.

'Drink?'

'I thought you were closed.' Falk pulled up a stool and sat down.

'I am. This one's on the house.' The barman set a beer in front of Falk then poured one for himself. 'Call it a thank you.'

'For what?'

'I've seen Grant Dow have a go at a lot of people, and more often than not it ends with me cleaning up someone's blood. Because that's not the case tonight, I can kick back and have a cold one with you.' He held out a hand. 'David McMurdo.'

'Cheers.' Falk took a swallow of beer, surprised by how easily it went down. He'd had more to drink that week than he normally had in a month. 'Sorry about all that. I know I said there'd be no trouble.'

'My friend, if all the trouble round here was handled like that, I'd be a happy man,' McMurdo said, stroking his beard. 'Unfortunately it's weighted a wee bit too much towards the hands-on kind in this place.'

'How long have you been in town?'

'Coming up to ten years. A lot of them still see me as fresh off the boat, though. Born and bred here, or forever an outsider, seems to be the Kiewarra way.'

'Born and bred isn't a free pass either,' Falk said with a grim smile. 'How'd you end up all the way out here anyway?'

McMurdo paused. Rolled his tongue over his teeth. 'What reason do you give for leaving Kiewarra?'

'Career opportunities,' Falk said drily.

'Well. Think I'll say the same and leave it at that.' McMurdo gestured around the empty bar with a wink. 'Still. Seems to have served you well. Your pal Luke could've used some pointers from you on dealing with Dow, to be honest. Too late now, of course.'

'They had run-ins?'

'Like clockwork,' McMurdo said. 'Used to make my heart sink when one would be here and the other would walk in. They were like – I don't know, a pair of magnets. Siamese twins. Jealous ex-lovers. Something. Neither of them could ever leave the other one alone.'

'What did they fall out about?'

McMurdo rolled his eyes. 'What wasn't it about? You name it. The weather, the cricket, the bloody colour of their socks. Always picking at each other. Any excuse.'

'What are we talking? Fist fights?'

'Occasionally,' McMurdo said. 'It got vicious a few times, but not so much recently. Last few years it was more scuffles, heated rows. Don't get me wrong, there was no love lost. But I think they both enjoyed it in a way. Have a barney. Blow off some steam.'

'I've never understood that.'

'Me neither. I'd rather have a nice drink myself. But it must work for some blokes.' He wiped the counter like a man who knew the health inspectors weren't watching. 'To be fair to Dow, it can't be easy looking after that uncle of his.'

Falk remembered how Mal Deacon had mistaken him for his father.

'Do you know what's wrong with him?'

'A wee bit touched in the head these days. Whether it's the drink or something more medical, I couldn't say. But it tends to keep him quiet, whatever it is. He wanders in and sits here with a drink sometimes, or potters around town scowling at folks with that dog of his, but that's about it.'

'Grant Dow's never seemed the Florence Nightingale type. Does he care for his uncle full time?'

McMurdo grinned. 'God, no. He's a labourer. Does odd jobs, plumbing, bit of building. Whatever keeps him in beer money. But it's amazing what the promise of a windfall does, eh? Deacon's leaving the farm to him, or that's the story anyway. It could be worth a fair bit with those Asian investment groups always sniffing round for land. The drought won't last forever. Apparently.'

Falk took a sip. Interesting. The Hadlers' land backed onto Deacon's property. He had no idea what the market price would be but two parcels together were always more valuable to the right buyer. Provided the Hadlers' place came up for sale, of course.

A scenario far less likely when Luke was alive and at the helm than it was now. Falk filed the thought away for future consideration.

'So is the grapevine accurate about you looking into the Hadlers' deaths?' McMurdo was saying.

'It's not official,' Falk said, for the second time that night.

'Gotcha,' McMurdo said with a knowing smile. 'Probably the best way to get anything done round here anyway.'

'That said, anything happened that I should know about?'

'You mean did Luke have a massive bust-up the night before he died? Did Grant Dow declare in front of the entire pub that he was going to shoot the family in cold blood?'

'That would be helpful.'

'Sorry to disappoint you, mate.' McMurdo flashed a mouthful of yellowing teeth.

'Jamie Sullivan said he was in here with Luke the night before the killings,' Falk said. 'Making plans to shoot rabbits.'

'That sounds about right.'

'Was Dow in here too?'

'Yeah, of course. He's here most nights, that's why he hates being barred. For all the good it does me. It's more of an annoyance for him than anything. Too difficult for me to enforce, and he knows it. Whenever I try, him and his gormless mates plonk themselves on the porch outside with a pile of tinnies. I get all the trouble with none of the revenue, you know? Anyway.' McMurdo shook his head. 'To answer your question, Grant Dow was here that last night Luke was in. Along with nearly everyone else, mind. The cricket was on TV so it was packed.'

'Did you see him and Luke talk? Interact at all? Either of them have a go at the other?'

'Not that I remember. But like I said, it was a busy night. I was run off my feet.' McMurdo thought for a moment as he downed the last swallow of his beer and suppressed a small burp.

'But who can say with those two? You could never tell from one night to the next what was going to happen. I know Luke was your mate and Dow's a dickhead, but in a lot of ways they were quite similar. Both bolshy, larger than life, got tempers on them. Two sides of the same coin, you know?'

Falk nodded. He knew. McMurdo took the empty glasses, and Falk took his cue to leave. He climbed off his stool and said goodnight, leaving the barman to switch off the lights and plunge the downstairs into darkness. As Falk half-trudged, half-tottered upstairs, his mobile flashed with a new voicemail. He waited until he was locked in his room and lying flat on his bed before clumsily punching the buttons. He closed his eyes as a familiar voice floated from the handset.

'Aaron, answer your phone, will you?' Gerry Hadler's words were rushed in his ear. 'Look, I've been thinking a lot about that day Ellie died.' A long pause. 'Come out to the farm tomorrow if you can. There's something you should know.'

Falk opened his eyes.

Chapter Eighteen

The Hadlers' farm looked different as Falk pulled up. The tattered yellow crime scene tape had been removed from the front door. On either side, the curtains and blinds were pulled wide and every window was propped ajar.

The mid-morning sun was already fierce and Falk reached for his hat as he stepped out of the car. He tucked the box of Karen's and Billy's school things under his arm and walked up the path. The front door was open. Inside, the smell of bleach had eased a little.

Falk found Barb crying in the master bedroom. She was perched on the edge of Luke and Karen's queen-size bed, the contents of a drawer upended onto the pale green duvet. Balled-up socks and crumpled boxer shorts mingled with loose coins and pen lids. Tears slid from Barb's cheeks onto a piece of coloured paper in her lap.

She jumped when Falk knocked gently, and as he went to

her he could see she was holding a handmade Father's Day card. She wiped her face on her sleeve and flapped the card in Falk's direction.

'No secret's safe from a good clean-out, is it? Turns out Billy was as bad at spelling as his father.'

She tried to laugh but her voice broke. Falk felt her shoulders heave as he sat down and put his arm around her. The room was stiflingly hot as sweltering air seeped in through the open windows. He didn't say anything. Whatever the windows were letting out of that house was more important than anything they could let in.

'Gerry asked me to come by,' Falk said when Barb's sobs subsided a little. She sniffed.

'Yes, love. He said. He's clearing out the big barn, I think.'

'Did he say what it was about?' Falk said, wondering when, if ever, Gerry would see fit to confide in his wife. Barb shook her head.

'No. Maybe he wants to give you something of Luke's. I don't know. It was his idea to do this clear-out in the first place. He says it's time we faced it.'

The final sentence was almost lost as she picked up a pair of Luke's socks and dissolved into fresh tears.

'I've been trying to think if there's anything Charlotte might like. She's pining so badly.' Barb's voice was muffled behind a tissue. 'Nothing we do seems to help her. We've left her with a sitter, but Gerry actually suggested bringing her with us. See if being around her old things calmed her. There's no way I'm allowing that, I told him. There's no way I'm bringing her back to this house after what happened here.'

Falk rubbed Barb's back. He glanced around the bedroom while she cried. Apart from a layer of dust, it was neat and clean. Karen had tried to keep the clutter under control, but there were enough personal touches to make the room inviting.

Framed baby photos stood on top of a chest of drawers that looked of good quality but was probably second- or even third-hand. Any money for decorating had clearly been channelled towards the children's rooms. Through a gap in the wardrobe, Falk could see rows of clothes suspended on plastic hangers. On the left, women's plain fitted tops hung next to blouses, work trousers, the odd summer dress. Luke's jeans and t-shirts were crammed with less thought on the right.

Both sides of the bed appeared to have been slept in regularly. Karen's bedside table had a toy robot, a tub of night cream and a pair of reading glasses on top of a pile of books. A phone charger was plugged in on Luke's side, next to a dirty coffee cup, hand painted, with the word 'Daddy' spelled out in spidery letters. The pillowcases still had the shadows of dents in them. Whatever Luke Hadler had been doing in the days before he and his family died, Falk thought, it hadn't been sleeping on the couch. This was definitely a room for two.

An image of Falk's own bedroom flashed into his mind. He mostly slept in the middle of the bed these days. His bedspread was the same navy blue he'd had as a teenager. No-one who had seen it in the past couple of years had got comfortable enough to suggest something more gender-neutral. The cleaning service that came to his flat twice a month often struggled to find enough to do, he knew. He didn't hoard, he didn't keep much for sentimental reasons and he'd made do with whatever furniture he'd been left with three years earlier, when his two-person flat had become home to just one.

'You're a closed book,' she'd said one final time before she'd left. She'd said it a lot over the two years they'd been together. First intrigued, then concerned, finally accusing. Why couldn't he let her in? Why *wouldn't* he let her in? Did he not trust her? Or did he not love her enough? His response to that question hadn't come fast enough, he'd realised too late. A fraction of a moment's silence had been long enough for both of them to hear the death knell. Since then Falk's own bedside table traditionally held nothing more than books, an alarm clock and, occasionally, an aging box of condoms.

Barb sniffed loudly, bringing him back into the room. Falk took the Father's Day card from her lap and looked around in vain for somewhere suitable to put it.

'See. That's exactly the problem,' Barb said, her red eyes watching him. 'What on earth am I supposed to do with all their things? There's so much and there's nowhere to put anything. I can't fit it all in our house, but I can hardly give everything away like none of it matters –'

Her voice was high-pitched as she started snatching up odd items within reach and clutching them to her chest. Underpants from the bed, the toy robot, Karen's glasses. She picked up the books from the bedside table and swore loudly. 'Oh, for God's sake, and these are bloody library books. How overdue are these going to be?' She turned to Falk, red-faced and angry.

'No-one tells you this is how it's going to be, do they? Oh yes, they're all so sorry for your loss, all so keen to pop round and get the gossip when it happens, but no-one mentions having to go through your dead son's drawers and return their library books, do they? No-one tells you how to cope with that.'

With a flash of guilt, Falk pictured the extra box of Karen's and Billy's belongings he'd left outside the bedroom door. He plucked the books from Barb's hands, put them under his arm and steered her firmly out of the bedroom.

'I can look after that for you. Let's just –' He ushered her straight past Billy's room and emerged with some relief into the bright kitchen. He guided Barb to a stool. 'Let's get you a cup of tea,' he finished, pulling open the nearest cupboards. He hadn't the slightest idea what he might find there, but even crime scene kitchens usually had mugs.

Barb watched him for a minute, then blew her nose and climbed off the stool. She patted his arm.

'Let me, I know where everything is.'

In the end they had to settle for instant coffee, black. The fridge hadn't been emptied in over two weeks.

'I never thanked you, Aaron,' Barb said, as they waited for the kettle to boil. 'For helping us. Opening an investigation into what happened.'

'Barb, I haven't done anything like that,' Falk said. 'You understand that what I'm doing with Sergeant Raco is off the record, don't you? We're just asking a couple of questions. Nothing official.'

'Oh yes. Of course, I completely understand that,' she said in such a way that he could tell she didn't. 'But you've got people wondering. That makes all the difference. It's stirred things up.'

An image of Ellie flashed through Falk's mind, and he hoped Barb wouldn't come to regret that.

'Luke was always so grateful to have you as a friend,' she said as she poured boiling water into three mugs.

'Thank you,' he said simply, but Barb looked up at something in his tone.

'He was,' she insisted. 'I know he wasn't good at saying it, but he needed someone like you in his life. Someone calm, with a sensible head on their shoulders. I always thought that's partly what attracted Luke to Karen. He saw the same sort of qualities in her.' She automatically opened the right drawer and found a spoon. 'Did you ever meet Karen in the end?'

Falk shook his head.

'It's a shame, I think you really would have liked her. She reminds – reminded – me of you in a lot of ways. I think sometimes she worried that she was a tiny bit . . . I don't know, dull, maybe. That she was the only thing standing between Luke and his big ideas. But she wasn't. She was steady, and really bright, that girl. And she was exactly what he needed. She kept my son grounded. You both did.' Barb looked at Falk for a long moment, her head cocked to the side a little sadly. 'You should have come back for their wedding. Or any time. We missed you.'

'I –' He started to say he'd had to work, but something in her expression stopped the words on his lips. 'Honestly, I didn't feel like I'd be welcome.'

Barb Hadler took two large steps across the kitchen that had once been hers, reached out her hands and pulled Falk into her arms. She held him firmly until he felt a tension buried deep inside him start to waver.

'You, Aaron, are always welcome in my family,' Barb said. 'Don't ever let yourself think otherwise.' She pulled away and for a moment she was the Barb Hadler of old. She placed two steaming mugs of coffee in his hands, tucked the library books under his arm and nodded to the back door with a matriarchal glint in her eye.

'Let's take these out to my husband, so I can tell him that if he wants this house cleared he can stop hiding in the barn and do it himself.'

Falk followed Barb out of the back door and into the blinding sunlight. He narrowly avoided sloshing coffee on his wrist as he sidestepped an abandoned toy cricket bat.

Is this what his own life could have been like? Falk wondered suddenly. Kids' cricket bats and coffee in farmhouse kitchens?

He tried to imagine it. Working side by side with his dad in the open air, waiting for the moment when his old man would shake his hand and pass him the reins. Spending Saturday nights in the Fleece with Luke, eyeing up the mostly unchanged pool of talent until one day his eye stopped wandering. A brisk but beautiful country wedding, the first baby arriving nine months later. The second a year after that. The fatherhood role wouldn't come entirely naturally to him, he knew, but he would make the effort. They say it's different with your own.

His children would be friends with Luke's son, inevitably. They'd all have to take their chances at that shambolic country school, yes, but they would also have acres and acres of land where they could stretch their legs.

Days working on the land would be long, of course, but the nights at home would be warm and full of noise and chaos and laughter. Love. There would always be someone waiting for him with the light on. Who could that have been? he thought. Ellie?

Straight away, the image started to blur and fade. If she'd lived. If he'd stayed. If everything was different. The idea was a complete fantasy. There were too many lost chances for that vision to have played out.

Falk had chosen his life in Melbourne. And he was happy with it, he thought. He liked being able to walk down the street, surrounded by people but without a single soul recognising him. He enjoyed work that taxed his brain rather than his back.

Life was give and take. His flat may be quiet and empty when he returned at the end of each day, but he wasn't watched by curious eyes that knew every last thing about him. His neighbours didn't judge him, or harass him and spread rumours about his family. They didn't leave animal carcasses on his doorstep. They left him alone.

He knew he had a habit of keeping people at arm's length, collecting acquaintances rather than friends. But all the better should one of them ever again float bloated and broken to the surface of a river, a stone's throw from his family home. And yes, he battled the daily commute to work, and spent a lot of his days under fluorescent office lights, but at least his livelihood didn't hang by a thread on the whim of a weather pattern. At least he wasn't driven to such fear and despair by the blank skies that there was even a chance the wrong end of a gun might look like the right answer.

Luke Hadler may have had a light on waiting for him when he came home, but something else from this wretched, desperate community had seeped through that front door and into his home. And it had been rotten and thick and black enough to extinguish that light forever.

Falk's mood was low as they reached Gerry, who was leaning on a broom outside one of the barns. He looked up in surprise as they approached, and cast a nervous glance towards his wife.

'I didn't know you'd arrived,' he said as Falk handed him one of the mugs.

'He's been inside helping me,' Barb said.

'Right. Thanks.' Gerry sounded uncertain.

'There's still plenty to do, when you've finished messing around out here.' Barb gave her husband a small smile. 'It looks like you've made even less progress than I have.'

'I know. I'm sorry. It's harder being here than I realised.' Gerry turned to Falk. 'I thought it was time we came and faced it. Confronted things.' He looked towards the house. 'Listen, is there anything in there you'd like? Photos or anything? You'd be welcome.'

Falk couldn't imagine wanting to take a single souvenir from that terrible house into his own life. He shook his head.

'I'm good, thanks Gerry.'

He took a large gulp of coffee, swallowing so rapidly he nearly choked. He felt desperate to get away from this place. He wished Barb would leave so he could speak to Gerry alone.

Instead they all drank in silence, watching the horizon. In the distance, Falk could make out Mal Deacon's farm sitting squat and ugly on the hillside. He remembered the barman's comment about Deacon's property going to his nephew.

'What will you do with this place?' Falk asked. Gerry and Barb looked at each other.

'We haven't really decided,' Gerry said. 'We'll have to sell it, I suppose. If we can. Put the money in a trust for Charlotte. We might have to bulldoze the house though, sell it as land only.' Barb made a small tutting sound and Gerry looked at her.

'Yeah, I know love.' A defeated note had crept into his voice. 'But I can't see anyone round here wanting to live in it after all this, can you? And it's not like outsiders are lining up to move here.'

'Have Deacon or Dow mentioned anything about joining forces?' Falk said. 'Parcelling up both properties for Asian investors?'

Barb turned to him, her face a picture of disgust. 'We wouldn't sell those two a five-dollar note for ten bucks, let alone team up with them. Would we, Gerry?'

Her husband shook his head, but Falk suspected he had a more realistic view of the state of the Kiewarra property market.

'We've had nothing but thirty years of grief from that side of the fence,' Barb went on, her voice a little louder. 'We're not about to help him now. Mal used to sneak out in the night and move the boundaries, did you know that? Like we'd be too stupid to notice. Helped himself to anything he could find that wasn't nailed down. I know it was him who ran over Luke's dog all those years ago, no matter how much he denied it. Do you remember that?'

Falk nodded. Luke had loved that dog. He'd been fourteen and had cried openly as he'd cradled it by the roadside.

'And he always had a houseful of town blokes hanging round until all hours when he was younger, didn't he, Gerry? Drinking and tearing up and down the roads in their trucks. Blasting their music when he knew we had to be up at the crack of dawn to keep the farm going.'

'That was a while ago now, love,' Gerry said, and Barb turned on him.

'Are you defending him?'

'No. God, no. I'm just stating a fact. He's not been able to get up to much like that for a while, has he? You know that.'

Falk thought about his strange encounter with Deacon at the pub.

'Sounds like he has some sort of dementia.'

Barb snorted. 'Is that what they're calling it? A miserable life-time of bad deeds catching up with the drunken bastard, if you ask me.'

She took a sip of coffee and looked up at Deacon's land. When she spoke again Falk could hear the regret.

'It was Ellie I felt most sorry for. At least we could shut the door on him, but the poor girl had to live with it. I think he did care for her in his own way, but he was so defensive. Remember the upper paddock, Gerry?'

'We couldn't prove that was him.'

'No, but it was. What else could it have been?' Barb turned to Falk. 'It was when you kids were about eleven, not long after Ellie's mum did a runner – not that I blame her. The little girl was forlorn, wasn't she, Gerry? She was so thin, she wasn't eating properly. And she had this look in her eyes. Like it was the end of the world. Eventually I went up there to tell Mal that she wasn't right and he needed to do something, or she'd be making herself sick with all that worry.'

'What did he say?'

'Well, he showed me the door before I could barely get the words out, as you'd expect. But then a week later our upper paddock died. No warning, nothing. We did some tests and the soil acidity was all wrong.'

Gerry sighed. 'Yeah. It can happen, but –'

'But it happens a lot easier if your neighbour dumps a round of chemicals on it,' Barb said. 'It cost us thousands that year. We struggled to keep afloat. And it never properly recovered.'

Falk remembered that paddock, and he remembered the tense conversations around the Hadlers' dinner table that year.

'Why does he always get away with it?' he asked.

'There was no proof it was him,' Gerry said again. 'But –' He held up a hand as Barb went to interrupt. 'But you know what it's like here, mate. It takes a lot for people to be willing to stand up and rock the boat. It was the same then as it is now. We all needed each other to get by. Mal Deacon did business with a lot of us and we all did business with him. And he collected favours, let the odd payment slide so he had a hold over people. If you fell out with Deacon, it wasn't only him you fell out with. Suddenly doing business and having a peaceful beer in your own town become a hell of a lot harder. Life was already hard enough.'

Barb stared at him.

'The girl was so unhappy she drowned herself, Gerry.' She gathered their empty mugs together with a clash of ceramic. 'Stuff the business and the beer. We should all have done more.

I'll see you inside. There are a thousand jobs waiting when you're ready.'

She turned and stalked off towards the house, wiping her face with her sleeve as she went.

'She's right,' Gerry said, watching her go. 'Whatever happened, Ellie deserved far better.' He turned to Falk, his eyes drained of emotion. Like he'd burned through a lifetime's supply in the past few weeks. 'Thanks for sticking around. We heard you'd been asking questions about Luke.'

'Started to.'

'Can I ask what you think? Did Luke kill Karen and Billy?'

'I think,' Falk said carefully, 'there is a possibility he didn't.'

'Jesus, are you sure?'

'No. I said possibility.'

'But you do think someone else might be involved.'

'Maybe, yes.'

'Is it connected with what happened with Ellie?'

'I honestly don't know, Gerry.'

'But maybe?'

'Maybe.'

A silence. 'Christ. Listen, there's something I should have told you from the start.'

Gerry Hadler was hot but not unhappy about it. He tapped a light rhythm on the steering wheel, whistling to himself. The evening sun warmed his forearm through the window as he drove along the empty road. They'd had a solid rainfall that year, and out on the farm these days he liked what he was seeing.

Gerry glanced at the bottle of sparkling wine lying on the passenger seat. He'd popped into town to pick up some supplies and had spontaneously nipped into the bottle shop. He was taking it home to surprise Barb, who he hoped at this moment was making her Friday night lamb casserole. Gerry turned on the radio. It was a song he didn't recognise, but it had a deep jazz beat he liked. He nodded his head in time, and pressed his foot to the brake as a crossroad appeared ahead.

'I knew you and Luke were lying about your alibis for the day Ellie Deacon died.' Gerry's voice was now so quiet Falk had to strain to hear it. 'The thing is, I think someone else knew it too.'

Gerry was still twenty metres from the crossroads when the familiar figure flashed across on a bike. His son's head was down and he was pedalling furiously. From that distance, Luke's hair looked slicked back and shiny in the low sunlight. It was a change from his usually floppy style, Gerry noticed vaguely. It didn't really suit him.

Luke sped through the crossroads without as much as a glance in either direction. Gerry tutted under his breath. He'd have to have a word with that boy. Fair enough, the roads were usually empty, but that didn't automatically mean it was safe. Behaving like that, Luke would get himself killed.

'He was coming from the south, from the direction of the river. Nowhere near the paddocks you boys said you were in. You weren't with him. He didn't have his shotgun.'

'The river's not the only thing to the south,' Falk said. 'There are farms, for one. The bike trails for another.'

Gerry shook his head. 'Luke hadn't been on any bike trail. He was wearing that grey shirt he loved at the time. You know, that awful shiny button-down one he always saved for best. My impression was that he looked pretty fancy that afternoon. Like he was dressed for a date or something. His hair was slicked back. I told myself at the time he was trying a new style.' Gerry put his hand over his eyes for a long moment. 'But I always knew his hair was wet.'

Luke was well through the crossroads by the time Gerry pulled up. As if to prove a point, Gerry brought his truck to a complete stop and checked both ways. To the right, his son's shadowy figure grew smaller. To the left, he could see only as far as a bend in the road. All clear. Gerry eased his foot onto the accelerator and moved through. As he cleared the crossroads and pulled away, he glanced in his rear-view mirror.

The image in the reflection was there and gone in less than a second. It had disappeared almost as soon as he saw it: a white ute flashing through the crossroads. From the left. Following in the direction of his son.

Falk was silent for a long moment.

'You didn't see who was driving?' Falk watched him closely.

'No. I couldn't tell. I wasn't paying attention, and it went by so fast I couldn't see. But whoever it was, I bet they saw Luke.' Gerry wouldn't look at Falk. 'They pulled that girl's body out of the river three days later, and it was the worst day of my life.' He gave a small strange laugh. 'Well, until recently. Her photo was everywhere, do you remember?'

Falk nodded. It had felt like Ellie's picture had stared blank-eyed and pixelated from newspaper pages for days. Some shops had put it up as a makeshift poster, collecting money for the funeral expenses.

'For twenty years I've lived in fear of that driver coming out of the woodwork. Knocking on the door of the police station and saying they saw Luke that day,' Gerry said.

'Maybe they really didn't see him.'

'Maybe.' Gerry looked at his son's farmhouse. 'Or maybe when they finally decided to knock, it wasn't on the police station door.'

Chapter Nineteen

Falk sat in his car by the side of the road, thinking about what Gerry had said. White utes were ten a penny in Kiewarra, both then and now. It could be nothing. If someone saw Luke coming from the direction of the river that day, Falk thought, why wouldn't they have said so at the time? Who would benefit from keeping the secret for twenty years?

One thought nagged at him like an itch. If the driver of the ute had seen Luke, was it not possible Luke had also seen the driver? Perhaps – the idea grew, demanding attention – perhaps it was the other way around. Maybe it was Luke who had kept someone else's secret. And maybe, for whatever reason, Luke had finally had enough.

Falk stared unseeingly at the bleak landscape as he turned the idea back and forth in his mind. Eventually, he sighed and pulled out his phone. He heard a rustle of papers down the line when Raco answered.

'Are you at the station?' Falk asked. It was a beautiful Sunday outside. He wondered what Raco's wife would make of that.

'Yeah.' A sigh. 'Going through some of the Hadler paper-work. For all the good it's doing. You?'

Falk filled him in on what Gerry had said.

'Right.' Raco breathed out. 'What do you reckon?'

'I don't know. It could be something. Could also be nothing. Will you be there for a bit longer?'

'I'm sorry to say I'll be here for a lot longer.'

'I'll head in.'

Falk had barely put down his phone when it buzzed again. He opened the text and his frown morphed into a small smile when he saw who it was.

Busy? Gretchen had written. *Hungry? Having lunch with Lachie in Centenary Park.*

Falk thought of Raco, flat out trawling through reports at the station, and of the coffee churning in his stomach since leaving the Hadlers' place. He thought about Gretchen's smile when she'd left him standing under the stars outside the pub. *That dress must be all for you, you dickhead.*

On my way, he texted. Thought for a moment. *Can't stay too long though.* It didn't really assuage the guilt. He didn't really care.

Centenary Park was the first place Falk had seen in Kiewarra that looked like it had had some dollars thrown behind it. The flowerbeds were new and had been carefully planted with attrac-tive drought-friendly cacti, giving the park a lushness Falk felt he hadn't seen in weeks.

The bench they'd spent so many Saturday nights on was gone, he noticed with a pang of regret. Instead, elaborate play equipment shone in glossy primary colours. It was crawling with children, and every one of the picnic tables bordering the edge was taken. Prams jostled for space with eskies as parents chatted, breaking off only to alternately berate and feed their offspring.

Falk saw Gretchen before she saw him and he stopped, watching for a moment. She was alone at a table on the fringe, sitting on a picnic bench with her long legs stretched out in front of her and her elbows resting on the tabletop behind. Her fair hair was pulled into a messy bun on top of her head, topped by sunglasses. She was watching the activity on the play equipment with an amused look on her face. Falk felt the warm bloom of familiarity. In the sunlight, in the distance, she could almost have been sixteen again.

Gretchen must have felt his eyes on her because she suddenly looked up. She smiled and raised a hand and he headed over. She greeted him with a kiss on the cheek and an open Tupperware container.

'Have a sandwich, Lachie'll never get through them.'

He selected a ham one and they sat side by side on the bench. She stretched out her legs again, her thigh warm against his. She had thongs on her feet and her toenails were a shiny pink.

'Well, this is absolutely nothing like I remember. It's amazing,' Falk said, watching the kids scrambling over the equipment. 'Where did the money come from for all this?'

'I know. It was a rural charity thing. We got lucky a couple of years ago from some rich do-gooders' fund. I shouldn't make fun, it's brilliant really. Nicest place in town now. And it's always packed. The kids love it. Even if I was heartbroken to see our old bench go.' She smiled as they watched a toddler bury his friend in the sandpit. 'But it's great for the little ones. God knows, they haven't got much else going for them round here.'

Falk pictured the peeling paint and lone basketball hoop in the school playground. 'Makes up for the school, I guess. That was more run-down than I remembered.'

'Yeah. Another thing you can thank the drought for.' Gretchen opened a bottle of water and took a sip. She tilted it towards him the same way she used to offer vodka. Easy intimacy. He took it. 'There's no community money,' she said. 'Everything this town gets from the government goes towards farming subsidies so there's nothing left for the kids. But we're lucky to have Scott as the principal over there. At least he actually seems to give a toss. But there's only so much you can do with an empty bank balance. There's no way we can ask the parents for any more.'

'You can't tap the rich do-gooders again?'

She gave a sad smile. 'We've tried that actually. We thought we were in line for a windfall this year. It was a different mob from the playground though. This was some private group, the Crossley Educational Trust. You ever heard of them?'

'I don't think so.'

'Typical bleeding-heart types, but it sounded right up our street. They give cash to struggling rural schools, but apparently there are other schools more rural or struggling than us, if you can believe it. God help them. We made the shortlist, but no dice this time. We'll look around, try again next year I suppose, but until then, who knows? Anyway –' She broke off to wave at her son, who was standing at the top of a slide trying to get their attention. He slid down as they watched. '– Lachie's happy there for now, so that's something at least.'

She reached for the Tupperware as the little boy ran over. Gretchen held out a sandwich, but her son ignored her, staring instead at Falk.

'Hi, mate.' Falk held out his hand. 'I'm Aaron. We met the

other day, remember? Your mum and I were friends when we were younger.'

Lachie shook his hand and grinned at the novelty of the action.

'Did you see me on the slide?'

'We did,' Gretchen said, but the question wasn't aimed at her. Falk nodded.

'You were really brave, mate,' Falk said. 'That looks pretty high.'

'I can do it again. Watch.' Lachie took off. Gretchen watched him go with a funny look on her face. The kid waited until he had Falk's full attention before he went. He ran straight around to do it again. Falk gave him a thumbs up.

'Thanks,' Gretchen said. 'He's obsessed with grown men at the moment. I think he's starting to see the other kids with dads and . . . well, you know.' She shrugged. Didn't meet Falk's eye. 'Still, that's what motherhood's about, isn't it? Eighteen years of crushing guilt?'

'His dad not involved at all?' Falk heard the note of curiosity in his own voice.

Gretchen heard it as well and smiled knowingly.

'No. And it's OK, you can ask. His dad's gone. No-one you knew. Not a local, just a labourer who passed through for a while. I don't know much about him other than he left me with this amazing kid. And yes, I know how that sounds.'

'It doesn't sound like anything. It sounds like Lachie's lucky to have you,' Falk said. But as he watched the child clamber athletically up the ladder he found himself wondering what his father had looked like.

'Thanks. It doesn't always feel that way. I wonder sometimes if I should make an effort to meet someone. For both of us, try and give Lachie a bit of a family. Let him see what it's like to

have a mum who's not stressed and exhausted all the time, whatever that looks like. But I don't know . . .' She trailed off and
Falk was worried she was embarrassed, when she flashed him
a grin. 'It's a bloody shallow dating pool in Kiewarra. Muddy
puddle at best.'

Falk laughed.

'So you never got married at all?' he said, and Gretchen shook
her head.

'Nope. Never did.'

'Me neither.'

Gretchen's eyes crinkled with amusement. 'Yeah, I know.'

Falk was never sure how, but women always seemed to know.
They looked sideways and smiled at each other. Falk imagined
Gretchen and Lachie living by themselves on the vast Kellerman
property she'd bought, and remembered the eerie isolation of
the Hadlers' property. Even Falk, who liked his own space more
than most, started to crave company after a few hours with
nothing but paddocks.

'You must get lonely on the farm on your own,' he said, and
could have bitten his tongue off. 'Sorry. That was a genuine
question, not a terrible pick-up line.'

Gretchen laughed. 'I know. With lines like that, you'd fit in
better round here than you think.' Her face clouded. 'But yeah.
It can be an issue. It's not really the lack of company, it's feeling
cut off that gets me a bit. I can't get reliable internet, and even
the phone coverage is patchy. Not that I've got loads of people
trying to call me anyway.' She paused, her mouth pressed into a
tight line. 'You know I didn't even find out what had happened
to Luke until the next morning?'

'Seriously?' Falk was shocked.

'Yep. Not one person thought to ring me. Not Gerry and
Barb, no-one. Despite everything we've been through, I guess

I –' she gave a tiny shrug, '– I wasn't a priority. On the afternoon it happened, I picked up Lachie from school, went home, had dinner. He went to bed, I watched a DVD.

'It was so ordinary and boring, but it was like the last normal evening, you know? Nothing special, but I'd give anything to go back to that. It wasn't until the next morning at the school gates and I turned up and *everyone* was talking about it. It felt like they all knew and –' A single tear slipped down her nose. 'And no-one had bothered to call me. I couldn't believe it. I mean, I literally couldn't believe what I was hearing. I drove past his property, but wasn't able to get anywhere near. The road was blocked and there were cops everywhere. So I went home. By then it was on the news, of course. No chance of missing it, then.'

'I'm so sorry, Gretch,' Falk said, putting a hand on her shoulder. 'If it helps at all, no-one called me either. I found out when I saw his face on a news site.' Falk could still feel the shock at seeing those familiar features attached to that terrible headline.

Gretchen nodded, and her gaze suddenly focused on something over his shoulder. Her expression clouded and she hastily wiped her eyes.

'Christ, watch out. Incoming,' she said. 'Mandy Vaser. You remember her? It was Mandy Mantel back then. Jesus, I cannot be bothered with this right now.'

Falk turned. The sharp-faced ginger-haired girl he remembered as Mandy Mantel had morphed into a neat, tiny woman with a shiny red bob. She had a baby strapped to her chest in a complicated sling that looked like it would be made from natural fibres and advertised as 'organic'. Her face was still sharp as she marched across the yellow grass.

'She married Tim Vaser. He was a year or two above us,' Gretchen whispered as she approached. 'She's got a couple of kids in the school. Also got her hands full as the self-appointed spokeswoman of the anxious mothers' group.'

Mandy stopped in front of them. She looked from Falk to the ham sandwich he was holding and back again, her lip curled in distaste.

'Hi, Mandy,' he said. She pointedly ignored him, other than to place a protective hand around the back of her baby's skull, shielding it from his greeting.

'Gretchen. Sorry to interrupt.' She sounded nothing of the sort. 'Could you pop over to our table for a moment? Just a quiet word.' Her eyes flicked smartly to Falk then away.

'Mandy,' Gretchen said without enthusiasm. 'You remember Aaron? From the old days? He's with the AFP now.' She emphasised the last words.

He and Mandy had kissed once, Falk remembered. At a youth disco, from what he could recall. She had surprised him by poking her fourteen-year-old tongue deep into his mouth, tasting strongly of cheap lemonade as mood lighting glowed against the walls of the school gym and a stereo blared in the corner. He wondered if she remembered. From the way she crinkled her brow and avoided eye contact, he was certain that she did.

'Nice to see you again.' Falk held out his hand, not because he particularly wanted to shake hers, but because he could tell it would make her uncomfortable. She stared at it, making a visible effort to resist the automatic polite response. She succeeded and left him hanging in midair. He almost respected her a little bit for that.

'Gretchen.' Mandy was losing patience. 'A word?'

Gretchen looked her straight in the eyes. She made no attempt to move.

'The sooner you say it, Mandy, the sooner I can tell you

to mind your own business and we can all get back to our Sundays.'

Mandy stiffened. She glanced over her shoulder to where a gang of mothers with similar hairstyles were watching from behind sunglasses.

'All right. Fine. I – *we* – don't feel comfortable with Aar – with *your friend* – being so close to our children.' She looked straight at Falk. 'We'd like you to leave.'

'Noted,' Gretchen said.

'So he'll leave?'

'No,' Falk and Gretchen said in unison.

Falk actually thought it probably was about time he headed to the station to find Raco, but he wasn't about to be pushed around by Mandy bloody Mantel. Mandy's eyes narrowed. She leaned in.

'Listen,' she said. 'At the moment it's me and the mums asking politely. But it can easily be the dads asking not so politely if you'd find that message easier to understand.'

'Mandy, for God's sake,' Gretchen snapped. 'He's police. Do you hear what I'm saying?'

'Yeah, and we also all heard what he did to Ellie Deacon.' Around the playground, parents were looking on. 'Seriously, Gretchen, you can't really be that desperate, can you? That you'd expose your *own son* like this? You're a mum now. Start acting like one.'

The man who had eventually become Mandy's husband had once written and publicly recited a poem for Gretchen one Valentine's Day, Falk recalled. No wonder the woman was relishing having the upper hand for once.

'If you're going to be spending time with this . . . person, Gretchen,' Mandy went on, 'I've half a mind to alert social services. For Lachie's sake.'

'Hey –' Falk said, but Gretchen spoke over him.

'Mandy Vaser,' she said, her quiet voice like iron. 'You think you're so all-knowing? Then do something smart for once in your life. Turn around and walk away.'

The woman straightened her spine, unwilling to yield ground.

'And Mandy? Watch yourself. If you do anything that causes my son to lose a single minute of sleep or shed one tear —' Gretchen's icy tone was one Falk hadn't heard before. She didn't finish the sentence, letting it hang in the air.

Mandy's eyes widened.

'Are you threatening me? That is aggressive language, and I take that as a threat. I can't believe you. After everything this town has been through.'

'You're the one threatening me! Social services, my arse.'

'I'm trying to keep Kiewarra safe for our kids. Is that too much to ask? Haven't things been bad enough? I know you didn't have much time for Karen, but you could at least show some respect, Gretchen.'

'That's enough, Mandy,' Falk said sharply. 'For God's sake, shut up and leave us in peace.'

Mandy pointed at Falk.

'No. You leave.' She turned on her heel and stalked away. 'I'm phoning my husband.' The words floated across the playground in her wake.

Gretchen's cheeks were flushed. As she took a sip of water, Falk saw that her hands were shaking. He reached out to touch her shoulder, then stopped, aware of people watching, not wanting to make it worse.

'I'm sorry,' he said. 'I shouldn't have met you here.'

'It's not you,' she said. 'Tensions are high. The heat makes everything worse.' She took a deep breath and gave Falk a wobbly smile. 'Plus Mandy's always been a bitch.'

He nodded. 'That's fair.'

'And for the record, I didn't not like Karen. We just weren't close. There are loads of mums at school. You can't be friends with all of them. Obviously.' She nodded at Mandy's back.

Falk opened his mouth to respond when his phone buzzed. He ignored it. Gretchen smiled.

'It's OK. Get it.'

With an apologetic grimace he opened the text. He was on his feet almost before he'd finished reading it.

Five words from Raco: *Jamie Sullivan lied. Come now.*

Chapter Twenty

'He's in there.'

Falk peered through a thick glass panel in the door into the station's sole interview room. Jamie Sullivan sat at the table staring miserably into a paper cup. The farmer seemed somehow smaller than when they'd been sitting in his living room.

Falk had felt guilty leaving Gretchen in the park. He'd wavered as she'd looked him in the eye and said it was fine. He hadn't believed her, so she'd given him a smile and a push towards his car.

'Go. It's OK. Give me a call.'

He'd gone.

'What've you found?' Falk asked Raco. The sergeant told him and Falk nodded, impressed.

'It was there in plain view the whole time,' Raco said. 'It just slipped through the cracks with everything else happening that day.'

'Yeah, well, it was a busy day. Especially for Jamie Sullivan, it seems.'

Sullivan's head shot up as they entered. His fingers were clenched around his cup.

'Right, Jamie. I want to make it clear to you that you're not under arrest,' Raco said briskly. 'But we need to clear up a couple of things we talked about the other day. You remember Federal Agent Falk. We'd like him to sit in on this chat, if you're willing for that to happen?'

Sullivan swallowed. He looked back and forth, not sure what the right answer was.

'I suppose. He's working for Gerry and Barb, right?'

'Unofficially,' Raco said.

'Do I need my lawyer?'

'If you like.'

There was a silence. Sullivan's lawyer, if he even had one, probably spent fifty weeks of his year dealing with property disputes and livestock contracts, Falk thought. This could well be fresh territory for him. Not to mention the cost per hour. Sullivan seemed to come to the same conclusion.

'I'm not under arrest?'

'No.'

'All right,' Sullivan said. 'Just bloody ask. I've got to get back.'

'Good. We visited you two days ago, Jamie,' Raco began. 'To talk to you about the day Luke, Karen and Billy Hadler died.'

'Yes.' There was a fine sheen of sweat on Sullivan's upper lip.

'And during our visit, you told us that after Luke Hadler left your property at about 4.30 pm, you stayed behind. You said –' He checked his notes. '*I stayed on the farm. I did some work. I had dinner with Gran.*'

Sullivan said nothing.

'Is there anything you want to say to us about that at this point?'

Sullivan swivelled his eyes between Falk and Raco. He shook his head.

'OK,' Raco said, and slid a piece of paper across the desk. 'Do you know what this is?'

Sullivan's tongue darted out and ran over his dry lips. Twice. 'It's a CFA report,' he said.

'Yep. You'll see here on the date stamp it's from the same day the Hadlers died. Every time the firefighters are called out, they log one of these. In this case, they were responding to an emergency alert. You can see that here.' Raco pointed to typed lines on the paper. 'And below, the address they were called to. Do you recognise the address?'

'Of course.' A long pause. 'It's my property.'

'According to the summary —' Raco picked up the report. '— the fire crew was called to your farm at 5.47 pm. They were alerted automatically when your gran activated her panic button. They arrived to find your gran alone in the house with the stove alight. It says here they put it out, calmed her down. Tried to call you, got no answer, but then you arrived back at the house. That was at 6.05 pm, according to this.'

'I was in the paddocks.'

'You weren't. I called the guy who wrote the report. He remembers you approaching from the main road.'

They all stared at each other. Sullivan broke away first, looking down at the table as though an answer might appear. A lone fly circled over their heads with a tinny drone.

'I was in the paddocks after Luke left at first, but then I went for a bit of a drive,' Sullivan said.

'Where?'

'Nowhere really. Just around.'

'Be specific,' Falk said.

'Out to the lookout. Nowhere near the Hadlers' place, though. I wanted some space to think.'

Falk looked at him. Sullivan tried to meet his gaze.

'That farm of yours,' Falk said. 'How big is it?'

Sullivan hesitated, sensing a trap.

'Couple of hundred acres.'

'Pretty big then.'

'Big enough.'

'So tell me why a man who spends twelve, fourteen hours a day on a couple of hundred acres of paddocks needs any more space to think?'

Sullivan looked away.

'So you reckon you went for a drive. Alone. What's your excuse for keeping that quiet?' Raco said.

Sullivan glanced at the ceiling, considering and rejecting his initial response. Then he held his palms out and looked them both in the eye properly for the first time.

'I knew how it would sound and I didn't want the hassle. To be honest, I was hoping you wouldn't find out.'

For the first time, Falk felt like he was hearing the truth. He knew from the file that Sullivan was twenty-five years old and had moved to Kiewarra ten years earlier with his late father and grandmother. More than a decade after the day Ellie drowned. Still.

'Does the name Ellie Deacon mean anything to you?' he asked. As Sullivan glanced up a look flashed across his face too fast for Falk to read.

'I know she died. Years ago. And I know –' He nodded at Falk. 'I know Luke and – and you – were friends with her. That's about it.'

'Luke ever talk about her?'

Sullivan shook his head. 'Not to me. He mentioned her once or twice, said that he had a friend and she drowned, but he didn't talk about the past much.'

Falk thumbed through the files until he found the photo he was looking for and slid it across the table. It was the close-up of the interior of Luke's ute cargo tray, zoomed in tight on the four horizontal marks near his body.

'Any idea what they are?' Falk said, and Sullivan stared at them.

Four lines. In two columns of two on the interior side of the tray, about a metre apart. Sullivan didn't touch the photo. His eyes ran over the image, as though trying to work something out.

'Rust?' he ventured. He was neither convinced nor convincing.

'OK.' Falk took the photo back.

'Look, I didn't kill them.' Sullivan's pitch rose. 'Luke was my mate. He was a good mate to me.'

'Then help us,' Raco said. 'Help Luke. Don't make us waste time looking at you if we should be looking somewhere else.'

Wet circles had seeped out under the arms of Sullivan's blue shirt. The whiff of body odour drifted across the table. The silence stretched out.

Falk gambled. 'Jamie. Her husband doesn't have to know.'

Sullivan looked up and for a second there was a ghost of a grin on his face.

'You think I'm shagging someone's wife?'

'I think if there's anyone who can confirm where you were, you need to tell us now.'

Sullivan went very still. They waited. Then the farmer gave a tiny shake of his head. 'There's not.'

Not quite right then, Falk thought. But he also got the feeling he wasn't entirely wrong.

★

'What's worse than being fingered for a triple murder?' Falk said half an hour later as they watched Sullivan get into his four-wheel drive and pull away. The interview had gone around in circles until Sullivan had folded his arms. He'd refused to say a word other than insisting he needed to check on his gran or call someone to make arrangements.

'Yeah, he's scared of something,' Raco said. 'Exactly what, is the question?'

'We'll keep tabs on him,' Falk said. 'I'm going to head back to the pub for a while, go through the rest of the Hadlers' files.'

When in doubt, an instructor of Falk's had always said, follow the money. It had been sound advice. Raco lit a cigarette and walked with him to his car, parked on a patch of land behind the station. They rounded the corner and Falk stopped dead. He stood and stared, waiting for his brain to process what his eyes were seeing.

Across the doors and the bonnet of his car, the message had been carved over and over into the paintwork. The letters flashed silver in the sun.

WE WILL SKIN YOU KILLER SCUM

Chapter Twenty-one

Gretchen stopped whatever she'd been saying, her mouth frozen mid-word as Falk drove his damaged car into the pub carpark. She was talking to Scott Whitlam on the pavement as Lachie played around her feet. In his mirror, Falk could see them staring as he parked.

'Bugger,' he said under his breath. It was only a few hundred metres from the police station to the pub, but it had felt like a long journey through the centre of town. He got out of the car, the silver scrapings in the paint winking at him as he slammed the door.

'Oh my God. When did that happen?' Gretchen ran up with Lachie in tow. The little boy waved at Falk before turning his wide-eyed attention to the car. He reached out a stubby finger to trace the carved letters, and to Falk's horror began sounding out the first word before Gretchen hastily pulled him away. She sent him to play on the other side of the carpark, and he reluctantly sloped off to poke things down a drain.

'Who's done this?' she said, turning back.

'I don't know,' Falk said.

Whitlam gave a low sympathetic whistle as he walked slowly around the car.

'Someone really went to town. What did they use? Knife or screwdriver or something?'

'Yeah, I really don't know.'

'Bunch of bastards,' Whitlam said. 'This place. It's worse here than in the city sometimes.'

'Are you OK?' Gretchen touched Falk's elbow.

'Yeah,' Falk said. 'Better than the car at any rate.' He felt a stab of anger. He'd had that car for more than six years. Nothing flash, but it had never caused him any trouble. It didn't deserve to be wrecked by some country moron.

WE WILL SKIN YOU.

Falk turned to Whitlam. 'It's about something from the past. This girl we were friends with –'

'It's OK.' Whitlam gave a nod. 'I've heard the story.'

Gretchen ran a finger over the marks. 'Aaron, listen, you need to be careful.'

'I'll be fine. It's annoying, but –'

'No. It's worse than that.'

'Yeah, well. What more are they really going to do? Skin me?'

She paused. 'I don't know. Look at the Hadlers.'

'That's a bit different.'

'Are you sure? I mean, you don't really know.'

Falk looked to Whitlam for support but the principal gave a shrug.

'It's a pressure cooker round here, mate. Little things become big things faster than you expect. You'd know that, though. It wouldn't hurt to be a bit careful. Especially with both things coming on the same day.'

Falk stared at him.

'Both things?'

Whitlam shot a glance at Gretchen, who shifted uncomfortably.

'I'm sorry,' he said. 'I thought you'd have seen them by now.'

'What?'

Whitlam took a square of paper from his back pocket and handed it to him. Falk unfolded it. A hot wind rustled the dead leaves around their feet.

'Who's seen this?'

Neither of them answered. Falk looked up.

'Well?'

'Everyone. They're all around town.'

The Fleece was busy, but Falk could hear McMurdo's Celtic twang rising over the cacophony. He stopped in the doorway behind Whitlam.

'I'm not entering into a debate with you, my friend,' McMurdo was saying from behind the bar. 'Look around. This is a pub. This is not a democracy.'

He was clutching a handful of screwed-up fliers in his large fist. They were the same as the one burning a hole in Falk's pocket and he had to fight the urge to take it out and look at it again. It was a crude reproduction, probably photocopied five hundred times at the town's tiny library.

Across the top in bold capitals were the words: *RIP Ellie Deacon, age 16.* Below was a photo of Falk's father aged in his early forties. Next to it was a hastily taken snap of Falk himself that appeared to have been shot as he left the pub. He was caught in a sideways glance, his face frozen in a momentary grimace.

Underneath the photos in smaller type were the words: *These men were questioned about the drowning of Ellie Deacon. More information needed. Protect our town! Keep Kiewarra safe!*

Earlier in the carpark, Gretchen had given him a hug.

'Bunch of absolute dickheads,' she'd whispered in his ear. 'But watch yourself, anyway.' She'd scooped up a protesting Lachie and left. Whitlam had ferried Falk towards the pub, waving away his protests.

'They're like sharks in here, mate,' Whitlam had said. 'They'll pounce at the first sign of blood. Your best move is to sit in there with me and have a cold beer. As is our God-given right as men born under the Southern Cross.'

Both now stopped in the entrance. A large purple-faced man, who Falk remembered had once turned his back on Erik Falk in the street, was arguing across the bar with McMurdo. The man stabbed a finger emphatically at the fliers and said something Falk didn't catch, and the barman shook his head.

'I don't know what to suggest, my friend,' McMurdo said. 'You want to protest about something, you get yourself a pen and paper and write to your MP. But the place to do it is not in here.' He moved to shove the fliers in the bin and as he did, he caught Falk's eye across the room. He gave a tiny shake of his head.

'Let's go,' Falk said to Whitlam and backed away from the entrance. 'Thanks anyway, but it's not a good idea.'

'Think you might be right. Unfortunately. Christ, it's like *Deliverance* round here sometimes,' Whitlam said. 'What are you going to do?'

'Hole up in my room, I suppose. Go through some papers. Hope it blows over.'

'Stuff that. Come and have a drink at mine.'

'No. Thanks, though. It's better if I lie low.'

'Nope, that doesn't sound better at all. Come on. But we'll take my car, eh?' Whitlam fished out his keys with a grin. 'It would do my wife good to meet you. It might help reassure her a bit.' His smile dimmed a fraction, then brightened. 'And anyway, I've got something to show you.'

Whitlam texted his wife from the car, and they drove in silence through the town.

'You're not worried about me being seen at your house?' Falk said eventually. He thought back to the incident in the park. 'The school mums won't be impressed.'

'Stuff 'em,' Whitlam said, his eyes on the road. 'Maybe it'll teach them something. "Judge not lest ye be judged by a gang of small-minded nut jobs" or however it goes. So. Who do you think's been sending out your fan mail?'

'Mal Deacon probably. Or his nephew Grant.'

Whitlam frowned. 'I think Grant's more likely. Apparently Deacon isn't all there these days. Mentally, I mean. I don't really know, I don't get involved with those two. Don't need the hassle.'

'You might be right.' Falk stared gloomily out of the window. He thought of his car, the silver words scratched into the paintwork. 'But neither of them are above getting their hands dirty.'

Whitlam looked at him, weighing up Falk's response. Then he shrugged. He'd turned off the main street and was navigating the warren that was the closest thing Kiewarra had to a suburban estate. The houses seemed tight and manicured after the sprawling farmhouses, and some of the lawns were actually green. No easier way to advertise you used fake turf, Falk thought. Whitlam pulled up on a paved courtyard outside a smart family home.

'Nice place,' Falk said. Whitlam made a face.

'Suburbia in the countryside. Worst of both worlds. Half the neighbouring places are empty, which is a pain. Security risk, you know? We get a lot of kids messing around. But everyone in farming lives on their land, and there's not much in town to attract anyone else.' He shrugged. 'Still, it's only rented. So we'll see.'

He led Falk through into a cool shining kitchen where his wife was making coffee with a rich, deep aroma on a complicated machine. Sandra Whitlam was a slender, pale-skinned woman with large green eyes that gave the impression that she was permanently startled. Whitlam introduced them and she shook Falk's hand with a vague air of suspicion, but pointed him towards a comfortable kitchen chair.

'Beer, mate?' Whitlam called to him as he opened the fridge.

Sandra, who was in the process of placing three china cups on the counter, paused.

'Didn't you just come from the pub?' Her voice was light, but she didn't turn to look at her husband as she spoke.

'Yeah, well, we didn't quite get inside in the end,' Whitlam said with a wink at Falk. Sandra pressed her lips into a thin line.

'Coffee's fine, thanks Sandra,' Falk said. 'Smells good.'

She gave him a tight smile and Whitlam shrugged and closed the fridge. She poured them each a cup and padded around the kitchen in silence, placing various cheese and cracker combinations on a plate. Falk sipped his coffee and glanced down at a framed family photo propped up near his elbow. It showed the couple with a small sandy-haired girl.

'Your daughter?' he said to fill the quiet.

'Danielle.' Whitlam picked up the frame. 'She'll be around here somewhere.' He glanced at his wife, who had paused mid-action at the sink when she'd heard the little girl's name.

'She's watching TV in the back room,' Sandra said.

'She OK?'

Sandra just shrugged and Whitlam turned back to Falk.

'Danielle's quite confused, to be honest,' he said. 'I told you she was friends with Billy Hadler. But she doesn't really understand what's happened.'

'Thank goodness,' Sandra said, folding the tea towel in her hands into a tight, angry square. 'I hope she never has to understand something as horrific as that. Every time I think about it, it makes me feel sick. What that bastard did to his own wife and child. Hell's too good for him.'

She reached over to the counter and cut a thin slice of cheese, forcing the knife hard through the block until it struck the board below with a sharp knock.

Whitlam cleared his throat lightly. 'Aaron used to live here in town. He was friends with Luke Hadler when they were younger.'

'Well. Maybe he was different back then.' Sandra was unabashed. She raised her eyebrows at Falk. 'So you grew up here in Kiewarra? That must have felt like a long few years.'

'It had its moments. You're not enjoying it then?'

Sandra gave a tight laugh. 'It hasn't exactly been the fresh start we were expecting,' she said, her voice clipped. 'For Danielle. Or any of us.'

'No. Well, I'm not the best person to defend this place to you,' Falk said. 'But you know what happened to the Hadlers was a once-in-a-lifetime incident. If that.'

'That may be so,' Sandra said, 'but it's the attitude around here that I can't understand. I hear some people almost *sympathising* with Luke Hadler. Saying how hard he must have been finding things, and I want to shake them. I mean, how stupid can you be? Never mind what Luke was going through. Who *cares*? Can you imagine what Billy's and Karen's last moments were like? But there's this – I don't know – parochial *pity* for him. And –' She pointed a manicured finger at Falk. 'I don't care if he took his own life as well. Killing your wife and child is the ultimate domestic abuse. Nothing more, nothing less.'

For a long moment the only sound in the kitchen was the coffee maker steaming away on the pristine counter.

'It's OK, love. You're not the only person who feels that way,' Whitlam said. He reached across the kitchen counter and put his hand over his wife's. She was blinking rapidly, her mascara smudging around the edges. She left her hand there for a moment before slipping it away to reach for a tissue.

Whitlam turned to Falk. 'It's been terrible for all of us. Losing a student. Danielle losing her little buddy. Sandra feels for Karen, obviously.'

Sandra made a small noise in her throat.

'You said Billy was supposed to come over to play the afternoon he died,' Falk said, remembering the conversation at the school.

'Yes.' Sandra blew her nose, and busied herself pouring more coffee while she almost visibly pulled herself together. 'We used to have him over quite a lot. And vice versa, Danielle would go to their place as well. They got on like a house on fire, it was quite sweet really. She really misses him. She can't understand that he's not coming back.'

'So this was a regular arrangement?' Falk asked.

'Not regular, but certainly not unusual,' Sandra said. 'I hadn't organised anything with Karen for that week, but then Danielle found this junior badminton set we got her for her last birthday. She and Billy were terrible at it, but they used to love messing about with it. She hadn't used it for a while but suddenly got completely fixated on it – you know how children are – and wanted Billy to come over as soon as possible to play with it.'

'So when did you speak to Karen to set something up?' Falk asked.

'I think it was the day before, wasn't it?' Sandra looked at her husband, who shrugged. 'Well, I think it was. Because, remember, Danielle was pestering you to put the badminton net up in the garden? Anyway, I called Karen that night and asked if Billy wanted to come home with Danielle the next day. She said, "Yes, OK", and that was it.'

'How did she sound?'

Sandra frowned as though taking a test. 'Fine, I thought,' she said. 'It's difficult to remember. Maybe a bit . . . distracted. It was only a short conversation, though. And it was late-ish so we didn't chat. I offered, she accepted and that was that.'

'Until?'

'Until I got a call from her the next day. Just after lunchtime.'

'Sandra Whitlam speaking.'

'Sandra, hi, it's Karen here.'

'Oh, hi. How are you going?'

There was a brief pause followed by a tiny noise, perhaps a laugh, down the line.

'Yes, good question. Look, Sandra, I'm so sorry to do this to you, but Billy can't come over this afternoon after all.'

'Oh, that's a shame,' Sandra said, suppressing a groan. Now she or Scott, or possibly both, would be on call for at least a couple of rounds of junior badminton that evening. She mentally drew up a list of potential last-minute stand-ins. 'Is everything OK?' she asked, a fraction late.

'Yes. It's just —' The line went quiet and for a moment Sandra thought they'd been cut off. 'He's been a bit under the weather lately. I think it's better if he comes straight home today. I'm sorry. I hope Danielle won't be too disappointed.'

Sandra felt a stab of guilt.

'No, honestly, don't be silly. It can't be helped if he's not a hundred per cent. Probably wise, especially with what Danielle's got in mind. We can rearrange.'

Another silence. Sandra glanced at the clock on the wall. Below, her to-do list fluttered against the corkboard.

'Yes,' Karen said finally. 'Yes. Maybe.'

Sandra had farewell pleasantries on the tip of her tongue when she heard Karen sigh down the line. She hesitated. Show her a mother of school-age children who didn't sigh on a daily basis, and she'd show you a woman with a nanny. Still, curiosity got the better of her.

'Karen, is everything all right?'

There was a silence.

'Yes.' A long pause. 'Is everything all right with you?'

Sandra Whitlam rolled her eyes and glanced again at the clock. If she left for town right now she could be back in time to put the washing out and ring around to find a replacement for Billy before the school run.

'Fine, Karen. Thanks for letting me know about Billy. I hope he's on the mend soon. Speak later.'

'I feel guilty every single day about that phone call,' Sandra said, refilling the coffee cups yet again like a nervous tic. 'The way I rushed her off the phone like that. Perhaps she needed someone to talk to, and I just . . .' She teared up before she could finish her sentence.

'You weren't to blame, love. How could you know what was going to happen?' Whitlam stood and put his arms around his wife. Sandra stood a little stiffly and glanced in embarrassment at Falk as she wiped her eyes with a tissue.

'I'm sorry,' she said. 'It's just that she was such a nice person. She was one of the people who made it bearable to be here. Everyone loved her. All the school mums. Probably some of the school dads.' She started to give a little laugh that she cut dead in her throat. 'Oh God, no, I didn't mean – Karen would never . . . I just meant she was popular.'

Falk nodded. 'It's OK, I understand. She was obviously well liked.'

'Yes. Exactly.'

There was a silence. Falk drained his coffee and stood up. 'It's probably time I made a move anyway, leave you in peace.'

Whitlam swallowed the last mouthful of his own coffee. 'Hang on, mate, I'll take you back in a minute, but I've got something to show you first. You'll like it. Come and see.'

Falk said goodbye to a still teary Sandra, and followed Whitlam through to a cosy home office. He could hear the muffled sound of a cartoon playing from somewhere down the hall. The office had a far more masculine feel than what he'd seen of the rest of the house, with furniture that was battered but well loved. Along the walls ran floor-to-ceiling bookshelves crammed with sports books.

'You've got half a library in here,' Falk said, scanning the contents of the shelves, which ranged from cricket to harness racing, biographies to almanacs. 'You're obviously a fan.'

Whitlam bowed his head in mock disgrace. 'My post-grad was in modern history, but to be honest, all my research focused on sports history. Racing, boxing, origins of match fixing, et cetera. So all the fun stuff. But I like to think I still know my way around your standard dusty and faded document.'

Falk smiled. 'I have to admit, I hadn't pegged you as the dusty document type,' he said.

'A common mistake, but I can mine those archives with the best of them. Speaking of which –' He pulled a large envelope out of the desk drawer and handed it to Falk. 'I thought you might find this interesting.'

Falk opened it and pulled out a photocopy of a black and

white team photo. Young men from Kiewarra's 1948 first XI
cricket side had donned their best whites and lined up for the
camera. Their tiny faces were washed out and fuzzy, but sure
enough there, seated middle of the first row, Falk saw a familiar
face. His grandfather. Falk felt a lift in his chest as he saw the
name typed neatly in the team list below: *Captain: Falk, J.*

'This is fantastic. Where did you find it?'

'Library. Thanks to my tightly honed archiving skills.'
Whitlam grinned. 'I've been doing a bit of research on Kiewarra's
sporting history. For my own interest really, and I came across
that. Thought you'd like it.'

'It's great. Thank you.'

'Keep it. It's only a copy. I can show you where to find the
original one day if you want. There'll probably be other photos
from around the same time. He might be in more of them.'

'Thanks, Scott, really. What a great find.'

Whitlam leaned against the desk. He pulled one of the crumpled anti-Falk fliers out of his back pocket and screwed it up. He
chucked it at the bin. It went straight in.

'I'm sorry about Sandra,' Whitlam said. 'She wasn't finding it
easy to adjust to life here anyway. The idea of a relaxing country
escape hasn't quite worked out like either of us thought. And this
terrible business with the Hadlers has made everything worse.
We thought we were moving here to get away from anything
like that. Feels like a frying pan–fire scenario.'

'What happened to the Hadlers is so rare, though,' Falk said.

'I know, but –' Whitlam glanced at the door. The hallway
outside was empty. He lowered his voice. 'She's hypersensitive
to any kind of violence. Keep it to yourself, but I was mugged
back in Melbourne and it ended – well, badly.'

He looked again at the door, but having started, seemed
to need to unburden himself. 'I'd been at a mate's fortieth in

Footscray and took a short cut through a laneway to the station, you know, like everyone does. But this time these four blokes were there. Still kids really, but they had knives. They blocked the way and me and this other man – I didn't know him, just some other poor sod taking a short cut – we were stuck. They did the whole routine, demanded wallets and phones, but somewhere it went wrong.

'They got spooked, lashed out. I was beaten up, kicked, fractured ribs, the works. But the other guy took a knife to the guts, bled out all over the asphalt.' Whitlam swallowed. 'I had to leave him there to go and find help because the bastards had stolen my mobile. By the time I got back the ambulance had arrived, but it was too late. Paramedics said he was already dead.'

Whitlam looked down and fiddled with a paperclip for a long moment. He shook his head as though to clear the thought.

'Anyway, so there was that, and then this. So you see why Sandra's not happy.' He gave a weak smile. 'But you could probably say the same about almost anyone in town right now.'

Falk tried to think of a single exception. He couldn't.

Chapter Twenty-two

Back in his room, Falk stood at the window and stared down at the empty main street below. Whitlam had driven him back to the pub and given him a friendly wave in full view of passers-by. Falk had watched him go, then walked around to the carpark to check if his paintwork looked as bad as he remembered. It was worse. The words scratched into the car had shone in the fading light, and for good measure someone had shoved a handful of the Falk fliers under the windshield wiper.

He'd slipped up the pub stairs unnoticed and spent the rest of the evening lying on his bed and going through the last of the Hadlers' files. His eyes were stinging. It was late, but he could still feel his nerves tingling from Sandra Whitlam's bottomless cup of coffee. Outside his window, he watched a lone car cruise by with its lights on and a possum the size of a small cat scuttle along a power line, her baby on her back. Then the street was quiet again. Country quiet.

That's partly what took city natives like the Whitlams by surprise, Falk thought. The quiet. He could understand them seeking out the idyllic country lifestyle; a lot of people did. The idea had an enticing wholesome glow when it was weighed up from the back of a traffic jam or while crammed into a garden-less apartment. They all had the same visions of breathing fresh clean air and knowing their neighbours. The kids would eat home-grown vegies and learn the value of an honest day's work.

On arrival, as the empty moving truck disappeared from sight, they gazed around and were always taken aback by the crushing vastness of the open land. The space was the thing that hit them first. There was so much of it. There was enough to drown in. To look out and see not another soul between you and the horizon could be a strange and disturbing sight.

Soon, they'd discover that the vegies didn't grow as willingly as they had in the city window box. That every single green shoot had to be coaxed and prised from the reluctant soil, and the neighbours were too busy doing the same on an industrial scale to muster much cheer in their greetings. There was no daily bumper-to-bumper commute but there was also nowhere much to drive to.

Falk didn't blame the Whitlams. He'd seen it many times before when he was a kid. Arrivals looked around at the barren-ness and the scale and the sheer bloody hardness of the land and before long their faces all said exactly the same thing. *I didn't know it was like this.*

He turned away, remembering how the rawness of local life had seeped into the kids' paintings at the school. Sad faces and brown landscapes. Billy Hadler's pictures had been happier, Falk thought. He'd seen them dotted around the farmhouse, colourful and stiff with dried paint. Aeroplanes with smiling people in the windows. A lot of variations on cars. At least Billy hadn't been sad like some of the other kids, Falk thought. He almost laughed out loud at the absurdity. Billy was dead, but at least he wasn't sad. Until the end. At the end he would have been terrified.

Falk tried for the hundredth time to imagine Luke chasing down his own son. He could conjure up the scene, but it was hazy and wouldn't quite come into focus. Falk thought back to his last meeting with Luke. Five years ago, on an unmemorable grey day in Melbourne. When the rain was still a nuisance rather than a blessing. By then, Falk had to admit to himself, in a lot of ways he'd felt he barely known Luke at all.

Falk spotted Luke immediately across the Federation Square bar. Harried, damp and straight from work, Falk was just another grey man in a suit. Luke, even freshly liberated from a lengthy suppliers' convention, still had an energy that was hard to miss. He leaned now against a pillar with a beer in his hand and an amused smile on his face, surveying the early evening crowd of British backpackers and bored youths dressed head to toe in black.

He greeted Falk with a beer and a slap on the shoulder.

'Wouldn't trust him to shear a sheep with a haircut like that,' Luke said without lowering his voice. He pointed his drink at a skinny young guy sporting a style that was half-shaved, half-Mohawk, and almost certainly expensive. Falk smiled back, but wondered why Luke felt he had to trot out the country-boy comments every time they met. He ran a complex six-figure agribusiness in Kiewarra, but played the country-mouse-in-the-big-city card without fail.

Still, it was an easy shorthand excuse for the gap that seemed wider to bridge every time they met. Falk bought a round of drinks and asked after Barb, Gerry, Gretchen. All were fine, apparently. Nothing to report.

Luke asked how Falk was coping since his father had died the year before. OK, Falk said, equal parts surprised and grateful his friend had remembered to ask. And that girl Falk had been seeing? Again, surprise.

Good, thanks. She was moving in. Luke grinned. 'Jesus, watch out for that. Once they've got their throw cushions installed on your sofa, you never get them out.' They'd laughed, the ice broken.

Luke's son Billy was one now, and growing fast. Luke pulled up photos on his phone. Lots of them. Falk scrolled through with the polite forbearance of the childless. He listened as Luke reeled off anecdotes about fellow suppliers at the conference, people Falk had never known. In return, Luke feigned interest as Falk spoke about his work, playing down the desk work and ramping up the entertaining bits.

'Good on you,' Luke would always say. 'Bang up those thieving bastards.' But he said it in a way that implied, very gently, that chasing men in business suits wasn't real police work.

On this occasion, though, Luke was more interested. It wasn't just men in suits this time. A footballer's wife had been found dead with thousands of dollars of cash in a pair of suitcases by the bed. Falk had been called in to help trace the bills. It was a weird one. She'd been found in the bathtub. Drowned.

The word slipped out before he could stop it and hung in the air between them. Falk cleared his throat.

'Has there been any trouble in Kiewarra for you lately?' He didn't have to specify what kind. Luke shook his head briskly.

'No, mate. Not for years. I told you last time.'

Falk felt an automatic thank you forming on his lips, but for some reason he couldn't bring himself to say it. Not again. Instead he paused and watched as his friend stared past him.

He wasn't sure what it was that made him want to push it, but this time he felt a flash of irritation. He was perhaps just fractious from work. Hungry and tired and keen to get home. Or maybe he was fed up with always having to feel grateful to this man. Feeling that whichever way the cards came up, Luke could be relied on to deal himself the stronger hand.

'You ever going to tell me where you really were that day?' Falk said.

Luke dragged his gaze back at that.

'Mate, I have told you,' he said. 'A thousand times. I was shooting those rabbits.'

'Yeah. All right.' Falk stopped himself rolling his eyes. That had always been the answer, ever since he'd first asked several years earlier. It had never rung completely true. Luke rarely went shooting alone. And Falk could still remember Luke's face at his bedroom window all those years ago. His memory of the night was coloured by fear and relief, that was true, but the story had always felt plucked from the air. Luke was watching him closely.

'Maybe I should be asking you where you were?' Luke said, his voice artificially light. 'If we're going down that road again.'

Falk stared at him. 'You know where I was. Fishing.'

'At the river.'

'Upstream, thanks.'

'But alone.'

Falk didn't answer.

'So I guess I'll have to take your word for it,' Luke said, and took a sip, his eyes never leaving Falk's. 'Luckily, your word is good as gold for me, mate. But seems it'd be better all round if you and I stuck to shooting rabbits together, don't you reckon?'

The two men watched each other as the noise of the bar rose and fell around them. Falk considered his options. Then he sipped his beer and shut his mouth.

Eventually they made their obligatory excuses about trains to catch and early starts. As they shook hands for what would prove to be the last time, Falk found himself struggling to remember, once again, why they were still friends.

Falk got into bed and turned off the light. He lay still for a long time. The huntsman had reappeared during the evening and its shadowy figure now crouched above the bathroom door. The night was dead silent outside. Falk knew he needed to get some sleep, but fragments of recent and long-gone conversations jostled for his attention. Traces of caffeine zipping through his system helped prop his eyes open.

He rolled over and switched on the bedside light. The library books he'd taken from Barb earlier that day were lying under his hat on a chair. He'd drop them through the returns chute tomorrow. He picked up the first one. A practical guide to growing an eco-friendly succulent garden. He yawned just reading the title. That would almost certainly do the trick, but he simply couldn't face it. The other was a battered paperback crime novel. A woman, an unknown figure lurking in the shadows, a body count. Standard stuff. Not quite to his taste, but he wouldn't be in the job he was in if he didn't enjoy a good mystery. He lay back against the pillow and started to read.

It was an obvious storyline, nothing special, and Falk was about thirty pages in before his eyes started to feel heavy. He decided to put the book down at the end of the chapter, and as he turned a page a thin slip of paper fluttered out and landed on his face.

He plucked it off and squinted at it. It was a printed library receipt showing that the novel had been lent to Karen Hadler on Monday, February 19. Four days before she'd died, Falk thought. She'd used the receipt to mark her place, and the realisation that this mediocre thriller could have been the last thing she'd read in her life made him feel deeply depressed. Falk had started to crumple the receipt before he noticed the pen markings on the back.

Curious, he smoothed out the slip of paper and flipped it over. He was expecting a shopping list. Instead, he felt his heart start to thud. He pressed the creases out more carefully now and thrust it under the bedside light to better illuminate Karen's looping cursive script.

At some point in the four days between when Karen Hadler borrowed the book from the library and when she was shot dead on her doorstep, she had scrawled two lines on the back of the receipt. The first was a single word, slightly messy, written in a hasty hand and underlined three times.

Grant??

Falk tried to focus, but his gaze was dragged down to a ten-digit phone number written underneath. He stared at the number until his eyes watered and the digits swarmed and blurred. The blood pounded through his skull with a throbbing, deafening roar. He blinked hard, then again, but the numbers remained resolutely in the same order.

Falk didn't waste a single moment wondering who the phone number belonged to. He didn't need to. He knew it well. It was his own.

Chapter Twenty-three

They found Grant Dow the next morning on all fours under a woman's sink. He had a spanner in hand and his fleshy crack on display.

'Oi, will he be back to fix that leak?' the woman asked as Dow was dragged to his feet.

'I wouldn't count on it,' Raco said.

The woman's children watched in wide-eyed glee as Dow was led out to the marked police car. Their expressions mirrored Raco's just a few hours earlier when Falk had produced the receipt. Raco had paced around the station, bouncing on the balls of his feet, the adrenaline pumping.

'*Your* number?' he said over and over again. 'Why did Karen Hadler want to talk to you? About Grant?'

Falk, who had been awake most of the night asking himself the very same thing, could only shake his head.

'I don't know. If she tried, she definitely didn't leave a

message. I've gone through my missed calls history. No match for Karen's home, work or mobile number. And I know I never spoke to her. Not just recently. Ever. Not once in her whole life.'

'She would've known who you were, though, right? Luke still spoke about you. Barb and Gerry Hadler saw you on TV the other month. But why you?'

Raco picked up the office phone and dialled the ten digits. He looked at Falk as he held the receiver to his ear. Falk's mobile trilled loudly in his hand. He couldn't hear the message as his answering machine clicked in, but he knew what it said. He'd listened to his own voice speak enough times overnight as he'd dialled the number from his room phone in disbelief.

'*You've reached Federal Agent Aaron Falk. Please leave a message,*' the recording said. Short and sweet.

Raco hung up and stared at him.

'Think.'

'I have.'

'Think harder. Grant Dow and Luke didn't get along, we know that. But if Karen was having problems with him, why didn't she call the station here?'

'Are you sure she didn't try?'

'No calls made to police or emergency services from any phone owned by any of the Hadlers in the week before their deaths,' Raco recited. 'We pulled the phone records the day the bodies were found.'

He picked up the novel and turned it over in his hands, examining the cover. He thumbed through the pages yet again. There was nothing else caught between them.

'What's the book about?'

'It's a female detective investigating a string of student deaths at a college in the US,' said Falk, who had stayed up most of the night speed-reading to the end. 'She thinks it's a disgruntled bloke from town targeting rich kids.'

'Sounds crap. Did he do it?'

'Oh, er, no. It's not what it seems. Turns out it was the mother of one of the girls in the sorority house.'

'The mother of −? Christ, give me strength.' Raco pinched the bridge of his nose. He shut the novel with a loud slap. 'So what do we reckon? Is this bloody book supposed to mean something, or what?'

'I don't know. I don't think Karen got to the end, for whatever that's worth. And I checked with the library as soon as it opened. They say she borrowed a lot of this type of thing.'

Raco sat down, stared blankly at the receipt for a moment, then stood straight back up again.

'You're sure she never called you?'

'Hundred per cent.'

'Right. Come on, then.' He grabbed his car keys from the desk. 'You can't tell us, Karen can't tell us, Luke can't tell us. So let's haul in the only person left who might be able to explain why his bloody name's written on a piece of paper in a dead woman's bedroom.'

They left Dow to stew in the interview room for over an hour.

'I called Clyde,' Raco said, calmer now. 'Told them some arsehole finance investigator from Melbourne had shown up to sort out the Hadlers' paperwork. Said you had a couple of questions about a document found at the property, did they want to come and babysit you while you asked them? They've declined, unsurprisingly. We're right to go ahead.'

'Oh. Nice work,' Falk said, surprised. It occurred to him that he hadn't even thought to call Clyde this time. 'So what do we know?'

'Dow's fingerprints weren't found anywhere at the property.'

'That doesn't mean anything. That's what gloves are for. How's his alibi for the murders?'

Raco shook his head.

'Solid and hollow at the same time. He was digging a ditch in the middle of nowhere with two of his mates. We'll check, obviously, but they'll all swear blind he was there.'

'All right, let's see what he says.'

Dow was leaning back in his chair, arms crossed, staring straight ahead. He barely glanced up as they entered the room.

'About time,' he said. 'Some of us have got a living to make.'

'You want your lawyer here, Grant?' Raco said as he pulled his chair out. 'You can.'

Dow frowned. His lawyer would probably come from the same theoretical firm as Sullivan's, Falk thought. Property and livestock fifty weeks of the year. Dow shook his head.

'Got nothing to hide. Get on with it.'

He was angry rather than nervous, Falk was interested to note. Falk laid out his folder on the table and paused for a moment.

'Describe your relationship with Karen Hadler.'

'Masturbatory.'

'Anything else? Bearing in mind she was found murdered.'

Dow shrugged, unfazed. 'Nup.'

'But you found her attractive,' Falk said.

'You seen her? Before she carked it, of course.'

Falk and Raco said nothing and Dow rolled his eyes.

'Look. She was all right, I suppose. For round here anyway,' he said.

'When was the last time you spoke to her?'

Dow shrugged.

'Can't remember.'

'What about the Monday before she died? Nineteenth of February. Or the following two days?'

'Seriously couldn't tell you.' Dow shifted and his seat creaked under his bulk. 'Listen, do I have to be here? Legally? I've got shitloads to do.'

'We'll cut to the chase then,' Falk broke in. 'Perhaps you could tell us why your name, Grant, was written by Karen Hadler on a receipt in the week she was murdered?' He slid a photocopy of the slip of paper across the table.

The only sound in the room was the hum of fluorescent lights as Dow stared at it for a long moment. Without warning he slammed his palm down on the table.

They both jumped.

'You are not pinning this on me.' Dow sent a fine mist of spittle across the tabletop.

'Pinning what on you, Grant?' Raco's voice was determinedly neutral.

'That bloody family. If Luke goes and shoots up his wife and kid, that's his business.' He pointed a thick finger at them both. 'But that has got bugger all to do with me, you hear me?'

'Where were you the afternoon they were shot?' Falk asked.

Dow shook his head, his eyes never leaving Falk's. His shirt collar was ripe with sweat. 'Mate, you can get stuffed. You did enough damage with Ellie. You're not going to take down me and my uncle as well. This is a witch hunt.'

Raco cleared his throat before Falk could answer.

'All right, Grant.' His voice was calm. 'We're just trying to get some answers. So let's make it as easy as we can. You've told officers from Clyde you were ditch-digging out along Eastway with your two workmates you've listed here. You stand by that?'

'Yeah. I was. All day.'

'And they'll back that up, will they?'

'They'd better. Seeing as it's the truth.' Dow managed to look them in the eyes as he said it. A fly droned in frantic circles around their heads as the silence stretched out.

'Tell me, Grant, what will you do with the property when your uncle dies?' Falk said.

Dow looked confused at the change of subject. 'Eh?'

'You're all set to inherit, I heard.'

'So what? I've earned it,' he snapped.

'For what, letting your uncle live in his own property while he's old and sick? That takes a big man.' Truthfully, Falk didn't see any reason why Dow shouldn't inherit, but the comment seemed to have hit a sore spot.

'Little bit more than that, smartarse.' Dow opened his mouth to say something, then thought better of it. He closed it before speaking again. 'Anyway, why not? I'm his family.'

'All that's left of it since Ellie died, eh?' Falk ploughed on as Dow sucked in a breath in outrage. 'So you'll sell the property when you can?'

'Too right I will. I'm not about to try and farm it, am I? I'm not a fool. Not when there's all those Chinese jumping out of their little yellow skins to buy land out here. Even shit land like ours.'

'And like the Hadlers'?'

Dow paused. 'I suppose.'

'Baby Charlotte's probably even less keen to lug around bags of fertiliser than you. I hear it'll come up for sale sooner or later. Two properties side by side.' Falk shrugged. 'That's a lot more attractive to overseas investors. Which is interesting in itself. But especially when the owner of one ended up shot in the head.'

For once Dow didn't open his mouth to reply, and Falk knew he'd come to the same conclusion.

'Let's get back to Karen.' Falk seized the advantage to change tack. 'You ever try it on with her?'

'What?'

'Romantically? Sexually?'

Dow snorted. 'Do me a favour. Right ice queen, that one. I wouldn't waste me breath.'

'You think she'd have knocked you back,' Falk said. 'That must have been annoying.'

'I get plenty, thanks, mate, don't you worry about me. The way you're panting round town after Gretchen, you've got enough on your plate worrying about yourself.'

Falk ignored the comment. 'Did Karen dent your ego? You argue with her about something? Things get a bit messy?'

'What? No.' Dow's eyes flicked left and right.

'But you fell out with her husband. Frequently, from what we've heard,' Raco said.

'So what? That was always about nothing. Just Luke being a prick. It had bugger all to do with his missus.'

There was a pause. When Falk spoke again, his voice was quiet.

'Grant, we're going to check your movements that day, and maybe your mates are going to back you up. The point is that some alibis are a bit like that plasterboard you work with. They hold up initially, but put them under pressure and they crumble pretty damn swiftly.'

Dow looked down for a moment. When he raised his head his attitude had shifted. He smiled. A calculating, full-bodied grin that hit his eyes.

'What, like your alibi, you mean? For why my cousin wrote your bloody name before she died?'

The silence stretched taut as three pairs of eyes looked at the photocopied receipt on the table. Falk had been far more shaken when his own name was discovered among Ellie's possessions than Dow seemed about this. He was wondering what to make of that when Dow barked a laugh.

'Good thing my yarn is built of solid brick, isn't it? You test it, mate, be my guest. Don't get me wrong, I had no time for the Hadlers. And yeah, I'll be selling my uncle's property the first chance I get. But I didn't kill them, I wasn't at that farm, and if you want to put me there, you're going to have to stitch me up. And you know what?' He banged the table with his fist. The sound was like a shot. 'I'm not sure you've got the balls.'

'If you were there, Grant, we'll prove it.'

He smirked.

'See you bloody try.'

Chapter Twenty-four

'**Y**ou're lucky we still have the footage, it usually gets deleted after a month.'

Scott Whitlam scrolled through the files on his computer until he found what he was looking for. The principal leaned back so Falk and Raco could see the screen. They were in his office, the sounds of the Monday afternoon school bustle drifting through the door.

'OK, here we are. This is the view from the camera at the main entrance,' Whitlam said. He clicked the mouse and CCTV footage started to play on screen. The camera appeared to be mounted above the large school doors, trained down on the steps to capture any approaching visitor. 'Sorry, it's not great quality.'

'No worries. It's better than what we got from the Hadlers' place,' Raco said.

'Cameras are only as much use as what they capture anyway,' Falk said. 'What else have you got here?'

Whitlam clicked again and the view changed. 'The other camera's over the staff carpark.' Again taken from a high vantage point, this footage showed a fuzzy row of cars.

'Those are the only two cameras in the school?' Raco asked.

'Yeah, I'm afraid so.' Whitlam rubbed his thumb and index finger together in the universal symbol for money. 'We'd have more if we could afford more.'

'Can we find Karen on her last day?' Falk said, although it wasn't primarily Karen they were looking for. It was Grant Dow. True to their word, Falk and Raco had spent several hours grilling Dow's mates over his alibi. They had backed him up to the hilt. It was nothing less than Falk expected, but it still pissed him off.

Whitlam enlarged the carpark image so it filled the screen. 'Karen usually drove in, so she'd probably be on this camera.'

He found the right recording and jumped through the timeline to the end of the school day. They watched the silent footage as pupils walked by in twos and threes, giggling and gossiping, set free for another day. A slim bald man walked into the frame. He went to one of the cars and opened the boot. He rummaged for a moment before retrieving a bulky bag. He heaved it over his shoulder and walked back off screen in the direction he'd come.

'The caretaker,' Whitlam said.

'What's in the bag?'

Whitlam shook his head. 'I know he has his own set of tools. I'd say it was that, at a guess.'

'He worked here long?' Falk asked.

'About five years, I think. For what it's worth, he seems like a good guy.'

Falk didn't reply. They watched for another ten minutes until the trickle of pupils had all but dried up and the carpark was quiet. Just as Falk was losing hope, Karen appeared.

Falk's breath caught in his throat. She had been beautiful in life, this dead woman. He watched as she strode across the screen, her pale hair blowing back off her face. The low-quality recording made it impossible to read her expression. She wasn't tall but had the posture of a dancer as she walked briskly through the carpark, pushing Charlotte in a stroller from the direction of the crèche.

Three steps behind her, Billy came into view. Falk felt a chill at the sight of the stocky dark-haired child who looked so much like his father. Next to him, Raco shifted his weight and cleared his throat. Raco had seen first-hand what horror was waiting for the boy.

Billy was pottering, fully engrossed in some toy clutched in his hand. Karen turned and silently called to him over her shoulder, and he ran to catch up. She bundled both children into her car, fastening them in, shutting the door. She moved fast, efficiently. Was she rushing? Falk wasn't sure.

On screen, Karen straightened and stood completely still for a moment, one hand on the car roof, her back to the camera. Her head tilted forward a fraction and she brought a hand to her face. Made one small movement with her fingers. Then another.

'Jesus, is she crying?' Falk said. 'Rewind that bit, quick.'

No-one spoke as they watched it again. Then a third time, and a fourth. Head down, two small flicks of her hand.

'I can't tell,' Raco said. 'It looks a bit like she could be. But she could as easily be scratching her nose.'

They let the tape run on this time. Karen lifted her head, took what could have been a deep breath, then opened the driver's door and climbed in. She reversed out of the space and was gone. The carpark was empty again. The time stamp on the tape showed she and her son had less than eighty minutes to live.

They stared at the footage, skipping over long stretches during which no-one came or went. The school receptionist emerged ten minutes after Karen, then nothing happened for about forty minutes. Eventually the teachers started heading to their cars one by one. Whitlam identified each as they appeared. The caretaker returned, put his bag back in the boot and drove away just after 4.30 pm.

Eventually Whitlam's car was the only one left in the lot. They sped ahead on the tape. Shortly after 7 pm, Whitlam himself appeared on screen. He was walking slowly, his head down and his broad shoulders slumped forward. In the seat next to Falk, the teacher exhaled. His jaw was clenched tight as he watched the footage.

'It's hard to look at this,' he said. 'By then, the Clyde cops had called to tell me Billy and Karen were dead.'

They watched on as Whitlam slowly got into his car and, after a couple of false starts, successfully reversed out and drove away. They let the tape run for another ten minutes. Grant Dow was nowhere to be seen.

'I'll be off then,' Deborah called from reception, handbag clutched over her shoulder. She waited a moment, but received only a vague grunt in response. Falk looked up and gave her a smile. Her manner towards him had thawed in the past few days and he felt they'd had a breakthrough when she'd brought him a coffee as she fetched one for the others. He suspected Raco had had a word.

Raco and Constable Barnes barely reacted as the station door slammed behind her. The three of them were each at a desk, staring at their computer screens as grainy images played out. They had taken all the available footage from both cameras at the school, then headed into town.

There were three CCTV cameras in Kiewarra's main street, Raco had told Falk. One beside the pub, one near the council offices and one over the door of the pharmacy storeroom. They'd collected the footage from each.

Barnes yawned and stretched, his bulky arms reaching towards the ceiling. Falk was poised for the grumbling to start, but Barnes simply turned back to his screen without complaint. Barnes hadn't known Luke or Karen, he'd confided to Falk earlier, but he'd given Billy Hadler's class a talk on road safety a couple of weeks before his death. He still had the thank you card from the class, including Billy's crayon signature, on his desk.

Falk stifled a yawn himself. They'd been at it for four hours. Falk was concentrating on the recordings taken from the school. He'd seen one or two interesting things over the hours. A pupil take a secret piss against the principal's front wheels. A teacher scraping a colleague's car with her own, then hastily driving away. But no sign of Grant Dow.

Instead Falk found himself repeatedly watching the footage of Karen. She had arrived and left three times that week – every day but Tuesday, which was her day off, and Friday, by which time she was dead. Each day was much the same. At about 8.30 am her car would pull up. She would get the children out, gather backpacks and sun hats and disappear off camera in the direction of the school. Shortly after 3.30 pm, the process would be reversed.

Falk studied her movements. The way she bent over to talk to Billy, one hand on the little boy's shoulder. He couldn't make out her face, but he imagined her smiling at her son. He watched the way she cradled Charlotte as she transferred her baby daughter from car seat to stroller. Karen Hadler had been a nice woman before she was shot in the stomach. Good both with children and finances. Falk felt certain Barb was right. He would have liked her.

He obsessively rewound the footage from the Thursday, the day Karen and her son had been murdered. He played and replayed the tape constantly, analysing every frame. Was that a slight hesitation in her step as she approached the car? Had something in the bushland caught her eye? Was she squeezing her child's hand tighter than usual? Falk suspected he was jumping at shadows, but he continued to watch over and over. He stared at the image of his dead friend's blonde wife and silently willed her to pick up her mobile and call the number she had scribbled on the receipt. He willed his past self to answer. Neither event happened. The script remained unchanged.

Falk was debating whether to call it a day when Barnes dropped the pen he'd been twirling and sat up in his chair.

'Hey, check this out.' Barnes clicked his mouse, winding back the grainy film. He had been combing through the material from the pharmacy camera, which was trained on nothing more exciting than a quiet back laneway and the door leading to their supply room.

'What is it? Dow?' Falk said. He and Raco crowded around the screen.

'Not exactly,' Barnes said as he set the footage running. The time stamp showed 4.41 pm on Thursday. Just over an hour before Karen and Billy Hadler were found dead.

For a few seconds the video looked like a still image, showing nothing but the empty laneway. Suddenly a four-wheel drive flashed past. It was there and gone in less than a second.

Barnes rewound the footage and slowed it down. He froze the image as the car reappeared. It was blurry and at an awkward angle, but it didn't matter. The driver's face was clear. Through the windshield, Jamie Sullivan stared back at them.

★

The light was fading by the time Falk and Raco got to the laneway, but there wasn't much to see. They'd let Barnes call it a day after a job well done. Falk stood under the pharmacy's CCTV camera and looked around. The small road was narrow and ran parallel to Kiewarra's main street. On one side it backed on to the real estate agent, a hairdresser's, the doctors' surgery and the pharmacy. On the other, parcels of scrub land had been turned into makeshift carparks. It was completely deserted.

Falk and Raco walked the full length of the lane. It didn't take long. It was accessible by car at both ends, and connected with the roads leading east and west out of town. In rush hour, it would offer a perfect rat-run to cut through town without hitting the main drag. But this was Kiewarra, Falk thought, and it didn't have a rush hour.

'So why did our friend Jamie Sullivan want to avoid being seen in town twenty minutes before the Hadlers were killed?' Falk's voice echoed off the brickwork.

'A few reasons come to mind. None of them good,' Raco answered.

Falk peered up at the camera's lens.

'At least we have some idea where he was now,' Falk said. 'He could have got from here to the Hadlers' place in the time-frame, couldn't he?'

'Yeah, no problem at all.'

Falk leaned against the wall and tilted his head back. The bricks had soaked in the heat of the day. He felt exhausted. His eyes were gritty when he closed them.

'So we've got Jamie Sullivan, who claims to be Luke's great mate, lying about where he was and caught sneaking around on camera an hour before his friend was shot dead,' Raco said. 'Then we've got Grant Dow, who admits he couldn't stand Luke, alibied to the back teeth while at the same time his name is in a dead woman's handwriting.'

Falk opened an eye and looked at Raco.

'Don't forget the driver of the mysterious white ute who may or may not have seen Luke Hadler cycling away from the river at the crossroads twenty years ago,' he said.

'And that.'

They stood in silence for a long while, staring up the alleyway as though the answer might be graffitied there.

'Stuff it,' Falk said, pushing himself away from the wall and standing straight. It was an effort. 'Let's work through methodically. First we drag Sullivan in again and ask him what the hell he was doing on camera in a back alleyway. I've had it up to here with that bloke messing us around.'

'Now?' Raco's eyes were red-rimmed. He looked as tired as Falk felt.

'Tomorrow.'

As they cut through a narrow passageway back to the main road, Raco's phone rang. He paused on the pavement and dug it out.

'It's my wife. Sorry, I'd better take it.' He put it to his ear. 'Hello, my beauty.' They'd stopped outside the milk bar. Falk jerked his head towards the shop and mimed a drinking gesture. Raco nodded gratefully.

Inside, the shop was cool and quiet. It was technically the same store Ellie had worked in, spending her evenings punching the price of milk and cigarettes into the till. They'd put up posters of her face in the window after her body was found, collecting for a funeral wreath.

The layout had changed so much since then it was almost unrecognisable. But Falk still remembered coming to chat to her behind the counter, as often as he could find an excuse to. Spending his money on things he didn't want or need.

The shop's ancient fridges had been replaced at some point by open chillers and Falk now lingered beside them, feeling some of the fieriness evaporate from his skin. His core remained uncomfortably high, like the hint of a lingering fever. Eventually he picked up two bottles of water and selected a slightly curled ham and cheese sandwich and a plastic-sealed muffin for dinner.

Falk turned to take his purchases to the counter and groaned silently when he realised he once again recognised the face behind the till. He hadn't seen the shopkeeper since they were both stuck behind desks in the same sweltering classrooms.

The guy had less hair now, but his heavy features were still familiar. He'd been one of those kids who was slow on the uptake and quick to anger, Falk remembered as he cast about desperately for his name. He suspected, with a flash of guilt, he'd been the punchline of Luke's jokes from time to time and Falk had never troubled himself to intervene. He forced a smile onto his face now as he walked up and put his goods on the counter.

'How are you going these days, Ian?' he said, managing at the last moment to pluck the guy's name from the ether as he pulled out his wallet. Ian something. Willis.

Willis stared at the items as though he'd forgotten what to do.

'Just these, thanks, mate,' Falk said.

The other man said nothing, but instead lifted his head and looked past Falk's shoulder.

'Next,' he called in a clear voice.

Falk looked around. There was no-one else in the shop. He turned back. Willis was still staring determinedly into the middle distance. Falk felt a hot flash of irritation. And something else. Shame, almost.

'All right, mate. I'm not trying to cause you any grief. I'll buy these, and I'll be out of your hair,' Falk tried again, pushing his dinner closer over the counter. 'And I won't tell anyone you served me, scout's honour.'

The man continued to stare past him. 'Next.'

'Really?' Falk could hear the anger in his voice. 'This town's dying on its feet and you can afford to turn down a sale, can you?'

The shopkeeper looked away and shifted his weight from one foot to the other. Falk was considering taking the items and leaving the money on the counter, when Willis opened his mouth.

'I heard you were back. Mandy Vaser reckons you've been bothering kiddies in the park.' He tried to sound disgusted, but couldn't disguise the malicious glee in his voice.

'You are joking,' Falk said.

His old classmate shook his head, resuming his stare into the middle distance. 'So I'm not interested in serving you. Not today, not ever.'

Falk stared at him. The guy had probably been waiting twenty years to feel superior to someone and wasn't about to waste his chance, Falk realised. He opened his mouth to argue, then stopped. It was the very definition of wasted energy.

'Forget it.' Falk left the items on the counter. 'Good luck to you, Ian. You'll need it round here.' The door chime rang behind him as he pushed out into the heat.

Raco had put his phone away and looked from Falk's empty hands to the expression on his face.

'What happened?'

'Changed my mind.'

Raco glanced at the shop and back to Falk, comprehension settling in.

'You want me to have a word?'

'No, leave it. Thanks anyway. I'll see you tomorrow. Work out the plan for Sullivan.'

Falk turned, feeling more unnerved than he wanted to admit about the exchange in the shop. He was suddenly keen to get away from there, even though all that was waiting for him was a long evening in his tiny pub room. Raco eyeballed the shop once more, tempted, then looked back at Falk.

'Look. Come for dinner. Round mine,' Raco said. 'My wife's been on at me for days to ask you.'

'No, honestly, it's OK –'

'Mate, either I argue the toss with you now, or I argue the toss with her later. At least I've got a chance of winning against you.'

Chapter Twenty-five

Forty minutes later Rita Raco placed a steaming bowl of pasta in front of Falk. She moved away with a feather-light touch on his shoulder and returned a moment later with a bottle of wine. They sat outdoors around a small pine table covered with a colourful cloth as the sky turned a deep indigo. The Racos lived in a converted former shop at the far end of the main street. Walking distance to the police station. The back garden housed a lavender bush and a lemon tree, and fairy lights strung along the fence gave the scene a festive glow.

Light spilled from the kitchen windows and Falk watched Rita as she disappeared inside to fetch this and that. He tried to help, but she waved him down with a smile. A tiny compact woman with a halo of shiny brown hair falling over her shoulders, she ran her hand unconsciously over the swell of her pregnant belly. She seemed to harbour a huge concentration of energy, and despite the pregnancy moved smoothly between any one of a dozen tasks with seamless efficiency.

When she smiled, which was often, a deep dimple appeared in her left cheek, and by the time she put the food in front of Falk he could see why Raco was in love with her. As they began to eat – a rich concoction of tomatoes and eggplant and spicy sausage washed down with a decent shiraz – he felt he was a little bit in love with her himself.

The night air was warm, but the dark seemed to soak up some of the heat. Rita sipped mineral water and looked with good-natured longing at the shiraz.

'Oh, what I wouldn't give. It's been so long,' she said, and laughed at her husband's disapproving expression. She reached out and stroked the back of his neck until he smiled. 'He's so worried about the baby,' she told Falk. 'So overprotective and she's not even here yet.'

'When are you due?' Falk asked. To his untrained eye she looked right on the verge.

'Four weeks.' She caught her husband's eye and smiled. 'Four long enormous weeks still to go.'

Over good food, the talk came easily. They spoke about politics, religion, football. Anything but what was happening in Kiewarra. Anything but the Hadlers. Only when Raco cleared the table and disappeared inside the house with the plates did Rita finally ask.

'Tell me,' she said to Falk. 'Honestly, please. Is everything going to be all right?'

She looked towards the kitchen door and Falk knew she wasn't talking just about the Hadler case.

'Look, it's never an easy job, policing a small community,' he said. 'You're on a hiding to nowhere in lots of ways. There are politics involved, too many people who know too much about each other. But your husband's doing an excellent job. Really. He's smart. Genuinely dedicated. The top brass recognise things like that. He'll go far.'

'Oh.' Rita made a gently dismissive noise and flapped a hand. 'He's not worried about that so much. His dad was a community officer his whole life. Out on a tiny dot on the map, somewhere near the South Australian border. You won't know it. No-one does.' Her gaze drifted towards the empty doorway again. 'He was highly respected though, I understand. He ran the town like a firm but fair patriarch, and they loved him for it. Up until the day he retired and beyond.'

She paused. Reached over and shared the dregs of the wine between Falk's glass and her own.

'Shh,' she said, and put a finger to her lips as she raised the glass. Falk smiled.

'Is that where you met? In South Australia?'

'Yes, but not in his town. No-one would ever go there,' she said matter-of-factly. 'It was in my parents' restaurant in Adelaide. He was working nearby. It was his first job with the force, and he was so *proper*. So keen to make his dad proud.' She smiled at the memory and drained her small glass. 'But he was lonely and used to come into our restaurant all the time, until I took pity on him and let him ask me out for a drink.' She rubbed a hand over her stomach. 'He waited while I finished my Master's and then we got married straight away. That was two years ago.'

'Master's in what?'

'Pharmacology.'

Falk hesitated. He couldn't think how to phrase the question. Rita saved him.

'I know,' she said with a smile. 'So what am I doing barefoot and pregnant in the middle of nowhere, when I could be putting my qualifications to use somewhere else?' She shrugged. 'It's for my husband, and it's not forever. His ambitions, you know, they're not the same as some others'. He worships his father, and he's the youngest of three boys so I think he feels – wrongly, in my opinion – that he always has to fight for his dad's attention. So we moved to this small rural town, and he had such high hopes that it would be like it was for his father, but almost immediately everything went so –' She hesitated. 'Wrong. He has a weight on him constantly. He was the one who found that little boy's body, did he tell you?'

Falk nodded.

Rita shivered, despite the heat. 'I tell him, all the time, I tell him: What's happening in this place, it's not your fault. This place is different. It's not like your dad's community.'

Rita raised her eyebrows at Falk and he nodded. She shook her head and flashed half a dimple.

'Still. What can I do? It's too complex for logic, isn't it? A man's relationship with his father?'

Raco reappeared in the doorway as she spoke. He was holding three mugs of coffee.

'I've put the pots in to soak. What are you talking about?'

'I was saying you put yourself under too much pressure to live up to your father's standards,' Rita said, and reached out to smooth his curly hair. The dimple flashed again. 'Your partner here agrees with me.'

Falk, who hadn't offered an opinion either way, decided Rita was probably right. Raco coloured a little, but moved his head to meet her hand.

'It's not quite like that.'

'It's OK, my love. He understands.' Rita took a sip of her coffee and looked over the rim of her mug at Falk. 'Don't you? I mean, that's partly why you're here yourself, isn't it? For your father.'

There was a mystified silence.

'My father's dead.'

'Oh, I'm very sorry to hear that.' Rita looked at him, her eyes sympathetic. 'But surely that doesn't make it any less true? Death rarely changes how we feel about someone. Heightens it, more often than not.'

'My love, what on earth are you on about?' Raco said, giving her a friendly nudge as he picked up the empty wine bottle. 'I knew you shouldn't have any of this.'

Rita frowned a little, hesitating. She looked from Falk to her husband and back again.

'I'm sorry,' she said. 'Perhaps I've got the wrong end of the stick. It's just that I heard the rumours, of course, about your young friend who died. They said your father suffered, was accused himself even, had to take you away, leave his home. That must have caused some . . . friction. And even now, those awful leaflets being scattered around town with his photograph.' She stopped. 'I apologise. Please ignore me. I'm always reading far too much into a situation.'

For a long moment no-one spoke.

'No, Rita,' Falk said. 'Actually, I think you've read it just about right.'

Mal Deacon's ute filled the rear-view mirror for more than a hundred kilometres along the road out of Kiewarra. Aaron's father Erik drove with one eye on the reflection and two hands clenched on the wheel.

Aaron sat mutely in the passenger seat, still reeling from his hasty goodbye to Luke and Gretchen. The Falks' household goods clunked and shifted in the back. Whatever they'd managed to fit in. Far behind them, their farmhouse had been locked up and secured as tightly as they could manage. The sheep flock had been divided between any neighbours willing to take them on. Aaron was afraid to ask out loud if the arrangement was for now, or forever.

Just once, near the start of the journey, Erik had slowed right down to encourage Deacon to pass. As if this were a normal drive on a normal day. Instead, the dirty white ute had advanced steadily until it shunted the back bumper with a jolt that sent Aaron's head snapping forward. Erik didn't slow down again.

Nearly an hour had passed when Deacon suddenly blasted his horn in one continuous bellow. He edged closer, his vehicle huge in Aaron's side mirror, the noise blaring and bouncing along the empty road. The sound crowded Aaron's head and he pressed his palms against the glove box, bracing himself for the inevitable jolt from behind. By his side, his father's jaw was set. The seconds stretched long, and when Aaron thought he couldn't stand it anymore, the noise stopped. The abrupt silence rang in his ears.

In the reflection, he saw Deacon wind down his window and slowly extend an arm and then a single middle finger. He held it there for an age, braced against the wind. And then he finally, mercifully, grew smaller and smaller in the mirror until he disappeared from sight.

'Dad hated Melbourne,' Falk said. 'He never really settled there. He found an office job managing the supply chain for an agribusiness, but it absolutely sucked the life out of him.'

Falk himself had been pointed in the direction of the nearest high school to finish his final year. Distracted and dismayed, he barely remembered picking up a pen, let alone raising his hand. He sat his final exams and emerged on the other side with grades that were strong, rather than outstanding.

'I managed to adjust a bit better than Dad. He was really lonely there,' he said. 'We never talked about it, though. We both kind of closed in on ourselves and got on with it. That didn't help.'

Rita and Raco looked across the table at him. Rita stretched out her hand and placed it over Falk's.

'I'm sure whatever sacrifices he made for you, he felt they were worth it.'

Falk inclined his head a fraction.

'Thank you for saying it, but I'm not sure he would agree.'

Aaron continued to watch in the mirror as they drove on in silence. Deacon didn't reappear. After an hour of nothing, his father abruptly braked, slamming Aaron against his seatbelt as he pulled the truck over at the side of the empty road with a squeal of tyres.

Aaron jumped as Erik Falk slammed a hand against the steering wheel. His dad looked paler than usual and his forehead glistened with a sheen of sweat. Erik swivelled in his seat and in one swift movement had reached out and grabbed his son's shirt. Aaron gasped as hands that had never once been raised at him in anger now twisted the fabric and dragged him closer.

'I'm going to ask you this one time, so tell me the truth.'

Aaron had never heard that tone in his father's voice before. He sounded sickened.

'Did you do it?'

The shock of the question rippled like a physical force through Aaron's chest and he felt like he was suffocating. He forced himself to gasp a breath, but his lungs were tight. For a moment he couldn't speak.

'What? Dad —'

'Tell me.'

'No!'

'You have anything to do with that girl's death?'

'No. Dad, no. Of course I bloody didn't.'

Aaron felt his own heart thudding against his father's grip. He thought of their best possessions knocking and grinding in a pile in the back of the ute, of his rushed goodbye to Luke and Gretchen. Of Ellie, who he'd never see again, and Deacon, who he even now checked for through the rear window. He felt a thrill of anger and tried to wrench his dad's hand away.

'I didn't. Jesus, how can you even ask me that?'

Aaron's father kept his grip. 'Do you know how many people have asked me about the note that dead girl wrote? Friends of mine. People I've known for years. Years. Crossing the street when they saw me. All because of that note.' He tightened his grip. 'So you owe it to me to tell me. Why was your name on it?'

Aaron Falk leaned in. Father and son, face to face. He opened his mouth.

'Why was yours?'

'We were never the same after that,' Falk said. 'I tried a few times over the years. He probably did too, in his own way. But we couldn't really fix things. We stopped talking about it, never really mentioned Kiewarra again. Pretended it didn't exist, none of it had happened. He put up with Melbourne, put up with me, and then he died. And that was it.'

'How dare you?' Aaron's father's eyes flared and there was an unnamable edge to his expression. 'Your mother is buried in that town. That farm was built up by your grandparents, for God's sake. My friends and my life are back there. Don't you dare throw this on me.'

Aaron felt the blood pumping in his head. His friends. His mother. He had left almost as much behind.

'Then why are we running?' He grabbed his father's wrist and wrenched it off his shirt. It came free this time. 'Why are you making us run with our tails between our legs? It only makes us look guilty.'

'No, that note makes us look guilty.' Erik stared hard at Aaron. 'Tell me the truth. Were you really with Luke?'

Aaron made himself meet his father's eyes. 'Yes.'

Erik Falk opened his mouth. Then he shut it. He looked at his son like he'd never seen him before. The atmosphere in the car had morphed into something tangible and putrid. He shook his head once, turned back to the wheel and started the engine.

They drove the rest of the way without exchanging a single word. Aaron, burning with anger and shame and a thousand other things, stared into the side mirror for the entire journey.

Part of him was disappointed that Mal Deacon never reappeared.

Chapter Twenty-six

By the time Falk had walked back from the Racos' place he'd felt an urgent need to cleanse himself. The past coated him like a layer of grime. It had been a long day and the evening felt later than it was. The bar had still been in full swing as he slunk past and up the stairs.

In the shower, his body bore the marks of exposure to the Kiewarra sun. The skin of his forearms, his neck, the V of his collar. What had been pale was now an angry red.

The first thumps on the door were almost inaudible over the running water. Falk shut off the taps and stood naked, listening. Another flurry of knocking sounded, louder this time.

'Falk! Quick!' The muffled voice was accompanied by another round of bangs. 'Are you in there?'

He grabbed a towel and nearly skidded on the wet floor. He flung open the door to find a breathless McMurdo with his fist raised to knock again.

'Downstairs.' The barman was panting. 'Hurry.' He was off, taking the stairs two at a time. Falk pulled on shorts, a t-shirt and trainers without bothering to dry himself and slammed the door behind him.

The bar was in chaos. Chairs were overturned and the floor glittered with broken glass. Someone was hunched in a corner, his hands over his nose slick with blood. McMurdo was on his knees trying to pry apart two men grappling on the floor. Around them, a semicircle of drinkers slowly wiped the smirks off their faces and stepped away as Falk took two strides into the centre of the room.

The abrupt drop in volume distracted the two men on the floor and McMurdo was able to get an arm in. He pulled them apart and they lay sprawled in their respective corners, breathing heavily.

Jamie Sullivan's eye was already swelling up, distorted into a bulbous shape. His bottom lip had split and he had scratch marks across his cheek.

Opposite him, Grant Dow grinned then winced, feeling his jaw tenderly. He seemed to have come off best, and he knew it.

'Right. You and you.' Falk pointed to two of the least drunk onlookers. 'Take Sullivan into the bathroom and help him wipe that blood off his face. Then bring him back here. Understand?'

They helped Sullivan up. Falk turned to Dow.

'You. Take a seat over there and wait and – no. Shut it. It's very much in your own interest that you keep that trap of yours closed for once. You hear?'

Falk turned to McMurdo. 'Clean cloth please and large glasses of water all round. Plastic cups.'

Falk took the cloth to the man in the corner who was doubled over, clutching his nose.

'Sit up straight, mate,' Falk said. 'That's the way. Here. Hold this.'

The man straightened and took his hands away. Falk blinked as Scott Whitlam's bloodied face appeared.

'Jesus, how'd you get mixed up in this?'

Whitlam tried to shrug and winced.

'Wrog place, wrog tibe,' he said, pressing the cloth to his nose.

Falk turned and looked pointedly at the onlookers.

'I suggest the rest of you make yourselves pretty bloody scarce,' he said.

Raco forced his way in as the room was emptying. He was wearing the same t-shirt he'd had on at dinner but his curly hair was sticking up on one side and his eyes were bloodshot.

'McMurdo rang. I was asleep. We need an ambulance? I've got Dr Leigh on standby.'

Falk looked around. Sullivan was back from the bathroom and glanced up, a concerned expression on his face, at the mention of the doctor. The other two were hunched over in their chairs.

'No. I don't think so,' he said. 'Unless you're worried about two of them being brain dead. What's the story?' He turned to McMurdo.

The barman rolled his eyes. 'Our friend Mr Dow over there seems to believe the only reason he's in the frame for the Hadlers' deaths is because Jamie Sullivan doesn't have the balls to confess. He decided now was an opportunity to encourage him to do so.'

Falk strode over to Dow. 'What happened here?'

'Misunderstanding.'

Falk leaned in close, so his mouth was right by Dow's ear. He could smell the booze several layers deep in his pores.

'If we're bothering you, Grant, all you need to do is give us a decent reason why she wrote down your name.'

Dow gave a bitter laugh. His breath stank.

'That's bloody rich, coming from you. You mean, like the decent reason you never gave for that note Ellie left? No.' He shook his head. 'I could give you a thousand reasons, mate, and you still wouldn't go away. You won't be happy until you pin the Hadlers on me or my uncle.'

Falk pulled back. 'Watch yourself. Keep talking like that and you'll be formally questioned and processed and find yourself in a whole heap of aggro, understand?' Falk held out his hand. 'Keys.'

Grant looked up in disbelief. 'No chance.'

'You can pick them up at the station tomorrow.'

'It's over five kilometres to my place,' Grant protested, cradling them in his palm.

'Tough. Enjoy your walk,' Falk said, plucking the keys from his paw and pocketing them. 'Now bugger off.'

He turned his attention to Sullivan and Whitlam, who were being inexpertly tended by McMurdo and Raco.

'You want to tell us what happened, Jamie?' Falk asked.

Sullivan stared at the floor out of his one good eye.

'Like he said. Misunderstanding.'

'I don't mean tonight.'

There was no reply. Falk let the silence stretch out.

'This is only going to get worse the further you let yourself sink.'

Nothing.

'Right,' Falk said. He was clammy, wet from the shower, and had had enough. 'Be at the station at ten tomorrow. We need to talk to you anyway. And fair warning, mate, I would have a good hard think overnight about where you were that day.'

Sullivan's features crumpled. He looked like he was about to cry. Falk exchanged a look with Raco.

'I'll drive you home, Jamie,' Raco said. 'Come on, let's get you up.'

Sullivan let himself be helped out of the bar. He didn't look at anyone. Finally Falk turned to Whitlam, who looked embarrassed behind his cloth in the corner.

'I think the bleeding's stopped,' Whitlam said, gingerly testing his nose.

'Let's see.' Falk peered at it and tried to recall his first aid training. 'Well, as long as it's not school photo day any time soon, you'll probably survive.'

'Cheers.'

'We don't need to get you down to the station tomorrow as well, do we?'

'Not me, guv.' Whitlam held up his hands. 'I'm an innocent bystander. I was coming out of the toilets and they barrelled into me. Didn't even see it coming. I lost my balance and whacked my face on a chair.'

'All right,' Falk said, helping Whitlam up. The man was a little unsteady. 'I'm not sure you should drive, though.'

'I'm on my bike.'

'Motor?'

'Jesus. I'm a schoolteacher. Pedal.'

'Right. Come on.'

It was tight but they squeezed the bike in the boot of Falk's car with some twisting of the handlebars. They drove mostly in silence through the deserted streets.

'Any luck with the CCTV?' Whitlam said finally, coughing as he tried to breathe through his nose.

'We're still working through it,' Falk said. 'Thanks for your help with that.'

'No worries.' His swollen face was a distorted reflection as he stared out of the window at the emptiness. 'Jesus, I hope this is all over soon. This place is like a nightmare.'

'Things will get better,' Falk lied automatically.

'Will they?' Whitlam said. He was slumped back down in his seat, touching his nose gingerly. 'I'm not sure. I remember when I used to worry about normal things. Footy scores and reality TV. Seems unbelievable. Now it's the school, and the funding gaps, always trying to find the money. Little kids turning up dead, for God's sake.'

Whitlam stared out of the window until they pulled up outside his house. A welcoming light glowed over the porch. Relief passed across his busted features. Home.

Falk, exhausted and uncomfortable in his sticky clothes, was hit with a fierce longing for his own flat.

'Thanks for this. You want to come in for a drink?' Whitlam asked as they got out of the car, but Falk shook his head.

'I'll take a raincheck, thanks. It's been enough for one day.'

Falk opened the boot and jostled the bike, twisting the handlebars until it came free.

'Sorry if it's made a mess,' Whitlam said, peering at the upholstery in the dark.

'Don't worry about it. You'll be OK from here? With the nose. And everything else?'

Whitlam swung his bike around. He attempted a smile. 'Yeah, I'll live. Sorry for being morose. It's the over-the-counter paracetamol talking.'

'It won't always be like this. You're just unlucky to be caught up in it.'

'That's the thing, though, isn't it? No-one can control the ripple effect of something like this.' Whitlam's voice sounded heavy. Falk wasn't sure if it was just the nose. 'It's almost funny.

I'm standing here feeling sorry for myself, but then I think about poor Billy. Talk about being caught in the wake. I tell you, whatever went on in that house – with Luke, the drought, the farm – whatever the reason, that little boy should never have been touched by it.'

At the top of the driveway, the front door opened and Sandra stood framed in the glow. She waved. Whitlam said goodbye and Falk watched as he wheeled his bike up the path. He still looked a little shaky. As Falk clambered back into the car, his phone beeped once. It was a text from Raco. Falk read the words and thumped the steering wheel in delight.

Want to know why Jamie Sullivan was in the laneway? Call me ASAP.

Chapter Twenty-seven

The man was already waiting patiently outside the station when Falk and Raco arrived early the next morning.

'Dr Leigh.' Raco introduced Falk. 'Thanks for coming.'

'That's fine. It'll have to be quick, though, if you don't mind. I've got a full surgery today. And I'm on call later.'

Raco said nothing, just smiled politely and unlocked the station door. Falk looked at the doctor curiously. He hadn't met the town's GP before, but recognised the name from the Hadlers' murder report. First medical attendee on the scene. He was in his mid-forties, had a full head of hair and the healthy glow of someone who practised what he preached.

'I brought the notes on the Hadlers.' Dr Leigh put a folder on the interview room table. 'That's what this is about, isn't it? Any progress?'

He sat down in one of the offered seats and crossed his legs, relaxed. He had an iron-rod spine and excellent posture.

'Some.' Raco's smile didn't quite reach his eyes this time. 'Dr Leigh, could you please tell us where you were on the afternoon of the twenty-second of February?'

Jamie Sullivan stood alone in his paddock and watched Luke Hadler's ute disappear in the distance. As it vanished, he took out his mobile and sent a single text. He waited. Within two minutes the phone buzzed with a response. Sullivan gave a tiny nod and headed to his own four-wheel drive.

Surprise darted across the doctor's face and he gave a confused smile.

'You know where I was that afternoon. I was with you at the Hadler murder scene.'

'And the two hours before that?'

A pause.

'I was at the surgery.'

'With patients?'

'Earlier, yes. Then I rested in the flat above the surgery for a couple of hours.'

'Why?'

'What do you mean? It's quite common when I'm on a split shift. Being on call early and late is exhausting. As you know well yourself, no doubt.'

Raco gave no reaction to the attempt at common ground.

'Can anybody confirm this?'

Sullivan drove the short distance to town. He passed no-one on the country roads and only a handful of vehicles as he got nearer the centre. Before he hit the main street he took a sharp right, turning onto a small laneway behind the row of shops. He was being overcautious, he knew. No-one would think twice about seeing his car parked in town. But the sense of secrecy was stitched through him like a scar, and it was impossible now to override. On a wall overhead, a CCTV camera outside the pharmacy blinked as he drove past.

Dr Leigh leaned in, frowning. His long fingers picked at the corner of the Hadler folder, unsure whether to open it. 'Seriously, what the hell is this about?'

'If you could answer,' Raco said. 'Were you alone in the surgery flat that afternoon?'

Leigh looked from Raco to Falk and back again. 'Should I call my lawyer? Does she need to be here?' There was a challenge in his voice.

'That,' Raco said, 'could be prudent.'

Dr Leigh pulled back from the table as though he'd been burned.

Sullivan parked his car in the garage that was always waiting empty and unlocked for him. He got out and pulled the roller door down to hide his vehicle from view, wincing at the scream of metal on metal as it closed. He waited a moment. Nothing reacted. The laneway was empty.

Sullivan went to the anonymous door next to the surgery's supplies entrance and rang the bell. He glanced left and right. A moment later the door opened. Dr Leigh smiled at him. They waited until they were inside and the door was firmly shut before they kissed.

Leigh closed his eyes and rubbed his index finger along the bridge of his nose. His excellent posture had bent a fraction.

'All right. I take it from all this you've been told the situation,' he said. 'Yes, then. I wasn't in the flat alone that afternoon. I was with Jamie Sullivan.'

Raco made a noise that was half frustration, half satisfaction, and sat back in his chair. He shook his head in disbelief.

'About time. Do you know how many hours we've spent – *wasted* – chasing Sullivan's story?'

'I know. I do. I'm sorry.' The doctor sounded like he meant it.

'You're sorry? Three people died, mate. You were there with me. You saw the bodies. That poor kid. Six years old and his head shot off. How could you let us chase our tails? Who knows what damage you've done?'

The doctor swayed a little in the chair like he'd been hit by a physical force.

'You're right,' Leigh said. He bit his thumbnail and looked close to tears. 'Don't you think I wanted to say something straight away? As soon as I found out you'd been at Jamie's place asking questions? Of course, he should have told you then. *I* should have told you then. But we panicked, I suppose. We didn't speak up immediately and then more time passed and by then I – we – didn't know how.'

'Well, I hope the delay was worth landing Jamie with a busted face last night,' Raco said.

Leigh looked up, shocked.

'Oh, didn't you know?' Raco went on. 'Yeah, he was involved in a pub fight. It's the only reason he told me what was going on. It was his head rather than his conscience that took a whack. You could've saved us all this trouble days ago. Shame on you both.'

The doctor put his hand over his eyes and stayed there for a long minute. Falk got up to get him a cup of water and he gulped it down gratefully. They waited.

'So you felt you couldn't tell us then. It's time to tell us now,' Falk said, not unkindly.

Leigh nodded.

'Jamie and I have been together about eighteen months. Romantically. But – obviously – we've kept it quiet,' he said. 'It started when he began having to bring his grandmother in more often. She was getting worse and he was struggling on his own. He needed support and someone to talk to and it grew from there. I mean, I'd always suspected he might be gay, but around here –' Leigh broke off and shook his head. 'Anyway, I'm sorry, none of that matters. The day the Hadlers were killed I had open surgery until four o'clock and then had a break. Jamie sent me a text and I told him to come over. It was a fairly usual arrangement. He arrived, we chatted for a while. Had a cold drink. Then we went to bed.'

Sullivan was in the tiny bathroom drying himself off from the shower when the flat's emergency phone rang. He heard Leigh pick up. The muffled conversation was brief and urgent. The doctor put his head around the bathroom door, his face clouded with worry.

'I've got to go. There's been a shooting accident.'

'Oh shit, really?'

'Yeah. Listen, Jamie, you should know, it's at Luke Hadler's place.'

'You're joking. I was just with him. Is he OK?'

'I don't know the details. I'll call you. Let yourself out. Love you.'

'You too.'

And he was gone.

Sullivan got dressed with shaking fingers and drove home. He'd seen a shooting accident once before. A friend of a friend of his father's. The acid copper stench of blood had slithered up to the back of his nostrils and lingered for what had felt like months. The memory of it was almost enough to conjure up the hot sick scent again, and Jamie was blowing his nose when he arrived home to find two fire trucks outside. A firefighter in protective clothing met him as he ran to the door.

'It's all right, mate, your gran's OK. I'm afraid your kitchen wall's another story.'

'After you went to Jamie's asking questions he called me, scared,' Leigh said. 'He said he'd been caught off guard and had lied to you about where he was.'

Leigh looked them both in the eye. 'There's no excuse for that. I know that and he knows that. But I ask you, please don't judge us too harshly. When you've been lying about something for so long it becomes second nature.'

'I'm not judging you for being gay, mate, I'm judging you for wasting our time when a family's lying dead,' Raco said.

The doctor nodded. 'I know. If I could go back and do things differently, I would. Of course I would. I'm not ashamed of being gay,' he said. 'And Jamie – he's getting there. But there are plenty of people in Kiewarra who would think twice about letting themselves or their kids be treated by a poof. Or want to sit next to one in the Fleece.' Leigh looked at Falk. 'You've seen first-hand what happens when you stand out here. That's all we wanted to avoid.'

They sent the doctor on his way. Falk thought for a beat, then jogged out of the station after him.

'Hey, before you go. I want to ask you about Mal Deacon. How bad is his dementia?'

Leigh paused. 'I can't discuss that with you.'

'One more thing for the list, eh?'

'I'm sorry. I would. But I really can't. He's a patient.'

'I'm not asking for specifics. General observations will do. What kind of things can he remember? Ten minutes ago but not ten years ago? Vice versa?'

Leigh hesitated, glancing back towards the station. 'Very generally speaking,' he said, 'patients in their seventies with symptoms similar to Mal's tend to suffer fairly rapid memory deterioration. The distant past may be clearer than more recent events, but often the memories blend and get muddled. They're not reliable, if that's what you're asking. Generally speaking, that is.'

'Will it kill him? Last question, I promise.'

Leigh's expression was pained. He looked around. The street was virtually empty. He lowered his voice. 'Not directly. But it complicates a lot of things healthwise. Basic personal care, nutrition, it all gets compromised. I'd suspect a patient at that stage would have a year or so, maybe a little more. Maybe less. It doesn't help if the patient's had a drink or three every day of his adult life either. Generally speaking, of course.'

He nodded once like a full stop on the conversation and turned. Falk let him go.

'They should both be charged. Him and Sullivan,' Raco said when he returned to the station.

'Yeah. They should.' They both knew it wouldn't happen.

Raco leaned right back in his chair and put both hands over his face. He gave an enormous sigh.

'Jesus. Where the hell to now?'

To kid himself that they weren't stuck in yet another dead end Falk put in a call to Melbourne. An hour later he had a list of all the light-coloured utes registered in Kiewarra in the year Ellie Deacon had died. There were 109.

'Plus anyone from out of town could have been driving through,' Raco said gloomily.

Falk ran his eyes down the list. There were a lot of familiar names. Former neighbours. Parents of his old classmates. Mal Deacon was on there. Falk stared at that name for a long time. But so was everyone else. Gerry Hadler himself, Gretchen's parents, even Falk's dad. Gerry could have seen half the town at the crossroads that day. Falk closed the file, fed up.

'I'm going out for a bit.'

Raco grunted. Falk was glad he didn't ask where.

Chapter Twenty-eight

The cemetery was a short drive out of town, on a large plot shaded by towering gum trees. On the way, Falk passed the fire warning sign, the danger now elevated to extreme. Outside, the wind was up.

The burial itself had been a private one so he hadn't been to the Hadlers' graves, but they were easy to find. Brand new, the polished headstones looked like indoor furniture accidentally left outside among their weather-beaten neighbours. The graves were ankle deep in a sea of cellophane, stuffed toys and withered flowers. Even from several feet away, the pungent smell of floral decay was overpowering.

Karen's and Billy's graves were piled high, while the offerings under Luke's headstone were sparse. Falk wondered if it would be Gerry and Barb's responsibility to clear the graves when the gifts crossed the line from tribute to trash. Barb had had enough trouble in the farmhouse, let alone on her knees with a bin bag, wretchedly sifting through the withered bouquets and trying to decide what to keep and what to throw away. No way. Falk made a mental note to check.

He sat for a while on the dry ground by the graves, ignoring the dust that coated his suit trousers. He ran a hand over the engraving on Luke's headstone, trying to shake the unreal sensation that had nagged him since the funeral. *Luke Hadler is in that coffin*, he repeated in his head. *Luke Hadler is in this ground.*

Where was Luke the afternoon Ellie died? The question resurfaced like a stain. Falk should have pressed him when he had the chance. But he'd truly believed Luke's deception had been for Falk's own benefit. If he'd known what was going to happen —

He cut the thought dead. It was a cry that had come from too many lips since he'd returned to Kiewarra. *If I'd known, I would have done things differently.* It was too late for that now. Some things had to be lived with.

Falk stood and turned his back on the Hadlers. He headed deeper into the cemetery until he found the row he was looking for. The headstones in this part of the lot had lost their shine years ago, but many were as familiar as old friends. He ran his hand over a few of them affectionately as he passed, before stopping in front of one particular sun-bleached stone. There were no flowers on this grave and it occurred to him for the first time that he should have brought some. That's what a good son would do. Bring flowers for his mother.

Instead he stooped and with a tissue wiped her engraved name free from dust and dirt. He did the same with her date of death. He'd never needed a reminder of the anniversary. As far back as he could remember, he'd known that she'd died the day he was born. *Complications and blood loss*, his father had told him gruffly when he was old enough to ask, before looking at his son in a way that made Falk feel that he was almost, but not quite, worth it.

As a kid he'd taken to cycling out to the cemetery alone, at first standing solemnly for hours in penance at his mother's grave. Eventually he realised nobody cared whether he stood there or not, and their relationship had thawed into something of a one-way friendship. He tried hard to feel some form of filial love, but even then it had seemed like an artificial emotion. He simply couldn't ignite it for a woman he'd never known. It made him feel guilty that deep down he felt more for Barb Hadler.

But he'd liked visiting his mother and she was a hell of a listener. He'd started bringing a snack, books, homework, and would loll about in the grass by the headstone and chatter in free-flowing monologue about his day and his life.

Before fully realising it, Falk found himself doing that very thing now, stretching out his limbs and lying back in the stubby grass alongside the grave. The shade from the trees took the edge off the heat. He stared at the sky and in a voice barely above a murmur, he told her all about the Hadlers and his home-coming. About seeing Gretchen again. About the heavy feeling in his chest when he'd seen Mandy in the park and Ian in the shop. He spoke about his fears that he might never find out the truth about Luke.

After he had run out of words, he closed his eyes and lay still beside his mother, cocooned by the warmth of the ground at his back and the air all around him.

When Falk woke the sun had moved in the sky. With a yawn, he stood up and stretched his stiff joints. He wasn't sure how long he'd been lying there. He shook himself off and set out through the cemetery towards the main gates. Halfway, he stopped. There was one more grave he needed to visit.

It took him far longer to find this one. He had only seen it once, at the funeral, before he'd left Kiewarra for good. Eventually he stumbled across it almost by accident: a small stone huddled anonymously among a crowd of more ornate memorials. It was overgrown with yellow grass. A single bunch of dead stalks wrapped in tattered cellophane lay under the headstone. Falk took his tissue and reached out to wipe the grime from the engraved name. Eleanor Deacon.

'Don't touch, you mongrel.'

The voice came from behind and Falk jumped. He turned and saw Mal Deacon sitting deep in the shadows at the feet of a huge carved angel in the row behind. He had a beer bottle in his hand and his fleshy brown dog asleep at his feet. It woke and yawned, exposing a tongue the colour of raw meat as Deacon hauled himself to his feet. He left the bottle at the foot of the angel.

'Get your hands off her before I cut 'em off.'

'No need, Deacon, I'm leaving.' Falk stepped away.

Deacon squinted at him. 'You're the kid, aren't you?'

'Eh?'

'You're the Falk kid. Not the dad.'

Falk looked at the old man's face. The jaw was set with aggression and the eyes seemed more lucid than they had the last time.

'Yeah. I'm the kid.' Falk felt a pang of sadness as he spoke. He started walking.

'Right. Pissing off for good this time, I hope.' Deacon moved after him, shaky on his feet. He pulled his dog's leash tight after him and the animal yelped.

'Not yet. Mind your pet.' Falk didn't break stride. He could hear Deacon trying to follow. The footsteps were uneven and slow over the rough ground.

'Can't leave her in peace even now, eh? You might be the kid, but you're just like your dad. Disgusting.'

Falk turned.

There were two distinct voices coming from the yard. One loud, one calmer. Twelve-year-old Aaron dumped his schoolbag on the kitchen table and went to the window. His father was standing with his arms crossed and a fed-up look on his face as Mal Deacon prodded a finger at him.

'Six of 'em missing,' Deacon was saying. 'Coupla ewes, four lambs. Few of those same ones you were looking over the other week.'

Erik Falk sighed. 'And I'm telling you they're not here, mate. You want to waste your time walking over to check, you be my guest.'

'So it's a coincidence, is it?'

'More a sign of your shoddy fence line, I reckon. If I'd wanted your sheep, I would have bought them. Weren't up to scratch, to my eye.'

'Nothing wrong with 'em. More like why buy 'em when you could nick 'em from me? Isn't that right?' Deacon said, his voice rising. 'Wouldn't be the first time you've helped yourself to something of mine.'

Erik Falk stared at him for a moment, then shook his head in disbelief.

'Time for you to leave, Mal.' He went to turn but Deacon grabbed him roughly by the shoulder.

'She called from Sydney to say she's not coming back, you know. You happy now? Make you feel like a big man, does it? That you talked her into buggering off?'

'I didn't talk your missus into anything,' Erik said, shoving his hand away. 'I'd say you did a good enough job of that yourself with your boozing and your fists, mate. Only surprise is she stayed as long as she did.'

'Oh yeah, real knight in shining armour, you are. Always here for a shoulder to cry on, dripping poison in her ear. Talk her into leaving and talk her into bed while you're at it, eh?'

Erik Falk's eyebrows shot up. He laughed, a pure genuine burst of amusement.

'Mal, I didn't shag your missus if that's what you're worried about.'

'Bullshit.'

'No, mate, it's not bullshit at all. It's the truth. OK, so she'd pop round for a cup of tea and a bit of a cry when she'd had enough. Needed a bit of time away from you. But that's it. She was nice enough, don't get me wrong, but she was nearly as mad on the booze as you. Maybe if you took better care of things — your sheep, your own wife — they wouldn't bloody wander off on you.' Erik Falk shook his head. 'Honestly, I've no time for you or your missus. It's your daughter I feel sorry for.'

Mal Deacon's punch came like a dog out of a kennel and caught Erik in a lucky blow above his left eye. He staggered and fell backwards, his skull landing with a sharp crack against the ground.

Aaron ran outside with a shout and bent over his father, who was staring at the sky with a dazed expression. Blood was trickling from a cut in his hairline. Aaron heard Deacon laughing, and he sprang towards the older man, ramming his chest. Deacon was forced to take a step backwards, but his large frame kept him grounded and steady on his feet. In an instant, Deacon reached out and grabbed Aaron's upper arm in an iron grip, pinching the skin as he twisted it and dragged Aaron's face close to his own.

'Listen here. When your old man gets up from the dirt, you tell him that'll seem like a pat on the head compared with what's coming if I find him — find either of you — messing around with what's mine.'

He shoved Aaron to the ground, then turned and strode across the yard, whistling through his teeth.

'He begged me, you know?' Deacon said. 'Your dad. After you did what you did to my Ellie. He came to me. Wasn't trying to tell me you didn't do it. That you couldn't have done it. Nothin' like that. He wanted me to tell everyone else in the town to back off until the police made up their minds. As if I'd give him the steam off my piss.'

Falk took a deep breath and made himself turn and start walking away.

'You knew that, did you?' Deacon's words came floating behind him. 'That he thought you might have done it? Your own dad. Course you knew. Must be a God-awful thing, to have your old man think that little of you.'

Falk stopped. He was almost out of earshot. *Keep walking*, he told himself. Instead he looked back. Deacon's mouth curled up at each side.

'What?' Deacon called. 'You can't tell me he bought that bullshit story you and the Hadler kid cooked up. Your dad may have been a fool and a coward, but he wasn't stupid. You ever manage to make things right with him? Or did he suspect it until the day he died?'

Falk didn't answer.

'Thought so.' Deacon grinned.

No, Falk wanted to shout at him, they had never made things right. He took a long look at the old man, then, with a physical effort, forced himself to turn and walk away. Step by step, weaving through the long-forgotten headstones. At his back, he could hear Mal Deacon laughing as he stood with his feet firmly planted on his own daughter's grave.

Chapter Twenty-nine

The shot bellowed across the distant paddock, the echo rippling through the hot air. Before silence could settle, another crashed out. Falk froze in the driveway of Gretchen's property, one hand stilled mid-motion as he went to slam his car door.

His thoughts fled to the Hadlers' raw scrubbed hallway, the stained carpet. He imagined a blonde woman lying bleeding on the ground, only this time not Karen, but Gretchen.

Another blast rang out and Falk was off, running across the paddocks towards the noise. He tried to follow the sound but it bounced and echoed off the hard ground, leaving him disoriented. He scanned the horizon frantically, eyes watering against the blinding sun, looking everywhere, seeing nothing.

At last he spotted her, her khaki shorts and yellow shirt almost invisible against the bleached paddocks. He stopped dead, feeling a rush of relief followed by a wave of embarrassment.

Gretchen turned her head and stared at him for a moment, then propped the shotgun on her shoulder and raised her hand in a wave. He hoped she hadn't seen him running. She started over the paddock towards him.

'Hey, you got here fast,' she called out. Pink ear defenders hung around her neck.

'I hope that's OK.' He'd phoned from outside the cemetery. 'I felt like I needed to see a friendly face.'

'It's fine. It's good to see you. I've got an hour before I need to pick up Lachie from school.'

Falk looked around, buying a moment while his breathing steadied. 'Nice place you've got here.'

'Thanks. The rabbits seem to think so too.' She nodded over her shoulder. 'I need to get a few more before I call it a day. Come on, you can be my spotter.'

He followed her across the paddock to where she'd left her kit bag. She rummaged in it and pulled out another pair of ear defenders. She reached in again, and pulled out a box of ammunition. Winchesters. Not the Remingtons found by the Hadlers' bodies, Falk thought automatically. He felt relieved, then immediately guilty for noticing. Gretchen opened the barrel of the shotgun and loaded a round.

'The warren's over there.' She pointed, squinting in the sun. 'Point when you see one.'

Falk put his ear guards on and everything was muffled, like being under water. He could see the gum trees moving silently in the wind. The sounds in his head became amplified; the blood pumping through, the slight click of his teeth.

He stared at the area around the warren. Nothing moved for a long while, then there was a twitch on the landscape. He was about to gesture to Gretchen when she steadied the gun against her shoulder, one eye squeezed shut. She centred the gun, tracking the rabbit with a smooth arc. There was a muffled boom, and a flock of galahs rose in unison from a nearby tree.

'Good, I think we got him,' she said, pulling off her ear guards. She strode across the paddock and bent down, khaki shorts stretching tight for a moment. She stood triumphantly, dangling a limp rabbit carcass.

'Nice shot,' he said.

'You want a go?'

Falk didn't particularly. He hadn't shot rabbits since he was a teenager. But she was already holding out the gun, so he shrugged.

'All right.'

The weapon was warm as he took it from her.

'You know the drill,' Gretchen said. Then she reached up and replaced his ear guards for him. Falk's neck tingled where her fingers brushed it. He squinted down the sights towards the warren. There was blood soaked into the ground. It reminded him of the mark left by Billy Hadler and the memory made his spine go cold. Suddenly he didn't want to be doing this. Up ahead, there was a movement.

Gretchen tapped his shoulder and pointed. He didn't react. She tapped his arm again. 'What's wrong?' he saw rather than heard her say. 'It's right there.'

He lowered the shotgun and pulled off his ear guards.

'Sorry,' he said. 'I guess it's been too long.'

She stared at him for a moment then nodded.

'Fair enough.' She patted him on the arm as she took the gun off him. 'You know I'm going to have to shoot it anyway, don't you? I can't have them on the land.'

She raised the gun, steadied for a brief moment, then fired.

Falk knew before they even walked over that it was a hit.

★

Back at the house, Gretchen gathered up papers that had been neatly laid out across the kitchen table.

'Make yourself at home. Try to ignore the mess,' she said, putting a jug of iced water in a clear space. 'I've been filling out applications for the school board to get some more funding. Charities and things. I was thinking about trying the Crossley Trust again, even though Scott reckons they're a waste of time. See if we get further than the shortlist this year. The problem is, before anyone'll give you any cash they want to know everything.'

'Looks like a lot of paperwork.'

'It's a nightmare, and not my forte, I'm happy to admit. It's not something the board members have had to do ourselves before.' She paused. 'That's why I shouldn't complain. It used to be Karen's job actually. So, you know . . .' She didn't complete the thought.

Falk glanced around Gretchen's kitchen as he helped her stack the papers on the sideboard. He wasn't sure what he'd been expecting, but it was a little more down at heel than he'd imagined. The kitchen was clean, but the units and appliances had clearly seen better days.

A framed photo of Gretchen's son Lachie stood in pride of place among the ornaments. He picked it up and ran a thumb over the kid's toothy smile. He thought of Billy, ambling through the carpark behind Karen on the CCTV footage. Just eighty minutes left in his short life. He put the frame down.

'Strange question, but did Karen ever mention me?' he said, and Gretchen looked up in surprise.

'You? I don't think so. We didn't really talk, though. Why? Did she even know you?'

Falk shrugged. Wondered for the thousandth time about the phone number in her handwriting.

'No, I don't think so. I was just wondering if my name had ever come up.'

Gretchen watched him closely, her bright eyes unblinking.

'Not that I know of. But like I said, I didn't know Karen that well.' She gave a small shrug. A punctuation mark to indicate the end of topic. There was a slightly awkward pause, broken only by the clink of ice as she poured glasses of water.

'Cheers,' she said, raising hers. 'Not often, but sometimes, this is better than wine.' Falk watched the tiny muscles in her throat as she took a long gulp.

'How's the investigation going anyway?' Gretchen said when she resurfaced.

'Looks like Jamie Sullivan's in the clear.'

'Really? That's good, isn't it?'

'Good for him. I'm not sure it puts us a whole lot further forward.'

Gretchen cocked her head to one side like a bird.

'But you'll stay until it's resolved?'

Falk shrugged. 'At this rate, I doubt it. I've got to get back to work next week.' He paused. 'I ran into Mal Deacon before.' He told her about the encounter in the cemetery.

'Don't let him get to you. That man is off his head.' Gretchen reached over the table, her fingertips brushing against his left hand. 'Twenty years on and he's still trying to blame you for what happened to Ellie. He's never been able to accept that you and Luke were together.'

'Gretchen, listen –'

'If anyone's to blame, it's Deacon himself,' she ploughed on. 'It's his fault his daughter was unhappy enough to drown herself. He's been looking for years for someone else to point the finger at.'

'You've really never doubted it was suicide?'

'No.' She looked surprised. 'Of course not. Why would I?'

'Just asking. I know Ellie was acting a bit odd towards the end, keeping herself to herself a lot of the time. And there's no question, living with Deacon must have been a nightmare. But I never realised she felt that hopeless. Certainly not enough to kill herself.'

Gretchen's laugh was dry.

'God, you boys were blind. Ellie Deacon was miserable.'

Ellie threw her maths book in her bag at the end of class. She'd started automatically copying down the homework from the board but stopped, her pen frozen. What was the point? She'd considered skipping school altogether today but in the end had reluctantly decided against it. It would only draw attention to her. And she didn't need any of that. It was better to do what she always did. Keep her head down and hope for – well, if not the best, then not the worst either.

Out in the crowded corridor a group of boys jostled around a portable radio listening to the cricket. Australia versus South Africa. A six prompted a cheer. Friday afternoon and all was well. They had that weekend glow already.

How long, Ellie wondered, had it been since she'd felt like that? She honestly couldn't remember. If weekdays were bad enough, the weekends were even worse. They stretched out interminably, the end seeming like it was always just over the horizon.

Not this weekend, though. She cradled the thought in her chest as she pushed her way down the corridor. After this weekend, everything would be different. This weekend had an end firmly in sight.

Still clouded in thought, Ellie jumped as someone grabbed her arm. It caught a small bruise, and she winced at the pressure.

'Hey. Where's the fire?' Luke Hadler looked down at her.

'What do you mean?' Falk stared at Gretchen.

'You know what I mean, Aaron,' she said. 'You were there.

You saw exactly the same things I did. How weird she was in those last few weeks. When she actually spent any time with us, that is. She was hardly around. She was always working at that crappy job, or – well, I don't know what. Not hanging around with us anyway. And she'd completely stopped drinking, do you remember? She said it was to lose weight, but with the benefit of hindsight that sounds like bullshit.'

Falk nodded slowly. He did remember that. He'd been surprised because she'd probably been fonder of the booze than the rest of them. Not entirely surprising given her family line.

'Why do you think she'd stopped?'

Gretchen gave a sad shrug. 'I don't know. Maybe she didn't trust herself with alcohol. Wasn't sure what she might do. And I hate to say it, but Luke had a point, that night when we had that big argument at the lookout.'

'What are you talking about?'

'I don't mean he was right to trick us,' she said hastily. 'That was a horrible move. But what he said about Ellie not being able to take a joke anymore. He shouldn't have said it, but it was true. She really couldn't. She didn't have to laugh at that stupid stunt, obviously, but by then she wasn't laughing at anything. She was always sober and serious and disappearing off on her own. You remember.'

Falk sat in silence. He did.

'And I think –' Gretchen stopped.

'Think what?'

'I think if you're honest with yourself, you've suspected for a long time now that Ellie Deacon was abused.'

Ellie pulled her arm out of Luke's grip and rubbed the mark. He didn't seem to notice.

'Where are you racing off to? You want to go into town and get a

Coke or something?' Luke's voice was overly casual. Ellie had lost count of the number of times he'd tried to engineer one-on-one time with her since the fight at the lookout. So far she'd always brushed him off. It had occurred to her that he might be trying to apologise, but she couldn't summon the energy or interest to find out. That was Luke through and through, she thought. You had to put yourself out even to get a sorry from the guy. Anyway, even if she wasn't still pissed off with him, today was never going to be his lucky day.

'I can't. Not now.'

She deliberately didn't apologise. She did wonder briefly if she should try to bury the hatchet, for old times' sake. They'd known each other for years. There was history there. Then his face clouded and by the sulky way he looked at her she knew it wasn't worth the effort. Ellie Deacon had enough men in her life who wanted more from her than they gave back. She didn't need another. She turned away. Better to forget it. Luke Hadler was who he was, and that would never change.

Falk looked down as guilt and regret swelled in his chest. Gretchen reached out and touched his arm.

'I know it's not easy to admit,' she said. 'But the signs were there. We were just too young and self-centred to read them.'

'Why didn't she tell us?' Falk said.

'Maybe she was scared. Or felt a bit embarrassed, even.'

'Or maybe she felt no-one cared.'

Gretchen looked at him. 'She knew you cared, Aaron. That's why she was drawn to you over Luke.'

Falk shook his head, but Gretchen nodded.

'It's true. You were so stable. Someone she could rely on. You would have listened if she'd tried to talk. OK, yes, Luke was flashier and smoother than you. But that's not always a good thing. Luke was the star, but most people don't like just being the afterthought in their own life. It's not like that with you. You've always cared more about other people than yourself. Otherwise you wouldn't still be here in Kiewarra.'

'Hey, Ellie.'

She was halfway down the hall, feeling Luke's eyes on the back of her neck, when she heard the voice from an empty classroom. Inside, Aaron Falk was packing labelled potted plants into a large cardboard box. She smiled to herself and went in.

'How'd the presentation go? More top marks?' she said, curling an escaping fern tendril around her finger and tucking it back into the box.

Aaron shrugged modestly. 'I don't know. OK. Plants aren't really my thing.' He wouldn't say it, Ellie knew, but he would have aced it. When it came to all things academic, Aaron barely had to lift a finger. She'd also been barely lifting a finger this past year, but with markedly different results. The teachers had stopped bothering her about it a while ago.

He closed the box and hoisted it up, awkwardly balancing it in his long arms. 'This is going to be a pain to get home. Fancy giving me a hand? There's a Coke in it for you.'

His voice was as casual as Luke's had been, but he coloured slightly and avoided her eyes. Things had been a little weird ever since they'd kissed at the rock tree. The fight at the lookout hadn't helped. She felt an urge to explain herself but couldn't think of the words. Instead, she wanted to take his face in her hands, kiss him again and tell him he had done everything he could.

He was still waiting and she wavered. She could go with him. It wouldn't take long. But no, she told herself firmly. She had made her decision. She had somewhere else to be.

'I can't. I'm sorry,' she said, meaning it.

'No worries.' His smile was genuine and she felt a pang of deep regret. Aaron was one of the good guys. He always made her feel safe.

You should tell him.

The idea popped into her head, unbidden. She shook her head once. No. She couldn't tell him. That was stupid. It was too late. He'd only try to stop her now. But then, when she looked at his open face, she felt her insides wrench with a loneliness that made her wonder if maybe, in fact, that was exactly what she wanted.

'Poor Ellie,' Falk said. 'Christ, we were supposed to be her friends and we all let her down.'

Gretchen looked at her hands. 'I know, I feel guilty about it too. But try not to beat yourself up too much. Other people must have suspected and turned a blind eye. You were a kid. You did the best you could. And you were always good to her.'

'Not good enough, though. Whatever she felt she was going through, it was happening right under our noses and we barely even noticed.'

The kitchen was comfortable and quiet and Falk felt like he would never have the energy to drag his heavy limbs up and leave. Gretchen gave a small shrug and put her hand on his. Her palm was warm.

'It's a lesson we've all had to learn the hard way. There was a lot going on back then. It wasn't all about Luke.'

Ellie looked up at Aaron, and he smiled. Tell him, the little voice in her head whispered, but she shut it down. Stop. It was decided. She would tell nobody.

'I've got to go.' Ellie started to move away, then paused. The thought of what was to come sent a wave of recklessness crashing over her. Before she really knew what she was doing she stepped in, leaned over his box of plants and kissed Aaron lightly on the lips. They felt dry and warm. She stepped back, bumping her hip painfully on a desk in her rush.

'OK. See you round.' Her voice sounded false to her own ears and she didn't wait for his response.

As Ellie spun around to the classroom door, she nearly jumped in fright. Leaning up against the doorframe, watching without making a sound, stood Luke Hadler. His face was unreadable. Ellie took a breath and forced her features into a smile.

'See you, Luke,' she said as she edged passed him.

He didn't smile back.

Chapter Thirty

Falk sat on his bed with a dozen sheets of paper spread out in front of him. Below, the pub was quiet. The last patrons had left hours ago. Falk stared at his notes on the case. He scrawled connecting lines back and forth until he ended up with a tangled cobweb and a bunch of dead ends. He took a fresh sheet of paper and tried again. Same result. He picked up his mobile and dialled.

'I think Ellie Deacon was being abused by her father,' he said when Raco answered.

'What's that? Hang on.' The voice on the other end was sleepy. The line went muffled and Falk could hear a muted conversation. Rita, Falk guessed. He looked at his watch. It was later than he thought.

A minute passed before Raco's voice came back on. 'You still there?'

'Sorry, I didn't notice the time.'

'Never mind, what was that about Ellie?'

'Just something Gretchen I were talking about before. About Ellie being unhappy. Not just unhappy, miserable. I'm sure Mal Deacon was abusive.'

'Physically? Sexually?

'I don't know. Maybe both.'

'Right,' Raco said. There was silence.

'Deacon doesn't have an alibi for the afternoon the Hadlers were killed.'

Raco sighed heavily down the line. 'Mate, he's in his seventies with mental problems. He may be a bastard, but he's a doddery old one.'

'So? He can still hold a shotgun.'

'So,' Raco snapped, 'I think your view on Deacon is coloured by the fact you hate his guts for what happened to you over twenty years ago.'

Falk didn't reply.

'Sorry,' Raco said. He yawned. 'I'm tired. We'll talk tomorrow.' He paused. 'Rita says hello.'

'Hello back. And sorry. 'Night.'

The line went dead.

It felt like only minutes later when the room's landline woke Falk with a sharp plastic trill. He prised open one eye. It was barely seven. He lay with his forearm over his face, struggling to make himself respond. He'd looked at his notes until falling into a clammy disturbed sleep, and now his head was pounding in protest. Unable to bear the noise, he summoned the energy to reach out and pick up the receiver.

'Jesus, at last,' McMurdo said. 'Did I wake you?'

'Yes.'

'Whatever, my friend, it doesn't matter. Listen, you need to come down right now.'

'I'm not dressed —'

'Trust me,' McMurdo said. 'I'll meet you round the back. I'll give you a hand as best I can.'

Falk's car was awash with shit. Streaks and smears covered the paintwork, pooling around the wheels and under the windscreen wipers. The mess was already dry in the early morning sun and had settled into the words scratched into Falk's car. SKIN YOU, spelled out in shit rather than silver.

Falk ran over. He had to hold his shirt over his nose before he got anywhere near. The smell was almost solid in his mouth. The flies were in a frenzy and he swatted them away in disgust as they landed on his face and hair.

The inside was worse. A funnel or hose had been wedged into the tiny gap of window Falk tended to leave open on the driver's side to let heat escape overnight. The revolting sludge was splattered across the steering wheel and radio and collected in murky pools in the seats and footwell. None of the other cars in the lot had been touched. McMurdo was standing off to the side with his forearm pressed across his mouth and nose. He shook his head.

'Bloody hell, mate. I'm so sorry. I was bringing the empties out and found it. They must have come in the night.' McMurdo paused. 'At least it's animal. Mostly. I think.'

Still holding his shirt over his nose, Falk walked around the car silently. His poor car. Scratched, and now destroyed. He felt a surge of rage course through him. He peered through the streaked windows, holding his breath. Careful not to get too close. Through the grime, he could see there was something else inside the car. He stepped back, not trusting himself to speak.

Plastered to the seats and smeared with shit and stench were hundreds of fliers appealing for information about the death of Ellie Deacon.

The mood at the station was bleak.

'I'll read Dow and his uncle the riot act, mate,' Raco had said to Falk before picking up the phone. 'You know what the car's worth? Could be some compensation.'

Falk had shrugged distractedly as he sat at a desk looking blankly at the Hadler files. Across the room Raco now hung up the phone and put his head in his hands for a moment.

'Looks like Deacon's making a pre-emptive strike,' Raco called over to Falk. 'He's put in a complaint. Against you.'

'Really.' Falk crossed his arms and looked out of the police station window. 'And yet my car's the one covered in shit.'

'He says you've been harassing him. Tampering with his daughter's grave or something? He's coming in with a lawyer.'

'Right.' Falk didn't look around.

'Do I need to ask –?'

'I wasn't, but there were no witnesses. So it'll be his word against mine. And I do have an axe to grind, so . . .' Falk gave a shrug.

'You not bothered about it? It's serious, mate. I'll have to process it but it'll go to someone independent. Career could take a hit.'

Falk looked over.

'Of course I'm bothered. But that's Deacon all over, isn't it?' Falk's voice was so quiet Raco had to lean forward to hear him. 'Leaving a trail of destruction and misery. He used to smack his wife around, probably did the same to his daughter. He had a hold over this town and used it to drive me and my dad away. His nephew's done God-knows-what to make Karen Hadler write down his name days before she died. That pair are dirty. And no-one ever calls them on it.'

'What do you suggest?'

'I don't know what to suggest. I'm just saying Deacon deserves to be strung up by his balls. Getting him on a vandalism charge is too good for him. He's as guilty as sin for something bigger. The Hadlers, his daughter. Something. I know it.'

In the front office they heard the station door slam. Deacon and his lawyer had arrived.

'Mate, listen to me now,' Raco said. 'You don't know it. You get caught saying stuff like that outside of this station and that harassment charge is going to stick, so watch your mouth. There's nothing linking Deacon to the Hadlers' murders, no matter how much you want there to be.'

'Ask him.'

'Tunnel vision is a dangerous route.'

'Just ask him.'

The lawyer was young and infused with a deep passion for her client's rights. Raco listened to her patiently as he escorted them both into the interview room. Falk watched them go, then leaned back in his chair, frustrated. Deborah came out from behind the reception desk and handed him a cold bottle of water.

'Not ideal to be stuck out here with Mal Deacon in there,' she said.

'Yeah.' Falk sighed. 'Procedure. It works for you until it doesn't.'

'You know what you need to do? Make yourself useful while you're waiting.' She nodded to the hallway. 'The storeroom could do with a clear-out.'

Falk looked at her. 'I don't think —'

Deborah regarded him over her glasses. 'Follow me.' She unlocked a door and ushered him inside. It was musty, with shelves of paper and office supplies stacked around. She held a finger to her lips then touched her ear. Through an air vent above the shelves, Falk could hear voices. Muffled, but audible.

'For the tape, I am Sergeant Raco, present with my colleague Constable Barnes. Please state your names for the record.'

'Cecilia Targus.' The lawyer's voice was bright and crisp through the vent.

'Malcolm Deacon.'

In the storeroom, Falk stared at Deborah.

'This has to be fixed,' he whispered, and she gave him the shadow of a wink.

'I know. But it won't be today.'

She pulled the door to behind her and Falk sat down on a box to listen.

Deacon's lawyer tried to kick things off. 'My client –' she began, and stopped.

Falk could imagine Raco holding up his hand to silence her.

'You've given us the written copy of the complaint against Federal Agent Falk, thank you.' Raco's voice drifted through the vent. 'As you're aware, he is technically off duty and not a member of this police force, so that will be directed to the appropriate member in his chain of command.'

'My client would like assurances that he will be left in peace and –'

'I'm afraid I can't give any assurance of that kind.'

'Why not?'

'Because your client is the nearest neighbour to a house where three people were shot dead, and currently remains without an alibi,' Raco said. 'He's also a suspect in the vandalism of a car last night, as it happens. We'll come to that later.'

There was a silence.

'In regards to the deaths of three members of the Hadler family, Mr Deacon has nothing more to add to –' The lawyer was cut short by Deacon this time.

'I had bugger all to do with that shooting, and you can put that on your record,' he piped up.

Cecilia Targus's high voice cut in. 'Mr Deacon, I advise you –'

'Oh shut it, love, will you?' Deacon's scorn was blistering. 'You've no idea how it works down this way. These blokes'll pin it on me in a heartbeat given half the chance, and I don't need you getting me slammed up.'

'Nevertheless, your nephew has asked me to advise –'

'What's wrong? Those tits make you deaf as well as stupid?'

There was a long silence. Falk, sitting alone, smiled despite himself. Nothing like old-fashioned misogyny to make the ignorant turn down good advice. Well, Deacon couldn't say he wasn't warned.

'Maybe you could tell us again about that day, Mal. Please.' Raco's voice was calm but firm. The sergeant had a good career in front of him, Falk thought – if this case didn't kill his enthusiasm stone dead before it really started.

'Nothing to tell. I was round the side of the house fixing that fence and I see Luke Hadler's ute come up his driveway.'

Deacon sounded more alert than Falk had ever heard him, but his words had the sing-song quality of a story memorised rather than remembered.

'Hadler comes and goes all the time, so I pay no attention to it,' Deacon went on. 'Then I hear a shot from down their farm. I go inside my house. Then a bit later there's another shot.'

'Did you do anything?'

'Like what? It's a bloody farm. Something gets shot every day. How was I to know it was that woman and her kid?'

Falk could picture Deacon shrugging.

'Anyway, I told you before, I wasn't paying attention, was I? 'Cause I was on the phone.'

There was a shocked silence.

'What?'

Falk heard his own confusion echoed in Raco's tone. There had been no mention of a phone call in Deacon's statement. Falk knew. He'd read it enough times.

'What?' said Deacon, seemingly unaware.

'You took a phone call? During the shootings?'

'Yeah,' Deacon said. 'I told you.' But his voice had changed. He sounded less sure.

'No, you didn't,' Raco said. 'You said you went inside and that's where you heard the second shot.'

'Yeah, I went inside *because* the phone was ringing,' Deacon said, but he hesitated. His voice was slower now, and he stumbled a little over the final word. 'It was the bird from the pharmacy calling to tell me my prescription was ready.'

'You were on the phone to a woman from the pharmacy when you heard the second shot?' Raco asked, his disbelief evident.

'Yeah,' Deacon said, sounding not at all certain. 'I was. I think I was. 'Cause she asked what that bang was and I said it was nothing, farm stuff.'

'Were you on your mobile?'

'No. Landline. I get a crap signal on the mobile up there.'

There was another silence.

'Why didn't you tell us this earlier?' Raco asked.

There was a long silence. When Deacon spoke again he sounded like a little boy.

'I don't know why.'

Falk knew. Dementia. In the storeroom, he leaned his forehead against the cool wall. On the inside he was shouting with frustration. Through the vent he heard a tiny cough. When the lawyer spoke she sounded pleased.

'I think we're finished here.'

Chapter Thirty-one

Raco kept Deacon in the interview room for another twenty minutes, quizzing him about the damage to Falk's car, but it was a lost cause. He eventually let the old man leave with a warning ringing in his ears.

Falk took the keys to the police car and waited behind the station house until Deacon drove away. He gave it five minutes then slowly drove the route to Deacon's property. Along the way, the fire warning sign advised him the danger was still extreme.

He turned at a faded sign pointing to the ambitiously named Deacon Estates and rumbled along a gravel driveway. A few ragged sheep raised their heads hopefully as he drove past.

The property was high on a hill and offered a breathtaking view of the surrounding countryside. On Falk's right he could clearly see the Hadlers' home some distance below in the shallow valley. The rotary washing line was a cobweb on a stick and a couple of garden benches looked like dolls' furniture. Twenty years ago he had loved that view, on the occasions he'd visited Ellie here. Now he couldn't stand to look at it.

Falk pulled up outside a dilapidated barn as Deacon was attempting to lock his car. The man's hands were shaking and he dropped the keys in the dust. Falk folded his arms and watched Deacon bend slowly to retrieve them. Deacon's dog trotted over to his master's feet and growled in Falk's direction. The old man glanced up. The aggression in his face had for once been replaced with something else. He just looked exhausted and confused.

'I just left the police station,' Deacon said, but he didn't sound sure.

'Yeah. You did.'

'So what do you want then?' Deacon stood straight, as best he could. 'You going to take a pop at an old man while no-one's around? You're a coward.'

'I'm not going to waste a career-ending punch on you,' Falk said.

'What, then?'

It was a good question. Falk looked at Deacon. For two decades, the man had loomed larger than life. He'd been the bogey-man, the spectre at the feast, the monster under the bed. Standing in front of him now, Falk could still taste his own anger in the back of his throat, but it was diluted with something else. Not pity, definitely not pity.

Instead, Falk realised he felt cheated. He'd left it too long to slay the beast and over time it had shrivelled and wasted until it was no longer a fair fight. Falk took a step forward and for a second Deacon's eyes registered fear. A stripe of shame flashed through him. Falk stopped in his tracks. What was he doing here?

He looked Deacon in the eye. 'I had nothing to do with your daughter's death.'

'Bullshit, your name was on that note. Your alibi was a fairytale –' The words again had the hollow ring of learned repetition. Falk cut him off.

'How do you know? Deacon? Tell me. Why have you always been so sure Luke and I weren't together the day she died? Because I tell you, from here it seems like you know a lot more about that day than you've let on.'

There was no smell of dinner in the air when Mal Deacon let himself into the farmhouse and he felt a hot flash of irritation. In the living room his nephew was lying on the old brown couch with his eyes closed and a beer can balanced on his gut. The cricket was blaring from the radio. The Aussies were chasing the South African side.

Deacon kicked Grant's boots off the couch and his nephew prised open one eye.

'No bloody tea on yet?' Deacon said.

'Ellie's not back from school.'

'You couldn't have started something, you lazy bastard? I've been out there up to my eyes with those ewes all day.'

Grant shrugged. 'Ellie's job.'

Deacon grunted, but he was right. It was. He snapped a beer from the six-pack by Grant's side and went through to the rear of the house.

His daughter's bedroom was clinically neat. It stood silent and almost aloof from the chaos of the rest of the house. Deacon stood in the doorway and took a swig from the can. His eyes roamed over the room like beetles, but he was hesitant to step inside. Poised at the threshold of the pristine room, he felt the uneasy sensation of misalignment. A loose thread. A crack in the pavement. It looked perfect, but it wasn't right.

His eyes flicked to the white bedpost and he frowned. There was a tiny circular dent in the wood and the paint there had cracked and flaked. The pink carpet below the post had been scrubbed in a small and imperfect circle and was now one, or at most two, shades darker than the rest. Barely noticeable, but there.

Deacon felt a cold spot form in his stomach, like a tiny ball bearing. He stared at the silent room and the dent and the spot as the alcohol carried the first threads of anger through his veins. His daughter was supposed to be there and she wasn't. He clutched the beer in his palm and waited for its cool solid weight to calm him.

Later, he would tell the police that was the moment he knew something was seriously wrong.

Falk watched Ellie's father closely.

'You might be able to claim your hands are clean when it comes to the Hadlers,' Falk said, 'but you know something about what happened to your daughter.'

'You watch your mouth.' Deacon's voice was quiet and tight, like a coiled spring.

'Is that why you were always so keen to pin Ellie's death on me? If there's no suspect to hand, people start looking for one. Who knows what they'd start to uncover if they looked too closely at you. Neglect? Abuse?'

The old man lunged at Falk with surprising force, taking him by surprise and knocking him flat to the ground. Deacon's grubby hand mashed against his face. The dog circled, barking frantically.

'I will gut you,' Deacon was shouting now. 'I hear you breathe one word like that, and I will gut you like an animal. I loved her. You hear me? I loved that girl.'

Luke Hadler's heart was in his throat. He paused with one hand on the radio as the South Africans nearly took a wicket. Batsman restored and panic over, he switched it off.

He sprayed body mist liberally over his bare chest, and flung open his wardrobe. Automatically he reached for the grey shirt she'd admired once. Luke checked his reflection in the mirror and flashed his teeth as he buttoned it. He liked what he saw, but he knew from experience that meant bugger all. It took a mind-reader to know what was going through those girls' heads half the time.

Today, for example. The image of Ellie pressing her hot mean mouth on Aaron in the classroom popped into his head and his reflection frowned. Was that the first time it had happened? Somehow he felt sure it wasn't. Luke felt an intense flash of something like jealousy and gave his head a sharp shake. What did he care? He didn't give a stuff. But Jesus, Ellie Deacon could be a little bitch sometimes. Ignoring him and then running off to Aaron. Not that it bothered him, but Christ, you only had to look at that picture to know there was something seriously wrong.

Deacon's long fingers gouged painfully against the flesh of Falk's cheek and Falk grabbed his wrist, wrenching him off. He flipped Deacon onto his back and stood up, stepping away. It was over in a matter of seconds but both men were panting, the adrenaline kicking into overdrive. Deacon stared up at him, the corners of his mouth white with spit.

Falk leaned over him, ignoring the dog as it bared its teeth. He stood over an ill man lying on the ground. Later he would hate himself for it. At that moment, he didn't care.

Aaron's arms were aching under the box of plants by the time he got home, but the grin was still fixed on his face. His good mood was tempered only by a pang of mild regret. Maybe he should have followed Ellie out of the classroom. That's what Luke would have done, he thought. Kept the conversation flowing, convinced her she did want that Coke after all.

He frowned and dumped the box on the porch. Ellie had definitely smiled at Luke as she left the room. They were barely speaking these days, but she still managed a smile for him?

Aaron had braced himself for a smirk and a cheeky comment from his friend after Ellie left, but Luke had merely raised his eyebrows.

'Careful with that one,' was all he'd said.

Aaron had suggested they head to the main street, hang around for a while, but Luke had shaken his head. 'Sorry, mate, got somewhere to be.'

Ellie had said she was busy too. Doing what? Aaron wondered. If she was working she would have said, wouldn't she? He forced himself not to wonder too hard what both his friends were doing without him.

Instead, for something to do, he fetched his fishing poles. He'd head to the river. Upstream, where the fish had been biting. Or, he thought suddenly, he could go to the rock tree, just in case Ellie was there. He debated. If she'd wanted to see him, she would have said. But she was so difficult to read. Maybe if they spent a bit more time together one on one, she'd realise. He would be good for her. If he couldn't even make her see that, something was seriously wrong.

'You think I killed your daughter that day?' Falk said, looking down at Deacon. 'You think I held her body under water until she drowned, then lied to everyone, to my own dad, all these years?'

'I don't know what happened that day.'

'I think you do.'

'I loved her.'

'Since when,' Falk said, 'has that ever stopped anybody from hurting someone?'

'Give me a bloody clue then. On a scale of one to jail, how much shit have you stirred up?'

Raco was shouting down the phone. Falk realised he'd never really heard him angry before.

'None. Look, it's fine. Leave it,' Falk said. He was sitting in the police car a kilometre down the road from Deacon's place. He'd had eight missed calls on his phone from Raco.

'None?' Raco said. 'You think I came down in the last shower, mate? You got a complaint against you. You think I can't guess exactly where you are? I'm just some thick country plod who hasn't got a clue?'

'What?' Falk said. 'No. Raco, mate, of course not.' He was shaken up by his own lack of control. It felt wrong, like he was wearing a costume.

'You bugger off the minute the interview's over – I know you listened in, by the way – and I can hear in your voice you've been up to something with Deacon. *In a police car.* So it's not fine, is it? I'm still in charge round here last I checked, and if you've been harassing someone who's already complained, for God's sake, then we've one serious problem, mate.'

There was a long silence. Falk could imagine Raco pacing around the station, with Deborah and Barnes listening in. Falk took a few deep breaths. His heart was still pounding, but common sense was starting to return.

'We haven't got a problem,' Falk said. 'I'm sorry. I snapped for a minute. If there's any fallout, I'll cop it, not you. Promise.'

The line was silent for so long Falk wasn't sure if Raco was still there.

'Listen, mate.' Raco's voice was lower. 'I think all this might be getting too much for you. With your background here.'

Falk shook his head even though there was no-one to see it. 'No. I told you. It was a moment of madness. No harm done.' No further harm, anyway.

'Look, you've done everything that could have been asked of you. More,' Raco was saying. 'We've got further than I ever would have alone. I absolutely know that, mate. But maybe it's time we called it a day. Call in Clyde. I blame myself for that, I should have done it ages ago. This isn't your responsibility. It never was.'

'Raco, mate –'

'And you're obsessed with Deacon and Dow. You're obsessed with pointing the finger at them. It's as if you need to get them for the Hadlers to make up for whatever happened to Ellie –'

'It's not about that! Dow's name was in Karen's handwriting!'

'I know, but there's no other evidence! They've got an alibi. Both of them now.' Raco sighed down the phone. 'Deacon's phone call at the time of the Hadler shootings looks like it's legit. Barnes is getting the phone records now, but the girl from the pharmacy has backed him up. She remembers it happening.'

'Shit.' Falk ran a hand over his head. 'Why didn't she mention it before?'

'She was never asked.'

There was a pause.

'Deacon didn't do it,' Raco said. 'He didn't kill the Hadlers. You need to open your eyes, and fast. You're staring so hard at the past that it's blinding you.'

Chapter Thirty-two

Falk felt the tension in his shoulders finally start to lift around the time Gretchen poured the third glass of red. A weight that had pressed on his chest for so long that he'd almost stopped noticing at last began to ease. He could feel muscles in his neck loosen. He took a mouthful of wine and enjoyed the sensation as his cluttered head gave way to a more pleasant type of fog.

The kitchen was now dark, the remains of dinner cleared from the table. A lamb stew. Her own, she'd said. Animal, not recipe. They'd washed the dishes together, her hands deep in suds, his wrapped around a tea towel. Working together in tandem, and revelling self-consciously in the domesticity.

Eventually they'd moved through to the living room where he'd sunk, satiated, into a deep old couch, glass in hand. He'd watched her move around the room slowly, turning on low lights on side tables, creating a deep golden glow. She hit an invisible switch and discreet jazz filled the room. Something mellow and indistinct. The maroon curtains were open, flapping in the night breeze. Outside the windows, the land was still.

Earlier Gretchen had picked him up from the pub in her car.

'What happened to yours?' she'd asked.

He'd told her about the damage. She'd insisted on seeing it and they'd walked to the carpark where she'd gingerly lifted the tarpaulin. The car had been hosed down, but the inside was still destroyed. She'd been sympathetic, laughed gently as she rubbed his shoulder. She made it seem not as bad.

As they'd driven along the back roads, Gretchen told him Lachie was sleeping at the babysitter's overnight. No further explanation. In the moonlight her blonde hair gleamed.

Now she joined him on the couch. Same couch, at the other end. A distance he would have to breach. He always found that bit difficult. Reading the signs. Judging it just right. Too early and it caused offence; too late, the same. She smiled. Maybe he wouldn't find it too difficult tonight, he thought.

'You're still managing to resist the call of Melbourne, then,' she said. She took a sip. The wine was the same colour as her lips.

'Some days it's easier than others,' Falk said. He smiled back. He could feel a warmth bloom in his chest, his belly. Lower.

'Any sign of wrapping things up?'

'Honestly, it's hard to say,' he said, vague. He didn't want to talk about the case. She nodded and they lapsed into a comfortable silence. The blue notes of the jazz were swallowed up by the heat.

'Hey,' she said. 'I've got something to show you.'

She twisted around, reaching up to the bookshelves behind the couch. The movement brought her close, exposing a flash of smooth torso. Gretchen flopped back, holding two photo albums. Big books with thick covers. She opened the first page of one, then discarded it, putting it off to the side. She opened the other. Scooted closer to Falk.

The distance breached. Already. He hadn't even finished his glass.

'I found this the other day,' she said.

He glanced at it. He could feel her bare arm on his. It reminded him of the day he'd seen her again for the first time. Outside the funeral. No. He didn't want to think about that now. Not about the Hadlers. Not about Luke.

Falk looked down as she opened the album. It had three or four photos to a sticky page, covered with a plastic sheet. The first few pictures showed Gretchen as a small child, the images bright with the hallmark red and yellow tones of a chemist's developing room. She flipped through.

'Where is – ah. Here. See,' she said, tilting the page towards him and pointing. Falk leaned in. It was him. And her. A picture he'd never seen before. Thirty years ago, him bare-legged in grey shorts, her wearing a too-large school dress. They were side by side amid a small group of uniformed kids. The others were all smiling, but both he and Gretchen were squinting suspiciously at the camera. Childhood blondes – hers lit with gold, his white. Posed under duress at the instruction of the person behind the camera, Falk guessed, judging by his mutinous expression.

'First day of school, I think.' Gretchen looked sideways and raised an eyebrow. 'So. It would appear that, in fact, you and I were friends before anyone else.'

He laughed and leaned in a little as she ran a finger over the image from the past. She looked up at him, in the present, red lips parting in a smile over white teeth, and then they were kissing. His arm around her back pulled her in closer and her mouth was hot on his, his nose against her cheek, his other hand in her hair. Her chest was soft on his and he was keenly conscious of her denim skirt pressed against his thighs.

They broke away, an awkward laugh, a deep breath. Her eyes were almost navy in the low light. He brushed a strand of hair from her forehead, then she was moving in again, closer, kissing him, the scent of her shampoo and the taste of red wine in every breath.

He didn't hear the mobile ring. Only when she stopped moving did he register anything outside of the two of them. He tried to ignore it, but she held a finger to his lips. He kissed it.

'Shh,' she giggled. 'Is that yours or –? No, it's mine. Sorry.'

'Leave it,' he said, but she was already moving, pushing herself up out of the couch, away from him.

'I can't, I'm sorry, it might be the babysitter.' She smiled, a little witchy smile that made his skin tingle where she'd been. He could still feel her. She looked at the screen. 'It is, I'll be back. Make yourself comfortable.'

She actually winked. A playful, ironic nod to what was to come. He grinned as she left the room. 'Hi Andrea, everything OK?' he heard her say.

He blew out his cheeks, rubbed his eyes with his knuckles. Shook his head, took a slug of wine, sat up straighter on the couch. Waking up a little, but not too much, trying not to break the spell, anticipating her return.

Gretchen's voice was a low murmur in the other room. He leaned his head back on the couch, listening to the indistinct sounds. He could hear the cadence, up and down, soothing. Yes, the thought popped into his head unbidden. Maybe he could almost get used to this. Not in Kiewarra, but somewhere else. Somewhere grassy and open where it rained. He knew how to handle the wide open spaces. Melbourne and his real life seemed five hours and a million miles away. The city might have got under his skin, but for the first time he wondered what was hidden in his core.

He shifted on the couch and his hand brushed against the cool covers of the photo albums. In the other room, Gretchen's voice was a dull murmur. No urgency in her tone, she was patient, explaining something. Falk pulled the album into his lap, opening it half-heartedly, blinking away the heaviness from the wine.

He was looking for the photo of the two of them, but realised immediately he'd picked up the wrong album. Instead of the early childhood snaps on the first page, Gretchen was older in this one, nineteen or twenty maybe. Falk started to close the cover then stopped. He looked at the pictures with interest. He'd never really seen her at that age. He'd seen younger, and now older. Nothing in between. Gretchen was still looking a little suspiciously at the camera, but the reluctance to pose was gone. The skirt was shorter and the expression less coy.

He turned the page and felt a jolt as he came face to face with Gretchen and Luke, frozen in time in a glossy colour print. Both in their early twenties, intimate and laughing, heads close, smiles matching. What had she said?

We dated for a year or two. Nothing serious. It fell apart, of course.

A string of similar pictures spanned two double pages. Days out, holidays by the beach, a Christmas party. Then all of a sudden, they stopped. As Luke's face was changing from a twenty-something bloke to a man nearing thirty. About the age Luke had met Karen, he disappeared from Gretchen's album. That was OK, Falk told himself. That was fine. That made sense.

He flicked through the remaining pages as Gretchen's muffled voice floated through from the other room. He was about to close the book when his hand stilled.

On the very last page, under the yellowing plastic protector, was a photo of Luke Hadler. He was looking down, away from the camera, with a serene smile on his face. The picture was cropped close, but he appeared to be in a hospital room, perched on the edge of a bed. In his arms, he held a newborn baby.

The tiny pink face, dark hair and chubby wrist peeked out from the folds of a blue blanket in his arms. Luke held the child comfortably, closely. Paternally.

Billy, Falk thought automatically. He'd seen a thousand similar photos at the Hadlers' place. The name hit a dud note the moment it landed. Falk leaned in, over Gretchen's photo album, rubbing his eyes, wide awake now. The picture was not a good one, taken in a dim room with a heavy flash. But the focus was sharp. Falk shoved the album under the tableside lamp, the mood lighting revealing the image more clearly. Nestled in the blue blanket, circling the baby's fat wrist, was a white plastic bracelet. The child's name was written on it in neat capital letters.

LACHLAN SCHONER.

Chapter Thirty-three

In the black windows, Falk could see his reflection warp and shift. Gretchen's voice drifted down the hall. It sounded suddenly different to his ears. He grabbed the other album and flicked through. Photos showed Gretchen alone, Gretchen with her mother, on a night out in Sydney with her older sister.

No Luke. Until – he nearly missed it. He turned back a page. It was another bad photo, hardly worth including in an album. Taken at some community event. Gretchen was in the background of the action. Standing next to her was Karen Hadler. And standing next to Karen was Luke.

Over his wife's head, Luke Hadler was looking straight at Gretchen. She was looking back with the same little witchy smile that she'd just flashed at Falk. He turned to the photo of Luke with Gretchen's baby son. The son who, with his dark hair and brown eyes and sharp nose, had grown up to look nothing like his mother.

Falk jumped as Gretchen spoke behind him.

'It was nothing,' she said. Falk spun around. She smiled, put down her mobile and picked up her wineglass. 'Lachie just needed to hear my voice –'

Her smile faded as she saw the look on his face and the photo album open in his hand. She looked back at him, her expression a mask.

'Do Gerry and Barb Hadler know?' Falk heard the edge in his own voice and didn't like it. 'Did Karen?'

She bristled, instantly defensive. 'There's nothing to know.'

'Gretchen –'

'I told you. Lachie's dad's not around. Luke was an old friend. So he visited. Spent a couple of hours with Lachie now and again. So what? What's wrong with that? It was a male role model thing. It was nothing.' Gretchen was babbling. She stopped. She took a deep breath. Looked at Falk. 'Luke's not his father.'

Falk said nothing.

'He's not,' she snapped.

'What does it say on Lachie's birth certificate?'

'It's blank. Not that it's any of your business.'

'Have you got a single photo of Lachie's dad? One picture you can show me?'

She met the question with silence.

'Have you?' he said.

'I don't have to show you anything.'

'It can't have been easy for you. When Luke met Karen.' Falk didn't recognise his own tone. It sounded distant and cold.

'For God's sake, Aaron, he's not Lachie's father.' Gretchen's face and neck were flushed. She took a slug of wine. A pleading note had crept into her voice. 'We hadn't slept together for – Jesus, it had been years.'

'What happened? Luke didn't want to settle down with you, has one eye on the road. Then he meets Karen and –'

'Yeah, and what?' she interrupted. The wine sloshed against the side of her glass. She blinked back tears, and any earlier tenderness was gone. 'OK, yes, it pissed me off when he chose her. It hurt me. Luke hurt me. But that's life, isn't it? That's love.'

She stopped. Bit the tip of her tongue between her front teeth.

'I wondered why you didn't like Karen,' Falk said. 'But that would well and truly do it, wouldn't it?'

'So? I don't have to be her best friend –'

'She had all the things you wanted. Luke, the security, the money, at least what there was of it. You were here on your own. Your child's father had moved on. Left town allegedly. Or was he actually down the road playing dad and husband to other people?'

Gretchen rounded on him, tears spilling over now. 'How can you ask me this? If I had an affair with Luke while he was married? If he's the father of my son?'

Falk stared at her. She had always been the beautiful one. Almost ethereal. Then he remembered the stain in Billy Hadler's room. He remembered Gretchen raising her gun and shooting those rabbits down.

'I'm asking because I have to ask.'

'Jesus, what is wrong with you?' Her face had hardened. Her teeth were stained from the wine. 'Are you jealous? That for a while I chose Luke and he chose me? That's probably half the reason you're here now, isn't it? Thought you might finally manage to get one up on Luke now he's gone.'

'Don't be stupid,' he said.

'I'm stupid? God, look at you,' she said, louder now. 'Always following him around when we were younger like a lapdog.

And now, *even now*, you're hanging round in a town you hate because of him. It's pathetic. What kind of hold has he got over you? It's like you're obsessed.'

Falk could almost feel the eyes of his dead friend watching them from that album.

'Jesus, Gretchen, I'm here because three people were killed. All right? So I hope for your son's sake that lying about your relationship with Luke is the worst thing you've done to that family.'

She pushed past him, knocking his wineglass off the table as she went. The stain seeped like blood into the carpet. She flung open the front door and a gust of hot wind blew in a flurry of leaves.

'Get out.' Her eyes were like shadows. Her face was flushed an ugly red. On the doorstep she took a half-breath as though she was about to say something more then stopped. Her mouth twitched up in a cold little smile.

'Aaron. Wait. Before you do anything rash – I've got something to tell you.' Her voice was almost a whisper. '*I know.*'

'Know what?'

She leaned in so her lips were almost at his ear. He could smell the wine on her breath.

'I know your alibi for the day Ellie Deacon died was bullshit. Because I know where Luke was. And it wasn't with you.'

'Wait, Gretchen –'

She gave him a shove.

'Looks like we've all got our secrets, Aaron.'

The door slammed.

Chapter Thirty-four

It was a long walk back to town. Falk felt every step rico-
chet from the soles of his feet up to his pounding head. His
thoughts swarmed like flies. He re-lived conversations he'd had
with Gretchen, holding them up under this new stark light,
examining them, seeking out the flaws. He phoned Raco. No
answer. Perhaps he was still angry. Falk left a message, asked him
to call.

It was near closing time when he finally reached the Fleece.
Scott Whitlam was on the pub steps, fastening his bike helmet.
His injured nose looked better than it had the other night.
Whitlam took one look at Falk's face and stopped.

'You all right, mate?'

'Rough night.'

'Looks like it.' Whitlam took his helmet off. 'Come on, I'll
buy you a quick one.'

Falk wanted nothing more than to crawl up the staircase to

bed, but didn't have the energy to argue. He followed Whitlam inside. The bar was nearly empty and McMurdo was wiping the counter. He paused when they walked in and reached for two beer glasses without asking. Whitlam put his helmet on the counter.

'I'll get these. Put them on the tab, mate?' he said to McMurdo.

The barman frowned. 'No tab.'

'Come on. For a regular?'

'Don't make me say it again, my friend.'

'OK. Fine.' Whitlam pulled out his wallet and thumbed through it. 'I might be a bit – I might have to put it on the card –'

'I'll get it.' Falk cut across him and put a twenty on the counter, waving away Whitlam's protestations. 'It's fine, forget it. Cheers.'

Falk took a deep swallow. The sooner it was drunk, the sooner he could call it a night.

'What's happened then?' Whitlam asked.

'Nothing. I'm just sick to death of this place.'

It hurt me. Luke hurt me.

'Any progress?'

Falk thought for a wild moment about telling him. McMurdo had stopped cleaning and was listening from behind the bar. In the end, he shrugged.

'I'll just be glad to get out of here.' Whatever happened, he was due back in Melbourne on Monday. Sooner, if Raco got his way.

Whitlam nodded. 'Half your luck. Although –' He held up a hand and crossed his fingers. 'I might be following your lead sooner than I thought.'

'You're leaving Kiewarra?'

'Hopefully. I've got to do something soon for Sandra. She's had it up to here. I've been looking at a new place, a school up north maybe. Bit of a change.'

'Weather's hotter up north.'

'At least they get the rains,' Whitlam said. 'It's the lack of water here. Makes the whole town crazy.'

'I'll drink to that,' Falk said, draining his glass. His head felt heavy. Wine, beer, emotion.

Whitlam took the hint and followed suit.

'All right, better run. It's a school night, after all.' Whitlam offered his hand. 'Hopefully I'll see you before you leave, but if not, good luck.'

Falk shook it. 'Thanks, you too. Up north.'

Whitlam left with a cheery wave and Falk handed the empty glasses to McMurdo.

'Did I hear you say you're heading out soon?'

'Probably,' Falk said.

'Well, I'll be sorry to see you go, believe it or not,' McMurdo said. 'You're the only one who reliably pays. Which reminds me –' He opened the cash register and gave Falk back his twenty-dollar note. 'I put the drinks on your room tab. Thought it would be easier to claim them on expenses or whatever you cops do.'

Falk took the twenty, surprised.

'Oh, right. Thanks. I thought you said no tabs.'

'I only said that to Whitlam. You're all right, though.'

Falk frowned. 'But not Whitlam? You must know him well enough.'

McMurdo gave a short laugh. 'Oh, yeah. I know him well enough. That's why I also know where he keeps his money.' He nodded to the poker machines flashing in the back room.

'Whitlam's a fan of the pokies?' Falk asked.

McMurdo nodded. 'And the rest. Horses, dogs. Always got one eye on the racing channel, the other on those apps on his phone.'

'You're kidding.' Falk was taken aback, but at the same time not surprised. He thought about the sports books in Whitlam's house. He'd come across a lot of gamblers in his career. There was no single type. The only thing they had in common was delusion and misery.

'He's subtle about it, but you see all sorts of things from behind a bar,' McMurdo said. 'Especially when it comes to being able to pay for drinks. And I don't think he actually likes the pokies much.'

'No?'

'Nah, I get a sense they're small fry for him. Still, doesn't stop him feeding his weight in gold coins into them every time he's here. That's what he was doing when he accidentally got clobbered the other night. When Jamie and Grant had their punch-up.'

'Is that right?'

'Anyway, I shouldn't be telling tales out of school,' McMurdo said. 'There's nothing illegal about pissing your cash away. Thank God. Otherwise I'd be out of business.'

'So would a lot of people.' Falk managed a smile.

'These gambling types are fair old suckers, though. Always looking for strategies and loopholes. End of the day, it only works if you back the right horse.'

Falk's room had never felt so much like a cell. He brushed his teeth without turning on the light and collapsed into bed. Despite the chaos in his head, he felt overwhelmed by exhaustion. Sleep was close.

Out in the street a tin can rolled along, its metallic clatter rattling in the quiet. Through his drowsiness, it reminded Falk of the artificial clang of the pokies. He closed his eyes. McMurdo was right about gambling. Like this case. Sometimes all the strategies in the world couldn't help.

It only works if you back the right horse.

A cog turned deep in Falk's brain. Lazily, because it was an ingrained one. Crusted over and tough to shift. It reluctantly clunked one move over then stopped, settled.

Falk opened his eyes slowly. It was too dark to see anything, but he stared into the inky blackness, thinking.

He pictured Kiewarra laid out in three dimensions. He imagined himself climbing, up to the lookout maybe, the scene below growing smaller the higher he went. When he reached the top he looked down. Over the town, the drought, the Hadlers. Noticing, for the first time, how things looked from a very different perspective.

Falk thought about that, with his eyes open, staring at the nothingness for long minutes. Testing the cog in its new position. Finally he sat up, fully awake now. He pulled on a t-shirt and slipped his feet into his trainers. He grabbed his torch and an old newspaper and crept downstairs and into the carpark.

His car was right where he'd left it. The stench of shit made his eyes water, but he barely noticed it. He peeled back the tarpaulin and, using the newspaper as a makeshift glove, popped open the boot. It was kept separate from the body of the car by the back seats, and had been protected from the shitstorm.

Falk clicked on the torch and shone it into the empty boot. He stood there for a long time. Then he pulled out his mobile and took a photo.

Back in his room, sleep took a long time to come. When morning broke, he woke and dressed early, then waited impatiently. The moment the clock ticked over to nine o'clock, Falk picked up the phone and made a single call.

Luke Hadler's palms were sweating on the steering wheel. The air conditioner was on overdrive but had barely made a dent since he'd left Jamie Sullivan's place. His throat was dry and he wished he had a bottle of water to hand. He made himself focus on the road ahead. He was nearly home. Just get there.

He had turned onto the final stretch when he saw the figure up ahead. Standing by the road all alone. Waving.

Chapter Thirty-five

Falk clattered into the station, panting. He had hung up the phone and run all the way from the pub.

'It was a smokescreen.'

Raco looked up from his desk. His eyes were bloodshot and he still had sleep in the corner of one.

'What was?'

'The whole thing, mate. It was never about Luke.'

'Great,' Luke muttered as he drove closer, his heart sinking as he was able to make out who was waving. For a moment, he wondered if he could keep going, but it was a scorching day. It had to have touched forty earlier, he reckoned.

He hesitated a moment longer, then touched the brake and brought the ute to a stop. He wound down the window and leaned out.

Falk opened the Hadlers' file with shaking fingers, both excited and frustrated with himself.

'We've been tying ourselves in knots trying to find connec-
tions to Luke – what was he hiding, who wanted him dead? And
what have we ended up with? Nothing. Well, nothing substantial.
Lots of minor motives, but not enough. And you were right.'

'Was I?'

'I did have tunnel vision. But we both did. We've been
backing the wrong horse the whole time.'

*'Looks like you've got some trouble here?' Luke leaned out. He nodded
at the object lying at the person's feet.*

'Thanks. I think so. Have you got any tools on you?'

*Luke killed the engine and climbed out. He crouched down to look
more closely.*

'What's gone wrong?'

*They were the last words Luke Hadler spoke as a heavy weight
smashed into the back of his skull. There was a wet thud and a sudden
stunned silence as all around the birds in their trees were shocked mute.*

*Breathing raggedly as he towered over Luke Hadler's slumped form,
Scott Whitlam looked down at what he had done.*

Falk rummaged through the file and pulled out a photocopy
of Karen Hadler's library receipt. The word *Grant??* stood out
above Falk's own phone number. He pushed the page across
Raco's desk and stabbed it with a finger.

'*Grant*. For God's sake. It's not a bloody name.'

★

*Karen shut the door to the principal's office behind her, muffling the
everyday sounds of the Wednesday afternoon bustle. She was wearing a
red and white apple print dress, and she looked worried. She chose the
seat closest to Scott Whitlam's desk and sat straight-backed with her feet
neatly crossed at the ankles.*

'Scott,' she began. 'I wasn't sure about coming to speak to you about this. But there is a problem. And I can't turn a blind eye to it.'

She leaned in, cautious, embarrassed even, and handed over a piece of paper. On the letterhead, the Crossley Educational Trust logo stood out against the white background. Karen peered up from under her blonde fringe, her eyes looking for one thing. Reassurance.

Somewhere in the deepest fight-or-flight part of Scott Whitlam's brain, a hidden door cracked open and offered the briefest glimpse of just how far he was prepared to go to stop her.

'Grant,' Falk said, pointing at the diary. 'Also known as a bursary, a fund, a windfall, a financial gift. Like the kind Kiewarra Primary applied for from the Crossley Educational Trust last year. And their claim was rejected. Except guess what?'

Raco blinked in disbelief. 'You're kidding.'

'I'm not. I was on the phone this morning to the head of the trust, and Kiewarra Primary was successfully awarded a financial grant of fifty thousand dollars this year.'

In hindsight, Whitlam could pinpoint the singular moment when he blew it. He had picked up the page, branded with its telltale letterhead, and examined it. It was a form survey, sent automatically to successful grant recipients to gather feedback on the submissions process.

It wasn't much of a smoking gun, which meant there was probably more paperwork, he guessed. Other things that she'd kept back. Karen was giving him a chance to explain or confess. Whitlam could tell by the way she looked at him, with those blue eyes begging for a reasonable answer.

He should have said, 'Yes, strange, I'll look into it. Perhaps we've been lucky after all.' Jesus, he should have thanked her. That's what he should have done. Instead he'd panicked. He didn't take enough time to read the letter before dismissing it.

It was never going to be an easy game for him to win, but it was at that moment that he lost. Snake eyes. All over, red rover.

'It'll be nothing,' Whitlam had said. Sealing his fate with those words. 'A mistake. Ignore it.'

But the mistake was his. He could tell by the way her back stiffened and she cast her eyes down. Distancing herself. If she hadn't known for sure when she walked in, she knew it as she walked out.

Karen Hadler's goodbye as she left was as dry as the paddocks.

'Scott Whitlam,' Raco said. 'Shit. *Shit*. Does that work?'

'Yeah. It works. He's got a gambling problem, I found out last night.' Falk told him what McMurdo had said. 'That's what tipped me off. Something McMurdo said made me realise we'd been looking in the wrong direction the whole time.'

'So what are we talking? Stealing funds from the school for what? Bad debts?' Raco said.

'Could well be. Whitlam turns up last year from the city. No connection to the place. Sticks around even though he clearly hates it. He told me some story about a mugging gone wrong back in Melbourne, a stranger got stabbed. I wouldn't be surprised if there was more to that than he says.'

They were silent for a moment.

'Jesus, poor Karen,' Raco said.

'We're idiots,' Falk said. 'We discounted her far too quickly. Her and Billy. We thought they were collateral damage. Luke was always the main player, he always attracted the attention. Ever since we were kids. He was the perfect cover. How could anything ever be about his boring wife when it could be about Luke?'

'Christ.' Raco closed his eyes, running through the case as they knew it. Shaking his head as pieces dropped into place. 'Karen wasn't being stalked by Grant Dow. She wasn't afraid of her husband.'

'If anything, Luke was probably worried about what she thought she'd discovered at the school.'

'You think she told him?'

'I think she must have,' Falk said. 'Why else would she have my phone number?'

Karen went straight from Whitlam's office to the girls' toilets. She locked herself in a cubicle and put her forehead against the door before she let the angry tears come. Right up until that meeting there had been a glimmer of hope. She'd wanted Whitlam to look at the letter and laugh. 'I see exactly what's happened,' he'd say before explaining it in a way that made perfect sense.

She'd been desperate for him to say that, and he hadn't. Karen wiped her eyes with a shaky hand. What now? Part of her still couldn't quite believe Scott had stolen that money, even though she now knew it to be true. She'd known it before, if she admitted it to herself. She'd gone through the account records herself. The errors that had cropped up were his, not hers. A trail of breadcrumbs exposing his deceit. His theft. She tried the word out. It felt so wrong.

Karen believed suspicion was not the same as certainty, but her husband's view of the world had always been more black and white.

'Babe, if you think the bastard's nicked the money, then call the cops and report it. I'll report it if you don't want to,' Luke had said two nights ago.

Karen had been sitting up in bed, a new library book open across her lap. She wasn't getting very far with it. She watched her husband take his clothes off and throw them in a heap on a chair. He stood there naked and arched his broad back as he yawned. He flashed her a sleepy smile and she was struck by how lovely he looked in the half-light. They spoke in whispers so the sound didn't carry to the kids' rooms.

'No, Luke,' she'd said. 'Don't interfere. Please. I can do it myself, but I want to be sure. Then I'll report it.'

Part of her knew she was being overcautious. But the school's principal was part of the bedrock of the community. Karen could imagine how the parents would react. Tempers were so fraught, a part of her worried they might actually harm him. She couldn't let loose an accusation of that scale without solid proof. Kiewarra was fragile enough as it was. This had to be done right. Then there was her job to consider. She'd lose that in a heartbeat if she was wrong.

'I should talk to Scott first,' Karen said as her husband climbed in next to her and put a warm hand on her thigh. 'Give him a chance to explain.'

'Give him a chance to hide it, more like. Karen, babe, let the cops handle it.'

She was silent, mutinous. Luke sighed.

'All right. If you won't report it, at least get some advice on getting whatever this proof is you think you need.' Luke rolled over and reached out for his mobile phone. He scrolled through until he found a contact and passed the phone to Karen. 'Call this guy. That friend of mine who's a cop. He does something with money with the Feds in Melbourne. He's a good bloke. Really smart. Plus he kind of owes me one. You can trust him. He'll help you.'

Karen Hadler didn't say anything. She had told Luke she would sort it out, and she would. But it was late and easier not to argue. She found a pen among the clutter on her bedside table and picked up the first piece of paper to hand, the library receipt she was using for a bookmark. That would do. She turned it over and wrote a single word of reminder before copying down Aaron Falk's number. Then, because her husband was still watching, she tucked it carefully into the book she was reading and placed it by the bed.

'So it won't get lost,' she said, turning off the lamp and lying back against the pillow.

'Call him,' Luke said as he reached out and slipped his arms around his wife in the quiet night. 'Aaron will know what to do.'

Chapter Thirty-six

Ninety minutes later, Falk and Raco watched the school from the front seat of the station's unmarked police car. They were parked up a hill on a side street, their vantage point offering a decent view of the main building and front playground.

The back door of the car opened and Constable Barnes climbed inside. He'd jogged up the hill and was out of breath. He leaned through the gap between the front seats and held out his palm, proudly displaying two brand new Remington cartridges.

Raco picked up the ammunition and inspected the make. He nodded. It was the same brand found by the bodies of Luke, Karen and Billy Hadler. Forensics could probably match it more closely, but for now, that was good enough.

'It was locked away in the caretaker's shed, like you said.' Barnes was almost bouncing in his seat.

'Any trouble getting in?' Falk asked.

Barnes tried and failed to look modest. 'I went direct to the caretaker. Used the old "routine inspection" line. Licences, safety bullshit. He let me straight in. Too easy. I managed to find enough wrong that he'll keep it to himself. Said I'd turn a blind eye if he got it sorted before my next visit. He'll be telling no-one.'

'Good work,' said Raco. 'As long as he doesn't tell Whitlam for a few hours we'll be right. Backup from Clyde's about forty minutes away.'

'I don't see why we don't just roll in there and lift the bastard,' Barnes grumbled from the back seat. 'Clyde hasn't done anything to deserve the credit.'

Raco looked over. 'We'll get credit where it's due, mate, don't worry,' he said. 'They're not going to get much glory for securing his house and grabbing his bank statements.'

'Wish they'd hurry up then,' Barnes said.

'Yeah, me too,' Falk said.

All three turned back to stare at the building in the distance. A bell rang and the school doors opened. A gaggle of children trickled out, forming groups, running around, revelling in their temporary freedom. Behind them, Falk could make out a figure leaning against the main doorway. Hat on, coffee mug in hand, a flash of red tie visible against his shirt. Scott Whitlam. Falk felt Barnes shift behind him.

'Fifty grand. It's a grubby amount to kill three people over,' Barnes said.

'It'll be less about the money than you'd think,' Falk said. 'Gamblers like him are always chasing something else. I've seen it get pretty desperate pretty fast. They think every roll of the dice is a second chance. The question is, what was Whitlam chasing?'

'Doesn't matter what it was. It can't justify this,' Barnes said.

'No, but that's money for you,' Falk said. 'It can get bloody disgusting.'

★

Whitlam stood in the school doorway cradling his mug between his hands. The wind was up again. He felt the dust stick to the sweat on his skin. The kids shrieked and ran in the playground in front of him, and he wondered if he could start to breathe again. A couple of days and Falk would be gone, maybe sooner with any luck. He would breathe then, he decided. Not before.

A few more months. Keep his head down, keep his luck up and he could disappear to that job up north. Part of him couldn't believe he'd made it to this point. He'd nearly had a heart attack when Raco had mentioned they had security footage from the Hadlers' property. He'd had no idea the farmhouse had a camera, and he'd sat in a cold sweat between the two cops as he contemplated how near he'd come to being discovered.

He had to get away from here. He would have to convince Sandra to give him one last chance. One more fresh start and this time he would stop gambling. He promised. He had said the words to her last night, and through his tears he'd felt that for the first time he really meant them. She had watched in silence. She'd heard those words before. Right before they'd moved to Kiewarra, and at least twice before that. But this time he had to make her believe it. More than that, he told himself, he had to do it. He had to stop. Because this time there was so much more at risk than he could bear to lose.

Just the thought of it made his guts churn. Sandra was so worried, and yet she had no idea of the real weight of the axe dangling over them. She thought having a bank account constantly in the red was the worst of her problems. The secret shame of having to buy the weekly groceries on credit cards. Having to keep up appearances behind a veneer of rented houses and hire-purchase coffee machines. She thought the problems ran day to day, but not much further. She didn't know about the trail of debts that stretched from here to Melbourne. Or the

horrors waiting for her and their daughter at the end of that trail
if he didn't pay.

Whitlam almost smiled, a wild loopy grin at the idea of
telling her the truth. The promise of the nail gun alone would
be enough to send her racing up north.

They had delivered the message to his house. Here in
Kiewarra. Two thick-necked steroid junkies from Melbourne,
showing up on his tidy suburban-like doorstep in person to tell
him their boss was getting twitchy. Pay. They'd brought the
nail gun with them to show him. Whitlam had been paralysed
with fear. Sandra and Danielle were in the house. He could hear
the sounds of his wife and daughter chatting idly in the kitchen
as the two men detailed in low tones what they were going to
do to them if he didn't come up with the cash. It was a horrific
soundtrack.

The notification of the Crossley Educational Trust funding
had come through two days later. The letter was addressed to
Whitlam directly. It had arrived with the claim form on Karen's
day off and landed on his desk unopened.

He'd made the decision in less than a heartbeat. They gave
away millions. Fifty thousand was a drop in the ocean for those
rich bastards. He could earmark it for something vague and
tricky to quantify, training courses perhaps, support programs.
That would tick their boxes. For a while. But that was all he
needed. A while. Borrow it now to pay Melbourne; repay it,
well, later. Somehow. It wasn't enough to clear his debt, not by
a long way, but it was enough to buy him some breathing space.

He hadn't let himself think about it too closely as he'd
diverted the money. He'd simply swapped the school's account
details for his private one. The one Sandra didn't know about.
He kept the school's account name on the form. Banks used only
the numbers, not the names. Whether the two corresponded

was never checked, he knew. The plan had been OK, he told himself. Not great, not even good, but holding water. Then Karen Hadler had knocked on his door one afternoon, holding that Crossley Trust form.

Whitlam remembered the look in her eyes and, making a fist, he lightly, discreetly, punched the wall next to him until his knuckles were raw and weeping.

Whitlam watched Karen leave. As his office door clicked closed behind her, he rotated in his chair and silently vomited into the wastepaper bin. He could not go to prison. He couldn't pay off what he owed in prison and the people he owed weren't the kind to care about why. Pay, or his family paid. That was the deal. Signed and sealed. He had seen the nail gun. They'd made him touch it. Feel its leaden weight in his hand. Pay, or his – No. There was no alternative. He would pay. Of course he would pay.

He sat alone in his office and forced himself to think. Karen knew. Which meant she'd probably tell her husband, if she hadn't told him already. How soon would she blow the whistle? She was a cautious woman. Almost overly diligent in many ways. It slowed her down. Karen Hadler would want to be one hundred per cent certain before she committed herself to action. Luke, however, was a different story.

He didn't have much time. He couldn't let this get out. He could not let this get out. There was no alternative.

The end of the school day came and went, but brought with it no real answer. Whitlam waited as long as he could, then did what he always did in times of stress. He took all the cash he had, and some he didn't, and went to the pub's pokie room. It was there, cocooned in the glow of the lights and the optimistic jangling sounds, that the first stirrings of a solution came to him. As they so often did.

Alone and tucked out of sight among the pokies, Whitlam heard Luke Hadler's voice from a table round the corner. He froze, hardly

daring to breathe as he waited for Hadler to tell Jamie Sullivan about the
school money. He felt sure it was coming, but the secret remained unsaid.
Instead, they bitched about rabbits, planned a shoot on Sullivan's land
the following day. Times were arranged. Luke would bring his own
shotgun. Interesting, Whitlam thought. Perhaps the game was not quite
over. Not yet.

Another hundred dollars in gold coins pushed through the machine
and he had the skeleton of a plan. He ran it over and over in his head
until there was some flesh on the bones. It was OK. Not perfect. Not a
sure thing. But maybe fifty–fifty. And Whitlam would take those odds
any day of the week.

Down in the playground, Whitlam watched as a group of tiny
children hurtled past him, his own daughter in the mix. For a
second he thought he saw Billy Hadler in the crowd, not for the
first time. Whitlam's head jerked involuntarily, a sort of spasm
from the neck. He still felt sick when he thought about the boy.
For what it was worth.

Billy was never supposed to be there. Whitlam's scraped fist
clenched around the coffee cup as he made his way back to his
office. The boy was supposed to be out of the house. It was
all arranged. He'd made sure. He'd deliberately dug out that
badminton set. After that it had needed only a subtle suggestion from him for Sandra to get on the phone and organise that
last-minute playdate with Billy. If the boy's stupid mother hadn't
cancelled, stuffed up the plan, then Billy wouldn't have been
caught up in it. She only had herself to blame.

Whitlam himself had tried to save that kid. No-one could say
any different. He took a swig of coffee and winced as the liquid
burned his mouth. He felt it trickle down his gullet, turning his
insides sour.

Guts writhing, Whitlam had left the pub and passed a sleepless night picking holes in his plan. The next day, he sat in his office in a blank-eyed stupor, waiting for the inevitable knock on the door. Karen would have spoken up. Surely. Someone would come, he just didn't know who it would be. The police? The school board chairman? Karen herself again, perhaps? He both feared and longed for that knock. A knock meant Karen had told. It meant it was too late. And he wouldn't have to do what he was planning.

He didn't need to ask himself if he could go through with it. He knew he could. He'd proved it with the guy in the Footscray alley. That was a guy who should have known better. He was supposed to be a professional.

Whitlam had come across him once before. Then, the man had cornered him in a carpark, relieved him of his wallet and delivered his message via a sharp blow to the kidneys. It was supposed to play out the same in Footscray, Whitlam guessed. But then the man had grown angry, started waving the knife around and demanding more than they'd agreed. Things got messy fast.

The guy had been sloppy, and almost certainly under the influence of something. He'd heard the word 'teacher' and underestimated Whitlam's athleticism. A poorly timed lunge was countered with a lucky rugby tackle and they hit the concrete with a crack.

The blade had flashed orange in the streetlight and Whitlam felt the point slice across his belly, leaving a warm red line. Adrenaline and fear rushed through him as he grabbed the man's knife hand. He held and twisted it, using his own weight to force it back towards his attacker's torso. The man wouldn't drop the knife. He was still holding it as it slipped into his own body. He grunted wetly into Whitlam's face as the teacher pinned him down, feeling the slowing rhythm of the blood pumping out onto the road. He had waited until the man had stopped breathing, then waited a full minute more.

Whitlam had had tears in his eyes. His body was trembling and he was terrified he might pass out. But somewhere, buried many layers *down, was a pinpoint of calm. He'd been driven into a corner and he'd acted. He'd done what was needed. Whitlam, so familiar with the sick free-falling sensation every time he reached for his wallet, had, for once, been in control.*

With shaking fingers, he'd examined his own torso. The cut was superficial. It looked far worse than it was. He bent over his attacker and dutifully performed two rounds of CPR, making sure his finger-prints smeared in blood reflected his civic actions. He found a house in a neighbouring street with its lights on, and let forth the emotion he'd been holding back as he asked them to report a mugging. The attackers had fled but quick, please, someone was badly injured.

Whenever Whitlam now thought about the incident, which was more often than he expected, he knew it had been an act of self-defence. This new threat may involve an office rather than an alleyway, paper instead of a knife, but at its heart he felt it was not so different. The guy in the lane. Karen on the other side of the desk. Forcing his hand. Compelling him to act. It came down to them, or him. And Whitlam chose himself.

The end of the school day came and went. The classrooms and play-ground cleared. No-one came knocking on the office door. She hadn't reported it yet. He could still salvage this. It was now, or it was never. He looked at the clock.

It was now.

Chapter Thirty-seven

'How did Whitlam get to the Hadlers' property?' Barnes asked, leaning forward between the front seats. 'We turned our eyes square watching that school CCTV footage and I thought his car didn't move from the school parking lot the whole afternoon.'

Falk found the photos of Luke's body sprawled in his ute's cargo tray. He pulled up the close-cropped shot of the four horizontal streaks on the tray's interior. He passed it to Barnes, along with his phone showing the photos he'd taken of his own car boot the night before. On the boot's felt upholstery were two long stripes.

Barnes looked from one to the other.

'The marks are the same,' he said. 'What are they?'

'The ones in my boot are new,' Falk said. 'They're tyre streaks. He rode there on his bloody bike.'

Whitlam didn't tell anyone in the front office he was going. He slipped out of the fire door unseen, leaving his jacket on his chair and his computer switched on – the universal symbol for 'on the premises, back in a tick'.

He nipped out to the sheds, avoiding the limited range of the two cameras. Thank God for lack of funding, he caught himself thinking, then almost laughed at the irony. Within minutes, Whitlam had unlocked the ammunition store and pocketed a handful of shells. The school had a single shotgun for rabbit control, which he placed in a sports bag and slung over his shoulder. He would only use that as a last resort. Luke Hadler would have his own gun, Whitlam begged silently. He'd been shooting with Sullivan. But ammunition? No idea.

Whitlam jogged to the bike sheds. He'd driven in early that morning and parked in a quiet street near the school. Pulling his bike from the boot, he'd cycled the short rest of the journey. He'd chained his bike up where he knew it would soon be surrounded by others. Hidden in plain sight. Then he'd walked back to his car and driven it into the school carpark, choosing a prime spot well within the camera's range.

Now, he unlocked his waiting bike and moments later was cycling along deserted country roads towards the Hadlers' property. It wasn't far and he made good time. He stopped a kilometre from the property and picked an overgrown spot by the side of the road. He pushed his way into the bushes and waited, whispering a silent, feverish prayer that he'd timed it right.

After twenty-five minutes he was sweating, convinced he'd missed his chance. Not a single vehicle had come along. Eight more minutes ticked by, nine. Then, just as Whitlam was sliding his eyes sideways towards the end of the shotgun and wondering if there wasn't in fact another way out for him, he heard it.

A ute engine rumbled in the distance. Whitlam peered out. It was the one he needed. He felt lightheaded as he sent up a silent prayer of thanks. He stepped out onto the side of the road, dumping his bike at his feet.

He stood next to it and put out his arms, waving wide and wretchedly, like the drowning man that he was.

It looked for a terrible moment like the ute wasn't going to stop. Then, as it drew closer it slowed, pulling to a halt where he stood. The driver's window rolled down.

'Looks like you've got some trouble here?'

Luke Hadler leaned out.

Whitlam's elbow jarred painfully as he brought the sock packed with stones crashing down on the back of Luke's skull. It connected with the top of his neck with a gritty crunch and Luke crumpled face first into the dirt and settled with a dead weight.

Whitlam pulled on rubber gloves pocketed from the school science lab and opened the ute's cargo tray. With the speed of an athlete he shoved his hands under Luke's armpits and hauled him clumsily into the back.

He listened. Luke's breathing was shallow and ragged. Whitlam raised the sock and brought it crashing down twice more. Felt the skull crunch. There was blood now. Whitlam ignored it. He covered Luke loosely with a tarpaulin he found in the tray and flung his bike on top. The dirt-caked wheels came to rest against the side panel.

Luke's shotgun was in the passenger seat. Whitlam felt dizzy with relief and leaned his forehead against the steering wheel for a full minute while the sensation passed. The weapon was unloaded. Fine. Whitlam took the school's Remington ammunition from his pockets and loaded Luke's gun.

The die was cast.

Chapter Thirty-eight

Morning break time had been over for thirty minutes and all was still. The playground in the distance was deserted and Falk was stifling a yawn when his mobile rang. Raco and Barnes jumped as it trilled loudly in the silence of the car.

'Federal Agent Falk?' a voice said as he answered. 'It's Peter Dunn here, Crossley Educational Trust director. We spoke this morning?'

'Yes,' Falk said, sitting up a little straighter. 'What is it?'

'Look, it's a bit awkward, but that claim you asked about, for Kiewarra Primary?'

'Yes.' Falk wished the man would get to the point.

'I know you said it needed to be hush-hush, but I've discovered that my assistant – she's new, still trying to find her feet – it seems she passed it on to another team member who didn't quite grasp the confidential nature and –'

'And what?'

'And she appears to have contacted the school in question about twenty minutes ago to check –'

'No.' Falk reached over and buckled his seatbelt, frantically gesturing for Raco and Barnes to do the same.

'Yes, I know. I'm sor–'

'Who did she speak to?'

'As it was rather a large sum she went straight to the top. The principal, Mr Whitlam.'

Falk hung up the phone.

'School. Now.'

Raco slammed his foot on the accelerator.

Luke's body juddered a little under the tarpaulin as Whitlam trundled along the short distance to the Hadlers' farm. Whitlam dragged his eyes away from the rear-view mirror and gripped the wheel tight, his hands sweating inside the plastic gloves. At the farmhouse, he pulled Luke's ute to a stop and jumped out before he had time to think what was ahead. Only at the front door did he hesitate.

Whitlam didn't know the layout of the Hadlers' house and grounds well at all. Certainly not enough to go searching for Karen. Struck by the sudden madness of it, he saw his hand reach out and press the doorbell. He would bring her to him. The shotgun hung by his side, snug against his thigh.

Karen Hadler opened the door, blinking once in recognition and surprise. She drew a breath, her tongue curling behind her teeth for the sibilant 's', the hard 'c' forming in her throat, then his name was cut short as he raised the gun in a swift movement and pulled the trigger. He closed his eyes as he did it and when he opened them she was falling backwards, her stomach red and raw. Whitlam winced as her elbow caught the tiled floor with a loud crack and her head snapped back. Her eyes flickered eerily and a long alto moan sounded from deep in her chest.

Whitlam's ears were ringing and he could hear nothing.

'*Mummy?*'

No. No. He could hear nothing else.

'*Mummy?*'

Nothing but the breath in his chest and the ringing in his ears, and definitely not Billy Hadler shrieking like a bird from the shadow of the hallway, a toy dangling from one hand and his mouth stretched wide in horror.

'*Mummy?*'

Whitlam couldn't believe it, he could not believe it. The kid was here. The kid was here. Why the hell wasn't he far away, safe on the other side of town, playing in Whitlam's own backyard? Instead he was here. And he'd seen, and now Whitlam had to make it as though he hadn't seen and there was only one way he could think of to do that, and are you happy now, you nosey bitch, *he screamed at Karen's body as Billy turned and belted down the hall, too scared to cry so making ghoulish gasping little sighs instead.*

Whitlam felt as though he'd stepped out of his body. He followed and burst into the bedroom, almost unseeing as he flung open cupboard doors, ripped off the bedspread. Where was he? Where was he? He was angry, furious, at what he was being made to do. A sound came from the laundry basket, and Whitlam couldn't remember pushing it aside, but he must have because there was Billy. Billy, pressed against the wall, his face in his hands. But Whitlam remembered pulling the trigger. Yes. Later he would remember that well.

There was the dreadful ringing in his head again, and again — oh dear God, please no — something else. He thought for a hideous moment the cries were coming from Billy, who was missing half his head and chest. He wondered if he was making them himself, but when he put his hand to his mouth it was closed.

He followed the noise, almost curiously, across the hall. The child was in the nursery, standing in her cot, bawling. Whitlam stood in the doorway and thought he might vomit.

He positioned the barrel of the gun towards his own chin and held it there, feeling the heat radiate off the metal, until the urge passed. Slowly, he turned the weapon around. It wobbled as he trained it on the baby's yellow jumpsuit. He took a breath. The chaos in his head was deafening but amid the noise was a single urgent note of reason. Look! He made himself pause. He blinked once. Look at her age. And listen. She's crying. Crying, not talking. No words. She couldn't speak, she couldn't tell.

It scared him that in that instant, he was still tempted.

'Bang,' he whispered to himself. He heard a scary laugh but when he looked there was no-one else around.

Whitlam turned and ran. Over Karen's body and out to Luke's ute and then behind the wheel and roaring out onto the country road. He passed no-one and drove until the jitters got too strong for him to hold the wheel. He took the next turnoff he saw. A pathetic track leading to a small clearing.

Whitlam climbed out and dragged his bike from the ute, his teeth chattering in his skull. With shaking hands he threw back the tarpaulin, obscuring four horizontal streaks left against the paintwork as the bike's wheels had shifted and moved during the journey.

Whitlam steeled himself and leaned over the body. There was no movement. He peered at Luke's face, so close that he could see where the other man had cut himself shaving. He felt no whisper of air. Luke had stopped breathing.

Whitlam pulled on new gloves and a plastic rain poncho, then dragged the body to the edge of the tray. He hauled it with some trouble into a slumped seated position. Shotgun between Luke's legs, his fingertips pressed to the weapon, the barrel propped against his teeth.

Whitlam was terrified the body would slip and crumple, and had the bizarre thought that he should have practised this somehow. Then he closed his eyes and pulled the trigger. Luke's face disappeared and his body fell backwards. The blow to the back of his skull was lost in the mess. *It was done. Whitlam crammed his gloves, poncho and the tarpaulin into a plastic bag to burn later. Then he took three deep breaths and wheeled his bike onto the empty road.*

As he rode away, the blowflies were already starting to circle.

Chapter Thirty-nine

Whitlam's office was empty. His wallet was gone, along with his keys and phone. His jacket still hung from the back of the chair.

'Perhaps he's popped out,' said a nervous secretary. 'His car's still here.'

'He hasn't,' said Falk. 'Barnes, you get to his house. If his wife's there, detain her.' He thought for a moment. Turned back to the secretary.

'Is Whitlam's daughter still in class?'

'Yes, I believe s–'

'Show me. Now.'

The secretary was forced to jog down the corridor to keep pace with Falk and Raco.

'Here,' she said breathlessly at a classroom door. 'She's in here.'

'Which one?' Falk said, searching through the small window for the child he'd seen in Whitlam's family photo.

'There.' She pointed. 'Blonde girl, second row.'

Falk turned to Raco.

'Would he leave town without his child?'

'Hard to say. But I don't think so. Not if he could help it.'

'I agree. I think he's close.' Falk paused. 'Call Clyde. They must be nearly here. Get roadblocks out, then gather everyone we can get with search and rescue experience.'

Raco followed Falk's gaze out of the window. Behind the school the bushland sprawled dense and heavy. It seemed to shiver in the heat. It gave nothing away.

'Going to be some bloody hunt,' Raco said, putting the phone to his ear. 'Best hiding place in the world out there.'

The search and rescue crews formed up shoulder to shoulder, a splash of high-vis orange along the bushland track. The gums were whispering and rattling overhead as the wind tore through. Gusts whipped up the dust and grit, forcing them to squint and shield their eyes. At their backs, Kiewarra sprawled out, squat and shimmering under its heat haze.

Falk took his place in the line. It was midday, and already he could feel the sweat pooling under his reflective vest. To his side, Raco was grim-faced.

'Radios on, ladies and gents,' the search and rescue crew leader called through a megaphone. 'And it's tiger snake territory here so watch your feet.'

Overhead, a chopper wapped hot air down. The leader gave the word and the orange line stepped forward almost as one. The bushland closed behind them, swallowing them tight. Towering gums and thick scrub growth separated the team as they delved deeper, and within a few paces Falk could see only Raco to his left and one orange jacket in the distance to his right.

Probe searching, the leader had explained to them with definite impatience. Good for dense bush. The searchers would line up and each walk directly into the bush ahead, checking along their own line until their path was blocked.

'Theory is if we can't get through, your principal's not about to either. You get blocked, you turn around and come back to the path,' the leader had said, thrusting a jacket at Falk. 'Just keep your eyes open. It can get hairy in there.'

Falk pushed onward. It was strangely silent apart from the crackle of dry twigs underfoot and the wind whipping through the branches. The sun was high and white, forcing its way through occasional gaps in the trees like a searchlight. Even the noise of the chopper seemed muffled as it swooped high overhead like a bird of prey.

Falk stepped cautiously, the patchy sunlight playing tricks on the ground. He wasn't completely sure what signs he should be looking for, and felt sick at the thought of missing them. He hadn't done a full-scale bush search since his police training. But he'd spent enough time among these trees when he was younger to know they dragged you in far more easily than they let you go.

A heavy bead of sweat stung the corner of his eye and he wiped at it impatiently. The minutes ticked on. Around him, the trees seemed to get closer together with every step, and Falk found himself having to lift his feet higher as he waded through the tall grass. Straight ahead, he could see a thicket, sprawling and overgrown. Even from that distance it looked tangled and impassable. He was nearly at the end of his line. No Whitlam.

He took his hat off and ran a hand over his head. No shouts of success had made their way along the row of searchers. The radio on his belt was silent. Had they missed him? The image of Luke lying flat on his back in his ute flashed in Falk's head.

He put his hat back on and pushed forward, forcing a path through the overgrowth towards the thicket. The going was slow and he'd gained only a few metres when he felt a stick bounce off his jacket.

Falk looked up in surprise. Some distance to his left and a few paces ahead, Raco had stopped and turned towards him. He was holding his finger to his lips.

'Whitlam?' Falk mouthed silently.

'Maybe,' Raco mouthed back, raising one hand in an uncertain gesture. He lifted his radio to his lips and murmured something.

Falk scanned the surrounds for any other splash of orange. The nearest searcher was a distant spot behind a curtain of trees. Falk crept towards Raco, wincing as his footsteps crunched loudly against the undergrowth.

He looked to where his friend was pointing. A fallen log had created a hollow in front of the thicket. Barely visible but so very out of place against the backdrop, something pink and fleshy peeped out. Fingertips. Raco pulled out his police issue pistol.

'I wouldn't.' Whitlam's voice floated out from the log. He sounded oddly calm.

'Scott, mate, it's us.' Falk forced himself to match the tone. 'Time to give it up. There are fifty people in here looking for you. Only one way out.'

Whitlam's laugh floated up.

'There's always more than one way out,' he said. 'Jesus, you cops lack imagination. Tell your mate to pocket his weapon. Then he can get back on that radio and tell the others to back off.'

'Not going to happen,' Raco said. His pistol was aimed at the log, steady in his hands.

'It is,' Whitlam stood up suddenly. He was filthy and sweaty, with a web of fine scratches standing out purple against his ruddy cheek. 'Steady there,' he said, 'you're on camera.'

Whitlam pointed one finger overhead to where the police chopper loomed against the cloudless sky. It appeared and disappeared against the gaps in the treetops as it circled in a wide arc. Falk wasn't sure if it had seen them. He hoped so.

Whitlam suddenly thrust his arm out straight in front of him like a low Nazi salute, and took a step away from the log. He was clutching something in his fist.

'Stay back,' he said, rotating his hand. Falk caught a first glint of metal and his brain screamed *gun*, while a deeper part flitted frantically, trying to process what he was seeing. Raco tensed next to him. Whitlam unfolded his hand finger by finger, and Falk's breath left his chest. He heard Raco groan long and deep. A thousand times worse than a gun.

It was a lighter.

Chapter Forty

Whitlam flicked the lighter open and the flame danced dazzling white against the dull bushland. It was the stuff of nightmares. It was a tangled parachute, failed brakes on the motorway. It was a premonition, and Falk felt the fear flood from his core until it prickled against his skin.

'Scott –' Falk started, but Whitlam held up a single finger in warning. It was an expensive lighter, the kind that stayed lit until it was closed manually. The flame shivered and danced in the wind.

In one movement, Whitlam reached down and whipped a small flask out of his pocket. He flipped off the cap and took a sip. His eyes never leaving theirs, he tilted the flask and poured a trickle of the amber liquid on the ground around him. The whiskey vapours hit Falk a moment later.

'Call it an insurance policy,' Whitlam shouted. The spark fluttered as his outstretched arm shook.

'Scott,' Raco yelled. 'You stupid bastard. You'll have us all with that. You included.'

'Then shoot me, if you're going to. But I'll drop it.'

Falk shifted his weight and the leaves and branches under his feet cracked and snapped. Two years without decent rainfall and now doused in alcohol. They were standing on a matchbox. Somewhere behind them, invisible but linked by an unbroken chain of gums and grass, lay the school and the town. Fire would barrel along that chain like a bullet train, he knew. It surged and jumped and gorged itself. It raced like an animal. It ravaged with inhuman efficiency.

Raco's arms were shaking as he trained the pistol on Whitlam. He turned his head a fraction towards Falk.

'Rita's somewhere down there.' His voice was low and his teeth clenched. 'I will shoot him dead before I let him light this place up.'

Falk thought of Raco's vivacious wife, weighed down by her pregnancy, and raised his voice.

'Scott. There's no chance of you getting out of here if that flame hits the ground. You know that. You'll be burned alive.'

Whitlam's head jerked in a tiny spasm at the suggestion and the lighter jolted in his hand. Falk sucked in a sharp breath, and Raco took half a step back and swore.

'Christ, bloody watch that thing, will you?' Raco shouted.

'Just stay back,' Whitlam said, regaining control. 'Put your gun down.'

'No.'

'You haven't got a choice. I'll drop it.'

'Close the lighter.'

'You first. Gun down.'

Raco wavered, his finger white on the trigger. He glanced at Falk, then reluctantly bent and placed his gun on the ground.

Falk didn't blame him. He'd seen what bushfires could do. A neighbour had lost his home and forty sheep one summer when a controlled burn had got out of hand. Falk and his father had tied rags across their faces and armed themselves with hoses and buckets as the noon sky turned red and black. The sheep had squealed until they hadn't anymore. The fire had screamed and roared like a banshee. It was terrifying. It was a flash of hell. The land was drier now than it had been then. This would be no slow burn.

In front of them, Whitlam was flipping the lighter open and closed like a toy. Raco followed the action in mesmerised horror, fists clenched. The helicopter hovered directly overhead, and in his peripheral vision Falk could see a handful of orange vests dotted in the trees. They'd been warned to keep their distance, no doubt.

'So you worked it out then?' Whitlam sounded more interested than angry. 'The trust money.'

He flicked the lighter open and this time left it burning. Falk's heart sank. He tried not to look at the flame.

'Yes,' he said. 'I should've seen it before. But you hid the gambling well.'

Whitlam sniggered, an odd, sinister little noise whipped away by the wind. 'I've had a lot of practice at that. Sandra warned me. She said I'd pay for it one day. Hey –'

Whitlam pointed the lighter at them and Raco made a primitive sound in the back of his throat.

'Listen. Sandra had nothing to do with this, right? She knows about some of the gambling, but she didn't know how bad it was. Or about anything else. Promise me you understand that. *She didn't know.* Not about the school funds. Or the Hadlers.'

His voice stumbled at the mention of the family and he sucked in a sharp breath.

'And I'm sorry about the little boy. Billy.' Whitlam winced as he said the child's name. He looked down and pushed the lighter lid closed. Falk felt a first flutter of hope.

'I never thought Billy would get hurt. He wasn't even supposed to be there. I need you to believe me. I tried to keep him safe. I want Sandra to know that.'

'Scott,' Falk said. 'Why don't you come with us, mate, and we can go and find Sandra and tell her that.'

'As if she'll have anything to do with me now. After what I've done.' Whitlam's cheeks shone with tears and sweat. 'I should have let her leave me years ago, when she first wanted to. Let her take Danielle and get far away from me and be safe. But I didn't and now it's too late.'

He wiped his hand over his face and Raco seized the chance to reach towards his gun.

'Oi!'

Before Raco could touch the weapon, Whitlam had set the flame dancing once more. 'We had a nice arrangement going.'

'All right,' Falk said. 'Just keep calm, Scott. He's worried about his family. Same as you are.'

Raco, frozen with one hand outstretched and his face a mask of fear and fury, slowly straightened up.

'Scott, she's pregnant,' he said, looking right at Whitlam. His voice cracked. 'My wife is due in four weeks. Please. Please just close the lighter.'

Whitlam's hand shook. 'Shut up.'

'You can still turn this around, Scott,' Falk said.

'I can't. It's not that simple. You don't understand.'

'Please,' Raco said. 'Think about Sandra and Danielle. Close the lighter and come with us. If you won't do it for yourself, do it for your wife. For your little girl.'

Whitlam's face twisted and the scratches on his cheek turned an ugly shade as his colour darkened. He tried to take a deep breath but his chest was heaving.

'It *was* for them!' he screamed. 'All of it. This whole mess has been *for them*. I wanted to protect them. What was I supposed to do? *I saw the nail gun*. They made me touch it. What choice did I have?'

Falk didn't know for sure what Whitlam was talking about, but he could guess. Beneath the rising panic, he felt strangely unmoved. Whitlam might be able to justify his actions to himself, but his monstrous acts were spawned by a beast of his own creation.

'We'll look after them, Scott. We'll take care of Sandra and Danielle.' Falk said the names loudly and clearly. 'Come with us and tell us what you know. We can make them safe.'

'You *can't*! You can't protect them forever. I can't protect them at all.' Whitlam was sobbing now. The flame shook as his grip tightened, and Falk's breath caught in his throat.

He tried to still the swarm in his mind and think through the danger clearly. Kiewarra, huddled behind them in the valley with its secrets and its darkness. The school, the livestock, Barb and Gerry Hadler, Gretchen, Rita, Charlotte, McMurdo. He ran frantic calculations. The distances, the number of homes, the routes out. It was no good. Fire could outrun a car, let alone a man on foot.

'Scott,' he shouted. 'Please don't do this. The kids are still in the school. Your little girl is down there. We saw her ourselves. This whole place is a powder keg, you know that.'

Whitlam glanced in the direction of the town and Raco and Falk took a fast step forward.

'Hey!' Whitlam barked, waving the lighter. 'No. No more, stay back. I'll drop it.'

'Your daughter and those kids will burn to death running for their lives.' Falk tried to calm his voice. 'This town – Scott, listen to me – this town and its people will burn down to the ground.'

'I should be given a bloody medal for putting Kiewarra out of its misery. This town is a shitheap.'

'Maybe so, but don't make the kids pay.'

'They'll save the kids, the fireys will go there first.'

'What fireys, you dickhead?' Raco yelled. He pointed to the orange jackets dotted about in the bush. 'They're all out here looking for you. We'll all be killed *with you*. If you drop that lighter, we're all lost, your wife and your daughter included. I promise you that.'

Whitlam crumpled forward like he'd been punched in the stomach, the flame wavering in his hand. His eyes flashed with pure fear as they met Falk's and he wailed, raw and primitive.

'*I've lost them anyway!* I can't save them. I never could. Better this than what's waiting for us.'

'No, Scott, that's not –'

'And this town. This rotten *ruined* place,' Whitlam screamed as he raised his hand with the lighter. 'Kiewarra can burn –'

'Now,' Falk shouted, and he charged forward with Raco, arms out, pulling the fabric of their jackets wide like a blanket, hurling their bodies on Whitlam as he threw the lighter to the ground. A flash of white heat licked up Falk's chest as they tumbled to the earth, rolling, jackets flailing, boots hitting the dirt, ignoring the searing sensation up his calf and thigh. He had a handful of Whitlam's hair and he held it, his grip screaming with pain until the hair withered and his hand was raw pink and creped and holding nothing.

They rolled and burned for a thousand hours until a pair of thick gloved hands reached down and hauled Falk back by the shoulders. He gave an animal screech as his raw skin hummed and crackled.

A heavy blanket engulfed him and he choked and gulped as water was splashed over his head and face. A second pair of hands dragged him away. He collapsed onto his back and a water bottle was pushed to his lips but he couldn't swallow. He tried to twist away from the agony until someone held him down gently and he cried out as the pain licked his limbs. The stench of burned flesh hung in his nostrils and he blinked and snorted, eyes watering and nose running.

He turned his head to one side, pressing his wet cheek against the earth. Raco was hidden as a wall of vests crouched around him. Falk could see only his boots clearly. He was lying perfectly still. A third group had surrounded a hunched and screaming form.

'Raco,' Falk tried to say, but someone was pressing the bottle to his lips again. He struggled to turn his head away. 'Raco, mate. You OK?' No answer. 'Help him.' Why weren't they moving faster? 'Jesus, help him.'

'Shh,' a woman in a reflective vest said as he was strapped to a gurney. 'We're doing everything we can.'

Chapter Forty-one

He would live, the doctors told him when he woke up in the Clyde hospital burns unit. But his days as a hand model were over. When he was allowed to see the damage, he'd been both fascinated and revolted by his own body. The pale milky skin had given way to glistening red tissue, weeping and fresh. They bandaged up his hand, arm and leg and he hadn't looked again.

Bedbound, he had a stream of visitors. Gerry and Barb brought Charlotte, McMurdo smuggled in a beer, and Barnes sat by his side for long stretches without saying much. Gretchen didn't visit. Falk didn't blame her. Once allowed up, Falk spent most of his time by Raco's bed as he slept, sedated while they treated major burns on his torso and back.

He would also live, the doctors said. But they didn't make any jokes as they had with Falk.

Rita Raco pressed one palm to her belly while the other held Falk's good hand as they sat silently by her husband's side.

Falk told her that Raco had been brave. Rita just nodded and asked the doctor once more when he would wake up. Raco's brothers arrived from interstate one by one. They looked like variations of the same person. They shook Falk's hand and even as they threw bossy orders at their sleeping brother to get out of bed, he could tell they were terrified.

Raco eventually opened his eyes, and the doctors ushered Falk out for a full day. Family only. When he was allowed back in, he found Raco flashing a weak but familiar grin beneath his bandages.

'Real baptism of fire, eh?'

Falk managed a laugh. 'Something like that. You did well.'

'I had Rita to look out for. But tell me the truth.' Raco beckoned him closer. 'Weren't you a tiny bit tempted to let Kiewarra burn to the ground after everything it's done to you?'

Falk smiled, properly this time.

'I couldn't do that, mate. My house keys were back at the pub.'

Whitlam had been transferred to the Alfred Hospital in Melbourne, where he was under police custody for a string of charges, including the murders of Luke, Karen and Billy Hadler.

He was almost unrecognisable, Falk was told. The fire had caught his hair. He was lucky to be alive. Not so lucky, Falk thought privately. Prison wouldn't be easy for him.

When Falk was discharged, he was sent to recuperate under the Hadlers' grateful watch. Barb fussed and Gerry was unable to pass him by without shaking his hand. They insisted Falk spend as much time with Charlotte as possible. They told her how he had helped her daddy. Brought her real daddy – the good man, the loving husband – back from the dead.

Gerry and Barb's son was still gone, but they were lighter somehow. They could look people in the eye again, Falk noticed.

Falk went with them to the cemetery. Luke's grave in particular could now barely be seen for fresh flowers.

While Barb showed the cards and bouquets to Charlotte, Gerry stood off to one side with Falk.

'Thank God it had nothing to do with the Deacon girl,' Gerry said. 'I want you to know, I never really thought – I mean, Luke would never have –'

'I know, Gerry. Don't worry.'

'Any idea what happened to her?'

Falk made a non-committal noise as Barb wandered back.

As soon as Falk felt strong enough, he walked all the way to Gretchen's place. She was out the back shooting again and as he approached, she turned the gun on him and held it for a couple of beats longer than necessary.

'Gretchen. I'm sorry,' Falk called across the paddock. He held out his hands. 'That's all I want to say.'

She looked at his bandages and lowered the gun. She sighed and came closer.

'I didn't visit you in hospital.'

'I know.'

'I wanted to, but –'

'It's OK. Are you OK?'

She shrugged and they stood in silence, listening to the cockatoos in the trees. She wouldn't look at him.

'Luke loved Karen,' she said eventually. 'He really did. And before that, Ellie.' As she looked around the paddock, her eyes were wet. 'I don't think I was ever his first choice.'

Falk wanted to tell her she was wrong, but knew she was too smart for that.

'And the day Ellie died?' he said.

Gretchen's face creased.

'I always knew Luke had lied for you.' Her voice was tight as the tears spilled over. 'Because he was with me.'

'Did you hear that?' Gretchen opened her eyes and squinted at the sunlight filtering through the trees. The scrub grass tickled her back.

'Hear what?'

She could feel Luke's breath against her neck as he spoke. He didn't move. His hair was still wet and his voice was sleepy and muffled. Gretchen tried to sit up but was weighed down by his bare chest pressed against her. Their clothes were in an untidy heap at the base of a tree.

They had stripped down to their underwear before diving into the cool river. Gretchen had felt the heat of Luke's body through the water as he kissed her hard and pressed her up against the bank. The underwear had come off and was now drying on a flat rock.

The river was high and the water babbled and splashed as it gushed over the rocks downstream. Still, Gretchen heard the noise again. A dry snap deep among the trees. She stiffened. Another one.

'Oh, shit,' she whispered. 'I think someone's coming.'

She pushed Luke off and he sat up, frowning and blinking.

'Quick.' Gretchen threw his jeans at him and tried to fasten her bra, hooking it wrongly in her haste. 'Get dressed.'

Luke gave a wide yawn which turned into a laugh at her expression. 'All right, I'm moving.'

He checked that his boxers were the right way round before pulling them on. The path was some distance away and hidden by a thick curtain of trees, but they could hear the footsteps more clearly now.

'Please, will you get your pants on,' Gretchen said. She dragged her top over her wet hair. 'We should go. It could be anyone. It could be my dad.'

'It's not likely to be your dad,' Luke said, but pulled his jeans on all the same. He slipped on his shirt and shoes and they stood shoulder-to-shoulder in silence, peering through the heavy canopy towards the mouth of the path.

Gretchen almost laughed when the slight figure emerged from the tree line.

'Jesus, it's only Ellie. She almost gave me a heart attack.' She realised she was still whispering.

The girl was walking fast, with her head bowed. At the river she stopped. She stared at the swollen water for a few moments, one hand pressed to her mouth, then turned away.

'Is she down here on her own?' Gretchen said, her voice swallowed by the rush of the river. She thought for a moment she heard another snap, but the path beyond Ellie remained empty.

'It doesn't matter.' Luke was whispering. 'You're right. We should go.' He put his hand on her shoulder.

'Why? Let's say hello.'

'I can't be bothered. She's so weird lately. Besides, I'm all wet.'

Gretchen looked down. Her damp bra had soaked through her shirt.

'So what? So am I.'

'Let's just go.'

Gretchen stared at him. The water may have washed away the smell of sex, but the act was written all over his face.

'Why exactly don't you want her to see us?' she said.

'I don't care if she sees us, Gretch.' But he was still whispering. 'She's a stuck-up bitch. I don't have the energy today.'

He turned and pushed his way quietly through the trees, away from Ellie. He ignored the path she'd taken, instead heading the opposite way, along the small dirt track that led back to Gretchen's parents' farm. Gretchen took a step after him, then turned, looking back towards Ellie. She was beside a strange-looking tree, crouching down with her hand against a rock.

'What's she doing?' Gretchen said, but Luke was gone.

'When I heard she'd collected stones for her pockets, I didn't sleep for three nights.' Gretchen blew her nose on a tissue.

'I saw her. If I'd gone to her, I could have stopped her. But I didn't.' Her words were almost lost in her tears. 'I left. Of course. For Luke.'

Gretchen caught up to him a short way along the track.

'Hey.' She pulled at his arm. 'What is going on?'

'Nothing, babe.' He took her hand, but didn't stop walking. 'It's just time I got back.'

Gretchen pulled her hand away.

'She knows you and I are together, you know. Ellie, I mean. It's not a secret.'

'Yeah, babe, of course I know.'

'So why didn't you want her to see us? Why does it matter if the others know we're serious now?'

'It doesn't. Let's drop it,' Luke said, but he stopped and turned to face her. He leaned in for a kiss. 'Look, it doesn't matter. But what we have is so great. I just want it to stay something special. Between the two of us.'

She stepped away.

'Yeah, right. What's the real reason? You think there might be someone better on offer?'

'Gretch, come on.'

'Is that it? Because if so, Ellie's right back there waiting –'

Luke made a noise in his throat and started walking again.

'And there are a lot of guys round here who –'

'Don't be like that.' His voice floated over his shoulder. She stared after him. She loved those shoulders.

'What, then?'

He didn't answer.

They emerged from the track into the back paddock of her parents' farm and walked in silence to the house. Gretchen knew her mum and sister were still out. She could hear her dad knocking around in the back barn.

Luke grabbed his bike from where he'd left it against a tree and climbed on. He stretched out a hand and after a moment, she took it.

'I want to keep some things between us,' he said, looking into her eyes. 'But there's no point if you're going to act like a princess every time.'

He leaned in but she turned her head away from his kiss. He watched her for a moment, then shrugged. She burst into tears as he rode away.

Gretchen let the tears slide down her beautiful face for exactly as long as it took her to realise he wasn't coming back. She felt a surge of anger and, wiping her cheeks, ran into the empty house. She snatched up the keys to the farm truck. She hadn't passed her test, but she'd driven around the paddocks for years.

Gretchen jumped behind the wheel and took off in the direction Luke had headed. How dare he treat her like that? She spotted his bike ahead of the crossroads. She pulled the ute back a little, keeping her distance, not yet sure what she would say when she caught him. Up ahead, a car trundled over the crossroads across her path and she touched the brake. A moment later, she flashed through the intersection in her white ute.

Luke Hadler would not speak to her like that, she told herself. She deserved better. Luke took a sudden left turn and for a heart-stopping moment she thought he was heading back towards the river and Ellie. If he did that, Christ, she would seriously kill him. She followed at a distance, holding her breath. At the last moment he slowed, guiding his bike into his own driveway.

Gretchen stopped some distance away and watched from the road as he opened the front door and went inside. She could see the outline of his mother hanging up washing out the back.

She turned the ute, and cried all the way back.

'When I heard Ellie hadn't gone home, I went back to the river myself to check. I half-expected to find her holed up with a sleeping bag, keeping out of her dad's way. There was no sign of her.' Gretchen chewed her thumbnail. 'Luke and I argued about whether we should say something. But we weren't really worried at that point, you know? She'd been keeping to herself so much by then, I honestly thought she'd turn up when she was ready.' She said nothing for a long moment. 'I never once imagined she'd be in that water.'

She turned to look at Falk.

'When they said she'd drowned, I couldn't forgive myself. What if we'd stayed and spoken to her? I'd thought something wasn't right, and I'd turned my back. I was so ashamed. I just shut down. I made Luke promise not to tell anyone we'd seen her. I didn't want anyone to know how badly we'd let her down.'

Gretchen wiped her eyes.

'Then when I thought things couldn't get worse, everyone started pointing the finger at you. Even Luke got scared. If they thought you were involved, what would they say if they knew we were down there? Luke came up with this plan. He'd say he was with you. It would help you, it would help us. And I could pretend for the rest of my life that I hadn't been there. That I hadn't gone to Luke when I should have gone to her.'

Falk handed Gretchen a clean tissue from his pocket. She took it with a small smile.

'You're not responsible for what happened to Ellie Deacon,' he said.

'Maybe. But I could have done more.' She shrugged and blew her nose. 'I don't know what it was about Luke. He wasn't a bad guy, but he was pretty bad for me.'

They stood side by side for a while and looked out over the paddocks, both seeing things that were long gone. Falk took a breath.

'Listen, Gretchen, it's none of my business, but Gerry and Barb, and Charlotte, they –'

'Luke's not Lachie's father.'

'But if –'

'Aaron. Please. Just stop it.' Her blue-eyed gaze met his, but only for a moment.

'Fine.' He nodded. He'd tried. Enough. 'It's OK, Gretch. But they're good people. And they've lost a lot recently. So have you. If there's a chance to rescue something positive from all this misery, you should take it.'

She said nothing, just stared back at him, her face giving nothing away. Finally, he held out the hand that wasn't burned. She looked at it, then, to his surprise, reached out and pulled him into a swift hug. Not flirty, not even friendly, but perhaps peaceful.

'See you in another twenty years,' she said.

This time, he thought that was probably about right.

Chapter Forty-two

Falk's family home now looked even smaller than he remembered. Both from childhood and a few weeks ago. He set off past it towards the river, skirting around the edges of the property. He wasn't too worried about seeing the owner this time.

In the hospital, McMurdo had rolled his eyes as he told Falk how a lot of people had swiftly changed their tune. Started to feel downright disapproving of those fliers all of a sudden. Twenty years ago was twenty years ago, for God's sake. Water under the bridge and all that.

Falk tramped through the paddocks, his head clearer now. Twenty years was twenty years, but some things shouldn't be swept away. Ellie Deacon. She more than anyone had been a victim of this town. Its secrets and lies and fear. She had needed someone. Needed him maybe, and he had failed her. Ellie was the one at risk of being forgotten in all the chaos. Like Karen nearly was. Like Billy.

Not today, Falk thought. Today he would remember Ellie, at the place he knew she'd loved. He reached the rock tree as the sun was starting to dip in the sky. It was nearly April now. The summer fierceness was fading away. They said the drought might break this winter. For everyone's sake, he wanted them to be right this time. The river was still gone. He hoped one day it would come back.

Falk sat on the rock and pulled out the penknife he'd brought. He found the point where the secret crevasse opened, and started carving. Tiny letters, E. L. L. The knife was blunt and the going was slow, but he persevered to the end. Finally he sat back against the rock and wiped his forehead. He ran his thumb over the letters, admiring his handiwork. His burned leg felt like it was on fire from the pressure of kneeling.

The pain jogged a thought. With a grunt, he turned and reached into his crevasse, feeling for the ancient lighter he'd left there last time. Nostalgia was one thing, but after recent events, he didn't want to leave temptation around for anyone to find.

Falk knew he'd placed it deep and at first his good hand found nothing but dirt and leaves. He reached in further, stretching out his fingers. He felt the metal of the lighter as his thumb brushed against something soft but solid. He jumped, knocking the lighter away. Annoyed, he reached back in and paused as his hand hit the same object. It was rough but pliable and fairly large. Man-made.

Falk peered into the gap. He couldn't see anything and hesitated. Then he thought about Luke and Whitlam and Ellie and all the people who had been hurt by buried secrets. Enough.

Falk thrust his hand in and scrabbled around until he got a firm hold. He gave a tug and the object came free with a sudden jerk. He fell backwards, his chest screaming in pain as it landed on him with a thump. He looked down and sucked in a breath when he saw what he was holding. A purple rucksack.

It was covered in cobwebs and dirt, but he recognised it at once. Even if he hadn't, he would have known who it belonged to. Only one other person knew about the gap in the rock tree and she had taken the knowledge with her into the river.

Falk opened the bag. Laying the items on the ground, he pulled out a pair of jeans, two shirts, a jumper, a hat, underwear, a small bag of makeup. There was a plastic wallet with an ID of a girl who looked a little bit like Ellie Deacon. It said her name was Sharna McDonald and she was nineteen. A roll of money, tens, twenties, the occasional fifty even. Saved, scraped.

At the very bottom of the backpack was another item, wrapped twenty years ago in a raincoat to protect it as she packed. He took it out and held it in his hands for a long while. It was tattered and curled around the edges, but the writing beneath the hard-backed cover was there to read, in black and white. Ellie Deacon's diary.

He called her by her mum's name, the first time he hit her. She could see in her dad's cloudy eyes that the word had just slid out, as slippery as oil, as his fist slammed into her shoulder. He was drunk, and she was fourteen, with looks that were on the turn from child to woman. Her mum's photo had long been removed from the mantelpiece, but the woman's distinctive features were returning to the farmhouse each day as Ellie Deacon grew older.

He hit her once, then after a long while it happened again. Then again. And again. She tried watering down the booze. Her father realised from his first sip, and she never made that mistake again. At home she wore tops that showed her bruises but her cousin Grant just turned on the TV and told her to stop winding up her old man. Her schoolwork deteriorated. If the teachers noticed, it was with a sharp comment about her lack of attention. They never asked why.

Ellie began to speak less and discover more what both her parents liked so much about bringing a bottle to their lips. The girls she thought were friends looked at her strangely and whispered when they thought she couldn't hear. They had enough problems of their own, with their skin and weight and boys, without Ellie making them look even more out of place. A few teenage tactical moves later and Ellie found herself out in the cold.

She'd been on her own in Centenary Park on a Saturday night with a bottle in her bag and nowhere else to be when she'd heard the two familiar figures laughing in low voices from the bench. Aaron and Luke. Ellie Deacon felt a flutter, like finding something she'd forgotten but once held close.

It took them all a little getting used to. The boys looked at her like they had never seen her before. But she liked it. Having two people in her life doing as she said rather than telling her what to do suited her fine.

When they were much younger, she had preferred Luke's exhilaration and bravado, but now she found herself more drawn to Aaron's subtle thoughtfulness. Luke was nothing like her dad and cousin, she knew that, but she couldn't shake the feeling that hidden deep in his fabric there was a small part of him not completely unlike them either. It was almost a relief when Gretchen turned his head at least part of the way with her radiant siren call.

For a while it was good. More time with her friends meant less time at home. She got a part-time job and learned the hard way to hide her money from her cash-strapped dad and cousin.

She was happier, but it made her careless and cocky around her dad. It wasn't long before her sixteen-year-old face, with a smart mouth shaped so much like her mother's, was forced against a couch cushion until she thought she would pass out.

A month later, a filthy tea towel was pulled across her nose and mouth while she clawed at her dad's hands. When at last he let go, her frantic *first intake of air smelled like the booze on his breath. That was the day Ellie Deacon stopped drinking. Because that was the day she decided she would run. Not immediately, and not from one bad situation to something worse. But soon. And for that, she would need a clear head. Before it was too late.*

The catalyst came in the middle of a dark night, as she awoke in her room to find his weight on top of her and his jabbing fingers everywhere. A stab of pain and his soused voice slurring her mother's name in her ear. Finally, mercifully, she was able to push him off, and as he left he shoved her hard, sending her head snapping backwards and connecting with a crack against her bedpost. In the morning light, she ran her finger over the dent in the wood and groggily scrubbed the spot of blood from the pink carpet. Her head was aching. She felt the sting of tears. She didn't know where she hurt most.

When Aaron discovered the gap in the rock tree the next afternoon it was like a sign from above. Run. It was hidden, secret, and big enough to conceal a bag. It was perfect. Filled with a tentative spark of hope, she had looked at Aaron's face and let herself realise for the first time how much she would miss him.

When they'd kissed, it made her feel better than she thought she could, until his hand reached up and touched her sore head. She'd jerked away in pain. She looked up and saw the dismayed look on Aaron's face, and at that moment hated her dad almost as much as she ever had.

She wanted so badly to tell Aaron. More than once. But of all the emotions surging through Ellie Deacon's body, the most acute was fear.

She knew she wasn't the only person frightened of her father. His payback for any slight, real or perceived, was swift and brutal. She had seen him issue his threats then carry them out. Hoard favours, poison paddocks, run over dogs. In a community struggling to survive, people had to pick their battles. When every card was on the table, Ellie Deacon knew there was not one person in Kiewarra she could truly rely on to stand up to him.

So she made her plan. She took her saved-up money and she quietly packed a bag. She hid it by the river, in the place where she knew it wouldn't be found. Waiting for her when she was ready. She booked a room in an anonymous motel three towns away. They asked for a name for the reservation and she automatically said the only one that made her feel safe. Falk.

On a piece of notepaper, she scribbled his name and the date she had chosen and slipped it into the pocket of her jeans. A talisman for luck. A reminder not to back out. She had to run, but she only had one chance. If my dad finds out, he will kill me.

They were the last words she wrote in her diary.

There was no smell of dinner in the air when Mal Deacon let himself into the farmhouse and he felt a hot flash of irritation. He kicked Grant's boots off the couch and his nephew opened one eye.

'No bloody tea on yet?'

'Ellie's not back from school.'

Deacon snapped a beer from the six-pack by Grant's side and went through to the rear of the home. He stood at his daughter's bedroom door and took a swig from the can. It wasn't his first of the day. Or his second.

His eyes flicked to the white bedpost, with the dent in the wood and the mark on the pink carpet below, and he frowned. Deacon felt a cold spot form in his chest, like a tiny ball bearing. Something bad had happened there. He stared at the dent and a grotesque memory threatened to emerge. He took a long drink until it slid back silently beneath the shadowy surface. Instead, he allowed the alcohol to carry the first tendrils of anger through his veins.

His daughter was supposed to be here and she wasn't. She was supposed to be here, with him. She might be late, a rational voice barely whispered, but then he'd seen the way she'd been looking at him lately.

It was a look he recognised well. The same look he'd seen five years earlier. A look that said, enough. Goodbye.

He felt an acid wave surge through him and suddenly he was slamming open her wardrobe door. Her backpack was gone from its usual spot. The shelves showed one or two gaps in the neatly folded clothes. Deacon knew the signs. Her sneaking around. Keeping secrets. He'd missed them once before. Not again. He wrenched drawers out of the dresser, upending the contents on the floor, his beer spilling on the carpet as he rifled through for clues. Suddenly, he stopped still. He knew with cold certainty where she'd be. The same place her bloody mother used to run.

Little bitch, little bitch.

He staggered back to the living room, hauled a reluctant Grant to his feet and thrust the truck keys at him.

'We're going to get Ellie. You're driving.'

Little bitch, little bitch.

They took a couple of cans for the road. The sun burned orange as they tore along the dirt tracks towards the Falks' place. No way was she leaving. Not this time.

He was wondering what he would do if it was already too late when he caught a glimpse and his heart jumped in his throat. A single sudden movement as a pale t-shirt and familiar flash of long hair disappeared into the tree line beyond the Falks' place.

'She's there.' Deacon pointed. 'Heading towards the river.'

'I didn't see anything.' Grant frowned, but he pulled the truck to a stop.

Deacon jumped out, leaving his nephew behind as he ran across the paddock and plunged into the shadows of the trees. His vision was tinted red as he stumbled along the path in pursuit.

She was bending over by an odd-shaped tree when he caught her. Ellie heard the noise too late and looked up, the perfect 'o' of her mouth gaping wide in a scream as he grabbed her hair.

Little bitch, little bitch.

She wouldn't leave. She wouldn't bloody leave this time. But she was writhing, he noticed through his haze, and it was making it hard to hold her. So he clubbed her with an open palm, around the head. She staggered and fell backwards, landing with a soft groan on the edge of the bank, her hair and shoulders dipping into the black river water. Her eyes were looking at him in that way he recognised, and he thrust a hand under her chin until the murky water covered that face.

She'd fought when she realised what was happening. He stared at his own eyes reflected back at him in that dark river and held her harder.

He'd had to promise the farm to Grant as they searched the bank in the dying light for stones to weigh her down. He had no choice. Especially once his nephew found the note with Falk's name on it in her pocket. Suggested it might be a useful item to leave in Ellie's room. They searched until the last of the light disappeared, but they never did find her backpack.

It was only much later, when he was alone that first night and for many nights to come, that Mal Deacon wondered if he'd meant to hold his daughter quite so tightly.

If my dad finds out, he will kill me.

Falk sat for a long time after reading Ellie's words, staring out at the empty river. At last, he shut the diary and zipped it back into the bag with the other possessions. He stood and slung the backpack over his shoulder.

The sun was gone and night had fallen around him, he realised. Above the gum trees, the stars were bright. He wasn't worried. He knew the way. As he walked back to Kiewarra, a cool breeze blew.

Acknowledgements

I had never realised how many people were involved in bringing a novel to life and I am truly grateful to the many people who have helped me along the way.

A big thank you to my editors, Cate Paterson at Pan Macmillan, Christine Kopprasch and Amy Einhorn at Flatiron Books, and Clare Smith at Little, Brown, who have elevated the book through their intelligent notes, insight and advice. Thank you for offering me such a wonderful opportunity as a debut author.

I am also very grateful to all who worked so hard to get this book ready and onto the shelves, including the various talented copy-editors, designers and marketing and sales teams.

I feel lucky every day for the constant support and tireless work of my agents Clare Forster at Curtis Brown Australia, Alice Lutyens and Eva Papastratis from Curtis Brown UK, Daniel Lazar at Writers House and Jerry Kalajian at the Intellectual

Property Group. They have gone above and beyond at every turn.

Thank you to the Wheeler Centre in Melbourne and the judges, organisers and supporters of the Victorian Premier's Literary Award for an Unpublished Manuscript. The award is an invaluable opportunity for emerging writers, and winning in 2015 gave me a key that opened a thousand doors.

To get a book published, I had to write it first, and for that I will always be indebted to my fellow writers on the Curtis Brown Creative 2014 online course. Thank you for the wisdom of your collective talent; this book almost certainly would not exist in this form without you. Special thanks to teacher Lisa O'Donnell, my friend Edward Hamlin, and course director Anna Davis.

And thanks and love, of course, to my family, Mike, Helen, Michael and Ellie Harper, for making books such an important part of our life. And to my lovely husband Peter Strachan, who always believed in this novel.